TREETOPS

PETER BREMER

Cover design by Sarah Reed

To Siobhan who helps me climb ever higher.

The wonder of the world is o'er:
The magic from the sea is gone:
There is no unimagined shore,
No islet yet to venture on.

We dwindle down beneath the skies,
And from ourselves we pass away:
The paradise of memories
Grows ever fainter day by day.

from The Twilight of Earth
by George William Russell

In the wet dusk silver sweet,
Down the violet scented ways,
As I moved with quiet feet
I was met by mighty days.

On the hedge the hanging dew
Glassed the eve and stars and skies;
While I gazed a madness grew
Into thundered battle cries.

From The Memory of Earth
By George William Russell

PROLOGUE

SUMMER'S EVE

Clouds can be a stubborn thing. When they finally parted, late afternoon sunshine filtered in through the office window illuminating a framed degree from Penn State. Jackie frowned. She had never liked official titles. Some people wore them well. She was not one of them. Even though she was a college professor and held a PhD in comparative literature, she always told her students to skip any honorifics.

"Ms. Ashmore is fine," she would tell them at the beginning of the semester. "Better yet, just call me Jackie."

It wasn't because she didn't have pride in her accomplishments. The opposite was true. She knew how hard she had worked to get her degree. All those late nights studying after her daughter was asleep. Perhaps that was the reason she didn't need the accolades. Keeping things in perspective was one of the most important things she had learned as an adult. There was a natural balance between the extremes. If only she could go back and give her twelve-year-old self that advice. Would it have done any good?

She smiled at the bittersweet memory and the lines on her still-youthful face disappeared. Her hand hovered over the computer mouse. Of course not. Wisdom has to be earned. Knowledge comes cheap.

Jackie paused a moment longer and then clicked send. Her May term grades were submitted. The summer had finally arrived. Tomorrow was Riva's thirteenth birthday. There could be no more delays. No more busy work. She closed the laptop and sighed. The day she dreaded was almost here. She wasn't ready. Not even close.

If Jackie were being honest with herself, she knew the real reason why she didn't like titles. It wasn't that she thought they were pretentious or even unnecessary. It was simply the fact that she had found her own way without them. But even that wasn't the whole truth. There was still a small part of herself that felt it wasn't enough, that she somehow wasn't quite enough. Clouds swirled in her memories. She let them transport her back, if only for a little while.

"Roots"

CHAPTER 1

Jackie Ashmore sat with her back against the wall and her bare feet dangling off the side of her bed. Her thirteenth birthday party was about to begin, but she didn't really care. All she wanted was to be all grown up where she imagined things would make more sense. If she could fast forward through her life that would be the best present of all.

A candy bar wrapper drifted down to the floor as Jackie licked her fingers carefully before closing the page of the book she was reading. It was about disappearing dragons and a princess who tried to save them.

She had read a lot of books lately. Escaping was her favorite thing to do.

She hated it here in this new town and hated her father for dragging them to Minnesota. She missed her friends in Pennsylvania. Everything seemed wrong since her mother had died. Even the early summer sun spilling in through the window did little to lift her mood.

At least I don't have school for three months, she thought. Jackie's hazel eyes squinted at the window and hoped for rain.

Although her features were pretty enough, her nose was fierce, jutting out into the world like a challenge. Falling down over her ears were strands of fiery auburn-colored hair. Without meaning to, Jackie was drawn again to the picture of her mother which sat upon a desk in the corner. Tears welled up in her eyes.

A sudden knock on the bedroom door startled her.

"Party time birthday girl," her father said, knocking again gently on the door that was adorned with a poster featuring wizards and unicorns as well as a serpent's tail that coiled around and framed the design. In the center, featuring big, red letters, was a warning:

BEWARE! HERE BE DRAGONS.
ENTER AT YOUR OWN PERIL!

Jackie wiped her eyes quickly.

Then the door swung open to reveal a smiling middle-aged man with graying hair, a ridiculous birthday hat perched atop his head.

"Since it's your birthday, we really need you to make an appearance," her father said.

"Coming," she said with a sniffle and followed him downstairs into the living room.

Tied to arm chairs and table legs were a multitude of colorful balloons. Her little brother Dustin sat on the carpet, giggling and clapping his hands. A very large box with a yellow bow lay nearby.

"Open it," he told her smiling expectantly. "You're gonna like it."

"Don't ruin the surprise, buddy," her father cautioned. He had shared the news with Dustin just minutes before.

Jackie looked over at her father. He leaned forward in his chair as if to spur her on.

"Go ahead," he said. "We can have cake later."

Jackie removed the ribbon and lifted the edges of the flaps. They were taped, but came open without much effort. To her surprise and disappointment, the box was empty. She scanned the inside. On the bottom was a slip of paper that said, *Woof!*

"What's that supposed to mean?" she said crinkling her nose, but then noticed her father coming back into the room. In his arms was the most adorable puppy in the whole world.

"For me?" squealed Jackie.

David smiled broadly as he handed the puppy to his daughter.

"He's all yours."

Dustin reached out to pet the dog, then thought better of it as his sister scowled. He began to pout, but Jackie didn't notice.

"I love him!" she announced. All lonely thoughts were temporarily forgotten. The hurt inside of her temporarily receded. Jackie looked her present up and down, from speckled paws to floppy ears, and the joy she found there made all of her senses tingle with excitement. "You're the cutest thing in the whole world. Do you know that? I'll take you for walks around the block and to the park. I'm going to brush you and feed you, and pet you, and..."

"Take him out to the bathroom," her father interjected. "Your brother can help."

Jackie pretended she didn't hear him and said to the dog, "We'll have adventures," and held him close.

In response her new puppy licked her face wet and eagerly.

"Doggie kisses," laughed her little brother. "He likes you. He told me."

"Looks like he does," his father said. "Now there's only one thing for you to do, besides promising to get up at 3:00 in the morning to let junior out if he needs to go."

"I already know what I'm going to name him," Jackie assured him.

CHAPTER 2

There was a fairly small park only a block from the Ashmores' home. A sidewalk bordered the park, while a few smaller concrete paths cut through the greenery at regular angles. The grove of trees and underbrush at its center was unusually dense for a city park. Few open spaces intruded upon that wooded area and those that did seemed overrun with neglect. By night, of course, the whole area loomed larger, more mysterious, with moonlight and shadows dancing a deep, dark dance. It was then that the sidewalk seemed little more than a forgotten trail in a lonely wood. Even during the light of a June afternoon and high birdsong, the trees seemed to promise both mystery and slumbering danger if a person strayed from the path to explore what lay beyond the fringe of bright green leaves.

On this particular day though, at this particular time, the park was empty. Sunlight streamed through the canopy of trees and lay in golden pools on the forest floor, waiting for the rush of children. Fall seemed a lifetime away.

In a small hidden meadow surrounded by dense brambles, a rabbit sat on a stump and nibbled something of interest. Then it stopped, its meal unfinished. Alert, the animal perked its ears and wiggled its nose as if searching the air for an unseen menace.

The next moment, a giant form filled the clearing. It obscured the blue sky. It blocked the daylight. Where the old stump had been sat something very much alive—and very old.

CHAPTER 3

Jackie yawned. In her half-asleep daze, she imagined flames erupting from her mouth. She had been up too late reading a book about fiery beasts and had gotten up in the middle of the night to let Milky Way out. Her eyelids were heavy. Handsome, but foolish knights and powerful dragons still blazed hotly in her imagination while the princess's magic twinkled like cold stars. It was no surprise she didn't notice Milky Way trying to leap up on the bed until he started yipping impatiently.

Jackie smiled weakly and tried to sit up.

"Hello boy," she said.

Milky Way leaped up, his tail wagging frantically. Jackie pet the soft furry head affectionately before collapsing again. She was exhausted. With a sigh, she let herself drift off to sleep.

Jackie's room could almost be considered bare. She'd hung one poster—the Beatles' Abbey Road cover—on her wall. She didn't like them just because they were cute and wrote songs that made her heart melt. The songs were also funny, and sometimes sad, with melodies that were way better than most of the other stuff she heard on the radio or online.

No old toys littered the room (except for a lone tattered bear in the corner with a missing eye). Not counting a pair of tennis shoes lying where she had kicked them off, no fermenting laundry littered the floor. Her laptop sat unused in its case against the far wall. Most surprising was her cherry-colored cell phone, once always in her hand or pocket, now lay lifeless on her desk, its stored numbers only a memory. Papers in the room were few. Candy wrappers and books were many. Quite a few of the titles were fantasy or science fiction. Jackie loved stories that took her to fantastic places. Other books were about extinct or endangered animals, or brave explorers or pioneers.

The one bright spot of color in the room was an endless assortment of make-up accessories that glittered like a basket of jewels on her desk beneath an oval mirror. The eyeliner and blush, lipstick and polish had been a pre-birthday gift she had given herself, despite her father's objections. Every morning she practiced in the reflection until she was as beautiful and as mature as she desperately wanted to be. When she looked back at herself, she imagined that she was no longer a kid, but someone older, somebody without painful memories and aching loneliness. Everything else, all her reminders of her former life, were boxed up and shoved under her bed or deep in her closet.

There were only two things she could not bear to put away. The first was the picture taken many summers ago of her mother standing in the garden, a smudge of dirt on her face like a shadow to come. The other was more mysterious. It was about a foot tall and sat on the windowsill opposite her bed: a candle formed in the shape of a great oak tree, with vibrant green and yellow wax. Her mother had given it to her on her twelfth birthday, just a few months before losing her battle with breast cancer.

"To help light your way," Jackie's mother had said.

Down below, her puppy tried again to scramble up the steep side of the bed sheets and blanket but fell back to the floor, this time with a whimper, followed by a bark, and then another.

Reluctantly, Jackie awoke.

"Okay, okay," she said, opening her eyes. "I know, it's walk time. Let's go."

After a brief look in the mirror and a glance at her cell phone, she stuffed a candy bar in her pocket (the same pocket that held her lucky talisman: a Walt Disney World Animal Kingdom pressed penny featuring Safari Minnie Mouse) and made her way downstairs, with her puppy tumbling behind.

Jackie heard her father swear as she came out the back door into bright sunshine.

"Morning kiddo," greeted her father with a grimace as he nursed a small trowel wound.

"Where are you off to on your first day of summer vacation?" he asked. "It's a beautiful day for a girl and her dog."

His hands were filthy from replanting a row of white petunias with red geraniums and as he wiped the sweat from his forehead, he unknowingly left a streak of dirt in its place. A wedding ring adorned his left hand.

It was funny, she thought, how he seemed to be spending more time outside now. Back home, her mother had always tried to get him to work with her, planting and tending together, but he had always found other things to do like working late, balancing the checkbook, or playing geeky video games. Mom was the one that always liked growing things.

Jackie had always helped her mother plant, water, weed, and harvest. They made a good team, but Jackie felt like a poor second. It didn't help that she floundered trying to do the simplest things while her mother had moved about their spacious garden with effortless grace. Flowers and vegetables and herbs blossomed and thrived under her care. Sometimes her mother had even sung to the plants a sweet-sounding lullaby, although the words were strange.

Seeing her father struggle trying to do what her mother did

with ease only made Jackie more resentful. She certainly wasn't going to help him.

"What fantastic sights will you and Milky Way be seeing today?" her father asked.

"The park," Jackie answered as she attached the leash to Milky Way's bobbing collar.

"Can I come?" Dustin asked, eagerly poking his messy head out of the kitchen window that overlooked the backyard. He was wearing a bright red t-shirt and his eyes and face were alight as only a five-year-old's can be. "He's a good dog. He told me so. Please can I?"

Jackie shook her head. Sometimes her brother said the weirdest things. She didn't have to think about it. "No-oh," she replied sharply. Since her mother died, Jackie hadn't wanted to spend much time with anyone. But she especially didn't want anything to do with Dustin. He was always hanging on and getting in the way.

Her brother's smile faded away.

"Can you play with me Daddy?" he asked in his smallest voice.

"Not right now," her father answered with a hint of regret in his voice. "A little later, okay? Keep coloring like I told you or come hang with me outside. After I finish here, I need to do some work in my office, but then we can do whatever you want."

"When?" Dustin asked.

Jackie's father sighed. "Later," he said.

"It's always later," his son complained.

Jackie said nothing, but she silently agreed with her brother. Their father was more distant now and a lot less fun. She missed the way things used to be.

"That will do, buddy. Go and play. I'll be there when I can."

Dustin slumped in the window, all hope gone, and then retreated to whatever he had been doing inside. Like Jackie, he had gotten used to being alone, but he didn't like it.

Slowly, her father turned back to their conversation. Milky

Way tugged at the leash, eager to go. Jackie backed up, already making her escape.

"Well, be careful," her father said. "You know how busy those streets can be."

"I'm thirteen, Dad. *A teenager.* I'm not a little girl."

"I know, I know," he said. "Hey, wait a second. Before you go, I've got something for you."

"What?" she asked, coming to a reluctant stop.

"With all of the excitement yesterday, I thought it would be better to give this present to you today."

Curious, she walked back over.

Her father paused and for a moment, his jaw moved but no sound came. "It's from your mother," he managed at last. "She wanted to give it to you in person. I've been waiting for the perfect time, but I guess there isn't one."

Then he dug in his pocket and pulled out a ring case, brown and velvety.

Jackie's eyes widened and the world slowed down. "Do you know what it is?" she asked.

"Your mother said it was for you and you only."

"You didn't peek?"

"I didn't peek," smiled David.

Then he gave her the gift.

Holding her hand out, Jackie felt the object as it came to rest in her palm. It was soft and cool and surprisingly heavy.

She wanted to open it right then and there. Her whole body tingled with excitement. This was a connection to her mother. After all these long, lonely months with no friends and strange surroundings, the small velvety case felt like a glimmer of hope. Yet it didn't feel right somehow to open this last present with anyone else, even her father. After all, her mother had said it was for her and for her alone, hadn't she?

"Thanks!" she said brightening. An urge to hug her father rose up inside her, but she stuffed the case into her pocket instead. "I'll open it up when we get to the park. Is that okay?"

"Sure," David said.

Then a sudden wind came up, tossing her hair into her eyes. Her hair, the color of oak leaves in October, reminded her of Mom's hair. It only took her a moment to pull the strands back, but a pattern of freckles was visible just behind her ear that seemed, sometimes, when the light was just right, to be a winter tree; tall, spindly, and leafless. Her mother had a similar one, only fuller with a summer's shape. Jackie turned and began walking away.

"Have fun," her father said. "Make sure you have your cell phone."

"See ya later," she told him, clearly aware of what she didn't have.

A moment later Milky Way pulled on the leash nearly taking *her* for a walk.

The further away Jackie got, the more freedom she felt. Her mind raced with possibilities of what the gift could be. With her puppy out ahead of her, she veered off around the corner of the house and past the old stone hitching post that leaned like a weary traveler, finally escaping onto the sidewalk.

CHAPTER 4

It didn't take long to get to where they were going. The park was only a few blocks away and Milky Way, to her relief, seemed more interested in walking than stopping and sniffing everything in sight. His energy and eagerness were contagious. Jackie whistled a tune as Milky Way propelled her down the sunlit path. Yet in the back of her mind she couldn't help wonder.

What would her mother give her that her father couldn't see?

"Stop, boy," she commanded, tugging on the leash when he kept going anyway.

There before them was the wrought iron gateway to Highveil Park. The vine-like letters curled above the entrance. She had passed through it several times before but it always made her pause. Woven into the rusting architecture of the portal, carefully hidden, was an assortment of plant and animal life; beautiful blossoms, flying insects, rabbits, a solitary wolf, squirrels, birds of every description, a boy and a girl, and encompassing them all, a tree with flowering, spreading branches. Jackie took pride in the fact that while others regularly walked through the gate without knowing or caring she had taken the time and discovered the secret.

"C'mon, Milky Way," she said smiling. "Let's go see what we can see."

Together they passed under the archway and walked into the green world of sunlight and shadows of Highveil Park.

The sidewalk paths were almost deserted since it was a Monday morning. Jackie liked the illusion this created—that the park, encompassing several blocks, was hers and hers alone. She imagined being alone in the greenery, a space that grew bigger with every step until the park was a vast woodland of mystery and unseen danger that could only be revealed through her brave exploring.

Milky Way paused and looked back at her, as if to remind her that Jackie was sharing the adventure.

"Yes, and you too," Jackie added playfully, continuing the charade. "Magellan had his Malamute, Ponce de Leon his Pekinese, and I have you."

Eventually the path curved around the edge of a dense overgrown wood. The remains of an old fence sagged as the wind sighed. Where the rusting barbed wire dipped lowest, she could see a faint, but worn trail wind off into the trees. She tugged on her puppy's leash until he finally slowed to a halt.

"Well, faithful dog. Which way shall we venture? Around the edges of this great rainforest or straight into the heart of it?"

Milky Way gave two short yelps and strained impatiently.

"Straight ahead it is, faithful dog," said Jackie and they walked off into the thickening branches.

The light grew dimmer with each footstep she took. Still, it was only a small city park, and they were walking on a trail where others had been before. The trees that surrounded her were like familiar friends.

So why, she wondered, *am I getting this feeling that something's going to happen?*

Goosebumps rose down her arm.

"I wonder what's inside you?" she asked aloud trying to calm her worries.

Jackie took the ring case from her pocket and held it up into a ray of sunlight. The chestnut color of it was sprinkled with flecks of silver that only added to the air of mystery. Peering at the strange present, her pace slowed. There could be anything inside. Lost in a daydream, her fingers clutched the smooth case as the world around her receded. It took her a moment to realize that she was no longer moving.

"I guess it's now or never," she decided, speaking with as much confidence as she could muster.

Milky Way barked impatiently and tugged on his leash eager to keep going.

"Just a minute," she told him, pulling on his leash to make him stop.

She put down the leash and stepped on the end of it. Then she sank to her knees. Gently, she placed the case on the ground in front of her and took a deep breath.

"One, two, three," she counted slowly and then reached out to lift the lid.

Suddenly a white blur shot past her, a small creature of some kind. It brushed against her before scampering away. Milky Way gave a sudden growl, ferocious for such a young dog. Jackie's body shifted in surprise and confusion. A second was all it took.

Milky Way tore off like a little squealing rocket, dragging his leash behind him like a vapor trail. Before he disappeared into the underbrush and trees lining the trail, she had one last glimpse of her puppy as he yelped—in surprise or excitement, she couldn't tell. Then there were only the receding echoes of his chase as he continued speeding away from her.

Everything had happened too quickly. Whatever the animal might have been, it had been fast and she seriously doubted Milky Way could catch it. At the edge of her hearing, so faint it might not have been there at all, she thought she heard the distant murmur of water, metallic and twinkling with a hint of laughter. Then even that faint sound was gone.

I should have tied him to something, she thought.

Then she looked down at her present. The ring case was gone! Jackie spun in a circle, expecting to find it on the ground having tumbled out of her hands, but it wasn't there. Panicking, she began searching the nearby bushes and grass, crawling on her hands and knees with growing frustration. Finally, she was forced to admit it; her mother's gift had vanished. Even more unbelievable was the explanation. Somehow the little forest creature had taken it. Clenching her fists, she walked into the trees.

"Milky Way," she called anxiously into the gathering shadows, hoping to see him behind the next tree. "Milky Way!"

But however far she walked, she did not find him. The fading sound of his barking was the only way she could be sure he was still in the park. At any moment she expected it to stop completely and fall silent. Blind to the sharp branches that tore at her clothes and face, she began running with no thought to where she had been or where she was going. Mosquitoes buzzed in her ears, biting her exposed skin. The woods blended into one featureless blur as she leapt over stagnant pools of water, swerved around fallen logs, and then stumbled up one rocky slope only to race down the steep side of another. All the while the park, this forest, was getting darker and denser, with the light more feeble and the open spaces ever more constricted as if the bushes and trees themselves were conspiring to stop her progress.

What is this place? she wondered.

How long she wandered, Jackie had no way of knowing. She had no watch, no compass to guide her footsteps, and no phone either. An empty feeling grew in the pit of her stomach. She reached into her pocket and removed a candy bar.

At least I won't go hungry, she thought.

Tearing open the wrapper, she devoured the chocolate.

The air was getting cooler, she realized as she licked her lips. There was a chill in the woods that summer could not touch. It felt like the ancient heart of a glacier.

Jackie took another step, shivering. Then the barking stopped.

Immediately she froze and listened. But it did not resume or Milky Way was too far away. The thought of her puppy alone in the woods made her ache inside.

Standing by a line of thorn bushes ripe with berries, she wondered how on Earth she could have lost her dog. It didn't seem possible. Turning around to catch a glimpse of her furry birthday present, she saw a speck of light through the thick underbrush.

Still hungry she reached out and picked several blood red berries from the bush and placed them in her hand, remembering what her mother had taught about identifying edible foods in the wild. Satisfied she was safe, Jackie popped them in her mouth. Warmth spread through her body. Using her new-found strength Jackie gritted her teeth, closed her eyes, and pushed her way through the tearing wall of vegetation.

As her eyes adjusted to the harsh light of the open sky, she looked around. She had to be out of the park now. But she was not. Encircling her was a beautiful green meadow surrounded by forest and bramble on all sides. It was empty except for one thing. In the exact center of the grassy bowl there stood a tree, ancient and magnificent. But it was not just any tree, however grand. This was no sequoia or baobab. It was not of a kind or of a size she had ever seen before. Her eyes widened. From a knotty trunk massive enough to support a whole forest spread boughs laden with sun-sprinkled leaves and crowned with flowers the color of the purest snow. The uppermost branches, it seemed to Jackie, reached up to the very sky itself and then were lost in the misty clouds at their summit.

Following the wonder down from the fearful heights, she again looked at the base and this time saw what her unfocused eyes had missed before. There, curled up in the cooling shade at the foot of the tree was Milky Way, fast asleep.

For the longest time Jackie stared at the sight, trying to make sense and mesh the two images together. It reminded her of the time Dustin had snuck under the guard ropes in the dinosaur exhibit at the museum and when she had looked back, he was running under their mighty legs and climbing up their sweeping tails.

Clearing her head Jackie was left with two emotions: joyful relief and unbridled anger. She meant to give her dreaming dog a healthy dose of each. Striding through the soft, tickling grasses she bent down over her puppy and reached out to touch him. A sudden movement out of the corner of her eye interrupted her. From up in the jungle of branches, a perfectly white squirrel emerged, larger than most, with the edge of her mother's jewelry case tucked into its mouth. Skittering down the side of the trunk, it spat out the velvety box and then proceeded to scratch three times on the ground at the base of the tree. Then it scampered nervously back out of sight to the fading sound of bells and pocket change. Turning back to Milky Way, Jackie noticed that he was awake and looking at her with big, pleading eyes.

"Do you know what I had to do to find you? Do you?!" she demanded, wrapping her arms around him. "I thought I lost you. Why did you run away, huh? Haven't you ever seen a squirrel before?"

Milky Way blinked, looked up to the treetop, and then put his nose flat on the ground with his floppy ears covering both eyes. His front paws were crossed at the foot of the tree as if in some vain attempt for canine luck.

"You're a bad dog," continued Jackie. "A very bad dog!"

Then she buried her face in his fur.

"Don't do that again, okay?" she whispered.

Milky Way uncovered one eye and then another.

"Want to see something?" Jackie asked. "I've got a present."

Milky Way sat up and watched eagerly as Jackie picked up the object.

Holding the brown velvety case in the palm of her hand, she brushed it off and tried not to think of squirrel saliva. Once it was clean, however, she still didn't open it. Inside was the last present from her mother and she had almost lost it. This gift, whatever it might be, was precious. A part of her didn't want to open it. She wanted to make it last forever.

Eventually Jackie's curiosity got the better of her. Slowly, carefully, she lifted the edge of the lid. It wouldn't budge. She tried again, but without success. Frustrated, she turned it over in her hand and felt for any irregularities that might be a release mechanism. Finally, she found the switch buried deep in the velvety fabric.

"Gotcha!" she exclaimed. "You better be worth all this trouble."

With her thumb, she gave the switch a flick and the lid sprang open like a muffled pop.

Nestled inside was an almost perfect sphere swirling with colors of blue, white, and touches of green and brown. Although she knew it must be an illusion, it appeared that the markings were layered with one overlapping another. For a moment they even appeared to be moving. It was the most beautiful thing Jackie had ever seen.

Taking it out, she was amazed at how the object felt. She expected it to feel hard, like glass, but the soft sphere felt more like a raindrop with a thick skin. Afraid she would somehow damage it, despite the toughness it displayed, Jackie gingerly put the present back, noticing as she did so the small, folded note stuck to the inside of the lid like a miniature piece of origami.

"Jackie," it began with the unmistakable penmanship of her mother. *"I have seen that a tree that reaches past a person's embrace grows from one small seed. That is how you are to me. There are so many things I will never get to do with you. So many things I won't get to tell you or share with you. So many secrets you'll have to discover on*

your own. Be strong. I won't get a chance to watch you grow and blossom into the woman I know you can become. But I feel as if you've given me so much already. So much hope. Having you as my daughter has been more beautiful than I ever imagined it could be. You, and your smile, will always be in my heart. Remember that. I know you will be sad and angry for a while, but life goes on. That is the magic of life. Disease and death do not matter in the end, only love.

And don't be mad at your father for waiting to give this to you. I was going to wait a while longer yet, but as we know, circumstances changed. I've been hoping that, like a flower, you would be open by now, but each of us moves at our own speed. Each of us has talents we must discover on our own. I told your father that this seed would be your birthday present from me. What is it you ask? It is called an Amarantha, my darling, and it is very special. It needs help from those around it, just as we all do, but in turn, it can carry you far. You will know where to plant it when the time is right. It will need no tending, nor any water. Just you, if you are willing.

All my love,

Mom

P.S. Don't let your father near it. You know how he is with plants.

At the bottom of the page was the familiar hand-drawn leaf; black-lined and green tinged, her mother's way of ending all her letters. Only now, instead of conveying growth, it appeared to be falling.

Tears welled in her eyes and spilled down her cheeks as she read the words over and over again. Finally, she folded the note and wiped her tears away fiercely, afraid if she did not, the sadness would never stop.

Why did you have to die? Jackie thought. *Oh Mom, I miss you so much.*

This last emotion she may have spoken out loud because Milky Way got up and started barking as if eager for company again. The sudden sound of it shocked her senses and her mind reeled backwards to the words she had just read.

"She says it's a seed, boy," Jackie spoke aloud to Milky Way. "But what kind of seed doesn't need water or weeding?"

Shaking her head, Jackie folded the note up carefully and put it in her pocket. Then she picked up the object again from its case, turning it over in the palm of her hand. It certainly didn't look like anything her mother had ever planted. Not even the exotic hybrids approached the strangeness of this seed.

"What do you think, Milky Way? Where should we plant it?"

But a seed of an idea was already taking root, inside.

"Maybe we're not really supposed to plant it," she said and then put the seed back in its case. "I think it's just symbolic or something."

Milky Way gave a whimper and then craned his neck skyward as if suddenly catching an unlikely scent.

"No more high-speed chases," she chastised. "Time to get you home."

Jackie grabbed his leash securely and gave a tug, but Milky Way only barked in response, as in protest.

From up above came the sound of shaking leaves. Milky Way barely had time to skid out of the way as a strange bird—round with a large bill—crashed from the branches above in a feathery flutter, finally coming to a most ungraceful landing at the foot of the colossal tree. About the size of a penguin, but fatter, it proceeded to peck the ground with a dim-witted repetition, managing to dig a hole four or five inches deep. Then it stopped, lifted its beak-heavy head, and stared at Jackie as if waiting for some kind of response or reward.

"Well?" the dodo said unexpectedly, its voice heavy with sarcasm.

Jackie stared back in numb disbelief.

"Yes, yes I know. A talking extinct bird. But focus. Where do you think would be an especially ideal place to plant the gift you have been given? I'll give you a little hint."

The strange creature dipped its substantial beak into the cavity it had just dug.

"Why should I believe you?" Jackie managed, looking around for a movie crew to explain what she was seeing.

In response, the dodo gave her such a withering stare that Jackie looked away in discomfort. "Because I have nothing better to do than help clueless girls like yourself."

Jackie frowned. This thing, whatever it might be, was really getting under her skin. "Are you some kind of mechanical drone?" she asked.

"No, are you?" the creature retorted. "You do drone on without end. Quit wasting my time and answer the question."

"Right there?" she said meekly, looking over at the depression in the dirt.

"Good guess, Sherlock," congratulated the amateur avian. "A hole-in-one. Gotta fly!"

The dodo, its features forever frozen in awkward embarrassment, waddled around the tree, disappearing from Jackie's sight. Cautiously, Jackie followed, looking for the not quite flightless bird, but it was gone.

Had she really seen what she thought she'd seen? Had she really heard what she thought she'd heard? Perhaps it had all been a hallucination from those berries she had eaten. That would explain it.

Looking up into the dizzying growth as she circled the trunk again, she noticed differences in the canopy of leaves. Healthy green growth and snow-capped flowers blended into fiery explosions of color, which in turn changed into skeletal twigs and barren branches. Finally, completing her visual arc, she spied a section above her that was full of bursting buds. The tree, she realized, as she spun slowly in place, was like a carousel, turning in timeless precision from one season to another. Spring, summer, autumn, and winter. All were contained in the living branches spread out before her.

Milky Way, keeping close, bumped into her heels as she stopped and knelt by the little hole. The seed was in the open case, completely forgotten in the excitement of the past few minutes. Now she stared at it intently.

Is this really where you belong? She wondered. *Mom did say I was supposed to plant it.*

Taking the Amarantha between her fingers, she placed it in its new home and covered it carefully with handfuls of dark, rich earth from beside the colossal tree.

"There," declared Jackie. "I guess this is where you're meant to be."

It felt strange not to water it or anything, but she trusted her instructions and planned to return. Putting the case back in her pocket, she reached down and grabbed Milky Way's leash.

"C'mon," she told him anxiously. "Let's get going. You know how Dad gets when we're late."

Milky Way kept close and trotted beside Jackie as if his adventure had made him wary of the world. The journey back through lengthening shadows was surprisingly easy. Although troubled about what she had just seen, Jackie was confident she knew the way. It felt as if she carried within her an invisible compass. In this manner she avoided the thorns by finding a hidden path and managed to walk through the forest unharmed. Even the mosquitoes seemed to ignore her. Without knowing why or even thinking, she was able to make choices in the direction that brought her out of the trees and onto the dusky sunlit path within the space of a miracle. Looking back at the small tangle of trees, she had a momentary shiver of recollection but then it passed into the distant memory of a dream.

By the time she walked in the back door of her house, the extraordinary events of the day had been transformed into the ordinary and mundane. The World Tree was nothing more than a collection of trees in the park, the dodo only a bird, the albino squirrel just a timid forest creature, and the seed, if that's what it was, was nothing more and nothing less than the last birthday present from her mother.

In a furry blur, her puppy ran through her legs across the kitchen floor.

"Sorry I didn't make it back for lunch," she said, closing the door and eyeing the dishes. "Or dinner," she added, as she caught a glimpse of the oven clock.

Her father spun around from the sink, a plate nearly slipping from his wet and trembling fingers. Jackie caught a look of panic on his face as he turned.

"That was some walk you had. I was beginning to worry.," Her father said, an edge creeping into his voice. "I walked to the park twice looking for you."

"I'm sorry," Jackie began. "I am. Milky Way ran away from me in the park. I raced after him and I guess I got lost."

"What park did you go to? Highveil or Yosemite National Park?"

Jackie ignored her father's attempt at forced humor. She paused. Better to change the subject. "I opened up mom's present."

Her father closed his eyes for a moment seemingly lost in his own thoughts. "That's good. I'm glad you took as much time as you needed." Then he sighed. "Next time have your cell phone on and call if you're going to be late. Okay? I thought we had a deal."

Jackie looked at her dad and tried not to look disappointed that he didn't ask what her mother's gift had been.

"How about something to eat?" he offered. "I made your favorite."

Jackie yawned. She was hardly able to stand. The remnants of tangy grilled cheese smelled delicious, but she was suddenly overcome with fatigue.

"Later, I promise. I'm just really tired."

Dad put the dish he was still holding away in the cupboard.

"I hope you got a wonderful birthday present," he said

"Yeah, I think I did. I'm just not sure what it is."

Jackie yawned again; this time even bigger than before. Then she walked out of the kitchen, her head and body hanging forward like a marionette with its strings cut. Slowly she made her way up the stairs and into her room without bothering to close the door or even glance at her unfinished book. She was more exhausted than she had ever been in her entire life. Within minutes she was lying on her bed, shoes still on, fast asleep.

CHAPTER 5

Faster than a giant descending a beanstalk, Jackie rumbled down the steps, taking them two and three at a time. David and Dustin looked up just in time to see her come to a halt, her face red with anger.

"Who opened my door?" she demanded, leveling her gaze at Dustin. "My room is off limits!"

"Not me," said Dustin, lying on the living room floor as he flicked one of his large blue ants just wide of the plastic pants. His harmonica lay nearby. Milky Way bumped down the steps past her, and then curled up next to Dustin.

"Good morning, Sleeping Beauty," said her father as he worked on his own red insect invasion.

"Good shot," chuckled Dustin.

David glanced at his son. In the middle of the night, Dustin had crawled into his bed crying and then curled up in a little ball, still reeling from another one of his bad dreams. "The am-i-nuls hurt, Daddy. They don't know what to do," Dustin had told him tearfully. "I have an achy head."

Jackie was hurting too, he knew. She just expressed it in a different way.

At the bottom of the stairs, Jackie continued to fume.

“Doesn’t anyone care?” demanded Jackie. "Someone went into my room!" She stomped over like an eager detective about to expose a murderer.

"You did," her father explained carefully. "You left it open yesterday when you went into your bedroom. I'm surprised you made it to your pillow. We tried to wake you, but you wouldn't budge. Not even for breakfast this morning."

"We had scwambled eggs," smiled Dustin petting Milky Way.

"How long have I been sleeping?" asked Jackie running her hand through a tangle of unmade hair.

"Since you got home after dinner last night. Over sixteen hours. Dustin and I took Milky Way out for you. Three times.”

When Jackie made no response, he added, “You’re welcome.”

“Thanks Dad,” she said hurriedly.

“Anyway, you must be starving. I can fix you a sandwich if you like."

Jackie shook her head in disbelief. "I just laid down for a little while. I can't believe I slept that long.”

"We were getting concerned about you," said her father getting up from the floor. "But you didn't have a fever or any bumps to your head so I just let you be. How do you feel? I noticed you got some scratches."

"I’m fine," Jackie said, growing exasperated, but David noticed her knees wobble slightly and she looked pale. “I'm gonna go take a shower. I have to get out of these clothes."

David watched as his daughter tiredly walked back upstairs. Jackie always seemed to be escaping since Jillian had passed away. He wasn’t worried about all the books. That actually heartened him since she hadn’t read much before. Fits of anger were to be expected under the circumstances. That at least showed a spark. What bothered him was her distance. She felt so far away since they had moved to Minnesota. He listened to the sound of her fading footsteps, and almost wished she would slam the door, the way she used to after Jillian had died, but she left no trace.

"Good idea," observed Dustin holding his nose. "I hope she takes a long one. She stinks."

"Sometimes your sister *is* a stinker," he told him. "Uh oh."

"What?" Dustin asked with his worried voice. "Do you have to stop playing with me now?"

Feigning surprise, David put his hand to his mouth and tipped over the blue suspenders.

"The ants. They've gotten out. They're crawling all over you!"

"Get them off!" he laughed.

"I'm trying," smiled David tickling his son and noticing absent-mindedly the tree-shaped birthmark that was etched across his forearm. It was the same as his sister's, only smaller and full of leaves. His two children were alike in so many ways yet his daughter was becoming a stranger to him.

"Daddy, are you even trying?" Dustin asked, still giggling.

Milky Way began licking the boy's face, which only made his son roll around even more.

David let thoughts of Jackie go for the moment and instead raised his hands menacingly in the air, twitching his fingers in evil delight.

"I'm trying," he said. "I'm trying."

After a few more moments David stood up.

"No more ants," he said. "I got the last one."

Dustin was still giggling lying on the floor, dozens of colorful insects scattered around him, but David didn't smile. Ending their playtime was never easy and preparing his son with a five-minute warning never really helped. Sometimes it just made it worse.

"Daddy has to go into his office and do a little work, okay?"

His son stopped laughing and sat up crossing his legs.

"Do you *have* to?" he asked.

"Yes, I'm afraid I do. But I won't be busy long, I promise."

"Can we play just a little bit longer?" his son asked, eyes growing wide. "*Pleeeease*"

The puppy climbed up into his lap and laid down in contentment. Dustin stroked its fur gently.

"Why don't you find a book or play with Milky Way for a while?"

Dustin's face fell. "Milky Way is tired. He doesn't want to play right now. He told me so." Tears started welling up in the boy's eyes and he slunk down to the floor again displacing his furry guest.

"Did I do something wrong?" his son asked.

David wrapped his arms around him. "No, buddy, you didn't do anything wrong."

Somehow he had managed to make his daughter angry and his son cry all in the space of 15 minutes.

CHAPTER 6

After lunch, David was outside working in the garden again and still trying to figure out what *he* had done wrong earlier when Jackie came out the back door and down the steps wearing denim shorts and a dark green shirt. She was turning the ring case over in her hands like a puzzle she had somehow forgotten how to solve. Finally, she put it down on the picnic table and came over to where he was gardening. Involuntarily he readied himself for whatever his daughter was about to say.

"Why do you work out here so much anyway?" she said. It was a question wrapped in criticism.

"I don't know," David said. "Just trying to make things grow, I guess. These were your mom's favorite flowers. But a garden just isn't the same without your mom."

A pained look passed over his daughter's face and then was gone. Jackie said nothing for a long time. She looked down at the ground and then lifted her head abruptly and stared at the vibrant red, yellow, purple and white snapdragon blooms still in their plastic boxes. Then she looked over at what he knew was a pitiful garden.

"Want me to help?" she asked.

David raised his eyebrows in surprise.

"Sure. This computer programmer would be forever in your debt. I should have just planted seeds. It would have been less work."

"Well, first of all," she began a bit airily, "you need to make the hole wide enough so the roots have enough space to breathe and branch out. Like this."

Taking the trowel from his grip she expanded the hole he had already constructed.

"You already have it deep enough so now it's just a matter of putting the plant in. Unless you have any fertilizer, that is. Natural would be best."

David shook his head meekly and his daughter dismissed the omission as if she expected nothing less.

"Right," she said. "I guess you're ready then."

David reached out and picked up the Snapdragon, eager to finish the lesson.

"Don't knock off those clumps of dirt," she chastised. "That's good soil."

With careful movement he lowered the flower into the hole and filled the dirt in around it.

"Now just remember to get some fertilizer or manure, maybe even some peat and sprinkle it in. You know, to help it grow."

"Manure?" mouthed David with a questioning look. "You know, your mother always used that stuff. Said it was black magic. She'd have me pick up these 50-pound bags at the nursery. I never could understand how she could go through so much. I used to kid her that some of it must have ended up in the meals when it was her turn to cook."

He started to laugh. But then he noticed Jackie and the shadow that passed over her unsmiling face at the mention of her mother. It didn't last long, and then it was gone, but the mood had definitely changed.

"I'd better go in and check on Dustin," she said quickly. "He was pouting before about how I never take him on walks. One puppy's enough. I wish he could just take care of himself."

David looked at Jackie as she walked back to the house and a momentary spark of hope, of recollection, fired in his tired eyes. The decision was made without thinking or calculating. The words just sprang from his mouth.

"Have I ever told you how your mother and I first met?"

Jackie turned slightly but made no response and although she came no nearer, she didn't walk away either as David told the tale of the day he would never forget. It had been many years ago, but it still seemed like yesterday.

Each step I had taken along the forest trail seemed to bring another mosquito bite. I swatted at one bloodthirsty insect after another and then wiped the sweat away from my eyes.

Each year the company I worked for, NetTec, sent some of its more promising employees to a national seminar focusing on information age technology issues. That particular year, for reasons still unfathomable to me, the convention had decided to focus all its energies on the theme of technological isolationism and the need for meaningful human binary relationships or some such nonsense.

So me and a co-worker, Gary Lavlin, got on a plane and flew from Arlington, Virginia (the birthplace of the Internet) to Minneapolis, Minnesota where we soon left civilization behind, driving north into a world of pine trees where a resort was nestled.

Gary was one of those people who really needed to be your friend. It didn't matter how many ways and how many times you tried to tell him that you didn't need that sort of attention. He just kept right at it anyway following along everywhere.

"Sounds familiar," interjected Jackie sourly. "What about Mom?"

"I'm getting to that," said David. "Just listen."

After a particularly numbing day of workshops and seminars Gary asked me, smiling from ear-to-ear, if I would like to have dinner together. I think I managed to mutter something about needing some air and then excused myself. I knew full well that my Team Partner could not follow me outside due to an unexpected allergic reaction to everything Minnesotan. But just to be sure I decided to take a nature hike that some of the other resort guests had started on earlier that afternoon. It was supposed to be breathtakingly beautiful, with panoramic overlooks, an abundance of animal life, and even a small waterfall.

Almost an hour later, the only animal life I had seen were swarms of wretched mosquitoes.

I was thinking of heading back when I heard the sound of running water. Eager for a distraction from stinging insects I stepped off the path. A few minutes later I found the little stream and began following it, stepping carefully along the bush and tree-lined bank. Before long the faint sound of falling water met my ears. With each passing minute it grew noticeably louder as the tangy air enveloped my senses.

Tearing the branches away from my face, I stepped through the archway where two trees crossed and was suddenly standing on a small, grassy covered peninsula. It was otherwise barren except for an ancient looking tree, almost impossibly tall, which rose up from the edge of the opposite shore. Upstream, tumbling twenty feet or so in a silvery-white curtain of spray and foam, was the waterfall. A small rainbow sparkled in its midst.

But I only looked at that scene for a moment. Something else had captured my attention. A person leaned somewhat awkwardly against the great tree, a woman more breathtakingly beautiful than all of the nature surrounding her.

She was wearing blue jeans and a t-shirt. Long red hair fell down to her waist. Although she was short, almost schoolgirl height, her stature was somehow elevated by the way she carried herself, as if she carried a secret inside her. She reminded me of one of those forest creatures, an elf or a nymph perhaps. And like them, she appeared younger than her years. If it wasn't for her obvious maturity, I might have mistaken her for a lost child.

The next moment her legs gave away and she fell to the ground

Rushing through the long grass in a panic I leaped into the stream. It was cold, but only came up to my shins. I reached her moments later and bent beside her, dripping water.

She seemed disorientated.

"Where am I?"

The question seemed absurd. "We're in the middle of the woods near Ely, Minnesota."

Taking this information in, the woman looked up at me and smiled faintly.

"It moved. I didn't know it could. I'm glad. What year is it?"

I looked at her speechless, thinking it a joke. She asked me again so I told her.

"Thank you," she mouthed. "I'll be fine. Let me sleep—just a little."

Then she closed her eyes to the world and did just that.

During the next several hours she stirred only once and then only fitfully as if in a dream, mumbling nonsensical words of towering trees, creatures above the clouds, and other fairy tale things. Several times I reached out to check her forehead for fever or to gingerly feel for bumps on her head. Finding none, I waited. What else could I do? When she awoke and opened her eyes, I was right beside her.

With a start she sat up and put a hand to her temple.

"What's wrong?" I asked, worried that I had made a mistake in not insisting she seek medical attention immediately. I backed away to give her space.

"Bad headache," she replied thickly. "It will pass."

Slowly she stood up, wobbling for a moment as she found her balance. With a shaking hand she brushed the hair out of her eyes, revealing a strange tree-shaped birthmark on her neck. Taking a deep breath, she took a cautious step forward. Her movements seemed fragile and unsure as if she were an astronaut just returned to the Earth or an infant learning to walk for the first time.

"I don't understand," I began. "Were you drinking before? Are you ill or in need of medication?"

The woman tried to smile again, but failed. "Earth Fall," she breathed.

But that didn't make any sense. She must have said "waterfall" or just "fall."

I didn't know what else to say or what to do. She wasn't talking clearly. But in time her speech became more recognizable, more coherent. Soon she was able to walk without help.

She told him how she had gotten lost, how she had wandered for the better part of two days with no food and little water. How she had slipped and turned her ankle.

Then she thanked me again, always politely declining my repeated efforts to take her to a doctor. We parted back at Paul Bunyan's Pine Lodge Resort, but not before I talked her into staying overnight and resting in a room of her own. The management seemed happy enough to waive the cost of her room once they learned of her story. Late the next morning, when I went to knock on her door, I found only the maid finishing her chores and a note on the bedside table which read:

Write to me Prince Charming. I don't know your name.
Thanks again!
Jillian Gardner (now you know mine)

Her address in California was written below.

Feeling like a character in a nineteenth century novel I wrote to her, with pen and paper, telling her my name (finally), my work, my dreams, and more as the months went on. We wrote letters back and forth between the coasts (I was amazed that she didn't have a computer, and she preferred not to use the phone) until one day, almost a year later, on the first day of summer, I met your Mom again near her home in northern California. It was in a park again, Muir Woods, this time in the shade of redwood trees.

Six months later, after many more dates, we were married and living in Ambler, Pennsylvania where I began a new job in nearby Philadelphia.

"Not too long after that, you came along," finished David.

Jackie held herself still, not wanting to break the spell of the story.

"Hard to believe you hiked in the woods," she said smiling.

"Yes," her father said dryly, "I did all sorts of amazing things in my younger days."

Jackie wrinkled her nose at him and rolled her eyes.

"Do you know if mom liked trees?" She asked. "I mean *really* liked them?"

"She sure did. She planted them everywhere around the house after we got married. It was the only way I could get her to move back to civilization."

Jackie paused, opened her mouth as if to speak, and then closed it again.

"That place in Minnesota where you met mom in the woods. Is that close to here?"

"Not really. I figure it's a ways from here. Up north. At least a half-a-day's drive, I guess."

He paused.

"Funny thing is, when I went back the tree was gone. I must have gotten lost. Those woods all look the same. Hey, are you okay?"

Although she tried to hide it, Jackie's eyes were slowly filling up with tears.

"I'm fine," she said, wiping the tears away and unintentionally smearing her makeup.

David reached out a hand to comfort his daughter. To his surprise she didn't flinch. "Hey, what's wrong?"

"It's nothing," Jackie said. "I guess I just wanted to see that tree. It's stupid."

"No, it's not—" David began.

She shook her head. “I gotta go, okay?" Jackie said, standing up quickly. “Thanks for the story.”

Then she took off running along the side of the house toward the sidewalk and the street.

"Where are you going?" he called after her.

But his daughter had already disappeared around the corner of the house without her puppy. A lone monarch butterfly fluttered into view like an emissary from heaven. Wiping the dirt from his hands, he got up to check on Dustin. Sometimes that kid was so quiet you wouldn’t even know he was there.

CHAPTER 7

Jackie ran as fast as she could with her heart pounding in her chest like a warning bell. She ran to the park because she didn't know where else to go. Whenever she felt like this, she just had to get away. All the while she dashed down the sidewalk, she couldn't shake the feeling that there was something she was forgetting. Her father had mentioned it in passing.

Then it hit her. She came to a halt and leaned against a tree.

"A seed!" she thought in amazement.

That's what her mother's gift had been. How could she have forgotten? Her father's story had brought at least part of yesterday's events back. There had been a luminous seed and a great tree which resembled the one her mother had slept under. That couldn't be a coincidence! Her mother had always loved living things. She liked gardening and taking care of plants. Yet it went beyond that.

Another memory came back to her now, much more distant. She had been a little girl playing outside as her mother worked in the garden. With her dolls, she would spend countless hours amidst the towering flowers pretending to climb them or more often playing house with her scattered clothes and miniature plastic appliances.

"Do you see this one," her mother had said, pointing to a sagging flower that had bent in the wind. "I can fix it and I don't even need a needle and thread."

Reaching out she held the broken stem between two fingers and closed her eyes. Slowly, her mother began speaking, but the words were silly and they made Jackie giggle. Stronger and clearer came the sounds until they took on a melody all their own. *Sunaria Folium. Mortalisanimea. Nahla.* Now her mother was smiling. From the gaps between her fingers Jackie saw a glow like a firefly spread. It sparkled once, growing in intensity and then vanished.

"That should do it, I think."

Then she had removed her hand to reveal an unbroken green stem.

"Fixed," Jackie said, delighted at the transformation as only a small child could be. "Magic!"

"Yes, sweetie" her mother had answered. "Sort of."

Jackie held out one of her fingers. It had a Care Bears band aid wrapped around it. "Make better?"

Her mother's smile wavered, but only for a moment.

"I wish I could. Come here. Let me kiss it again."

Jackie watched as her mother kissed her finger up and down.

"Dollies have owwies too," Jackie said, holding up her favorite one.

"That's okay," her mother had said. "I've got lots of kisses."

As if one memory opened the door to another, Jackie remembered one more thing. It had been a bright sunny day with a blue sky above. She had been only a few years older. The wind battered a plastic kite. Jackie had hung on to the string with all her might. Suddenly the string broke and the kite drifted away high on the breeze. She began to cry. Then her mother had sung a strange song.

"Sunaria Springeldergreen. Hulunia Dansadew."

The wind quieted and her kite floated down, landing near her feet. Big, wise owl eyes stared up at her from the ground.

That was all she remembered for now, but it was enough. A surge of pride passed through Jackie. There had always been something special about her mother. When other gardens in their neighborhood were withering in heat or overrun by bugs, her mother's garden was always immaculate. Almost impossibly so.

Green thumb my foot! Jackie thought.

Suddenly she felt an overwhelming need to check on her birthday present. Racing around the corner she bolted across the road, a car horn blaring suddenly with a screech of brakes, and then she was passing under the arching gate of the city park. Just inside the green oasis, she allowed herself to rest momentarily and collect her thoughts. But all she had were questions and a growing desire to find the great tree again where she had planted the seed.

Unable to wait any longer, although her breath still came in rapid bursts, she took off running once again. Ignoring the path completely, she stepped toward the green-dark world of the quiet little forest.

And froze. Out of the corner of her eye, Jackie spied, or thought she did, a small figure coming up the path behind her, but when she turned around there was no one there. Shaking her head, she entered the milky shadows.

Jackie breathed deeply, her earlier exertion forgotten. She liked the peaceful feeling that came over her when she walked in the living green spaces and the world outside disappeared. With her body relaxed, she began walking through the trees at a vigorous pace; the only sound was that of her tennis shoes as they crunched on the ground below. It could have been a magical magnet pulling her along for she could never explain how she found the Tree again. There was no trail or markings nor did she have a clear idea which way she had gone before. But in short order (much quicker than last time it seemed to her), she walked into the flowering meadow for a second time, on this occasion bypassing the thorns entirely.

In front of her was the tree of trees. Its branches, thick as Atlas's arms, rose from a trunk so titanic, and yet so natural, that Jackie imagined its roots descending down into the very heart of the Earth itself or rising from it, like a sapling from a seed eternal. Spreading out and above the woody splendor were fingertips of life; whorls of emerald and mossy hues that reached up to touch the sky. All was as she had remembered it or rather remembered it anew. She was so taken by the sight that she didn't see at first the great green snaking vine that wrapped its way around the bark like a living ladder.

Running over she looked up and saw in amazement how the stalk disappeared and then reappeared, like a slithering serpent, higher and ever higher into the dizzying branches above. Finally, with a height incalculable, it winded its way into green oblivion with the sun-darkened leaves obscuring any further view.

But the marvel that most interested Jackie was at her feet.

There, at the foot of the mammoth plant, the remnants of her handiwork could still be seen: a gently curving rise of dirt that had formed the protective cover for the strange and beautiful seed she had planted here only a day before. The *Amarantha*.

"*It can't be*!" she wanted to shout. But she knew it was true. There was no other explanation.

Following the stalk up with her eyes, Jackie breathed a long, open-mouthed, "Wow!" and then sat down heavily in front of the Tree. She felt as if she had walked miles instead of only a few blocks to get here. She reasoned that her body was just tired from all her earlier running. But it hadn't seemed like she had worked that hard. Then again, when she really stopped to think about it, she couldn't remember exactly what she had done or how long it had taken to find her way here again. The sun was conveniently hidden behind the clouds, obscuring the time of day.

Confused, Jackie let out a healthy yawn and then another. She felt spent as if she had just run a marathon. Although she tried to resist, before she knew it, she was lying down in the soft meadow grass and her eyes began to close.

"Nobody has to fertilize you," she muttered dreamily to the skyscraper-sized vine.

Just before she fell into a deep sleep Jackie noticed the red X painted on the side of the tree.

Then dreams swept her away, but they were dark and troubling, featuring a towering figure clad in black who meant to take something precious away. Powerful arms reached out for her as a black dove alighted at the tips of his fingers.

Jackie awoke in a cold sweat.

"Wake up! Wake up!" said the familiar voice again as small hands shook her. "Naptime is over."

She opened her eyes. Disorientated from her already fading dream, she could only stare at her brother Dustin in disbelief as he took a step backward. He was wearing jean shorts and a red t-shirt. Reaching up he touched the great wrapping vine which disappeared up the trunk. Somehow she felt betrayed by his presence as if this was a sacred space, her own secret that he violated by being here.

"Sorry," he said meekly. "Did I scare you?"

"What are you doing here?" Jackie said. "You shouldn't have come."

"Followed you. In woods," he said proudly. "You were sleeping a long time."

Something of her dream came back to her at that moment. Not the details itself for those had already faded away, but a feeling nonetheless. Seeing Dustin, she was overcome with thankfulness and smiled despite her surprise.

"Hey kiddo," she said. "That was a big walk you went on. But you shouldn't have followed me. Not across the road and into the park. Definitely not here. Dad is going to be worried." *And he's going to blame me.* She sighed. "Do you understand?"

Dustin hung his head and his mouth curled into sadness as his eyes filled with tears. Looking at him a little bit more of Jackie's anger crumbled.

"Followed you," Dustin mumbled. "I miss you."

Jackie stood up, wiping the loose strands of hair from her face.

"I've missed you too. I haven't been a very good big sister lately, have I?"

"You don't play with me anymore," he said sadly.

"Look," she said, trying not to be defensive. "I know it's been hard. I've been busy. Thinking," she continued searching for an explanation. "Ever since Mom… You wouldn't understand. But I'll make you a promise," she began.

"No promises!" her brother interrupted. "Daddy's busy. You're busy. But I'm not," he said with a sniffle, wiping his eyes with the back of his hand. "Do you wanna see me climb? I was prac-ti-cing while you were napping. It's easy."

"Maybe later, okay? I got to get you home. C'mon, let's go."

"Not later. Watch me!" shouted Dustin.

Before she could stop him, he scrambled up the vine like he had been born to do it. Jackie grabbed for him, but he was already out of reach.

"Look!" he called down. "Look at me!"

Jackie swallowed with fear. She hated heights.

"Come down, Dustin. This isn't funny. You could get hurt."

In response, her brother climbed even higher.

"You get down right now or I'll never play with you again! Do you hear me?"

Her brother froze on the great vine.

"I'll tell Dad you followed me and I'll tell him you climbed up here and wouldn't come down. Is that what you want?"

Dustin inched up the tree further like a miniature acrobat, his sneakers nimbly ascending the thick twisting greenery.

"You better listen," she said putting her hands on her hips. "This is your last chance. Don't make me come up there."

She placed her hands tentatively on the thick stalk and looked up at her brother into the dizzying heights. She had always been afraid of high places. Even step ladders and scenic overlooks made her nervous. "Please," she said. *Don't make me go up there.*

Her head was already starting to spin and her stomach felt sick.

"God, I hate you when you act like this," she muttered under her breath.

But soft as her voice was, it carried across the distance. Something in the meadow amplified the words and Dustin heard—heard enough to know.

"I don't like you too," he cried.

A moment later, he took off up the vine, up the winding living stairs that wrapped around the tree again and again and again. Soon he would be lost to her completely.

Swallowing her fear, she stepped onto an old branch stub that stuck out low on the mighty trunk and then leaped to where the curving vine was wide enough to stand on. That was almost too much and her heart froze with the realization of what she had done, and what she still had to do. For a moment she was unable to move, her eyes closed tightly as her hands gripped the rough bark of the tree like a lifeline. But her brother was up there. Somewhere. That made her move.

Slowly, she began dragging one foot after another across the glistening, textured surface of the stalk that wound itself around the tree trunk in ever-spiraling arcs. One step at a time she made her way upwards. Soon the 'staircase' widened so that it was nearly half as wide as she was tall. Even so, her progress was torturous. It helped that the Amarantha's surface was sticky, giving her some small measure of safety. Yet it was the plant's curving form which made all the difference for Jackie. Rather than being simply flat, the vine's surface grew up on the sides to create a natural barrier, and more importantly, handrails. She used these extensively. Twisting ever skyward, the massive plant curved around the tree like a living helix. Translucent leaves bigger than elephant ears drooped just out of reach. When the sunlight struck a patch of emerald in just the right way, the leaf blossomed in momentary color.

"All from one tiny seed," Jackie thought in amazement.

Birdsong soothed her electrically charged senses and light filtered through the canopy of leaves as she climbed. When she finally gave in to the morbid desire and looked down, she realized with a small degree of comfort that she could not see the ground, obscured as it was, by the tree's dense foliage.

Even so, she was frozen in place, unable to climb up or down for fear of falling.

You have to do something, she told herself. *You can't stay here.*

"Dustin!" she called. "Can you hear me?"

There was no answer, but for a moment she thought she heard a distant rustle of leaves and peculiar chattering.

Taking a deep breath, she began walking as briskly as the sloping vine and her frayed nerves would allow.

Higher and higher she climbed into the gathering darkness of leaves and seasons. Through branches of summer, spring, barren winter, and fall she turned, her feet carrying her forward, past clouds of insects and fallen leaves, always looking for a sign of her little brother.

Surely, he couldn't have climbed so high.

A cold wind began to blow and the air seemed too thin as if she were leaving the Earth behind. The light grew dim. She stepped more carefully, more slowly. Her energy was nearly spent and her breathing was ragged. How long she climbed, she did not know. Time itself seemed to work differently here. When she thought for sure the sun was extinguished and was afraid to move any further for fear of stepping blindly off the tree, a hazy glow of light appeared above her. Relieved, she began working her way towards it. The illumination grew steadily stronger until finally she stood, panting and sweating, a hands-length under a sea of dusk-colored, translucent leaves. They looked so brittle, so thin, like the skin of an old man where one breath might blow them to dust. Carefully, so as not to disturb the veil, Jackie peered through.

There, on a sloping branch the size of a cafeteria table, sat a bright red squirrel. It had darting eyes, black and beady. When it spied Jackie, the creature began chattering incessantly. Away it bounded up the tree, still clicking in a gossip-like staccato, as if it were broadcasting burning news. Then it was lost in the shadowy and confusing foliage that continued high above.

"Dustin!" she called with equal parts frustration and worry. "Where are you?"

Leaving behind the light where the strange squirrel had been, Jackie climbed into crepuscular reaches nearly devoid of illumination. It was as if she were in the belly of a whale swallowed whole by the great tree, an insignificant pest already forgotten.

The darkness was nearly complete now. Her steps slowed to a halt and a warm feeling suffused with fatigue coursed through her body. It would be so easy to simply lie down and go to sleep. All her worries would be forgotten.

Jackie shook her head violently to banish the thought. Her brother was up there, somewhere, all alone, she reminded herself harshly. She had to bring him back down.

Moving with renewed determination she began climbing again. Soon the stalk narrowed and a vague glow appeared through the thinning branches.

With relief and trepidation Jackie popped her head through the canopy like a rabbit out of a hole and looked around.

Whiteness stretched complete and unbroken as far as she could see. It was as if she were standing on top of the world's largest marshmallow or the Antarctic wilderness.

Jackie's mouth hung open as she stared at the alien landscape.

Yet the more she looked, the more she discovered that there were other features as well, images that were more familiar. All around her, the whitescape rose in a high cumulous glow as if that were the source of the strange light. Sometimes the cloud terrain took on the form of a castle or minaret before falling away into billowy waves of sky-foam and stratus plains. Even as she reveled in these sights, a more somber specter drew her attention. Spread across the pure stratosphere valley, she noticed, were dark, stormy bands or lumps. *Like cancer,* she thought with foreboding.

Then she saw the movement. A small figure ran across the clouds.

"Dustin!" she yelled.

But he was too far away and running the wrong way.

"Dustin!" she yelled again, hearing her voice echo across the sky. "Come back!"

And for a moment Jackie thought that he might. Her brother slowed to a halt and turned his head, looking for the source of the sound. In that one moment he seemed utterly lost and alone like an explorer on an endless sheet of ice. But at least he wasn't running away anymore.

"Stay right there!" She shouted moving towards him, and then nearly screamed in fright as she realized she had climbed out of her hole. She was standing on *top* of the cloud. The places where her feet rested felt like super strong cotton candy and although she wasn't falling through at all, it seemed to her only a matter of time before she did.

When she looked up again, he was running. No yelling or pleading could make him stop. Precious seconds ticked by as she struggled with her fear of heights, unable to wade out into the quicksand of clouds. A few heartbeats later, she gathered her courage and took off after him. Jackie was so focused on Dustin that she didn't notice that they weren't alone. A figure, hardly more than a smudge, grew larger as it moved across the expansive cloud range. When it entered the inky tainted terrain, Jackie finally noticed the visitor, but it was nearly too late. Quicker than she thought possible it had covered half the remaining open distance and took on the vague shape of horse and rider. Both the mount and figure atop it were darker than death, a living shadow among the light. The rider rode in stark defiance with a single slit of blackness, a pennon streaming tattered from an upraised staff.

An unnatural shiver passed through her, although the temperature was pleasant. Her brother had seen it coming, she realized, and he was afraid, frozen where he stood.

"Run! Dustin!" Jackie yelled. "For God's sake run!" But her voice seemed small, constricted by a terror she could not name. Only her legs continued to move.

Within a handful of strides, Jackie could make out the clouds of frosty exertion exhaled by the midnight dyed horse as if the creature were freezing from within. Every falling hoof beat produced an accompanying crack of thunder that echoed in the air. The rider crossed the remaining distance as fast as lightning and as certain as disaster. She could see the storm-bent staff now as well as the gloved hand that wrapped itself around it. She watched the hooves beat in unstoppable repetition as she waited for the sound of the final thunderclap that would swallow her whole. But there was only silence. Suddenly an awful emptiness opened at the bottom of her stomach. It was as if she were watching a movie she had seen before and couldn't change.

One more stride, both horrible and fascinating, the rider turned his hooded face directly toward her. Somewhere from within those shadows she caught a glimpse of surprise or amusement in his eyes. Then he turned away. Too late, Dustin tried to turn around and run back towards her.

"Dustin!" she wailed, her voice breaking with emotion.

Even as she surged forward to shield her brother, Jackie knew the distance was too great. The climb had spent valuable energy and even her adrenaline wasn't enough.

Leaning ever so slightly in his saddle with his arm down lazily, as if about to pick a flower, the hooded figure plucked Dustin in mid-step, riding off with him across the cloud tops, finally disappearing into the vague mountain vapors on the opposite side. At that exact moment, something within Jackie broke and she fell to her knees.

CHAPTER 8

At first it was just a game. The quiet was just silence waiting to be broken. The emptiness was just space waiting to be filled. But by the last room, an eerie foreboding had taken a hold of David.

"Dustin, come out. This isn't funny anymore."

He kept expecting to see his son pop up or come running around a corner giggling with laughter, victorious at eluding detection for so long. Oh, how he loved playing hide-and-seek. But there was only the growing unease and the sound of his own rising voice threatening to break.

"I give up! Come out! Come out, wherever you are!" David called, his voice cracking and his worry overpowering his ability to sound playful. "Do you hear me? Come out! Game's…" "

David's voice cut off as if it had been strangled. There, written in bright red crayon and clipped to the fridge message board with thoughtful precision was a note from Dustin.

"**Be Bak soom**" was all it said.

CHAPTER 9

Jackie sat hunched over in disbelief. She couldn't believe her brother was gone. For the longest time she just stared at the last place Dustin had been before he disappeared. Tears flowed down her cheeks, but it felt as if someone else were crying them. When they finally subsided, she felt empty inside. No thoughts of anger or worry stirred within her. The expected panic did not rise from her gut. She formulated no plan of action. There was nothing for her to do since she couldn't accept that it had really happened.

"What is this," she murmured numbly, "some kind of fairy tale?"

"That is the stupidest thing I've ever heard," retorted a voice harshly.

Jackie turned around in slow motion and for a moment, saw nothing. Then she looked down. There was the creature again. It was the same strange bird that had appeared at the foot of the tree. Perhaps she hadn't imagined it after all.

The creature was much bigger than a turkey and decidedly more plump. Blue-gray plumage covered it like a tacky carpet. Its over-sized head sported a black bill ending in a reddish sheath that tapered off unmercifully to a hooked tip. Along each side of its body was a small, useless wing that looked like it had been put there as some sort of cosmic joke. Bearing the brunt of all this absurdity were two stout yellow legs. It was, without a doubt, a dodo bird, with a few unexpected abilities; namely that it had an attitude and was speaking to her again.

"Listen, deary," the bird continued, leveling its BB-sized pupils directly at her. With every word, the ridiculous creature managed to convey a sound directly opposite to birdsong. "I'm no Cheshire cat as you can plainly see and no Prince Charming is going to ride in on his steed to save the day. The boy is gone and if he isn't dead already, he'll soon wish he was. There is no escaping where he's been taken."

"I'm afraid Regnal's right," said a man's voice. It sounded like the wind rattling through October leaves; tired, coming at the end of the season.. "There's nothing we can do."

As Jackie watched, his form seemed to materialize from the wispy surroundings as if it were taking shape from some greater mystery. In front of her eyes, the shifting cloud canvas became a patchwork cloak of morning glories and creeping green vines that ended in a multitude of filigree roots. These in turn disappeared into the white clouds at his feet. On his head was a crown of bristlecone-pine with one small flower, a violet, growing from his forehead through the tangle.

The only place that wasn't covered with living green growth was on his face and hands. His skin was weathered. His fingers were knotted and bark-like and were wrapped tightly around a gnarled staff of wood. Deep lines, rivulets of time, stretched across his cheeks and under his eyes like tectonic struggles she could not begin to fathom. A long, thin beard the color of the mottled clouds covered his chin like a retreating glacier on a rock-strewn mountaintop. But it was the stranger's mouth and eyes that held her the most, for it was these alone that seemed to contain his essence. The former drooped like a flower gone to seed, but his eyes, sunk beneath frosty brows, still sparkled like deep pools of secret blue water.

"Who has taken him? Where is he?" she asked.

"Gaylon has taken him," explained the leafy figure with a touch of sadness.

"Gaylon *the Black*," corrected the dodo bird. "Taken him to Flood and the Arkanum."

The tall figure nodded solemnly like a tree bowing to the wind.

"Oh," mouthed Jackie, trying to stay afloat, but it was all too much, and she was drowning, becoming as tenuous as the clouds which swirled at her feet. When her legs gave way and she slipped into blessed oblivion it seemed like the next best thing to a happy ending.

Jackie awoke with a sudden start, her body rigid as if she had just fallen to the ground. Long strands of hair covered her face and she brushed them away. The first thing she saw when she opened her sleep-encrusted eyes was a gnarled old man covered in living growth. His face, as he leaned over her, was riddled with concern.

"So you're awake. Welcome back," the canopy of leaves said with undisguised relief. "You had quite a rest."

It was the strange leafy figure from her storybook dream. A dream she was evidently still having.

“We’ve been expecting you.”

But Jackie barely heard him. She barely saw him. Struggling to sit up, she at once began looking around frantically. There was something very important that she was supposed to do, but for the life of her she couldn’t remember. Nothing she saw reassured her.

"This isn't my bedroom," she said. "And this most definitely isn't my house."

Everything she saw was utterly wrong. She was in some kind of living enclosure. The walls were branches intertwined into undulating angles, an uneven sphere. Rising to her feet from a bed of sweet-smelling grass, she stared up at the ceiling only to find there was none. Instead, a multitude of stars blinked back at her amidst a ring of celestial blackness.

"Where am I?" she exclaimed as something light and nimble ran across her feet.

Looking down, Jackie saw a squirrel the color of fallen snow scamper across the dirt strewn floor. From a string tied around its neck dangled a single silver coin. As she watched the creature slowly circled her in ever decreasing arcs until it was wrapped, bushy tail and all, around her ankles in a playful pose.

"You feel real," murmured Jackie, not trusting her senses.

At those words the albino squirrel rested its furry nose atop her shoe and closed its eyes.

"It is a good sign," said the leaf covered old man with more hope than conviction.

"It is a sign we are not *completely* lost," said the dodo next to him. "Nothing more. Optimism is still close to extinction."

"What is this place?" asked Jackie, nervously looking around.

They both turned toward her. The man-sized leaf pile raised his mossy eyebrows in surprise.

"My manners and my senses desert me in these dark days," he said apologetically. "Please accept my condolences for your loss, Jackie. We have not been properly introduced. My name is Nimbus. I am the Keeper here, and this," he paused gesturing down to the clump of unruly feathers, "is Regnal. You must not take any great offense at him. The napping creature at your feet is called Pence. You are in HeartWood, my home of sorts. Be welcome."

He paused.

"We have been expecting a visit from a child of Jillian."

Jackie looked back dumbfounded.

"Is this some kind of joke?"

"I wish it were," replied Nimbus gravely. "So much pain and effort could be avoided."

"You're not making any sense," Jackie replied. "How do you know so much about me? I didn't know I was coming until I got here."

Obscured behind leaf and twig, the Keeper's eyes darted over to Regnal as if asking a secret question before responding.

"Most find us by intent rather than by accident," he replied carefully. "They come when it is time if they have the talent. Children receive many gifts from their mothers. Jillian had much to give. She was one of my best students."

"You mean she was *here*?" Jackie asked in disbelief. "What did she do? How long was she here?"

"Questions, questions," chided the Keeper. "So many questions. All in good time, yes? For now, let me merely say that Pence is my eyes and ears of the world below, and he is infinitely more reliable than that gossipy rodent you saw on your way up here."

Jackie remembered the blazing squirrel alight on the branches of the great tree. It had been the only creature visible during her ascent.

"Ratatosk," Nimbus was saying, "has a wagging tongue of flame, capable of spreading mischief faster than a wildfire. Pence favors me with his careful observations when it suits him, and they are invaluable, yet I would have to be blind and even more senile not to notice that you have your mother's eyes and spirit."

Jackie nodded, acknowledging the compliment while another part of her slipped away. It was all too much. In truth, she barely listened. Instead she shrunk into herself, retreating to a safer place where things made more sense.

"If I may," continued the Keeper, "allow me to ask one question of you. What talent do you possess?"

"I'm not sure what you mean. Mom said I was a really good gardener and I ace all of my spelling tests."

A troubled look passed over the Keeper's face.

"Did your mother have a chance to talk with you about this place before she passed," Nimbus asked gently.

A familiar sadness wormed its way into Jackie's voice and she shook her head.

"We're doomed," Regnal proclaimed. "She's as useless as my wings."

"There's no sense jumping to conclusions," the Keeper countered, but it seemed a half-hearted response.

As if raising a battered shield, Jackie covered her face with her hands and closed her eyes.

"I know it's lame, but would someone please tell me if I'm dreaming," she murmured.

"There she goes again," Regnal remarked.

Ignoring his flightless servant, Nimbus shambled over. Jackie watched him through the slits of her fingers as he gingerly reached into the midsection of his forest growth where a stomach should be. She imagined him pulling out one of his internal organs (if he had any) or some jungle monster from the dark depths. With trepidation, she steeled herself as a rustling of leaves and feathers became a pair of alabaster wings. In fascination and horror, she watched as a mourning dove alighted on his shoulder.

"Isn't this better than a dream?" he said with a glimmer of a smile.

Then he reached a leafy hand out to touch her shoulder.

Jackie flinched in sudden terror.

"Get away from me," she warned rising to her feet, startling and dislodging her furry freeloader. "Whatever you are, leave me alone."

Her tone was defiant and yet the remnants of her inner strength were crumbling fast. So much had happened and she didn't know how to make sense of it all. She needed help.

"I have to find my brother," she said as tears welled up in the corners of her eyes.

Turning, rather than be seen by whoever or whatever it was, she started walking away. Soon she was running across the mossy floor towards the edge of the enclosure looking for a way out. But whichever way she turned, she could not see a door or an opening which might let her pass. The tangle of wood and leaf was complete. All around her the air seemed stagnant and stale as if the weight of time accumulated here.

Out of the corner of her eye she spied, in the center of the room, something that looked like a window in the floor. With her heart pounding in her chest she made for it, gulping air as if she couldn't get enough. It was a raised circle, easily ten feet in diameter, containing a pool of glasslike liquid. Clouds swirled at her feet but when she tried to touch them, they were out of reach. Water rippled gently but the image remained untroubled. It was only then that she noticed the ribbons of blue and the unmistakable patterns of dusky continents as they coalesced and drifted into view through the bands of white.

She was looking down at the Earth.

This was more than she could take and so she ran again, but this time without purpose. She needed time, she needed space, and she needed to escape.

Unseen behind her, the Keeper raised a leafy digit and traced an invisible circle in midair.

An arched doorway suddenly appeared where before there had been only an unbroken wall of tightly woven branches. Fresh air filled her lungs as she plunged down the tunnel-like exit. For the first time, she realized how rich smelling everything was, how alive. Branches whizzed past her, tugging at her clothes, scraping at her skin, and she imagined herself back in the park, scampering through the trees. But there was no sun visible, only a faint light that broke through the dark wall of leaves like an afterglow without warming her skin. Layer after layer of foliage dropped away in ever decreasing density until, with a final wave of her hand, she pulled back the last branch and peered out on a vast cloudscape valley filled with a multitude of animals beyond counting. It was like a colossal puzzle with the pieces all jumbled. Overhead a golden and radiant chariot arced its way across the sky heralding another day.

"Welcome to Treetops," toned Nimbus from her side as if he had never left it.

"Treetop"

CHAPTER 10

David sat on the stylish ottoman with his head in his hands wondering what he hadn't thought of, where else he could look. He had walked the neighborhood calling their names. He had been to the park three times. He drove the streets of Rockwood. There was no sign of either one of them. And of course he had checked the backyard tree house; the place Dustin loved so much. Not a clue, anywhere. It was as if they had vanished off the face of the Earth.

A lifetime ago back in Pennsylvania, he had made a tree house for Jackie because she begged him to, but then she had been too timid to actually climb up it. Dustin was a different story. Without any fear, his son defied gravity to new heights every chance he could get, whether on the playground, around the house, or in trees. David always had to keep an eye on him to make sure he wasn't getting into trouble. Somehow he had let his son down.

Running his hands through his thinning salt and pepper hair, David stood up and walked over to the window. Pulling the curtains aside he gazed into the deepening darkness, trying to probe its secrets. A car drove by, but it did not slow down. Nervously he tapped his fingers on the windowsill. He had never been good at waiting. There was no moon or even stars out and he quickly sat back down, unwilling to stare into the void. At his feet Milky Way lay in a small furry ball and whined low and mournfully.

His one bright hope was that Dustin and Jackie were together, and she had just lost track of time. He imagined them noisily opening the back door amid a flurry of yawns and apologies. But that reassurance was fading with every creep of the minute hand. It was almost 10:30 PM he realized, glancing at his watch again.

Not even a phone call, David thought with growing alarm. Worse, there was no way for him to call. Jackie had forgotten or purposefully left her cell phone at home. He felt completely cut-off.

The sudden knock froze his heart. He leaped for the door and opened it wide.

"Good evening," said the police officer. His features were obscured by the darkness.

But David said nothing in response. He only stared back with a drained and vacant look on his face.

"Are you Mr. David Ashmore?" the officer asked.

David nodded his head weakly. Good news never came from an officer of the law standing on your doorstep.

"Did you call concerning two missing children?"

"Oh, yes. I did. Of course," he blurted out like a revelation. "Nearly an hour ago. Have you found out anything? Where are they?"

"Mr. Ashmore, can I step inside please? I just need to ask you a few questions. It will only take a few minutes."

The living room light revealed a young officer, hardly more than a boy, David thought, although the gun holstered at the man's waist certainly looked real. His uniform, although smartly pressed, hung loose and long on his legs and arms, as if he were expected to literally grow into his new position. Yet when David looked at his face and listened to his voice, he noticed no indecision of procedure or of character. Sewn above a silver badge was the officer's name.

"Perhaps we could sit down," said Officer Lindquist politely but firmly.

"Yes, yes of course," stammered David, leading the way to a matching leather chair and sofa.

"Just for the record, Mr. Ashmore," the officer began opening a small notebook. "Please state the children's full names and birth dates as well as your relationship to them."

David did so and watched as his words were written down.

"Are you the sole parent?"

"Yes. Their mother passed away last year."

Over the course of the next half-hour David described Jackie and Dustin, starting with their ages. He specified their hair color and eyes, height and approximate weight. Then he shared the most current picture of them both that he could find. He told the officer what they were wearing and the last time he had seen each of them as well as what their interests were and where they might have gone. The list wasn't long. No friends or family in the area. Then he detailed his own searching, both outside and inside the house, scouring the park as well as the city. Finally, he showed the note from Dustin.

"Has he ever done anything like this before? Ever run away?"

"No. Never," said David.

The officer scribbled something in a black little book.

"How about your daughter Jackie? Has she ever run away before?"

"No," he said. "Not really."

"What do you mean?"

"She's never run away," David said. Then he paused. "Yesterday she took her dog for a walk, though, and was gone all day. She didn't come home until after dinner. That's not like her."

Officer Lindquist nodded.

"Any reason why she would take Dustin? Any reason at all? Have you noticed any change in behavior?"

"Jackie would never hurt her brother, if that's what you mean. But yes, I've noticed a difference. She's been withdrawn and moody," David began. "Normal teenage behavior except she's also dealing with the death of her mother. She barely talks, even on the phone. I don't think she's made any friends here yet."

The officer looked up from his writing. "When did you first notice this change?"

"About nine months ago. After her mother, Jillian died. We moved here from Ambler, Pennsylvania in early December."

"Why did you come here?"

"My wife made me promise that we would make a new start. We met in Minnesota years ago."

"I see," the officer said. Then he made another note on his paper. "Anything else?"

David was reluctant to go on, feeling exposed to all his parental failures. Swallowing hard he continued. "It's been getting worse."

"Any reason to think she would go back home?"

David nodded. The thought had occurred to him, of course. "That's where all her friends are. Her whole former life. It wouldn't be like her to just leave, though."

"Does she have any serious boyfriends?"

"She just turned thirteen. She's not dating boys."

"You'd be surprised," Officer Lindquist said. "Is anything missing?" he asked evenly. "A suitcase, clothes? Anything like that?"

"No, nothing like that. All her belongings are still here. It's just her. And Dustin."

"I'll need names and numbers of friends she knew back in Pennsylvania as quickly as you can round them up. Tomorrow is fine."

"Sure," he said mechanically. The situation was spiraling out of control.

"Do you know of anyone who would want to take your children? Anyone who holds a grudge? Someone you're dating? Have you noticed anyone suspicious in the neighborhood?"

David swallowed as a pit in the bottom of his stomach opened up. "I'm afraid not. No one at all. It's just been Jackie, Dustin, and me."

Officer Lindquist stared at David for a long moment. Then he clicked his pen abruptly and put it away. "Okay. We'll get the word out to other departments and check the bus stations and highways. But I think that the park is as good a place as any to start with. From what you've said, your son may have simply followed your daughter over there. Could be they got lost or distracted. Kids have two hands, but they don't always run like clockwork." He chuckled and then immediately grew serious as if he had broken one of the laws he had sworn to protect. "If they're in there we'll find them. Highveil Park's not *that* big."

"Thank you," mouthed David. "If there's anything I can do..."

"You've done everything you could," interjected the patrolman as he stood up and put a hand on David's shoulder. "We'll take it from here, okay?"

David nodded and walked him to the door.

The officer paused. "There's one more thing. I'll file a missing person's report for your children tonight. After that we can issue an AMBER Alert if the situation dictates it. You mentioned on the phone to the dispatcher earlier this evening that the last time you saw them was approximately 2:00 this afternoon. Is that correct?"

"Yes, that's right," stammered David, although it felt like days rather than mere hours.

"We'll do everything we can. Someone will be by in the morning. Good night," toned the officer stepping back out into the darkness. "Try and get some sleep."

"Good night," said David hollowly. Then the words spilled out of him. "You know, Dustin's only five years old. But he always..."

His voice caught with emotion. "He's always liked to climb trees; the bigger the better. You might want to shine a light up..."

"You mentioned that. We'll look both high and low. I promise."

David watched the policeman get in his car. He stood and listened as the engine started up and saw the lights turn on. Slowly the squad car drove away. Long after it had turned a corner and disappeared from sight, David finally closed the door and went back inside.

Milky Way lay on the floor with his head down; he had barely moved since the officer's arrival.

Oh my God... David thought, standing in the middle of the suddenly very empty room. The house seemed eerily quiet.

Where are my children?

Nightmare visions called to him even as he tried to shake them off. David imagined accidents and injuries, lonely bus rides and terrifying abductions. All of his choices were suddenly in question. Doubts about the judgments and promises he had made clambered for his attention. But he never allowed himself to think, even for a moment, that he would never see them again. Some thoughts were just too terrible.

CHAPTER 11

Standing at the edge of the stone path leading to Nimbus' abode, Jackie Ashmore looked out from her high vantage point to the vast cloudscape valley sloping away from her. It should have been impossible, but it wasn't. Marvels sprung to life all around her as if from one of her favorite books.

"Wow!" she exclaimed, unable to hide her enthusiasm.

High overhead, as if heralding the spectacle below, a chariot raced across the pale blue sky drawn by four fiery winged horses. A tall figure crowned with a brilliant helm of light stood in the golden carriage, his arms outstretched as he held tightly to the reigns.

"That's Helios, of course," explained Nimbus. "The Sun God. His path mirrors the cycle of light and dark on the Earth below, although in Treetops there is no true night to speak of."

"You have gods?" Jackie asked. "I have to admit, that's pretty cool."

"Yes," smiled the Keeper. "Most of them, however, are forgotten or asleep in their own realm. They do not concern me."

"What does concern you?" asked Jackie, her wariness returning as she wondered how immortal beings could be unworthy of attention.

Nimbus pointed a gnarled and woody finger at the landscape below.

There she beheld the valley sloping away like a basin of all Creation. From its depths, soft colors glowed faintly, like hidden gems scattered across a skein of white. Their beauty was so pure that she almost overlooked the few dark blotches that dotted the valley like shadows of something to come. There was so much to see, though, and it was the teeming life covering the cloudscape that held her spellbound.

Without turning her head Jackie spotted a myriad of animals, all in pairs. It was as if someone had left all the animals in all the zoos loose. A cacophony of sounds rose up from the valley's inhabitants.

Some of the creatures were immediately recognizable. Most were not. Nameless, in that first bright, wonderful moment, the creatures spread out across the great valley like an evolutionary chess game run amok. Some walked, some flew, while others remained motionless or appeared to "swim" in midair. Most had four legs. Some had two or no legs at all. Others had wings instead. But all had a mate, a single companion of its species, no less and no more.

One of the most amazing wonders that sprang into view were the dinosaurs. Fearsome tyrannosaurs waded through the menagerie while long-necked apatosaurs and duck-billed iguanodons kept a watchful eye. A pair of windmill-backed stegosaurs stood in the corner of the valley as two triceratops leveled their horns at some menacing velociraptors. Overhead a pteranodon glided silently, followed by another.

Everywhere Jackie looked produced another marvel. Wooly mammoths and mastodons lumbered slowly, while feral saber-toothed cats prowled, and a pair of armored glyptodons stood still as giant rocks. But there were other surprises as well, species she would not have been able to identify at all if not for her mother and her own obsession with endangered Earth life.

She spied Tasmanian forester kangaroos and Komodo dragons, white rhinos and flying foxes. There were Florida cougars and giant sable antelopes, moon bears, and fierce looking kestrels. Black-faced impalas peered out of the mist while brightly painted kakapos streamed through the air like winged rainbows. Ibex and hartebeest, freira and cormorant, tapirs and aye-ayes all dazzled her senses. So much life! The more Jackie looked, the more she decreased in stature and significance. Who was she when compared with all this abundance? Even her own fears and confusion seemed to lessen amidst the spectacle before her. And still the explosion of life continued.

Arctic foxes patrolled the valley's perimeter while an Andean condor drifted silently overhead. Into this already busy spectacle, a new movement arose. As Jackie watched, the vast sea of animals became agitated and began to move in two different directions. At first it wasn't clear what caused the disturbance. There was too much chaos and the cloudscape obscured many of the details. Then she saw. Down the vacated channel of ghostly terrain swam a blue whale. Its massive tail, almost transparent, undulated like the rhythm of the tide and a jet of vapor erupted from its blowhole before it descended into the cloudscape seemingly gone forever. Then another emerged and repeated the colossal disappearing act. A moment later, the animals of Treetops came back together as if nothing at all had happened.

"Is this some kind of zoo?" Jackie asked.

Regnal waddled up next to the Keeper. "Oh yes," he said. "It's exactly like a zoo except for the cloud terrain, the absence of any internal barriers, and a dodo on staff."

Nimbus ignored the comment. Perhaps he was used to it. He seemed to ponder the question carefully. When he finally did speak it was in a slowness bordering on geological time.

"There are many things you need to know, child," he began awkwardly.

Jackie cringed. She hated that word. She was tired of being a child.

"So many things," the Keeper was saying. And then he paused for a second time and for a moment, Jackie feared he would not speak again, not tell her the things she desperately needed to know, and she realized as she waited that she was shaking; trembling to know and not to know, all at the same time.

"Treetops," Nimbus continued, "is a place unlike any other. It is not on the Earth, but it is of the Earth and encompasses the very heart of it. Here the animals, the plants, the insects—from the largest creature to the most infinitesimal organism—abide and are remembered."

"Are there people here too?" Jackie asked. Of course, she was really wondering about her mother. It was all she could do to keep from blurting out her real question.

"Now you speak of fairy tales," Nimbus chuckled. "There is, as I recall, an ancient legend of an ever-changing, ever-moving city called Necrowane where the dead go to live. Loved ones wave from windows never to walk back out through the door. But that is just a story. Nothing more."

Jackie tried not to let her disappointment show.

"Everything and everyone have their time," the Keeper told her as if reading her thoughts. "Love and life must have boundaries."

Jackie sighed. There were always so many rules.

"Consider the animals here. Every one of them is extinct or close to extinction. They come here as they must, to reside in Treetops and then only in twos. For everything in Life has its opposite, its match. Look there." Nimbus directed, pointing a leafy finger.

Jackie looked down into the vast, teeming herd of species but could not find what the Keeper wanted her to see.

"Come," he said, motioning for her to follow as he walked

closer to the sloping edge of the cumulous rise that overlooked the myriad of animals below.

"There," quavered Nimbus again leaning on his staff, "away from the others, towards us, the giant pandas, do you see them now?"

"Uh, yes I see them!" exclaimed Jackie.

They looked just like giant black and white teddy bears, as soft as giant summer clouds and about as substantial. Both were leaning against a vapory tree eating something. Suddenly, in mid-munch they faded, becoming transparent as they shifted to the edge of invisibility and then back.

"What happened?" Jackie asked in alarm.

Regnal took the tip of his wing and drew it horizontally across in front of his feathery neck. The irony was not lost on Jackie.

"Another panda down Below has died," explained Nimbus somberly. "Every time an animal in Treetops wavers like that it means another of its kind has perished. In a strange way, though, that is a good sign. When they stop shifting at all and are solid and static that signifies that the last one has left the Earth. Then the dying is finally over."

"That's horrible," replied Jackie, making a face. "Can't you do anything?"

"I do what countless Keepers have done down the centuries—I preserve what has been lost and cherish what has been abandoned. I tell each new animal that I will keep it safe and free from harm. There is no higher service I can perform."

"That's not doing anything," Jackie protested, her voice rising with emotion. "That's just waiting. Every creature is here because you didn't do anything to save it! It's like a horrible cemetery."

Memories—flashes of pain and hospital rooms, her mother wasting away before her eyes cut through her pounding pulse. In an instant she was transported back to the worst day of her life. "No more," her mother had said, her voice weak but resolute. "Take me home."

Jackie shook her head trying to clear it of dark thoughts. For a moment she was as stunned as Nimbus at her sudden outburst. *What had she done? Where were her manners?* With a pang of self-consciousness, she brushed away the tears welling up in her eyes. Yet the pain and anger still flowed beneath her skin like molten lava ready to erupt again.

"No," Nimbus said at last. "I haven't done anything at all to save them though it hurts like an axe in the deep-wood to say it. That is not my purpose. All Keepers are bound by their duty to serve and preserve Treetops. How can I be any different? The Earth itself is not part of my realm, and so I must preside over a certain amount of loss. They are like dying stars, but their light goes on forever. It is in their memory that I do what needs to be done."

"And what is that?" Jackie asked, thinking Nimbus was as powerless as her father. All he could do was stand around as her mother wasted away. A moment later she felt guilty. All of a sudden, she missed her dad. He would know what to do. At the very least, he would distract her with a stupid joke.

"I learn from the Earth and train those that seek wisdom," the Keeper replied.

"Why?" she asked.

Nimbus seemed genuinely nonplussed.

"It has always been this way. It's what I was taught from the Keeper before me who learned it from their predecessor, and so on through the mists of time."

"Then how do you know it's the right thing to do?" Jackie wondered, trying hard not to sound combative. "Do you have an ancient book or big commandments carved into a tree?"

The Keeper cringed at the thought.

"We are Servants of the Earth. It is not a Keeper's place to question, and I would never hurt a plant in such a way."

Jackie rubbed her forehead trying to make sense of what she was hearing. Her patience was hanging by a thread. "Wait a minute. Are you telling me that the Earth itself tells you to sit around here and do nothing while the whole planet goes down the drain?"

"Take a care at whom you point fingers," Nimbus warned. "You know little of this world. Who are you to judge? What have you done?" he continued, his voice turning as cold as a January winter. "*You* are a PlanetWalker. Why don't you do something about it instead of complaining?"

"I did. I climbed here for help."

"Only indirectly," the Keeper toned with a hint of displeasure. "You came in search of your brother."

"Have you checked the Lost and Found?" Regnal interjected.

"Let me get this straight," Jackie began, her voice rising with emotion. "You can't save the animals and there's probably nothing you can do to help me get my brother back. Is there anything you *can* do?"

Nimbus's features tightened. His eyes grew dark while a sudden rage burned within him causing a host of his leaves to blacken.

"How dare you!" the Keeper exclaimed. "Your impertinence must end."

To Jackie, he seemed to suddenly gain stature as he towered over her. With a series of painful sounding words and a final flourish of his leafy hand, he eclipsed the light. Thunder echoed overhead and lightning blazed down into the valley, scattering the animals.

For once Regnal lost his sarcastic airs.

"No more, Keeper. The animals—they are frightened," quaked the dodo, surprised and visibly shaken by this display. Evidently such demonstrations of power were rare.

"Yes...yes, of course," said Nimbus as if he were remembering himself and stepping back from an imaginary precipice.

Before her eyes, he shrunk back down to his normal, frail self. Now he looked even older, almost wasted, as if the spectacle he had put on had wounded him in some way.

The light in Treetops was returning but Jackie was not soothed. When she looked up into the tangled mass of concealing leaves to his mossy eyes, she saw only power and was afraid.

"Forget what I said, okay? I'm a guest here. Don't kick me out." Jackie paused. "I don't have anywhere else to go."

The Keeper studied his new guest and then let out a long sigh.

"Under the circumstances we can forgive a lapse in manners. You are hurting, that much is plain to see. The little boy, your brother—we will do what we can to get him back."

At the mention of Dustin, panic rose up inside her. She still didn't have a strategy to rescue Dustin. Every moment seemed to carry him further away. Frustrated, Jackie swept the hair away from her eyes. Why was it always in her way lately?

"This is all new to me," she said. "I'm a bit overwhelmed. I don't want to be rude or anything, but I really have to find my brother. I can't wait much longer."

"I know, you are in a *hurry*," he said, pronouncing the last word as if it was strange to him. "Yet there is much to learn before you can help your sibling. It will not do to go running off across the clouds without a plan."

Jackie's face screwed up in barely contained anguish.

"Soon," Nimbus interjected, forestalling her objections. "We will leave soon. Rest assured. For now, let us return inside. New visitors usually see the Nexra, but time presses upon us cruelly and your need is raw. A brief respite first..." Nimbus trailed off. Then the Keeper turned back toward HeartWood and away from the pageantry in the valley below. "It is enough for one day."

Walking the bramble-lined path behind the slow shambling form of the Keeper, Jackie kept thinking of how her mother had walked these same worn stones. Turning the corner of Heart-Wood, she spied a narrow expanse of weeds and stumps stretching off towards the distant cloud-top mountains. A moment later, it dwindled from view as they approached the entrance to the Keeper's dwelling.

"What are all those stumps back there?" Jackie asked.

Nimbus paused, his gnarled staff at his side.

"The Keeper's Garden, I'm afraid," sighed Nimbus, "or what's left of it."

Jackie wanted to ask what happened to it, but she tried to be polite. Instead she said, "It sounds beautiful."

"If ancient tales can be believed, multitudes of lore-wise Keepers once tended the Garden containing all the world's plants. Sabine was the first and it was she who nurtured the Garden and expanded the greenery beyond imaginings, laying the groundwork for the network of *noventices* and Keepers that would tend the Garden. It stretched across Treetops in verdant profusion. This is all that remains. The knowledge of why the Garden and the tending was abandoned is lost." Nimbus paused. "You can see the scattered remains of the old Keeper dwellings stretching in a line from HeartWood."

Jackie followed the Keeper's gaze until she saw the faint markings. They were little more than clumps of stone.

"The village was long in ruin when I first came to Treetops." Then he started walking again.

When they reached the threshold of HeartWood, Jackie asked the Keeper the one question she had been dreading.

"Why did this Gaylon take my brother?" She whispered like she was sharing a secret. "Who would do something like that?"

"Yes, you asked a similar question when you first arrived. It is an important one." Nimbus paused and seemed to avoid her gaze. "Gaylon is a servant, and a misguided one at that. He does the bidding of Flood. By now your brother is leagues away in his master's fortress. It is no place for a small child."

The tears that Jackie had been valiantly keeping at bay burst forth again at the Keeper's words. She hardly noticed as Nimbus encircled her with his leafy canopy and forest embrace. For the first time she noticed the dark, loamy smell of the guardian. The scent was from deep in the earth. "There, there," he soothed, sounding like a grandfather she had once known when she was younger. "I promise. He will be returned. We are not without allies or hope, you know."

"Well," she began hesitantly like a child afraid of being punished again, "couldn't you just use your power and make it storm again?"

The Keeper sighed. "I am not what I once was. If anything, I am made weaker after each display of force. Our best course is one of diversity. Power is not our path."

Jackie frowned in disappointment. A retort blossomed on her lips, but Nimbus was faster.

"Please," he told her with an edge of pleading to his voice. "No more questions. You said something before about not believing in what a Keeper does. Such statements only reinforce your ignorance."

"It just seems kind of weird," Jackie replied. "No offense. I mean, the animals don't really need you, do they? Aren't they dead already?"

The Keeper looked down at her again but this time the slightest of smiles grew across his weathered face.

"Do you really want to know the answer?" he asked.

Jackie nodded.

"Let's go find out then," Nimbus said turning from the path. "Take my hand."

CHAPTER 12

Gaylon stood unmoving, tall and lanky, like a scarecrow sentinel without nearly enough stuffing, and watched from his perch. It was part of his daily routine. Atop the natural cliff tower rising from the ridge, he could see across the cracked cloudscape, dried and lifeless, in either direction. Black tendrils, the ragged ends of his shirt, trailed behind him in the warm gusting wind. On his bare arm was the mark of a swirling zephyr. His long, slender fingers shielded his eyes from the light of Helios. He was gazing toward the east and HeartWood in the unlikely event the Keeper would take action. It had been almost a year since he had left his post as a *noventice* in Treetops. Throughout his training, he had been instructed concerning the duties and mysteries of being a Keeper while in the service of the Earth. Gaylon was, until his departure, a promising student of the current Keeper, Nimbus.

With his keen eyesight, Gaylon could make out the Keeper, even to the expression on his face, as the elder walked down into the teeming Central Valley, the jewel of the shrinking domain of Treetops.

What a doting old fool you are, he thought. *Even now your power weakens. Once there were countless valleys, lush with cloud meadows and First Life. But now there is only one. The wasteland surrounds you and still the Earth animals come, a legacy to the dying and destruction down Below. And what will happen when they come no more?*

Gaylon had tried to tell the Keeper this in the weeks and months leading up to his exodus but the dithering dimwit wouldn't listen. He had tried to tell Nimbus, delicately, that his power was weakening. Surely the aging imbecile could see that. His Earthly disease showed for all to see in the desert that surrounded the Keeper's once fertile domain. But Nimbus feigned blindness again and again. Gaylon had even tried to warn him of the Return. 'Flood has rebuilt the Arkanum,' he told him, genuine fear in his voice. 'Soon the Call will sound and Earth's Retribution will follow.'

Brushing the raven black hair from his eyes he smiled and turned toward the west. He had been so naive. Now he knew better. The coming battle was not to be feared or prevented, but simply accepted. It was inevitable, like a storm, natural and terrible, that reminds people how small and insignificant they really are.

Looking over the dried sea bottom, he saw, perched high atop a dusty dark plateau, the grand curving outline of the ark. The sight was alien in its contrast. It was as if sometime in the dark dim past, the great ocean waters receded or diverted leaving the colossal vessel stranded, far from home, and utterly lost. But not lost for very much longer. Soon the vessel would reclaim her former glory.

Help is on its way, he thought. *The Earth will be healed.*

For an unexpected moment, Gaylon's mind drifted to the invisible homes down Below. In one of them, his nameless mother probably lived. There were people that she knew and cared about. He wondered what would happen to them when the Day of Retribution came.

Angry at himself, he shook his head as if to clear it of distraction and confusion. No one cared about him, least of all his mother who had given him up at birth. Instead of self-pity, however, Gaylon found himself thinking of the little boy he had taken from the empty cloud-tops, so alone and far from home. When he had plucked the nameless lad off the high meadow, he had felt something. It was hard to explain. It reminded him of the water in a lake, the part that changes suddenly from warm sun-charged bliss to cold untouchable fathoms. The boy had been terrified and for good reason. Gaylon was a vanguard, a dark stranger on horseback come to sweep away worlds. But the sensation Gaylon had felt had been more than merely fear. There had been power there. Then it was gone like a candle covered for protection. Now he couldn't be sure what he had sensed. With each passing day, his doubts grew.

Gaylon wondered if perhaps his master had erred. What if the child was simply a scared little boy and nothing more? He wasn't close to being of age, after all. Most boys were around 15 when they climbed the winding vine to Treetops. Girls were usually a little bit younger, around 13. Never had a child as young as Dustin ever arrived. He could still see the boy running as he closed in at full gallop. A small stab of guilt stung Gaylon over what he had done. The kid's family would probably worried sick.

He stopped himself. As an orphan, it felt strange to think that someone else could care. Gaylon had never known his mother and father. His childhood had been spent going from one foster family to another. He was a "problem," the agency said. Sometime just before high school, he stopped getting placed. The institution became his home. It hadn't been hard to leave when he felt the Call and then made his way to Treetops.

Individuals came when they were needed, usually one at a time, climbing to the clouds. After a brief initiation and testing by the Nexra (he cringed at the memory), an apprentice started their work under the Keeper, learning the ways of Treetops as well as their own special talent. An individual's length of stay varied, with the most ambitious and talented eventually replacing the current Keeper.

Gaylon had barely made it two years under the Keeper's forgetful tutelage. Instead of going back down to Planetside, he sought out Flood, a name only whispered by Nimbus and ancient texts. Even so, it wasn't hard to find him. You just needed to know where to look.

Since then, he had done his master's bidding, keeping watch and waiting for the visitor Flood said would come, a child. When the small boy emerged from the world below by the Portal Tree, Gaylon did as he was instructed and brought him to the Arkanum where his master could sort things out. It was out of his hands. Now he waited for signs of trouble from the only being in Treetops whom his master feared.

Once again he turned back to HeartWood to assure himself all was well on that front. A detail he had missed before in Treetops now caught his attention and nearly brought him to his knees. On the far side of the Keeper, nearly invisible to Gaylon, was a smaller figure. Together they walked onto the valley floor towards the grand herd of animals that congregated there.

A jolt of dismay surged through. If this new stranger were the one and not the boy then all was lost. Only hours before he had hand-delivered their salvation. Every fiber of his body demanded that he race to the Arkanum and tell Flood what he had seen. Yet he knew that was foolhardy. First, he must make sure. Yet he did not move. Instead, he remained rooted to the spot watching his past unfold in front of him.

This was how he had been indoctrinated as well; following Nimbus around and learning. His memory spun back to the dizzying climb and he recollected the awe he felt in meeting Nimbus and crossing the cloud meadows to Heartwood. More than anything else, he remembered the very moment the Keeper first took his hand. There had been a mossy sensation followed by...it was hard to explain...a connection. Then everything had changed.

A pang of jealousy stung Gaylon's heart. It didn't seem fair. He had only been trying to help! He wouldn't take the words back nor would he if he could. He had spoken the truth.

"The animals are dying," he had said. "The Earth is dying. If you will not stop it, I will. There is another way where the world is saved. We've just forgotten how to fight."

Nimbus looked at him for a long moment. His eyes held all the seasons but at that moment they glistened only with rain.

"Man is also of the Earth," the Keeper breathed. "You cannot take part away without lessening the whole. Interference, however well intentioned, only causes more ripples. It takes little to spawn storms that can sweep us all away. Recant your statement and recite the Vow."

But he could not. There could only be one thing to do. Leave. He had no other choice.

Yet in seeing the Keeper and the girl together, he knew he must return to HeartWood however it pained him. Who was the girl? A new recruit? What did she want? How were the boy and this stranger connected? And most of all, who was the real KeyStone? These were questions that Flood would want answered. It was always better, Gaylon learned, to jump at chances rather than wait to be ordered. There was more freedom that way, more opportunity for reward. Besides, he was curious too.

Gaylon stood up and pictured in his mind the smooth piece of mottled black and white crystal. Each facet was a hidden world that he could feel in his hands. He had found the rare material deep in the Lost Caves, and then had cut and honed the material himself, under Flood's tutelage. Holding it, he could catch glimpses of the lives of animals and experience their life through their own eyes. Over time, however, he became drawn to a darker power that Nimbus cautioned him against. One that could change him into a creature that represented the state of his soul, his heart, and his mind.

Now he turned the object over in his mind as he traced the language of transformation that was etched there. A sudden gust of wind ruffled his cloak. Rips began to appear in the fabric of his shirt and pants as his body contorted. Gaylon's face began to change. His thin lips curled back and his blue eyes darkened. From atop his thick ebony hair a metamorphosis advanced downward. It was as if a black shadow fell over his features. Painfully a beak emerged from the shadows and the shadows in turn became fur and feathers. His form contracted and refined until when he lifted his arms, he felt only the rush of air under his wings. Gone were his slender fingers. Only his feet remained. A moment later three-toed talons had taken their place. He was a man in a bird's body. The ground now felt unfamiliar to him. Dizziness gripped him, as it always did after a transformation. He waited a few moments for the worst of it to pass.

Satisfied the change was complete he took to the sky and circled once around the tower before diving down towards his target.

One or two strands of hair should do fine, cawed Gaylon. *A little flesh wouldn't hurt either.*

CHAPTER 13

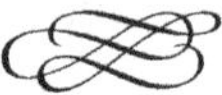

Exploding fireworks. That's what it felt like. In the split second it took Nimbus to take her hand, Jackie's world became transformed. Reality blossomed from uniform whiteness to a profusion of color that seemed to reach out to her as if she were wearing 3-D glasses. The spongy clouds were gone. In their place was a sweeping landscape of gold and brown dotted with tall trees topped with green.

From the bottoms of her feet, Jackie felt a sense of health and vitality rise through her. Her whole body seemed to be glowing in warmth. The same gentle breeze that blew through her hair bent the tall grasses that stretched out across the valley. She felt a connection, vast yet intimate, to the world around her. Land and sky were part of her and she was part of it.

Lush savannah swirled around her knees like a rising tide. Jackie reached out her free hand to clear a path, wondering where all the animals had gone.

"*No!*" warned Nimbus. "*Stay with me.*"

Jackie couldn't tell if the Keeper spoke out loud or in her mind. It was as if the distance between them had been eliminated with all the static removed.

She froze.

Something lurked in the vegetation just inches from her outstretched hand. Lying low in the shadows, avoiding the light, the animal was hard to see. But she could make out its form; slender and cat-like, a rod of coiled energy, feral and hungry. The pattern was unmistakable. Black spots surrounded by patches of light brown fur all undulating like the surrounding stalks in the wind as the animal's lungs rose and fell with air. She was looking upon a cheetah, swiftest of all runners and among the most effective hunters.

For a horrible second, Jackie imagined herself alone and a wave of fear gripped her. In desperation she tried to run through the blinding grass. But something had her and did not let go. Within two steps she boomeranged back, crashing into a leafy form like a child into a tree. Stunned she looked up. There was the Keeper, calm and unflinching, not looking at her at all. Following his gaze, she saw the cheetah again, just as motionless and seemingly unaware of her presence. Nimbus stared back into the creature's eyes.

Now Jackie became aware of a growing hunger coursing through the animal's veins. They were her veins too, she realized with amazement. Her own lifeblood pumped through them. Yet her cheetah heart was weak and the energy to live wilted under the hot summer sun. Her breathing labored to the point of failure. She hadn't eaten in weeks. If she didn't eat soon, it would be too late. She would die in these grasses. Deep in the pit of existence, she knew instinctively that there was only one more chance.

After what seemed like a lifetime, the animal blinked. All at once the world shifted, taking Jackie with it. Disorientated she struggled to comprehend. Perhaps she cried out.

"*Too deep,*" the Keeper said. "*You are a girl. Your name is Jackie. Look. Open your eyes!*"

Jackie saw it from within and without. She was herself, barely, but a new fear threatened to overwhelm her. It rose up and flooded her senses. Nothing else seemed to exist. In front of her, a brown gazelle with a white underbelly and rump crossed into the plain a short distance away. It had short curving horns. She took a deep breath and felt herself merge with the frightened creature. The animal paused; alert for danger. She walked in fitful starts and stops, finally standing motionless near the edge of the tall grass. A tall figure stood in the savannah, but she didn't fear it. There was something else. Trickles of sweat ran down her forehead and neck. Her whole body tensed to flee. All around a heightened sense of awareness spread out around her.

A wide range of smells filled the air. Different flowers, different plants, a rain shower just over the mountains to the west blown by the cooling wind. No smell or movement went unseen. The flights of individual insects were noted and then discarded as irrelevant. At the merest sound, her ears rose and fell with the gusts of the wind. Even while eating the slender leaves she was alert, poised for any threat. Unconsciously Jackie squeezed her free hand into a fist as nervousness gripped her like a mental seizure. Soon her body started twitching in time with the gazelle's frantic heartbeat.

Then she and the gazelle stopped, frozen again in mid-chew. Movement, unexplained, in the grasses came and went, holding her fast. Nothing existed except the memory of that motion and the resonance of peril. Although she searched, no more trace could be found. Finally, tentatively, she bowed her head to forage once again. Immediately the savannah erupted before her. Almost before she saw the bright yellow and black markings, she knew what it was. A split second after the cheetah had leaped, Jackie bounded away. Terror flooded through her mind. There was danger! She must run! Only Nimbus's hand on her shoulder gave her the anchor she needed to remain and remember who she was. But even as she remembered who she was, she could not deny that she was also the gazelle.

Deep in her chest, Jackie's heart pounded to the rhythm of the chase. With each stride the cheetah closed in on its prey until a claw length was all that separated them. Jackie felt sure she could feel the predator's hot breath on her heels. Turning like some wild carnival ride she mirrored the desperate movements of the sprightly creature as it zigzagged frantically in a last-ditch effort to shake its pursuer. But the cheetah, hungry almost beyond endurance, would not give in and with a swipe of its talons finally managed to bring its elusive meal down in a cloud of dust.

"NO!" screamed Jackie with all the force of her being. "NOOOOO!"

A heavy stabbing weight descended upon her throat, eclipsing the light, making it hard to breathe.

And then she was looking down at the gazelle's torn windpipe. Warm blood dripped off her open mouth. Far from satiated, she dipped her feline head again and quickly bit off another chunk of meat with razor sharp teeth, always on the lookout for other predators.

Wind beat at her ears unexpectedly amid a fluttering of feathers. Confusion and panic swirled through her heightened awareness. A stab of pain shot through her scalp.

"What! You dare carry out this dark service under my very nose!" boomed the Keeper like a clap of thunder as he let go of her hand.

At once the world changed from technicolor brilliance back to glacier white. Gone were the feasting leopard and fallen gazelle. The sweeping grassland also blinked out of existence as if a sudden gust of wind had blown it out like a candle. All that remained was the same unbroken waxy vista that had greeted her when she first popped her head out of the clouds.

Stranger still, the world askew. At the killing stroke she must have fallen just as the gazelle had fallen. Nimbus towered above her, but his attention wasn't directed at her at all. Far from concerned over her safety, he seemed to be struggling with something just out of sight in the sky above. Still disorientated, Jackie struggled to get up.

"Be still, child!" Nimbus commanded chancing a sharp glance in her direction. “Stay down!”

Without warning, green shards of lightning shot out from the foliage of the Keeper. Jackie recoiled in fear, but the vine missiles shot overhead were not touching her at all. The tendrils arced overhead toward a fleeing bird, a giant raven. It was black, as dark and despairing as lost dreams, and when it flapped its wings, the sun was obscured for a moment.

As she watched, one-by-one the living strands reached their limit just short of the avian intruder and then fell back to the ground. Miraculously, the last tendril reached its target, going taut and then tangling itself in a sticky embrace around the great bird’s leg. With a jolt the raven shrieked in surprise and flapped its wings violently.

"Now I have you," smiled the Keeper grimly and began drawing in the vine.

The bird clawed desperately at the green chain, the talons of its free foot raking back and forth over the Keeper’s lasso, even as the vine dug into its flesh, opening a ragged gash. Soon the lasso was in tatters. Nimbus pulled the creature downward as fast as his aged limbs allowed yet the raven was still out of reach when its talons finally succeeded in slicing through. Freedom! With wings beating furiously, the creature flapped into the sky and out of range of the Keeper's vines. In anger or in pain, it shrieked. Soon it was a dwindling speck on the horizon.

"Drought and devastation!" cursed the Keeper.

"What was that?" asked Jackie, bewildered at what had just happened.

"Gaylon," answered Nimbus with a sigh.

He reached down and extended a mossy hand to help her up. Jackie waved it off, not wanting to lose herself again.

"That's your old student, right? You didn't tell me he could turn into a bird."

"He had help," the Keeper muttered. "I taught Gaylon many things. Taking the shape of another living creature was not one of them. I hope *our* lessons end better."

"Why would he do that?" she asked. Her cheek and scalp still ached where the bird had scratched her.

"He took a sample of your skin to find out who you are and what you're doing here, I presume."

Jackie massaged her head gently. "Next time he can just walk up and ask."

"Yes, well, Gaylon has not been very polite as of late, I'm sorry to say."

The events of the last few minutes were too much for her. Jackie took a deep breath not knowing how to say what she felt or where to begin. But she had to try.

"Thanks for helping me. Both with Gaylon and with the animals. I know I was freaking out a bit. It was just so real. I *was* the gazelle and the cheetah. Somehow I kind of lost myself."

"What you saw and experienced was what the animals felt and did when they were alive on the Earth. First encounters are always confusing. There is no need for embarrassment. You are growing a perspective beyond yourself. Holding my hand allowed you to see things as I do."

Jackie frowned. "The animals in the valley are from all over the Earth. Why did I only see a small part of Africa?"

"You saw what your mind could handle," the Keeper explained. "I see and feel *all* the animals. Sometimes all at once."

"Next time warn me. That was some trip." A wave of dizziness passed over her and she swayed like a sailor trying to find her sea legs. To make matters worse, something wet and warm was running down her cheek. It stung.

"No more questions," instructed Nimbus. "You are injured."

Reaching deep into his leafy body, he pulled out a small oozing lump of what looked like sap. "This will help with the cut."

Jackie steadied herself as best she could.

"You are weak from the sight, but it will pass quickly," the Keeper told her.

Carefully he placed the goo on the wound where Gaylon's talons had dug in. Although she feared it would sting, it did not. Jackie held still as the Keeper applied the salve. The smell of autumn leaves hung in the air as she breathed in his presence. The medicine had an immediate effect. Coolness radiated out from the point of contact, neutralizing the discomfort and calming her nerves as well.

"That should help," soothed the Keeper.

"Thank you," Jackie said. "It feels better."

"Happy to oblige. Now, where were we?"

"Going to save my brother," she reminded, trying her best not to sound annoyed.

"Of course," agreed Nimbus, a trifle embarrassed. "That's right. But first you have some choosing to do. The make-up of any rescue party is very important."

Humming a fragment of a tune, the Keeper reached into his leaves and took out a short, knotty looking piece of wood. The bark was at once both shimmering and gnarled so Jackie could only guess whether it was from the last living branch of a Bristlecone Pine or merely a twig from a sapling planted yesterday. Putting it to his mossy lips the Keeper blew once, making no sound that Jackie could hear, and then stuffed it away again.

"There, that should do it," he remarked quite satisfied and walked off. "Now if I could only remember where that meeting place is."

"What meeting place?" Jackie asked.

"For the Choosing," Nimbus explained. "The animals are waiting for you."

"What animals would that be?"

"All of them," the Keeper replied matter-of-factly.

Jackie's jaw dropped in surprise and her eyes widened in amazement. Almost sheepishly she followed Nimbus out across the Central Valley hoping he knew where they were going.

CHAPTER 14

Dustin sat all alone in the darkness with his knees scrunched up and his head bowed down, afraid to move. For hours he had simply rocked back and forth against the rough wall. Once he peed in the corner. His stomach felt as empty as the room around him. He was so tired. No one had talked to him since he had been brought here. He wished he could sleep. His eyes were getting so heavy. Sleep would be so much better than the flashes of memories. A horse and dark rider. Jackie screaming. An ark that was so terribly big it made a lump in his throat. When it got too bad, he stopped thinking about everything and went back to simply rocking. It was better not to think about it. Thinking made the terror come. But he never cried out. Exhausted, he finally fell asleep. Dark, troubled dreams took hold of him and well before dawn he awoke, alone and scared.

It had all been a game. He could still hear Jackie calling out to him as he climbed up the tree. Racing out across the clouds had been fun—at first—until his legs felt like lead. He had run far away. It made him nervous. He slowed down. He meant to stop and go back to her then, across the strange top of the clouds.

That's when she had screamed at him to run. Something was coming for him.

The only warning had been the sound like a train clicking and clacking ominously on tracks, bearing down on him. He hadn't screamed when the dark rider swept him off the ground and carried him away. Perhaps he had been too shocked. He hadn't pleaded or protested as the white cloudscape swept underneath him in a dreamy blur. The only sound he made was a low moan so soft that the rider could not hear it.

"Jackie," he breathed, soundlessly mouthing her name like an incantation as he watched her form dwindle away in the distance.

The tears had come then, quickly turning into sobs. The frantic beating of his heart matched the pounding of the horse's hooves.

"Quiet!" snapped the stranger from behind over the whistle of the wind.

The rider squeezed him tighter as if trying to stop his emotions. Dustin watched as they skirted an edge of a great cloud valley and then rode across great basins bare and empty. They trotted through a long mountain pass as thin as a ray of cold sunlight and galloped across a wide plain. Eventually the plain turned into a desert littered with half-buried objects, both strange and familiar.

From time to time the rider would stop so Dustin could relieve himself, but he always seemed irritated at the delay. With barely a pause they rode on, leaving a cloud of dust in their wake. Finally, as the sun set, they came to a black, skeletal ridge in the center of a vast desolate plain. On top of the rise lay a giant bone-white ship. It looked very old. Black portholes ran in a horizontal line along the side. Scattered around them were thousands of skulls that made up the vessel's great hull, but in the dim light Dustin could not see this. To him, the unusual boat reminded him of what an ark might look like, only much bigger.

Suddenly the horse reared up, flaring its nostrils and neighing.

"Whoa!" commanded the horseman pulling on the reins and uttering some words Dustin didn't understood.

Slowly the animal settled down and Dustin relaxed, no longer worried about being thrown off. The rider drove his heels into the horse's flank and the animal continued up the side of the barren ridge toward the vessel.

Closer to the ship, details became clearer to Dustin. The ground surrounding the ark was filled with bones of every shape and size. Some were as large as dinosaur fossils. Others were as small as finger bones from a child. They stuck out at odd angles like seashells scattered in a forgotten sea. A clear path led through them to the edge of the rocky rise where a pair of curving ivory tusks formed an arch to the vessel's grisly hull. Without warning they stopped and the darkly clad stranger slid down from the saddle.

"This is the Arkanum," the hooded figure said looking at Dustin. Then he lifted him off the horse to the ground. Some half-hidden fear played along the corners of stranger's mouth. "You are expected."

Immediately, as if the man had said a magic word, a giant doorway slid into view above them and a wooden ramp silently unfolded itself. Slowly it worked its way down to the bone-littered ground until it stopped in front of Dustin.

"Fun's over," the man said. "This is your new home now. Be a good boy and walk up."

Dustin stood still as a stone.

From the depths of his hooded cloak, the stranger chewed his lip nervously. "Go on. Don't be afraid."

In response, Dustin nodded and then in the tiniest of voices started to repeat names over and over again like a mantra. "Daddy, Daddy, Jackie, Jackie, Mommy, Mommy, Daddy, Daddy, Jackie, Jackie..."

The figure shifted in the inky shadows. "Is that your family? Of course, it is. You're a lucky little boy to have them. They're waiting for you. Inside. I promise."

"Daddy, Daddy, Jackie, Jackie, Mommy, Mommy, Daddy…" he repeated.

"What's your name, kid?" The question was gruff, a tinge of impatience in the enunciation.

Dustin stopped abruptly and then stared back saying nothing.

Softer this time: "C'mon, it's okay. What's your name?"

"D-u-s-tin," he had said slowly as if he were revealing a great secret.

He wondered what the man's name was and what he looked like. Every single inch of the rider was covered in black. Even his hands had been covered in midnight-colored gloves. The stranger's face remained lost in the folds of shadowy fabric.

"How come I can't see you?" Dustin asked.

"If I show you what I look like," the stranger had replied, "will you go up the ramp?"

Dustin made no response.

"Suit yourself," the rider said.

Hesitating only for a heartbeat, the man scooped Dustin up and carried him the length of the ramp to the dark vault-like doorway, while Dustin screamed and thrashed in his arms. They entered another world. A long torch-lit corridor stretched off in either direction. The stranger turned right without hesitation as if he had come this way a hundred times before. The doorway disappeared. That's when Dustin kicked the stranger as hard as he could.

The kidnapper gasped.

"That wasn't very smart," the figure said as he tightened his hold and pulled Dustin closer. "I think it's time for bed. You've been a bad little boy."

Pulling out a pouch, the stranger sprinkled a glittering black powder into his hand. Then he blew it into Dustin's face. A sudden tiredness came over Dustin. Slowly his eyes closed and his thrashing slowed, finally stopping completely. Barely awake, he looked up into the shadowy face of his abductor.

"What's your name?" Dustin asked, not expecting an answer.

"Gaylon," the stranger replied at the edge of hearing. "Nighty-night." Then the darkness swallowed him up.

When he opened his eyes, he found himself here, sitting against this wall. Alone.

He had been here all night and it was getting cold. Dustin wished he had a blanket to curl up in. The air had a chill to it as if he were underground. There was no light to speak of aside from a faint strip of brightness marking the bottom of the door. Dustin clung to that golden sliver and tried to imagine his father walking through to take him home.

CHAPTER 15

The house was a mess. Reams of printed posters lay scattered on tables. Pictures of Dustin and Jackie peeked out from behind permanent markers and rolls of scotch tape. Stray underwear, shirts, and socks lay strewn like clumps of snow; dropped and forgotten on the way to the laundry room. The kitchen was even worse. Half-eaten meals and dirty plates along with bags and wrappers of greasy smelling fast food littered the sink and countertops. Little notes and reminders covered nearly every flat surface in sickly yellow. The most recent ones lay unfinished by his cellphone and listed, in almost unreadable cursive, people he needed to call or places he needed to look.

Milky Way's empty dish still haunted the corner even though the puppy had been delivered to a comfortable kennel for temporary safe-keeping days ago. David told himself it was because he was on the road a lot lately, talking to anyone who would listen, but the truth of the matter was he couldn't even take care of himself. It simply wasn't fair to the dog.

Jackie's dog, he reminded himself quickly. With any luck Milky Way would be home soon. But soon couldn't come quickly enough. Maybe it never would. And then where would he be?

Bereft of his wife, a father without his children, and not even a puppy to his name. He had lost everything he cared for. Worse than that, he seemed incapable of holding onto the things he loved. They slipped through his hands when he wasn't looking. He should have done so much more.

"Are you still there, Mr. Ashmore?" a voice said in his ear.

"I'm here," David said. "Can you repeat that?"

David stood in the kitchen doorway and gripped his cell phone focusing on each word the F.B.I. agent was saying as if he were a mountain climber frozen on a rock face. He hadn't slept in days and it showed in his blood-shot eyes and hollow expression. It took all of David's strength to concentrate on what was being said.

"...despite our best efforts over the last several days, we have not found any leads that would direct us to the whereabouts of your missing son and daughter."

David's heart sank in response and he felt one of his hands come loose from the mental ledge he was hanging from.

"I am instructing the agents on this case," continued the man with a Spanish accent, "to redouble their efforts and go over every scrap of information again. We will also be enlarging the search area to include adjoining states and will immediately post your children's biographical and photographic information on various regional as well as national missing persons search lists and law enforcement databases. We are continuing to do everything in our power to find them."

The agent paused and cleared his throat. "Would it be possible, Mr. Ashmore," the voice continued levelly, "for one of our agents to stop by and question you again, at your convenience? It would be a significant aid in our..."

Another finger came loose from David's hold on hope and reality.

"Haven't you already questioned me twice?" interrupted David with rising frustration. "Hasn't the sheriff and the city police already asked me questions? Of course, I'll help any way I can, they're my children for God's sake, but I don't know what else I can tell you."

"We just have a few holes in the picture you've painted for us and Sheriff Stanek, that's all. A few concerns. I'm sure you could clear them up for us. For example, were you aware that your daughter missed 19 days of school this past year, unexcused, according to the district?"

"Yes, of course," he responded impatiently. "That was in the winter," David shivered at the very memory of it. “She didn't want to come here. It was right after the New Year. Her mother had died a few months earlier. You can understand that, can’t you?”

David paused.

“It was hard,” he continued. “I don’t blame her. She missed Pennsylvania and all her friends. But we worked through that,” David explained. Now his voice grew in intensity. “I got her back on track. She didn't miss school at all the rest of the semester. Her grades were okay too. Better. She wasn’t failing anymore. All her teachers said she caught up in record time."

"Are you also aware," continued the agent matter-of-factly, "that your daughter Jackie met with the school counselor half a dozen times in the months preceding her disappearance?"

At first David said nothing. His features were frozen in disbelief. Then common sense caught up with him.

"I suppose that's possible," he stammered. "During those first few months here, yes of course, she had a lot of anger and resentment. She was confused. But we've made progress since then. That's no longer..."

"Your daughter communicated," interrupted the agent forcefully, but coolly, "to former friends in Pennsylvania on several occasions via several social networking sites and texts that she felt lost and abandoned. She said her father had no time for her and that he was always working late or making excuses to run errands, leaving both her and her younger brother home alone for hours at a time in the evening or on weekends. Your daughter said that she felt like a professional babysitter. Even when home, she said that you were often detached or unapproachable. On several occasions Jackie commented that she felt like a second-rate citizen in her own house.

"Mr. Ashmore," the agent continued dryly, "your daughter also communicated two weeks prior to her disappearance that she wished her and Dustin could go back home."

"Both of them?" David asked.

"That's correct."

His tenuous mental hold on the situation shifted as another finger slipped in his mind and David almost dropped the phone. A chasm opened up beneath him and his mind spun with unforeseen implications.

"Mr. Ashmore, are you listening?"

Somehow David found his voice.

"Let me ask *you* a question. Do you have any teenage children? Any children at all?"

The agent didn't respond.

"Kids are constantly pushing boundaries," continued David. "They're trying to find their way. As a parent all you can really hope for is to minimize your mistakes and try to help them along. Most of the time nothing you do seems right. Once in a while you hit the jackpot. Jackie is one of those teenagers, though, where the regular rules don't apply. Her mother is gone. We're all struggling with that. Her friends are a thousand miles away. You can't really be surprised to get a less-than-glowing review from her."

"Mr. Ashmore, I have no choice but to take very seriously any comments made by your daughter and give them due consideration in light of the ongoing investigation."

David put his free hand over his face and then ran his fingers through his thinning hair.

"Let me get this straight," he began. "Are you saying my

daughter kidnapped my son because I neglected them? Is that what you're saying, Agent Bernal? That this is my fault?"

He had spoken in anger, but as he said the words he wondered if they might not be true in some way. Suddenly he felt like he was falling.

"Now hold on," directed the agent, his voice losing its professionalism for a moment. "I don't know what happened. All I know is two children are missing and there are few leads. Any questions that you can answer, Mr. Ashmore, will help the investigation. You want that, don't you?"

With an effort, David forced down his feelings of guilt and inadequacy. This was neither the time nor the place for self-pity. His children were at stake here.

"First of all," began David, slowly pounding out each word with a blacksmith's fiery precision, "they're *my* kids. *I'm* their father. There is no way you can possibly imagine what I'm going through right now. So don't even begin to insinuate that I caused this. God knows I'm far from perfect but something else is going on here. Not me. Not Jackie. Something or someone else. Do you hear me?" David's voice cracked with emotion.

"I hear you, Mr. Ashmore," replied the voice on the other end. "Go on."

"I'll answer any questions you have," declared David. "Send someone over any time you like. But it's been too long. If you can't find my son and daughter, then I'll find someone who can!"

Before Agent Bernal could respond, David slammed the phone down on the counter, cracking the cheap plastic casing. The situation felt intolerable. Even so, he had to keep it together. Picking the phone up again he touched the screen tentatively. When it came to life, he let a sigh of relief escape his lips. Then he typed in a search.

A strange, peacefulness came over him when he saw the listing.

"PRIVATE DETECTIVES" it said hopefully—big and bold at

the top of the page. Then it went on to list different cities, some nearby, some more distant. Names and telephone numbers were listed beneath. In his mind he wove the text together until they formed a parachute to slow his descent.

David scrolled through the listings. None seemed any better or worse than any other. He clicked on listing after listing, but none seemed right. Towards the bottom of the page he noticed some text that caught his attention. **Do you have a mystery that no one else can solve? Give Greenwold Private Eye a try.** David clicked on the link, but it was broken. The only other information was an address and a phone number. He punched the numbers in on his cell phone.

After four heart-stopping rings, a voice on the other end began speaking. It was a recording. The voice was tinny and hard to hear, but several things were clear. The detective's name was Hunter Greenwold. He specialized in unsolved mysteries and prospective clients were instructed not to leave a message.

David cancelled the call and considered his options. He could continue to beat his head against the wall here or he could spend an hour driving to the Twin Cities on what was almost assuredly a wild goose change to find an uncouth detective. Neither sounded very appealing. He didn't consider trying a different detective—it seemed like the choice was to use this one or no one. Instead he made a couple of calls to law enforcement, asking if they had heard anything about the private eye. To his surprise, they had. David read the on-screen information again and made his decision. After several minutes searching for his car keys, he walked out the door. What did he have to lose?

CHAPTER 16

With her hand no longer intertwined in the Keeper's, the long walk across the plain soon became visually monotonous for Jackie. They had long since left behind the valley and its almost endless pairs of inhabitants. Now they were moving across one giant cloud top that seemed to stretch from horizon to horizon. Nothing made sense. She still didn't understand Nimbus's explanation of what she had seen and felt but her heart still ached at the memory of it.

One thing she did know was that she would never want to vacation *here*. If the savannah had been overwhelming in its brutal intimacy and breathtaking detail, then Treetops without the living connection she had experienced felt barren and numbing. Without the Keeper's leafy back to break the white relief, she feared she would go crazy. There was nothing to be seen in any direction on the cloudscape. No animals crowded their passage as they had in the alabaster valley near the Keeper's home. If she didn't know any better, Jackie would have described the whole of Treetops as lifeless. At least Nimbus walked slowly. That helped a little. From time to time he rested heavily on his staff.

"Is it much farther?" Jackie asked wondering if you could die of boredom.

"Not too much further," replied the Keeper without turning around. "At least I think so. You're not tiring, are you?"

Jackie ignored the question. "I hope we're not lost. Something tells me you don't have GPS here."

All at once the Keeper stopped and Jackie almost ran into his leafy backside.

"Hey, warn me or something when you do that," she said.

The Keeper gave no indication that he heard her. Instead, he turned slowly in a circle with one vine-entangled finger upraised into the non-existent wind.

"Hmmmm," he muttered digging around in his mossy innards. Then he pulled out a large folded piece of paper, opening it with careful precision and patience.

It was no easy task. The object was unwieldy in size and seemed to have a will of its own. Each time the Keeper secured one corner and moved on to the next, the former immediately sprung back to its original shape. When he tried to lay it on the ground, he had to quickly step on it to keep it from wriggling away. Finally, by holding it out in front of him and pulling with Olympian effort, he managed to wrestle it into submission. The surface was dark and featureless but a moment later, as if in response to the glow of Helios, it blossomed into full color. Geographic shapes and lines formed across its flat surface in front of Jackie's eyes. A map!

A smile curled on the Keeper's face.

"Yes, of course," he muttered and shoved the living map back into his canopy of leaves. "This way. We're almost there."

Jackie struggled to keep up. Far from wandering aimlessly at a snail's pace, Nimbus began stepping boldly across the cloud-top. Step after step, mile after mile he kept up a ridiculous pace, his staff disappearing into the vapors in soundless staccato.

"Just a little bit farther," the Keeper remarked excitedly.

But Jackie barely heard him. She had fallen behind. Short on energy she called out to him to stop.

"Hold on," she yelled in between gasps. "Can we -- take a break? I need to..."

Her voice trailed off. One moment Nimbus had been walking ahead of her and the next, he disappeared into the growing mist.

"Keeper!" she called out. "Where are you?"

She began running to the last place she had seen him. Panic rose up inside her as she thought of the dark rider returning. Despite her fatigue and straining muscles, she willed her legs to move. Faster and faster she ran with the cloudscape rising like a flood around her. Each stride brought the whiteness higher and higher. Faint wisps of color came and went as the surface undulated around her. Swelling past her knees the vapors rose like a frothing tide to her waist and still she rushed ahead, calling out, until the clouds licked her shoulders and she had to crane her neck to see out. Unsettled, she slowed down, but it was too late. Her momentum carried Jackie over a rise and then down a gently sloping landscape into the swirling bank of clouds. The world disappeared.

Jackie felt as if she were underwater, sinking fast. Soon the ground levelled out, but still she couldn't see a thing. All of the Treetops' animals could be hiding within the wispy whiteness and she wouldn't have a clue. The feeling of being submerged combined with a wet clammy sensation made Jackie imagine that she was walking on the bottom of an ocean. A briny smell grew. Soon the cloudy mist thinned and a milky luminescence shone through. Two more strides and Jackie broke through into the open air.

She let out a gasp of relief and looked around. An isle of green spread out in front of her, curving away from the cloud-capped sea. Short, slender grasses tickled her ankles as she stood on the shoreline and stared at the grove of trees rising from the center of the great green enclave. Each tree resembled the one she had climbed to get here, only bigger. They were spaced at regular intervals forming two distinct lines in the center of the island and rose magnificently like flying buttresses of some colossal living cathedral to a lofty mosaic of bark and leaf and sky. So high were the tops of the boughs that Jackie imagined they held up the stars.

Between their massive trunks, the lost animals of the Earth, the denizens of Treetops, stood at attention, one row on each side, waiting. The only thing out of place seemed to be the glaring empty spaces signifying where a creature should have been.

Jackie walked into the sacred place afraid even a single breath would break the spell.

"Well if it isn't Little Red Riding Hood," grated Regnal from a nearby trunk and fluttered his wings impatiently. "Did you get lost in the woods?"

Speechless, Jackie stared back.

"You realize this is all for you, don't you?" continued the dodo. "But if it's a bad time I'm sure we can work something out. Tell the animals to go away. Maybe come back later."

Jackie opened her mouth to speak, to defend herself. *It wasn't her fault. Nimbus had not waited for her.*

"Enough!" commanded the Keeper. "The delay was mine." Striding through the trees and put a leafy hand on her shoulder. "You must choose now," he said gently.

"Why are some spaces left empty?" she asked. "If slower creatures need more time to get here, I don't mind waiting."

Nimbus looked troubled. "All creatures arrive at the same time for the Choosing. None are at a disadvantage. I do not know why some have not taken their places. It is very," and here he paused, as if searching for an answer that eluded him, "unusual."

"If you say so." Jackie looked down at the ground and saw Pence skitter nearby. "But how can I see any of this?" she asked. "I mean, I'm not holding your hand or anything."

"You don't need me to see the Grove of the Earth Trees," the Keeper chuckled. "A blind woodcutter has eyes enough for this."

"But what do I choose?" she asked. "I don't even know why my brother was taken in the first place."

The Keeper held his tongue. The girl was right of course. He owed her at least a partial explanation before she began.

"You must choose from the animals, of course," explained Nimbus. "As far as why he was taken, I cannot tell you. Gaylon the Black took your brother to the Arkanum. No doubt Flood saw some potential or gain from it. He must see something."

"But how did he know we were coming?" Jackie asked.

Nimbus sighed. "Have I not said that Flood has a willing servant and eyes that can see even on Planetside, should he choose? Perhaps he has the gift of foresight or the ear of creatures whose trade is mysteries. How should I know?"

"If you don't know what is going on then why are you helping me?" Jackie asked perplexed. "Why go to all the trouble? I'm just some kid."

"Even one life is worth the 'trouble' you speak of, child. And there is something bigger going here, something I should remember. That is why the animals have come. No one commands them. Not even me."

The Keeper raised his hand to silence her flurry of questions but Jackie had one other that would not be denied.

"Will Flood hurt him?" she asked quietly.

Nimbus took a deep breath to gather his strength.

"Samuel Flood is not evil. Nor is he without reason. This is what I have come to believe. But I do not understand him and he does not, I fear, understand me."

Jackie tried to make sense of the words and gain some degree of hope from them. But she found it hard to be comforted. Still struggling with things she couldn't change and with another thousand questions burning on her lips, she let Nimbus take her by the arm and guide her to the front of the waiting animals.

On her left an alligator, dusky gray, stared back silently across the millennia while on her right, an ape, black as a hunk of coal with dark eyes glittering, hunched stoically at attention. There were others nearby that she could not name, but their beauty was enchanting. A Blue Xerces butterfly fluttered in the air while a straight-horned saola stood with its head down next to a striped Tasmanian Tiger. Beyond these stretched an endless parade of creatures, each waiting for their turn and chance. Jackie stood frozen, overwhelmed by the spectacle before her eyes. She didn't know how to begin.

Nimbus leaned toward her putting his mossy lips to Jackie's ear.

"For your brother," he urged. "For your own blood and the waiting world, choose now. There is no other way, child."

Then the Keeper began to recite a poem, almost a song.

"Four for the seasons that turn in the sky. Three for the lost elements both low and high. Two for the Sun that shines and moon that glows. One for the Life that flows on rivers of tomorrow."

For Dustin's sake, Jackie stepped forward and began putting the strange rescue party together. It helped to pretend that she was just shopping.

But she had never gone on a spree like this and she had no list. Unsure what to do, she walked more than a quarter of the way down the lines without naming a single creature before Nimbus gently nudged her.

"You must pick something. It will not do to merely pick oneself."

"But I don't know what animals are best," Jackie complained. "What would you choose?" she asked hopefully.

"No," smiled the Keeper sadly. "I cannot choose for you. It must be your decision alone. But keep this in mind; the Arkanum is not without defenders or defenses. It will not be easily breached. A handful of insects and rodents will not suffice but neither will a fistful of allosaurs and saber-tooth tigers. Balance is the key."

Jackie nodded.

"All right," she said. "Some big and some small. I get it. With a couple in-between."

She walked a few steps more and then stopped in front of a great golden cat. It sat like a statue with its eyes sparkling. Parts of it seemed to be transparent.

"I choose you," began Jackie not sure exactly what to say. "To help me rescue my brother from Flood and his Ark? Is this okay with you?" she added timidly.

Nimbus shook his head but Regnal spoke first.

"Cut the speeches, Miss Windbag. Just say the name."

Jackie looked back at the animal. It still hadn't moved. The predator stood only a few feet from her soft flesh. She hesitated, not out of fear, but because it seemed presumptuous that anyone could name a creature so beautiful and imagine it contained by a label.

"Cougar," she said self-consciously.

Regnal buried his head deep within his feathers and the Keeper cleared his throat.

"Florida," the Keeper whispered trying not to break the mood any more than they already had. "You must call it a Florida Cougar. This is the name given to it, although it has a hidden name as well. Say it again and this time put your hand on top its head."

Jackie's eyes grew wide at the thought of touching the beast but the look she got from Nimbus told her there was no point in arguing.

"Right," she said swallowing and reached out her hand slowly until it touched ever so lightly on the top of the animal's warm furry head. Then she uttered the words.

At the sound of its name the animal stepped forward. Then it looked at Jackie and waited for her command as if it had been called from the dust of the earth to do nothing else. Before Jackie could move on, it wavered. Just once. But when its image settled down the cougar had become less transparent and more solid than before. Jackie walked on in amazement.

A Yangtze River dolphin caught her attention next and she picked the creature at once. The animal had a long, tapered nose and a curious expression as if it knew a joke but could never tell. Lost and lonely looking, the nearly blind dolphin squinted back at her with slits for eyes, its skin glistening in unwavering brilliance amid the Treetops sun as it floated in mid-air.

Next, she picked a white-tailed sea eagle. It had an alabaster head with a brown body and bronze chest. Nimbus told her it was from Madagascar. Following that she chose a Sumatran elephant with great dusky ears and ivory tusks. Walking along for a time she eventually chose a red-bellied monkey because she thought they would need an animal that could climb. Going down the other row Jackie found a black rhino and when she put her hand on it felt like armor, tough and indestructible. A few paces further, she stopped at the column-like leg of a seismosaurus and waited as the creature bent its long serpentine neck down toward her and then said the creature's true name (once more with help from the Keeper) in the smallest of voices. Still further, her legs getting tired, her senses overwhelmed, Jackie nervously crept past the tyrannosaurus and then stood transfixed in front of a pearly-white unicorn, a single horn protruding from its regal forehead. Somehow the mythological creature seemed more real than all the others. The poster hanging on her bedroom wall didn't even come close. Pure white, the unicorn stared back at her with intelligent eyes of liquid blue. Working up her courage Jackie touched the beast's silky mane. If there was anything softer in all the world, she had never felt it. As if a spell had been broken, the beast tipped its horn, acknowledging her choice with a bow. Last, she chose a wooly mammoth with a long tapering trunk and great curving tusks. A jet of hot steam shot out of the creature's mouth when she buried her hand in its thick, warm fur.

Jackie turned around, a fragile smile shone on her face for

completing the task. Looking at her chosen animals she felt more confident about the upcoming rescue attempt. She was no longer alone. Together they might be able to save her brother.

"That's only nine," quipped Regnal. "Can't you count? You must pick ten. Not eleven. Not nine. But ten."

"Regnal is right," said Nimbus diplomatically. "The rules are very simple. It must be ten."

Jackie sighed. "I don't know what else to pick. Can't we just call this close enough?"

Her stomach rumbled and Jackie wondered when she had eaten last. It seemed like days ago.

Regnal was just about to make a nasty retort when Pence ran over her shoelaces.

"Hi there," Jackie said weakly. "What do you want?"

The little white squirrel ran back across her feet.

"Hey!" exclaimed Jackie. "I can pick you, can't I?"

She put her hand on the animal's head and before Nimbus could intervene said, "Pence."

"Child, you don't know what you've done," toned the Keeper, trying to hide his alarm.

"I certainly do. It means I'm done and we can finally get started."

Jackie looked at her Chosen and exhaled. She hadn't realized how tense she had become.

Cradling her final pick close to her chest, she walked away from the long parade of animals and towering Earth Trees down to the shore where the cloud-sea lapped. She could feel Pence's heart as it beat quick and strong.

"Of all the ones, you're the best," she whispered.

Nimbus put a leafy hand on her shoulder. "By Xylum's Orb, that was well done," he told her. "Your Chosen will serve you, most of them anyway," he added glancing down at Pence. "Be careful to use them well. Respect them. Each animal in attendance would have been honored to accompany you."

Behind her, as if on cue, the parade of animals winked out of sight, reappearing faraway in the Valley of Treetops a moment later. Only her Chosen remained. Those creatures stood ready, still as ready and regal as ever but somewhat diminished in stature with the others gone. Reconciled to their fate, Jackie's Chosen gave no sign of impatience at being temporarily forgotten, but did what all Treetop creatures did best and simply waited.

CHAPTER 17

Samuel Flood sat in the bridge-tower high atop the Arkanum. Evening approached. Outside Helios cast a melancholy glow as the chariot made its way to the western horizon. The glass windows allowed Flood a panoramic view of the barren valley that stretched to the southeast, but his thoughts were turned inward.

Gaylon had returned carrying troubling news. He told of another interloper, a teenage girl in Treetops being tutored by Nimbus. This raised the obvious question: was he in possession of the true KeyStone? His servant had surprised him by delivering a sample of the girl's hair. That was unlike him. Usually Gaylon was impetuous and not inclined to clear thinking. Flood had rewarded his servant with a day's rest, after which Gaylon would take to the air again to keep tabs on Nimbus and the girl.

Flood twirled the auburn-colored strands around his massive fingers as if trying to probe their fundamental mystery. In actuality, he had analyzed them over an hour ago. The results were indisputable if unsatisfying. The girl and Dustin were siblings. He could tell that much from scrutinizing specimens from both of them, little good that it did him. He wouldn't know for sure if he had the ultimate weapon in his possession or simply a harmless little boy until the First Call. The prospect made him nervous.

Flood was patient. He had to be. Countless millennia had come and gone. Mountain ranges rose and fell while he waited, ever vigilant. What he could not abide was uncertainty. He raised his fist to strike the ancient table, carved from the One Wood when the stars were bright and new. At the last moment he stayed the mighty blow.

I am forgetting something, he reasoned. *Something that will ensure success.*

All around him the walls of the bridge were covered with clocks of every size and description, including several cuckoo clocks that never failed to amuse. His favorite, though, was an early Morbier grandfather clock, dark and stately, that presided over his personal sanctuary like an elder statesman. Each face read one minute to midnight. Taken all together, the accumulated ticking time pieces soothed his senses. The syncopation of the seconds relaxed his mind. This is where he came to think. The best ideas waited for him here. Time was his home, after all. It was also a useful tool.

Flood couldn't travel through time or divine the future, but he could manipulate time's dimension, coaxing things through it that were needed or desired. In this way, he was able to obtain countless books on subjects that were of interest to him such as genetic engineering and human psychology, as well as planetary habitability and weaponry through the ages. Such texts filled a cavernous library several levels beneath him. There were size limitations to what he could bring through, of course. Most importantly, he could only successfully transfer inanimate objects. That was a lesson he had learned the hard way, and one that had made his current predicament even more complicated.

One thing was certain; the girl would try and rescue her brother. With the aid of a Keeper, failing or otherwise, he could not discount her as a factor that must be reckoned with. New defenses must be readied.

Flood rose up from the high-backed ebony chair, every inch of its surface covered with fossils, and strode over to the great wooden wheel. More than simply a means of turning the Arkanum's ancient (and for the moment) useless rudder, it also allowed Flood the means to peer into different time eddies, pinpointing spots in history or the future and then pulling items through. Gripping the smooth worn wood, he began the laborious process of turning the wheel, slowly, to the right. Beads of perspiration blossomed on his forehead as his mighty hands strained to move it one millimeter and then another.

Almost there, he thought.

In the center of the wheel, where the great wooden spokes converged, he could see his prize forming, still hazy, but growing more solid steadily by the moment. It looked like a futuristic gun, eggshell white, about as big as a bazooka, but without a noticeable trigger. Metal rings were spaced evenly along its tapered barrel. He would need several more just like it to be on the safe side.

When he finally finished, Flood collapsed back in his chair and allowed himself a brief rest. The new glittering weapons piled in the corner were his insurance policy. If Dustin's sister came with that old fool Nimbus, he would be ready. And he had other, even more terrible methods of keeping unwanted visitors away too. Very soon he would pay a visit to his young guest. Come morning he would know if he held the fate of the world in his hands.

CHAPTER 18

Dustin woke with a start. Strange half-remembered dreams danced in his head like shapes in a fire. There had been scary shadows moving silently across a landscape, pools of bright blood and a gash in the sky. Thunder had crashed from above while a storm swept below like an invisible hand toppling mighty trees. And something else. A man, who didn't know himself.

The sound of a key turning in the door brought Dustin back to the moment. He just had time to scrunch up in the corner and wish his dad was there. Then the mammoth wooden door swung open.

Dustin blinked his eyes and squinted.

Sunlight.

It streamed in from the open doorway, illuminating a room made of cold stone. Dustin hardly noticed. He stared straight ahead at the creature that stood before him. The animal had great hairy arms, muscular and black, with a massive body. Dustin sat and stared at the gorilla too terrified to think. Eventually he noticed that something was odd. Instead of a fist-thumping chest, the creature was adorned with a spotted turtle's shell, smooth and shiny, that grew from its fur like a shield. Strangest of all was the red baseball cap perched high atop its head. The creature opened its mouth.

"Get up," the animal said in slow guttural tones. "Won't hurt you. Not you."

In its hand an assortment of keys dangled from a chain.

Gorillas don't talk. Dustin thought. *Not ever.*

"Me late," the gorilla muttered impatiently looking at the digital watch wrapped around its wrist. "No time. Come now!"

A watch? That gorilla has a watch! And it talks!

But still he didn't move.

"He really won't hurt you," said a deep, masculine voice from somewhere above. "I promise that you are perfectly safe."

Dustin looked around for the source of the sound. He found it in a speaker attached to the wall behind him. A camera pointed down from the ceiling nearby. The strong, but reasonable sounding voice continued.

"Just don't make him mad. He likes it when people listen to him. Isn't that right, Lancelot?"

The gorilla nodded its massive head like a child agreeing with a parent.

Slowly, Dustin got to his feet. A coldness hung in the air that his jean shorts and t-shirt did little to protect him from.

"Good, good," congratulated the voice. "Now we're getting somewhere. Come along. Follow Lancelot. There's something I want to show you. I think you'll like it."

Moving his feet as if he had rocks tied to them Dustin inched his way toward the doorway. The gorilla grunted in frustration. Then it turned and walked out. Dustin peered around the doorframe.

A long darkly timbered hallway stretched out in front of him. Lancelot waited at the end of it. Pale blue torches flickered high on the wall, but most of the illumination came from shafts of light streaming in through high open-air windows like bright laser beams. Dustin walked through the sunlight, half-expecting to be cut in two.

"Too slow," the gorilla said. "Walk faster."

His simian escort looked at its watch again. With a heavy grunt the animal turned and without bothering to say another word, disappeared around the corner.

Not wanting to be alone, Dustin hurried down the passage, his feet kicking up small clouds of dust from the soft, smooth rock. Already his tennis shoes were covered in a chalky residue. It grew noticeably colder and Dustin wrapped his arms around his chest. On his right were a series of steel doors, much more massive than the wooden one he had just come out of. They were cut in different shapes and sizes and spaced irregularly down the length of the hallway. All of them were closed tight. Dustin thought that they must have been made for giants. The knobs were set higher than he could jump. Dustin passed by nearly all of them without a glimpse of what lay inside.

Then he came to the last door at the end of the passage.

This door was not closed. It rested slightly ajar on rusted hinges. There was just enough of a crack to peek through. Dustin paused, curious, and then took a step towards it. Something erupted through the opening, pushing the massive steel aside as if it were tinfoil. He only glimpsed the creature as his senses screamed in terror. A mindless hunger radiated from it.

The thing lunged right at him. There was no name for such an abomination. The creature had a crocodile's head and jaws but the upright body of a grizzly bear. Huge bloody scabs covered the animal's fur while from other wounds a smelly yellowish puss seeped. The thing stank of death and decay. The desperation in its attempted escape took Dustin by surprise. A strange mournful cry tore from its scissor-shaped mouth.

Dustin must have screamed. But he never tried to protect himself. His hands never moved from his side. Frozen in place he watched the thing hurtle toward him in slow motion. The world stopped. Even his heart felt as if it had quit beating. At the last moment, he closed his eyes.

Hot breath stung his cheeks but the razor-sharp reptilian fangs never reached Dustin's face. The monstrous bear claws never ripped through his small tender stomach. Instead there was a blinding flash and a terrible explosion that left him exactly as he was, followed by the deep voice of a man who was used to getting what he wanted.

"Back! Back to your room!" commanded the imposing figure as he strode down the hallway, a gun pointed in his outstretched hand.

The man was giant, easily eight feet tall, with great arms and legs big enough to have carried the timbers Dustin had seen throughout the ship. With his huge free hand, he reached out and grabbed the wounded beast by the neck, holding it much too close to Dustin's trembling body. The creature managed to swat away the man's gun, but this only made the stranger tighten his vise-like grip. Immediately the thing shrieked, struggling against its fleshy prison. Its breathing came in ragged gasps.

"I feel the blood rushing in your veins," began the man, slowly containing his anger. "I see the hunger. But you will not eat this one. You will feed when it is time. Now go back to your room. Do you hear me?"

As if in response, saliva dripped from the creature's open mouth. It steamed when it hit the ground.

The stranger was dressed in a hoodless robe. Here and there it was stained with smudges of unknown substances, some of which might have been blood. On his feet were sandals, dusky and faded.

While Dustin stared, the creature lessened its struggle, still in the iron grip of the towering figure.

"Go!" said the man, hard and final. "Go or you will be punished."

The creature moaned once, long and terrible, as if asking for the release that only death could bring.

The man's eyes, blue as the sea, narrowed.

"Leave," he said quietly, the word hanging in the air like a warning.

Then he let it go.

For a moment longer, man and beast stared at one another. Then the horrible beast, pitiful beyond measure, turned slowly away and disappeared into the shadows of its cell. The stranger slammed the door shut, turning a skeleton key in the lock.

Deep red scratches were visible on his forearms like plow marks in a bleeding Earth. But he didn't seem to notice them.

"This cell was not secure," the man said turning to his servant. "It is not acceptable."

"I am sorry," Lancelot apologized, having returned during the struggle. "Door bad. My fault."

The man's fists were clenched in rage, but as Dustin watched, the stranger mastered himself.

"See to it that all doors are secured and strengthened. Nothing gets out unless I allow it. We have a very special guest. Is that understood?"

"Yes, Changer," the ape replied.

"I'm sorry you had to see that," the man said with a sigh, running his hand through his silver storm-tossed hair as he turned to face his little visitor. "Are you hurt?"

Dustin shook his head slowly.

"Thank goodness. I wish I had never made any of them. It was a terrible mistake, unjust and unwise. They were to be my army. Now they are nothing but an abomination and the source of my deepest regret. But they will have their release. Are you sure you're all right?"

Dustin stared back, vacant eyed, trembling and terrified of what he had just seen.

The man started to say something but then thought better of it. Finally, he stooped down, his head still towering above the boy.

"Did you ever have a dog and your mommy or daddy said it

was in great pain, that it was better for it to go to heaven, but you didn't want it too?" he asked more to himself than Dustin. "It's a terrible decision to have to make."

Dustin said nothing.

"But you're too young, aren't you? At least I hope you are. No one should see such things, let alone have to choose. Oh, what I would give to be in your shoes."

He smiled and then just as quickly let it fade away like a silly idea.

"Forgive me," he said almost in a whisper. "You are lost and scared. I wish it were not so. I wish many things were not as they are."

For a moment, his features betrayed a deep sense of tiredness that burrowed deeper than any wrinkle could ever go and then it was gone.

"My name is Samuel Flood, the Changer," the man said with heartfelt pride. "And this," he continued, stretching his arms out wide as if to embrace all of creation, "is the Arkanum. Welcome!"

Dustin stared back, his eyes growing wide. His fear did not depart, but it faded a bit like snow on a sunny March day.

"You mean, you're—I mean I heard all about you and everything in church, but I never..." Dustin stammered. "It was so neat how you saved all the animals."

The man called Flood stared back, not quite understanding what his small visitor meant. Then a smile split his face and a thunderclap of laughter broke the silence. In fact, he laughed so hard and so long that tears welled up in his eyes, spilling down his cheeks.

"You think I'm *him*?" the man began, “the pious shipbuilder...” but his own laughter, deep and uncontrollable, choked him off again.

"No," he finally managed. "I'm not the fairytale man you speak of."

Here he paused and a strange, electrically-charged silence descended on the scene, the kind you feel just before a storm hits.

"I'm better!"

Grabbing the boy's arm, he propelled him down the hallway like a thunderbolt unleashed.

“Come! Come!" he boomed, his voice echoing down the shadowy timbered passageways. "I have something to show you. Something wonderful."

Dustin whizzed past a multitude of great wooden doors, through archways and strange carvings and through portals of sunlight. After only a few turns, however, it became clear that they were going down. In a spiral of narrowing passageways, Dustin could feel the coldness descend upon them as the light began to fade from the diminishing windows on the walls. Soon there were no windows at all. It felt to Dustin as if they were deep underground.

Suddenly, Flood jerked to a halt. In front of them loomed a giant door made of metal. It had strange markings on it, exotic yet familiar, as if the artist had started in one language and then became tired of it, only to write in another. In the center of it all sat a golden crown.

Dustin could see no doorknob or handle.

“Allow me,” the Changer said. “You are too short. Let me lend you a hand.”

Then he hoisted Dustin up into the air, his fingers squeezing the boy like a vise.

"Go ahead," Flood urged. "Touch the crown."

Dustin cringed in discomfort.

"You're hurting me."

"I'm sorry," said Flood, loosening his grip. "I will let nothing harm you. I saved you back there, didn't I?"

Dustin nodded. Slowly, he reached out his hand and let it touch, ever so softly, the cool metal of one of the glittering crown's points. Flood put him back on the ground as gentle as a feather.

After a few metallic rumblings the door swung inward. Flood bowed slightly in an open sesame gesture. Stepping carefully across the tiled threshold, Dustin found himself standing on a balcony overlooking the lowest level of the Arkanum. Above it was the open air of a vast cavernous space. Muted blue light filled the expanse from a ring of great burning torches that made no smoke. Dustin stood on his tippy-toes but could not see over the curving wall to what wonders lay beyond.

"Here," Flood said. "Let me help you again. I will not let you go."

Then he lifted the boy high in the air above the balcony's wall.

"Wow!" Dustin exclaimed.

Down below, a multitude of animals surged this way and that, islands of teeming life amid an ocean of open spaces. There were pairs of mountain gorillas and pandas, snowy owls and killer whales, coyotes and kangaroos, manatees and spotted leopards, and many more that Dustin could not name. A sudden wind rushed past revealing two pteranodons gliding on great leathery wings. Flood held the boy tighter, but Dustin only smiled at the sight. His eyes grew wide as he took it all in.

In the corner of the Arkanum, a great red dragon flapped its leathery wings impatiently next to a griffin and a snowy-white pegasus. Near the center of the holding area, a cyclops and a basilisk engaged in a staring contest while a pair of minotaurs stood nearby.

All around strange animals walked, squawked, and occasionally even talked. And from some hidden portal, new animals kept coming, filling up the vast empty floor below. With each new creature, Dustin sensed something building, a growing feeling of resentment that he couldn't quite place.

"So, what do you think?" Flood asked as an amber-hued griffin flapped by their lofty perch. "Isn't this better than Disneyland?"

"I dunno," responded Dustin, thinking to himself that Mickey Mouse was pretty cool.

"Well, to get in there you have to pay money. You know what you have to do here?"

"What?" Dustin asked.

"Just blow this."

Attached to the lip of the terrace wall perched a golden horn. From its great curved opening to the long, slender neck it must have measured at least eight feet long. It dwarfed Dustin and looked as if you could unroll the twisting metal down to the floor below. In contrast, the mouthpiece on the instrument was no larger than a thimble set atop a corkscrew of metal. Dr. Seuss himself would have been proud.

Whether by design or coincidence, the object shone brilliantly in a shaft of sunlight that streamed down through the skylight far above.

Dustin had never seen anything like it. It captivated him almost as much as the fantastic animals congregating below.

This did not go unnoticed on Flood. He smiled.

"It's very nice, isn't it?" he said, carrying Dustin over to it until his face hovered mere inches from the tiny opening.

"Can it make a sound?" Dustin wondered.

Flood's smile widened and his blue eyes twinkled.

"It does indeed, although I have never heard it."

"How come?" asked the boy in amazement.

"The Horn of Calling or Callixar can only be played by one very special person called the KeyStone. At least that's what some very old stories say. That someone, dear Dustin, might be you."

"Me?" the boy asked.

"I think it might be," Flood told him. "Are you ready?"

Flood puckered his lips in mock demonstration and then uttered a little poem. It sounded like a nursery rhyme to Dustin.

"One little blow to make the Shadows go. Another and Treetops will show its blood. A third, and the Earth will rise up in flood."

He paused and glanced nervously at Dustin.

"And the fourth a mighty cow will chew its cud."

The boy laughed.

"After the third sounding, the process cannot be stopped, not even by the Wild One," Flood explained with growing glee. "Only the gods remember his name and they are sleeping. But enough! Story time is over, my boy. It is time to wake up the Earth. The Callixar, the Horn of Calling, has to be blown three times," Flood continued.

Dustin looked up at him not understanding.

"But why, you are wondering. I won't lie to you. Our little rhyme makes it all sound like fun and games. But it's not. Time is running out. Down in the world the animals and trees are in trouble. They are disappearing, never to return. Oceans are emptying. Forests are being cut down. The web of life is fraying. Animals are being pushed aside. People are hurting them. Not always on purpose, but hurting them just the same."

Dustin nodded. He knew this.

"Factories and cars are changing the very air that is breathed. Pollution and chemicals are poisoning the very seasons, altering the rhythm of nature. Humankind's actions are causing the ice to melt, the oceans to rise, and the planet to warm with no thought for the future except making more money. While people argue and fight, the planet dies a bit more every day. Machines march over everything. If it continues there won't be anything real left. What kind of world will that be without elephants or whales, redwoods or crystal-clear waters?" Flood asked.

Dustin stared back in shock. He didn't want to live in a world like that at all.

"Or even people," Flood went on. "Human beings are hurting themselves too. They depend on the Earth to survive. Some people don't care because they think the world around them is just fine. They're just fine. It's a world full of squirrels and oak trees and trips to the grocery store and it doesn't change so the world doesn't change either. But even their little world changes; they're just too busy or scared to notice."

"I *feel* it," said Dustin. "I dream about animals all the time. Sometimes they are happy but most of the times they are sad. They make me sad too."

"So, you do see," Flood said as he scrutinized the boy like an audience member trying to discern a sleight of hand. "I had feared that Gaylon erred in bringing you here."

He paused, considering the boy's revelation.

"How old are you?"

Dustin held up his hand and spread his fingers apart.

"That's very young," Flood remarked. "Do you ever talk to animals?"

"A little," Dustin said. "And sometimes they talk to me."

Flood scratched his chin until a ferocious grin spread across his face.

"You have a gift, my boy, a very special gift. Together we may be able to help the animals. Would you like that?"

Dustin nodded.

"Something must be done. We must be brave and quick before it is too late. The pavement must be broken and the planet awakened. Help me stop the killing of animals. And the toppling of trees for progress. A final stand can be made! And all," Flood paused to put his huge hand on top of Dustin's head, "because of you!"

Flood reached down and picked up Dustin. Slowly, like a towering carnival ride, he spun Dustin in his arms around and around. Soon the revolutions became a blur and the only thing that remained clear was the man's deep abiding laughter. But Flood's grip was strong and never wavered in holding Dustin securely in his arms. It had seemed forever since the boy felt so safe and wanted.

Finally, Flood slowed to a halt and gripping under the boy's arms, lifted Dustin effortlessly high into the air like a soaring bird. Then brought him down again until the boy was only inches from the Callixar's mouthpiece.

"What do you say?" he asked in a booming voice. "Shall we give it a try?"

Dustin said nothing and from all outward appearances merely looked disorientated and dizzy, but inside, where it really mattered, he was touched by what Flood had said to him. Long ignored by the only people that meant anything to him, the Changer's words soothed him. He felt as if someone understood. At the same time everything had happened so fast, and Dustin couldn't make sense of it.

"I'm scared," Dustin said at last in a tiny voice. "I want to go home."

"Of course you do, but if you can blow this Horn then your family will hear it and will know where you are. You want them to find you, don't you?"

Dustin thought about it and then nodded his head.

"My sis-ter," he said slowly accentuating each syllable. "She couldn't catch me."

"Then make a sound," Flood suggested. "Tell her where you are."

Dustin closed his eyes and took a very deep breath. Then he put his lips to the glistening metal and blew.

Nothing happened. Dustin thought he must have goofed. He hadn't. A chorus of sounds erupted from the instrument as deafening as a volcanic eruption. At first it was only excruciating noise, an orchestra of chaos. Soon, though, Dustin could make out individual calls, instruments of distinction amidst the clamor. They didn't speak to him, but he recognized them. Each communicated in the tongue of a different animal.

Dustin heard the cawing and chirping of a million birds. There were elephants trumpeting and the echoes of whales. Roars and howls, buzzing and clicking, chattering and rustling, and a multitude of other sounds all burst through the small little opening at once. It was as if the Earth itself had become a giant radio signal, not of man, but of the creatures and plants that lived there. He could hear the ocean under it all as it rose and receded like a living blue heartbeat. And through it all, thunder sounded.

Then it stopped.

Only the wind remained to whistle and cry.

Down below, at the bottom of the Arkanum, a dark shape in the corner slowly coalesced. It had four ebony limbs. Jagged spikes jutted out from its back. Claws much too big and teeth much too sharp glistened. As it moved cat-like, effortless, the other animals parted for it, cowering on either side. When it came to the edge of the curving timbered wall it stopped and waited. Soon others like it emerged out of the shadows and took their place beneath the round portholes of light. For a moment, the sound of the wind increased in pitch as the midnight creatures known as Cyclix took a step forward. Then they disappeared through the side of the ship, stepping into another place.

The next moment, the aching sound of the wind stopped and a strange silence descended as if the Earth itself held its breath.

CHAPTER 19

The Grove of Earth Trees felt like a dream to Jackie as they made their way back into the main valley of Treetops. A few more steps and she knew it would be out of sight, perhaps forever. She stopped and turned her head to capture one more memory, perhaps reassure herself that it had been real, but cloud-mist had already obscured it. Suddenly, she felt alone without the majesty of the trees and the solidarity of the animals.

"The Grove remains," the Keeper admonished. "The Chosen wait for your word."

Jackie looked at him in confusion.

"To communicate with them you will need the Orchlea," the Keeper continued. "It was fashioned by Barkabus, the first Guardian, from a fallen Earth Tree, split open to its ruined center by a fireball from the heavens. In that misty distant age, the grove was a forest, and the forest was the heartwood of Treetops. Its upper boughs bent toward the starlight and its roots reached deep into the world below. Even then the grove was ancient and covered all of the cloudscape and far beyond with its mysterious woodsong," Nimbus explained, an air of solemnity growing as his story wore on.

"When the time-swept winds whistled through the great branches, it carried the seeds away, scattering them until they rained down, falling to the mundane ground far below, somehow changed, and growing less than they were. These became the trees you know from your life down Below. Up here, in the land of Treetops, The Orchlea and the Grove of Earth Trees are all that remains of a lost age. Who's to say if it ever really was?"

With the story complete, the Keeper began searching his leafy mass for the named object. As he struggled, he became more and more agitated. For one terrible moment Nimbus seemed utterly lost. Bereft of his prize he looked terminally stumped. His quivering form bent over his mount as if it were the end of all trails. Then, at the very brink of some crisis, he straightened, and reached behind his ear with the flair of a natural magician.

"Ah, there it is! Leaf and root! The Orchlea."

The foot-long hollow object was made of ancient wood and narrowed upward in a twisting fashion finally tapering to an end that fanned out like a blossom opening. A thin leather cord was strung through a hole a third of the way from the top. At the other end, the Orchlea's base was thick with a small hole in the center. From deep within, the wood burned the hue of a half-remembered fire, as if the meteorite that struck it still burned in its core.

"Take it. Keep good care," the Keeper was saying. He extended the Orchlea to her. "The gift of the Earth's ear and tongue is yours as long as you hold it. Many initiates have used it before you."

Reaching out she took the Orchlea from his leafy hand and gripped it securely. A comfortable, warmth spread over her body, and her toes tingled.

"This isn't like when you touched me before, is it?" she asked, remembering what it had been like to be the starving leopard and the fleeing gazelle after Nimbus laid his hand on hers out on the vast Treetops valley.

"No, the Orchlea only allows for one-way communication from you to the animals you have Chosen. You will not experience the reality of those you speak with, although it can open up certain pathways. Remember to always talk through the hole at the bottom and point the tip towards your listener."

Jackie nodded with an air of relief and placed the strap around her neck. It was surprisingly light.

"Right," Jackie said feeling slightly overwhelmed. Then she turned back toward the invisible Grove and spoke with as much confidence as she could muster through the Orchlea. "Chosen, follow me."

Through the mist they appeared, one after another. When they were all accounted for, even Pence, she looked at Nimbus.

"Time is shorter than our needs," the Keeper said. "We must not delay."

Then she followed Nimbus into the thickening clouds, the motley assortment of animals trailing in her wake.

Jackie took another step forward and then the cacophonous sound hit her. It sounded like an orchestra had set up rehearsal in her eardrum. The concussion split her senses, eclipsing the world that surrounded her. The earth beneath her trembled. Jackie thought she heard something, an undercurrent of notes borne on the furious blast. Mostly, however, it was just noise to her. Abruptly as it began the cacophony faded away on the air, becoming mere echoes that rippled and then passed beyond the edge of hearing.

"What was that?" Jackie asked the Keeper through the ringing in her ears.

For a long moment the Keeper said nothing. She had never seen him look so helpless before, so at a loss. It scared her.

"The First Call. Yes, that's right." Nimbus stammered. "Weak I am. Old. Failing. I should have known. I should have remembered. There were signs yet I did not see. Not until the Choosing did I notice the missing animals. For years I have dreaded this moment and hoped it would not come."

Jackie didn't try to keep the fear out her voice. "I don't understand. Did something bad happen?"

"There is no time," the Keeper said, but he remained frozen in place. "At least the Chosen are immune, otherwise all would be lost."

"You're not making any sense," complained Jackie. "What is the First Call? Is that what that sound was? Tell me what's happening!"

Nimbus opened his mouth, but he made no sound. His whole form quivered, but eventually he composed himself.

"The First Call marks the beginning of The Last Battle," the Keeper explained as if remembering a fleeting dream. "Legends have it that the Earth will rise up and protect itself. That is what Flood is trying to bring about."

CHAPTER 20

Rain splattered the windshield as David Ashmore made his way down the darkening streets of Minneapolis. Buildings towered above him, reflecting the last rays of the evening sun into a brilliant stained glass mosaic of pinks and reds. David squinted and then glanced again at the GPS display on the dashboard. His hand gripped the steering wheel tightly. He needed sleep. When was the last time he had slept through the night? Or even part of the night, without waking up every hour drenched in sweat or reeling from a nightmare he couldn't escape. Rubbing his eyes, he took another swig of sugary soda. Soon his mind reactivated and he felt himself recharged with artificial life.

It had been nine days since his children had disappeared. Memories and fears raced through his mind again as he thought about them. Time and time again he pulled the wrinkled picture from his pocket and looked at their faces, trying not to think the worst.

What would you do, Jillian? He thought. *Tell me.*

The jarring sound of a car horn behind him sliced through his brain.

"Move it!" someone shouted.

Off in the distance sirens wailed.

Shoving the pictures back in his pocket, he dropped his foot on the accelerator and lurched through the intersection.

He had driven through the streets of Minneapolis (mostly for technology conferences and one family excursion) enough to know how to get lost. Today had been no exception, even with GPS, and the afternoon had somehow turned to evening. David fought down a sudden panic that time was running out.

To soothe his mind, David thought of the family trip—their first without Jillian—to the lighted parade that ran through the heart of Minneapolis last December. They had only been in Minnesota a short time, but David imagined that the festive lights and holiday cheer would help heal their wounds and bring the family together. It hadn't. Feeling like an ill-prepared band of refugees, they shivered through the spectacle on the cold mall sidewalk and then drove back to Rockwood in tired silence.

A truck horn blared and David jerked the car back into his own lane. *Hang on,* he chided himself. He was getting close. It couldn't be much farther. He turned at the next corner. Streets with names like Emerson, Colfax, and Girard flashed by. Leaving the brightly lit street behind, he drove down a darkened road as the sun sank behind the diminishing skyscrapers to the west. Soon rows of hunched dilapidated structures, none of them more than two or three stories tall, began to appear. Some were apartment buildings, others small stores with faded and rusting signs like Dollar Grocery and Hookah & Tobacco. All sat squeezed together block after block. People sat talking on well-worn steps, while others walked to the corner store or into the neighborhood bar. Two small African American children jumped-rope on the sidewalk as adults yelled in English and Spanish from windows above. David stopped to let a colorfully clad Hmong woman cross the street. He felt like an outsider far removed from his small-town sameness.

With a growing sense of uneasiness, he watched as phantom

intersections came and went. Countless blocks and several wrong turns eventually brought him to his destination, a narrow one-way street called Briar. There was no traffic and the surrounding area seemed strangely deserted. Rolling across old weathered bricks instead of asphalt, he slowly made his way, looking at each building number with increasing frustration. Five minutes later he turned off the ignition and craned his neck back and forth in a vain attempt to locate the address of the private detective. A dark, bloody glow on the horizon marked where the sun had been. The darkness gathered, making it hard to see.

"*It should be here*," he thought. In frustration he banged the dashboard.

But where it should have been, right between a pawnshop and a seedy-looking adult store, there was only a sliver of an alleyway leading to a dead end. David looked at the small piece of wrinkled paper where he had scrawled the address and name of the detective.

Had he written it down wrong?

Feeling defeated he got out of the car and walked along the broken cobblestones between the two shops. No one was around to ask for directions. Here in the narrow alleyway, the darkness was nearly complete. An unseasonably cool wind tore through his light t-shirt as he ambled down the uneven surface, deeper into the shadows. On either side of him loomed the bare and battered brick masonry of the adjoining stores from which crumbling battlements and roof work hung. Both walls were heavily besieged by what appeared to be an army of trash bags, discarded furniture, and broken-down appliances. From out of this refuse darted a cat in a bolt of black.

"Get!" David instinctively barked, his arms flailing, and the feline ran off, revealing a small purple flower growing in a crack. It looked like a miracle. Taking it as a sign that Jillian was guiding him, he walked on.

The alley continued to narrow. Finally, he saw a faint glow. It was so dim that he wasn't even sure it was a light at all and not a reflection from a car headlight or street lamp for it seemed to shift like a mirage. But as he came nearer, the glow grew stronger. A light burned in a small window on the bottom floor of the crumbling building. The illumination wavered with a warm candle flicker. David stopped at the foot of the door. A leaf-shaped sign hung above it. Greenwold Private Eye it read in worn letters.

There was no doorbell or knocker; only an engraving of a closed eye adorned the center of the door. The eye was without color or detail yet that same crudeness made it somehow even more realistic. Left to the imagination, it became alive. In the sputtering of the candle flame in the window, it appeared that it might open at any moment or perhaps it already had, watching him approach, only to feign sleep now. Shaking off the idea, David knocked soundly on the door with his knuckles in the heart of the eye. He waited, but nothing happened. He knocked again, harder. No footsteps approached.

He proceeded to call out, cautiously at first, but then more loudly.

Still no one came.

In desperation he began beating on the door, throwing his arm out like a prizefighter at the unflinching eye. When he finally took his hand away it was wet with blood. Cradling his torn knuckles, he sighed and turned to leave. He had failed. There was nothing left to do but drive back home.

Then the door creaked open.

Hesitantly, David opened the door wider and peered inside. The feeble candlelight did little to illuminate the surroundings.

"Hello?" he called. His voice was soft and tenuous.

Reaching into his pocket he groped for his phone and pulled it out, clicking on the flashlight setting. Then he stepped carefully into the darkness. Only the vaguest of forms could be made out as he shuffled his way ahead, the glow from his phone failing to penetrate more than a few feet into the inky blackness. What looked like a long rectangular table covered in fabric spread out on his left while in front of him, towering sections of walls arranged themselves like a Minoan maze. Through the tomb-like stillness he slowly wound his way, avoiding obstacles in the room. As his eyes adjusted some of the taller objects became recognizable.

Bookshelves, he thought, feeling an immediate kinship.

Ahead of him there appeared to be a counter and beyond that another door bathed in bright artificial light. So relieved felt David to be around something familiar that he misjudged the distance and smashed into the nearest shelf, catching it square on his left side. Off-balance, he ricocheted to the next unit like a pinball of destruction adding up pain points.

Crashing forward he felt the back of his pants tear as he snagged a sharp corner. Then everything went black for a moment as he buried his head into the unforgiving wood. A wave of dizziness swept over him and he toppled over.

Lying on the floor, gasping in shock, he opened his eyes and watched as the shadowy forms of shelves toppled over like misplaced dominoes. The sound of wood splintering rolled through the darkness until only the echoes remained. Finally, his eyes focused on one last movement right in front of him. It was the original shelf he had bumped into. Miraculously, it still stood, but just barely. As he looked up helplessly, it wobbled back and forth like a drunkard. For several precious moments he lay utterly transfixed. When he finally registered the danger, it was too late. David crawled backwards on hands and knees as the towering bookshelf fell toward him. At the last instant he lunged on his side in a feeble attempt at preservation. By doing so, he saved his skull from being crushed, but opened his body up to the full weight of the falling force. There was a moment of sharp pain and then the darkness mercifully swallowed him up.

CHAPTER 21

Nearby, in a back room, behind a door framed in milky light, a middle-aged man put a revolver to his head. His hand shook, both from fear and from drinking. His eyes were closed.

Recent years had not been kind to him. Pain circled his eyes and creased his brow. Unshaven, he wore his misery like a hair-shirt. Yet even this disguise could not completely obscure the once handsome features of his youth. Slowly, the stranger flexed the finger of his right hand and started to squeeze the trigger…

A wave of noise tore through his senses. Was it relief he felt or dread for what came next? In the very pit of his stomach, heavier than a black hole, his old regrets still festered. There were so many things he wished had gone differently. So many mistakes he would make right, but of course he couldn't. A pang of self-pity rose up inside of him but he beat it down without remorse.

Am I dreaming? Hunter wondered. *It should all be over now. I shouldn't be here.*

There was still no pain. He opened his eyes and instinctively looked at his wife's picture on the desk and asked her to forgive him for the marriage he had squandered, for a past he could not escape. But forgiveness was a scarce commodity. He had never known how to give it to himself.

Seeing her face brought him back to his senses. Made him feel the cold hard metal. In shock he looked out of the corner of his eye and saw the gun poised in midair aimed at his temple. Suddenly the weapon felt like a serpent in his hand.

Carefully, the man put the weapon down on the cluttered table. Then he allowed himself to breathe. For a long time, he just sat there.

His nails had grown long again, he noticed absently. They always grew so fast and sharp. Hunter grabbed the nail cutters from his desk and clipped them back one at a time.

He had just finished when a second explosion tore through his raw nerves. Although he glanced at the gun out of instinct, the sound had come from the vacant storefront. Now his senses were alert, his body automatically reacting. Old training kicked in. Standing up he grabbed the gun and ran to the door.

Collectors! He thought with a pang of fear and disgust. *Not even the week Baland had promised.*

Turning the doorknob, he kicked the door open, waiting for the gunfire that never came.

Satisfied that it wasn't a trap, he stepped cautiously through the lighted doorway and into the shadows. The gun in his hand steadied him.

"Hey! I got the money!" he yelled into the stillness. "Isn't that what you want?"

No one answered. The anticipated answering footsteps and revealing silhouettes did not appear.

Yet something had happened. That much was obvious. Shelves lay on top of one another like Tokyo after a monster melee.

Slowly he picked his way through the destruction.

"Damn it! Should have fixed these lights," he thought.

Even the candle in the front window flickered as if about to go out. It was his own feeble attempt at a memorial when he was sober enough to remember and light it.

The only substantial illumination came from his office, spilling from the open doorway like a ray of sunlight across the wreckage. He took a step forward and froze. A body lay underneath the fallen shelving. He could see the person's face and chest. The rest lay obscured beneath the bookcase.

No longer afraid but angry at his own timidity, Hunter walked over and bent down by the man.

He was no thug. Hunter knew that immediately. Baland's men weren't clumsy. They knew how to move and stay alive. This unlucky fellow wasn't a thief either. With his peppered grey hair, he was too old and his soft features hinted at a life that didn't demand physical labor. A pang of jealousy rose up in Hunter. This could have been his life; his comfortable storybook existence.

What are you doing here? Hunter thought, looking down at the unexpected visitor.

It didn't make any sense. Then Hunter saw it. There was a shadow, a sunken desperation to the man's countenance. It pressed down on him like the weight of the shelving. Just another desperate soul running out of options.

The stranger's eyes were closed but his mouth hung open as if he had just been talking. An awful stillness filled the air as Hunter cupped his hand next to the man's mouth. Faint breath warmed his hand.

Putting his hands under the bookcase, he lifted with protesting muscles, but could not raise it more than a few inches before having to set it back down. His second attempt fared better, but it wasn't not enough.

"C'mon," he scolded himself.

Feeling the world begin to spin Hunter lifted one final time. With a groan, he managed to heave the shelving clear of the mysterious man.

"You're welcome," Hunter muttered.

In the darkness he did his best to gauge the man's injuries. Satisfied that the man wasn't bleeding or fatally injured, Hunter turned to walk back to his office. Any conversation would have to wait until the stranger came to. He had taken only a single step when out of the corner of his eye he noticed the wallet lying on the floor. After a moment's hesitation, Hunter stopped and picked it up. It was fine black leather, not the kind of thing a poor man would carry around. With a quick glance at the still motionless figure, he opened the wallet up.

"Holy crap!" Hunter exclaimed under his breath.

Fingering the bills, he counted fifteen crisp Benjamin Franklins inside the fold.

With a last look inside, he closed the wallet. Then he wandered back into his office in search of something to drown his mind. A moment later he reappeared in the lighted opening holding a whiskey bottle. A sliver of light fell where the unconscious man lay. Then Hunter closed the door.

CHAPTER 22

For a long gray time, David Ashmore floated in dreams. In his imaginings he saw his children, smiling and safe, in their home back east. Jillian sat next to him, her hand on his, warm and constant. He reached over to kiss her, smelling the natural perfume of her hair, but she dissolved in the air in front of him. He reached out but a sudden stab of pain held him back, causing him to cringe.

From under a heavy weight, David stirred. His first conscious moment back in the land of the living consisted of red-hot torment that shot down his leg and another that pierced his head like a knife whittling its way deep into bone. He moaned, high and weak, almost sinking again into blessed oblivion.

Fighting to stay awake, he opened his eyes. He found himself in near blackness with a chaos of shadows all around him.

What had happened? Where was he? Then he remembered his earlier stumble and the destruction that followed. He had been walking and looking. He had driven all the way into the city to find someone. Then the pieces came together a private detective.

Full of purpose, David tried to sit up. Pain tore through his side again and down his leg spreading like wildfire. He probably had some broken ribs and his leg appeared to be in bad shape. It was twisted unnaturally. A wave of dizziness passed through him. Steadying himself, he gritted his teeth and managed to sit up despite the pain that coursed through his body.

He didn't know if he could do much more. He felt depleted and spent. Out of desperation he called out for help, but his ragged pleas went unanswered in the stillness. If there was anyone in the room nearby, they weren't coming out. Feeling the ground around him, his hand brushed over his cell phone. Hope flickered and then died. Even in with the lack of light, he could make out the smashed, lifeless screen.

Hell, David thought. *I guess it's the hard* way.

Using his arms and a fallen shelf as an anchor he leveraged himself up, inch by inch, until he was standing. Putting his weight on his good leg, he took a deep breath and hobbled forward. Pain shot through his side as he extended himself, but somehow, he kept his balance. He kept going for few steps and then threw his arms around a nearby bookcase for support. Another wave of dizziness hit him. Putting his hand to his forehead, it came away damp with blood.

More determined than ever, David made his agonizing way to the lighted door.

Not bothering to knock he pushed it open with one knee and staggered into the tiny office. The smell of smoke hung heavy in the room. The naked lightbulb in the ceiling glowed stark and unforgiving. The walls may have been white at one time, but now were peeling and yellowed. A small shelf hung crooked in the plaster halfway to the ceiling supporting what might have once been a beautiful plant, but now looked wilted and dying. Nothing else adorned the walls save for an old faded painting of an idyllic woodland with a little clearing near its center where a silver stream meandered. Taped above the meadow was a small black circle and an arrow pointing downwards. In crude magic marker were written three simple words: **YOU ARE HERE**.

David followed the arrow down to the man who sat at the desk, face down, surrounded by a pile of beer cans and bottles. Ashtrays adorned the desk loaded with cigarette butts. Somehow, despite the noisy chaos of the shelves, the man was snoring.

"Excuse me," said David leaning against the doorframe.

After a moment he said it again louder. When that failed to work, he managed to kick a can across the floor.

Slowly, the stranger stirred. He lifted his head wearily from the wreckage and looked at David with bloodshot eyes. His face was covered in stubble and wrinkled beyond its years.

In addition to the stranger's clear lack of hygiene, he wore a garish neon tropical shirt covered with coconuts and pineapples. It was loose-fitting to the point of being comical.

"I don't have the cash," the man said wiping his mouth. "Not yet. We agreed next week, right?"

Sitting up with what looked to be an awkward agreement with gravity, he swept as many cans as he could to the floor using his forearm. Now that a portion of the mess was removed, several items including a newspaper and a framed picture of a smiling woman wearing a straw hat were now visible.

"Listen," David began. "I think there's been a misunderstanding. I came here for help. I need a detective. I'm not here about money. I'm looking for someone called Hunter Greenwold, private eye," he finished, fighting through the pain.

The man relaxed almost at once and ran a hand through his thinning brown hair. After a fit of coughing and several unsuccessful attempts at finding a cigarette, he finally found a box that wasn't empty. Taking a lighter from his desk drawer, he lit the end of a Maverick and chuckled.

"You've found him," the detective said taking a deep drag. He leaned back in his chair. "I'm Hunter Greenwold. Heard you come in earlier. You make quite an entrance. What's your problem?"

"For starters, that's mine," David said pointing to his wallet on the desk.

Another wave of coughing wracked the detective causing him to double over.

"Oh this," he managed. "I was just keeping this for you until you were feeling better. Get a lot of nasty types in here sometimes. They'll rob you blind."

Hunter tossed the wallet over.

After a brief check to make sure all his money and credit cards were still present, David put it gingerly back in his pants pocket.

"You're a real good Samaritan, aren't you?"

"I'm a lot of things. What's the problem?" the detective asked again.

The question seemed to open up a giant hole under David. He found he couldn't speak.

Taking another drag of his cigarette, the man was overcome again with a fit of coughing. He grabbed one of the remaining beer cans off the desk and took a swig.

David looked around the office for inspiration. There wasn't any.

"Listen, if there's something on your mind just spit it out. I can't help you unless you tell me what it is."

"I think maybe I have the wrong address," David mumbled as he started to back away toward the exit.

The man leaned forward and smiled a thin razor blade smile.

"Didn't the big eye on the door clue you in? I'd make it clearer but I don't exactly want to advertise, if you know what I mean. I won't ask again. Why are you here?"

It was getting hard to avoid the obvious; *this* was the detective.

David stopped in his tracks. "No offense, but you're not what I expected."

"No need to beat around the bush. You can't believe somebody like me can help you," said the investigator finishing his cigarette.

The private eye looked David up and down. He shook his head and laughed bitterly.

"You're nothing special. I'm not either. I thought I was once, but not many of us are, not in the way we grow up believing. You know, being famous or heroic or somehow different than all the other poor schmucks. We just do what we can and most of the time it's not enough, but sometimes it is. Is that good enough for you?"

David tried not to let his disappointment show.

"I'm sorry to have bothered you."

Sighing, David turned and hobbled back out of the room.

"Finding people are my specialty," Hunter called.

David froze.

"Am I right? Or do you have a little lady on the side that's giving you trouble. No, you got the looks for it but you also got brains, I can tell. Come back when you wanna use em'."

David hesitated a moment longer and then made his decision. Step by painful step he made his way back through the doorway and into the office.

The detective motioned to a chair covered in dust.

"Sit down," he said brusquely. "You look like crap."

"I'll be fine," said David.

"Sure you will," Hunter muttered taking out another cigarette and lighting it. "These things will kill a person. So, when did the they go missing?"

"How did you know? I didn't tell you anything yet."

"You didn't have to. I guess I've been in the business long enough to see the signs, that's all."

But something in the detective's face and the way he looked away when he said it made David believe that there was more to it than just work experience.

"Anyway," Hunter began taking another drag of his cigarette. "Let's clear the air, shall we? Name's Hunter Greenwold. I'm a private investigator. My fees are not negotiable. I charge $500 dollars a day plus meals and gas. I don't drink or smoke when I'm on a case and I don't take orders. I expect the truth and I won't tolerate you being in my face. I work alone. I work fast and I get results. In addition, I will need wheels, a car of my own choosing. You can consider it a down payment of your good faith, I don't really care. Any questions?"

David sat there momentarily stunned.

"I'm worth every penny," the detective said. "Just ask around."

David finally found his voice. "You were kidding about the car, right?"

"Red Jaguar, 1967. No scratches and no dents. Working radio is an absolute necessity."

"Huh?" sputtered David. "You can't be serious."

"I was kidding about the sports car. A rental car will be fine. But it's another expense. You understand?"

"Sure," David said. He felt like a boxer who had just taken a punch but was still standing in the ring. "Is there anything else you need? Perhaps I could call up Phillip Morris and set you up with an account."

"I said I don't drink or smoke when I'm on a job."

"This is crazy. I'm not putting my children's lives in the hands of a..."

"A what?" Hunter asked, his eyes no longer hazy but sharp as knives. "A loser? A drunk? Let me ask you this. Which one of the private dicks dropped my name? Let me guess, Jeffries. "

"I found your information online," David managed. "But I've also talked with the police, the FBI and a bunch of private eyes. They all said you were unconventional, but that you got results when no one else could."

David paused.

"It sounds strange, but seeing your name, I just felt like you were the right person for the job. I didn't know what else to do. You are my last hope. Someone said you were the best."

Hunter's eyes flickered over the framed picture on the desk.

When the detective spoke, his voice was softer and full of longing —the kind that never quite goes away.

"I used to be a lot of things," Hunter said.

David didn't know what to say in response. The silence lengthened until it became uncomfortable.

"I think we got off on the wrong foot before," he managed finally. "My name's David Ashmore."

He felt Hunter's eyes study him as if they were trying to gauge his own worth and sincerity.

"Okay, David Ashmore," the detective said, his rough bravado back in full force. "Tell me all about it. There must be a really good reason why you're here."

"My children are missing," he began. "Jackie is thirteen and Dustin's five. I haven't seen them in over a week."

"Do you have a picture?" Hunter asked. "I'd prefer a print."

David dug in his wallet and retrieved the photo. It was tucked in the back fold, hidden behind a secret pocket.

"Let's have a look," the detective said.

For a moment David hesitated. It was his closest connection to Dustin and Jackie. He always carried around a photo of them even though he had countless more on his phone. It reminded him of what was important. But he handed the image over to the detective.

Hunter held it up close to his eyes for inspection. What he saw surprised him.

In the photograph, a teenage girl was sitting with her legs outstretched and smiling as a young boy sat on her lap. A sea of colorful pillows surrounded the pair. They looked happy. It was a standard family photo in every way. But there was something else. Some echo of familiarity that tugged at the detective.

"They look like good kids," Hunter said. "Mind if I keep this?"

For a moment David paused as if on a ledge. Then he said, "If it'll help, go ahead."

"Tell me what happened. Start at the beginning and don't leave anything out."

David nodded, took a deep breath, and told the detective everything he could bear, everything he could think of regarding his son and daughter's disappearance. To the hour and the minute, he relayed when events occurred as best as he could, when he first realized they were gone and what he had done to try and find them. He described his children in agonizing detail including Dustin's quietness and infectious laughter as well as Jackie's fiery personality and despondency following his wife's passing. He relayed their move from Pennsylvania to Minnesota. How hard it had been to leave and why they had done it. He even mentioned his children's strange birthmarks.

"What do they look like?" Hunter Greenwold asked.

"I don't know. A tree, I guess. Why?"

"Anything that stands out is potentially important, especially since both of your children have a similar birthmark. Could make it easier for someone to spot them. Go on."

Taking a deep breath David continued. It was hard to tell him about Jillian. Somehow, David felt that he had betrayed her. That he had done something wrong that she would never have done. And maybe he had. He must have or his children would not be gone and he wouldn't be sitting here in this broken-down bookstore at the end of the world telling a chain-smoking drunk his problems.

"Mr. Ashmore," Hunter said. "You were talking about the gift your wife gave Jackie. What was it?"

"I don't know what was inside. She never told me."

"Who never told you?" Hunter probed. "Jillian?"

"Yes, that's right. When my wife realized—finally accepted—that she was dying, she gave it to me with instructions to give it to Jackie on her next birthday."

"She never hinted at what it was?"

"No and I never asked."

Hunter started to respond and then caught himself. Instead he leaned back and began making popping sounds. After a minute, the sound was more than David could take.

"Well? What do you think?" David asked.

"Very interesting. I've never had a runaway quite like this before."

"I told you, they didn't run away. Something else must have happened."

Hunter paused and then closed his eyes for so long David thought he must be asleep.

"Where did you say she went when she walked the dog?" he asked suddenly. "The park?"

"Yes, that's right. Highveil Park. It's just a few blocks away from our home."

"And that's where she went the day she disappeared? Alone?"

"Yes, I believe so. Several witnesses said they saw her enter the park but none of them saw Dustin, except for a trash collector and he wasn't sure."

"Mr. Ashmore," said the detective, opening his eyes and leaning forward. "It seems likely that your son followed Jackie into the park and that the two of them disappeared while there. You've received no ransom note and although your daughter appears far from happy, it also is unlikely that she would run away, especially with someone so little as her brother. You say police have scoured the area, even brought in dogs to track their scent. I'd like to see this park for myself. It seems almost impossible that any one sick individual could control and kidnap two children at once without creating a commotion, unless they used one sibling to leverage cooperation out of the other."

Dark thoughts swirled in David's mind. If someone had harmed his son and daughter, he didn't think he could bear it. His hands bunched into fists. After a moment he realized that the detective was still speaking.

"Another possibility, of course, is that you, Mr. Ashmore, are somehow involved in all this."

Despite the pain in his leg, David reared himself up and threw himself toward the desk and the detective.

"How dare you!" he yelled. "I don't have to take this from anyone, least of all you! I didn't take it from the sheriff or the feds and I'm not taking it now. I wouldn't be here if I didn't love my children, Mr. Greenwold. I am nothing—*nothing*—without them. Do you hear me? They're all I have. If I have to crawl on my hands and knees halfway around the world to get them back, I will."

David wiped a tear away self-consciously and turned to leave for the second time in the last half-hour.

"However," accentuated Hunter, "observations fail to support your involvement, at least directly. You are innocent, Ashmore. Innocent! Now get back in here. There's something I want to show you."

David stood there teetering. Eventually curiosity got the better of him and he came and sat back down.

"What?" David grated.

"Do you know what this is?" asked the detective holding up a folded front page of a newspaper.

A small grainy picture and box of text was circled in black, but David was too far away to make out anything.

"I can't really see it."

"Then come closer. This is important."

The father stood up with effort and hobbled closer, his eyes straining to make out details. Taking a pair of reading glasses out of his shirt pocket, David put them on.

"Perfect!" he exclaimed, noticing the shattered lenses.

"Don't read," Hunter sighed. "Just look for Pete's sake."

Putting the useless spectacles away, David took a deep breath and then peered again.

"Looks like a big cat of some sort," David said, leaning over the desk at the grainy image. "But it looks odd."

Hunter nodded.

"Whatever it is has been sighted several times in the last few days. No one's been able to get close to it except the person that took this picture and he's now dead. Died before they could even get him to an ambulance. Bites, claws, scratches, punctures, trauma to the head, poison, you name it. Hard to believe it all came from one creature."

"So it's an escaped exotic animal from a zoo," David said dismissively. "What does this have to do with my missing children?"

"Let me ask you something, Ashmore. You're not a city boy, are you?"

"I grew up on a farm. Went to college in a big city, but have lived in small towns ever since. Rockwood is probably the biggest small town I've ever called home."

"I'm envious of your daily commute. So you haven't heard of this strange bit of local news? It's straight out of *Stranger Things*."

Hunter Greenwold unfolded the paper so the headline became visible. David recognized the familiar masthead immediately. Then the detective turned the paper over revealing the story title: **ROCKWOOD PHANTOM PANTHER STRIKES.**

"It happened three days ago," Hunter said. "I'm sure it's all the gossip in town."

"I had no idea," stammered David. "The daily news hasn't seemed so important lately."

"You'd do well to stay current," advised the detective. "Clues can come from unexpected places."

He tapped the newspaper for emphasis. "Just another schmuck who winds up dead. Happens all the time, right? Something tells me there's more here. It's not a big story yet, at least nationally. But it will be soon. Reports I've been able to get my hands on, mostly from news sites and Google hits, are sketchy, but it goes something like this. Similar creatures have been spotted in major cities around the world in London, Paris, Beijing, Moscow, New

York, Calcutta, Rio, Cairo, Tokyo, Nairobi…the list goes on. Indications are that there's even more activity in the less populated areas. They're like Bigfoot sightings, although no one seems to be laughing about these."

The detective tapped his fingers on the desk. "Details vary, but they all amount to the same thing. Someone sees an inky shadow, something strange and unsettling. Then it disappears. No one has managed to take a picture until yesterday. Rumors are that something similar has been spotted prowling around the Arboretum in Chaska just south of here."

David took a deep breath. "Do you think this creature has anything to do with my missing children?"

"I don't know," Hunter said. "But it seems like a pretty big coincidence."

Bereft of words, David could only nod grimly. A wave of pain wracked him and he stifled a curse. His leg wasn't getting any better.

"Time to get down to business," the detective said.

"Of course. I suppose you'll want payment now."

"That's right and in full," Hunter stated unequivocally. "A week's worth."

Reaching into his front shirt pocket, David removed his checkbook and opened it up glancing around for a pen.

"Cash only," the detective said. "No exceptions."

"That depends on how much you want."

"Seven thousand plus another five hundred for meals, gas and miscellaneous."

David shook his head. "Sherlock Holmes isn't worth that much. I'll give you a thousand now and $5,000 later when you find my kids."

Hunter smiled. "Let's make it $2000 with $5,000 later. It's my final offer."

Reluctantly, David took out his wallet and began placing hundred-dollar bills on the private investigator's desk until he counted up to 15. It hurt him to see so much money go to such a scum bag, but what choice did he have?

"That's all I have," he said. "I'll give you the rest when you find my kids."

"No deal," the detective said. "You must have some additional collateral. Something of value to make up the difference." His eyes fell on the father's wedding band.

"If you throw the ring in, we're good."

David's eyes widened. "You must be joking. It's the last thing I have of my..." he caught himself and brought his emotions under control. "There must be something else. What about my watch?"

Hunter shook his head. "It's the ring or nothing. Take it or leave it. You'll get it back as soon as I'm done." When David still hesitated, Hunter's voice softened almost unnoticeably: "I promise."

Swallowing his pride and stifling a curse, David began tugging at the silver and gold ring. He'd never taken it off, not even once through all his years of marriage. After his wife's passing, it gave him some comfort and a connection that he clung to. After several more tugs and turns, he finally managed to slip it off of his finger. He felt naked without it.

"This is for my kids, you understand," he said through gritted teeth. "You find them. You bring them back home safe."

The detective took the ring and held it up to the light for a moment before depositing it in his pants pocket.

"It looks like you've got a deal, Mr. Ashmore," Hunter said extending his hand across the desk.

David declined to shake it and chose instead to close his now much emptier billfold.

Hunter smiled and clasped his hands together.

"I'll do everything in my power to find them and bring them back," he said.

Despite grave reservations, something in the detective's voice made David believe that he really would.

"You made the right decision in coming here," Hunter told him.

"I'll expect updates, you understand. Every day. Keep me informed. I don't want to be in the dark about anything."

He reached out and passed his business card to the detective.

"My cell phone number is on the back. Call me day or night."

David watched as Hunter deposited the stack of bills in his desk drawer. Somehow it felt as if he had just sold his soul to the devil.

Slowly, as if he had all the time in the world, the detective put his feet up, leaned back and closed his eyes.

"Aren't you going to do something?" David asked with rising indignation.

"Plenty time for that. It's late and I got one heck of a headache. I'll need to be fresh for tomorrow."

Only his damaged leg prevented David from leaping across the desk and choking the investigator on the spot.

"You bastard! How did you ever become so low and worthless? Slime has more ethics than you. Get off your sorry..."

"Shut up." Hunter said suddenly alert. "Shut up now," His voiced sounded hushed and earnest.

David curled his hands into fists. "How dare you speak to me like that!" David yelled.

But the detective wasn't looking at him anymore. Instead he stared off to his left at the open office door.

"I hope I'm not interrupting something," said a voice.

David turned. One look at the man behind those words told him they were in trouble. You didn't have to be street smart to see the violence held in check by the corners of his mouth or the ripples of muscle underneath his pressed pants and suit.

"Having a nice day?" asked the man, smiling coldly at the detective.

Nothing about the stranger suggested that he ever asked for

anything. He had that cold, certain look of just taking when it suited him or when someone even more heartless told him to.

"Not even close," said Hunter, trying to keep his cool but only half-succeeding. "How's the family Malory? Can you believe the weather we've been having? Everything's out of whack if you ask me."

"Cut the crap. You know why I'm here. Let's have it. My kid has a soccer game in twenty minutes. Don't make this difficult."

The stranger seemed momentarily sincere.

"Sure. I understand. I just thought I had one more week, that's all. Don't I have one more week?" the detective asked, his voice shaking slightly.

"A week ago you had one more week. You don't have any more weeks. No more time, Weed. No more games. This time it will be worse than a little scratch."

Hunter had one hand clasped in the other, almost cradled, with just the tops of his fingers protruding out while the thug talked. Only David now noticed that his digits weren't all there—the very top of his ring finger was missing, cut clear through from where the nail should have been. In its place was a flat patch of skin. A corner of scab still clung there.

After a moment David realized that the well-dressed man was still talking.

"...always about the kid. It's a terrible thing but that's not our problem. Can't be. This is between you and Baland. Right now. One way or another you're going to pay what you owe," he said evenly, almost politely, making it sound like an offer Hunter couldn't afford to let slip by. "Which is it going to be?"

Hunter glanced at David, making eye contact.

"My client here just paid me to take on a case," he said at last. "Didn't you, Mr. Ashmore?"

What game was the detective playing at? Whatever it was he wanted no part. Yet he had to say something. Some displaced sense of politeness caused him to think that standing up might be a good idea. He immediately regretted it. The moment he put weight on his bad leg, he forgot all about formalities. A thousand curses hung on his lips but only a moan snuck past as his world spun around like a carnival of pain. He swayed like a ship lost at sea. When he finally opened his mouth to say something, it was too late.

The stranger took one quick look at him out of the corner of his eye and sized him up, bloody forehead and all.

"Doesn't look like it to me. Just more street trash."

Hunter remained calm and composed. "My friend here is nothing of the kind," he said with indignation. "In fact, he paid me quite handsomely for my services. I put the twenty grand right here in the drawer before you barged in. Allow me."

In an instant the stranger drew his gun. It had a silencer at the end of the barrel so there wouldn't be a sound. Where it came from, David couldn't tell. But the gun pointed right at Hunter.

"That will be the last lie you tell, Weed," the man said with a chilly edge to his voice. "Move away from the desk and put your hands where I can see them. I'll look through your treasure chest myself."

Hunter pushed himself away from the desk while his fingers gripped the knobs. It was a smooth move, quick and precise, made all the more impressive by his hangover and general malaise. It was also suicide. Rolling backward in his chair Hunter reached for the gun in the drawer lying across his lap.

The stranger didn't flinch or raise his eye in surprise. Nothing about him gave any indication that he was aware of the detective's actions except for the barest of smiles that curled at the edge of his lip.

Slowly, as if his target was not worth more than one bullet, the man squeezed the trigger.

The detective was still bringing his gun up to aim a wild shot when David moved. Ignoring the pain in his leg he lunged with his whole body like a battering ram and dove into the stranger headfirst, arms outstretched. It should have been easy. He was only a few feet away. But he couldn't push off with his leg adequately. He didn't have the speed and he didn't have a gun. All he had was the element of surprise.

Hurtling through the air, David let out a yell of desperation. His kids needed him. To find them, he needed the detective. No one was getting in his way. Somehow it wasn't enough. He saw the stranger whirl toward him. He saw the man's finger pull the trigger.

There wasn't anything he could do.

The bullet ripped through him without a sound. It could have been the wind. There was a moment of excruciating pain and then nothing.

Hunter watched as the father fall heavily to the ground with his hands still outstretched to their target. Already Malory was returning his focus to him. Forcing himself to ignore what happened to the father, Hunter aimed his gun. The hired thug shifted off balance from having to take a step away when David had jumped at him.

That all the time Hunter needed. He fired off two deafening explosions. The hired muscle fell to the ground. For a heartbeat the detective stood there and emptied his lungs.

Still holding the weapon, he walked around the desk, stepping on Malory for good measure and then knelt down grimly beside the middle-aged man who had stumbled into his office only a few short hours ago.

"Ah, hell," he muttered.

The bullet had ripped through Ashmore's side. A pool of blood slowly soaked into the dull grey carpet. Cupping his hand over Ashmore's mouth and laying two fingers strategically on his neck, the detective acted in accordance with his old training, even though he already feared the worst. A flash of memory seized him. He was driving down a sunny street. He remembered the shadows of the trees as they fell across the road. Everything was perfect. He was happy. Then everything changed in a heartbeat. Hunter blinked, his nightmare interrupted by the unexpected. It was faint and irregular, but it was there like a miracle. Ashmore had a pulse, although he didn't deserve to have one after his idiotic action.

"Why did ya have to go do that," Hunter muttered.

But he knew why.

There was a time when he would have done the same thing.

"Christ!" he said out loud as he took the picture out of his pocket and forced himself to look at it. A little boy and teenage girl smiled back at him.

Grabbing the old rotary dial phone off his desk with a Kleenex he spun the numbers with a slow determination. It would be so easy just to run.

When the emergency dispatch personnel answered, he had to force himself not to hang up.

"A man needs help," he told the woman.

Then he verified his street address making sure she understood where the abandoned store was. He described the nature of the emergency but did not give a cause. He did not leave his name. When he finished, he didn't hang the phone up but rather just waited for the connection to close and then let the receiver slip from his grip.

All the strength seemed to have drained from his body and the door seemed impossibly far away. On the floor in front of him were two men: one dead and the other dying. A pool of blood hung from each like a comic strip voice balloon with the father having less and less to say as he watched.

Walking back over, the detective knelt beside Ashmore like he was asking for forgiveness. Gently he unbuttoned the man's shirt until the wound was visible. Forcing himself not to look away, he grabbed a hold of the father's shirt and ripped a strip of fabric along the seam. Tying it in a bundle he applied pressure until the flow of blood lessened. He could do no more.

Standing up, he nearly lost his balance and had to grab on to the desk for support. Twice he crammed his pockets with cigarettes and small booze bottles and twice he took them out. Finally, he just let them be. This was a dead place, he decided. Time for new mistakes. But still he couldn't move.

Only the siren sounding like a grieving mother as it echoed through the streets reached him. Turning to go, he paused. Hunter could not bear to leave behind the framed picture of his former wife, but he left it where it was. That life was over. He took out the money Ashmore had given him out of his desk drawer and jammed it in his pocket. Then he left for the arboretum.

When the ambulance crew arrived on the scene a few minutes later, the first thing they saw was a candle flame in the window, flickering as if the slightest breeze could blow it out.

CHAPTER 23

There wasn't much to do as she and the Chosen marched. Here and there the endless white of Treetops was broken by a dark lesion, a blemish on an otherwise pristine landscape. She remembered seeing them in the valley by Heart-Wood and wondered again what caused them. They seemed to be getting worse. There was so much she didn't know.

Riding atop the woolly mammoth, Jackie began thinking of how she got here. She certainly wasn't a hero, no leader, no Joan of Arc. Truth be told, most of the time she felt like a villain for what she had done to her brother. It seemed a lifetime ago that she had been back in Pennsylvania. Everything had been perfect then, although she hadn't realized it.

A casual observer seeing her walk through the halls of William Penn Middle School with her books held close to her like a shield would probably have said she was just another girl pretty to everyone but herself. They might have added that she was probably blind to everyone else's problems because of being caught up in her own. The old Jackie, of course, would not have agreed. But she was no longer the same. It was more than just being a year older, of now being a teenager. There was even more to it than living in a new state. Her mother's passing had shaken Jackie to her core. At a time when most girls her age were thinking of boys and cementing friendships, she had been living in the past, angry and broken-hearted. She still was, but right now Dustin needed her. The task of finding her little brother helped focus her, yet she still felt twinges of self-pity.

What was wrong with her?

Dustin was gone, carried off by some dark rider high atop the clouds as she looked on, helpless to stop it. Too preoccupied with herself, she hadn't even noticed how lonely he had been, and how much he needed her.

Need.

Even thinking about that word was hard. The concept became tied up in heaviness and emotional pain. Unconsciously her shoulders sagged beneath an unbearable weight and she gave herself one moment of escape, closed her eyes and tried to make herself believe that everything was all right. Her mother was still alive. Her brother was sleeping down the hall, and they were all still living in Yardley, Pennsylvania. Everything was all right and she didn't have to save anyone.

She called up an image of her mother, already faded and stylized. There, in her mind, she found the smile she longed for, etched in amber. Long fiery hair draped past sylvan cheeks like the fall of night on a high mountain lake. Two sparkling eyes gazed at her and within them sparkled the promise and comfort of love, but the picture in her mind faded as she was jostled about and she couldn't hold on to the vision.

From high atop her perch on the wooly mammoth, Jackie watched as the clouds of Treetops swirled like an icy breath on a long-lost Pleistocene day. The force of air generated by the hairy behemoth as it lumbered along parted the vapors for the rest of their strange animal entourage. Behind her trotted the cougar, a smudge of mottled brown in a sea of white, while the Yangtze river dolphin meandered almost blindly in mid-air a safe distance away. Next was the two-ton forest elephant with its long snaking trunk, walking along the shifting trail with the cloud strata beneath it, like a miracle in motion. More believable was the red-bellied monkey, although it was a strange sight to see it riding atop the African heavyweight. Occasionally the monkey would leap like a sprightly trapeze artist and catch a ride from another passerby when the mood struck him.

The black rhino didn't seem to mind the simian interloper. Tough as an obsidian tank, it lumbered through the bright mist as if nothing could stop it. Its counterpart, yin for yang, was the pearly white unicorn. It was as if the sun itself had taken animal form, allowing one to gaze upon it at leisure, noticing all the intricacies of its beauty. The two walked side by side, in synchronicity, their horns gently bobbing in a common rhythm, but they never glanced at each other, never sniffed the air for each other's presence. They simply walked. They might as well have been a universe apart.

Sweeping behind, a parade of creation unto itself, was the seismosaurus. One hundred and twenty feet long from head to tail, pale green with brown markings, and weighing 30 tons, the creature seemed to span not only Treetops, but the whole Mesozoic Era itself. Staring back at it wide-eyed, Jackie was almost convinced that she and the fantastic dinosaur could rescue her brother alone without any other help at all. It was almost too much to believe, like a mythical sighting in lonely woods or deep loch. Looked at it from the side with its legs partially hidden beneath the clouds, the dinosaur was transformed into a particular Scottish fantasy, with a snake-like head, humps and serpentine tail. Riding on its great back, oblivious of its evolutionary debt to the earth-bound plant-eater, was the Madagascan sea eagle. From time to time it fluttered its wings as if impatient for the fog to break so it could take to the open sky.

Almost as an afterthought Pence followed behind, zigzagging between the terrible tree-trunk legs of the seismosaurus, like the daredevil rodent he was with a lucky coin jingling around his neck.

With Regnal keeping watch back at HeartWood, the journey had been a quiet one, and Jackie found she enjoyed the respite from the almost continuous harassment. Still, Nimbus seemed to take some comfort from Regnal and Jackie noticed that his absence seemed to make the Keeper even more out-of-sorts than normal. More than just a long day's travel weighed on him.

Where before the Keeper walked with a slow, measured purpose, now his limbs trembled with exertion. He looked like a herdsman right out of the Book of Genesis with a flood of animals pouring forth in his wake, except each movement seemed handicapped by doubt or doom. Each step he took seemed to carry him further away from the group. And yet he struggled on. Finally, he stopped and leaned on his staff as if it were the only thing keeping him standing. Breathing deeply, the Keeper gazed off into the distance.

Jackie was about to call out to him when she noticed the change. Her eyes widened in disbelief. The clouds were ending. The boundary of Treetops appeared up ahead. Beyond stretched a dry, unbroken landscape. They resumed walking and within minutes arrived at the demarcation stretching across the landscape.

Overhead the pale sun of Helios neared the end of its daily journey. True night never fell in Treetops, but a sort of twilight took its place.

"We rest here," said Nimbus.

So amazed was she, and so weary Nimbus, that neither noticed when Pence darted back into the milky veil and disappeared.

CHAPTER 24

Hunter Greenwold was having a nightmare again. It never changed. He was talking on his hands-free cell phone, driving down the freeway. Traffic was light. It was a beautiful evening in late summer and he was smiling, almost laughing. His boss was telling him the news he had been hoping for.

"It's not official yet, you understand," Mr. Hawkins said. "The committee still has to sign off on the paperwork but I wanted to be the first to congratulate you. It was unanimous. Nobody deserves this promotion and assignment more than you do."

For a moment or two Hunter let the words sink in and didn't say anything. This was what he'd been working for and dreaming about for five long years: a chance to investigate the most sensitive cases from an office in Washington D.C. He took a deep breath, noticing almost without irritation as the sign for his upcoming exit flashed by.

"Thank you, sir," he said. "That's very good news. I can't tell you how thrilled I am. What is my reassignment date?"

The pause on the other end of the line lasted just a little too long.

"End of the month, I'm afraid. Something has got the powers-that-be on edge. Some kind of X-Files baloney. They want answers."

"I see."

"Heck, you haven't bought that house yet, have you?" Hawkins asked in an overly casual tone, but he didn't wait for a reply. "And it's not as if you have a ball and chain or family to drag behind you. This couldn't have happened at a better time. Believe you me, there's nothing worse than a kid who doesn't want to change schools again."

"No sir. I'll be ready. You can count on it."

"I know," he said pointedly. "That's why we gave it to you."

Before Hunter could say goodbye or say thank you again, his boss hung up. Stifling a curse, Hunter took the next available exit. Soon the crowded freeway was replaced by neighborhoods, and tree-lined streets. Parked cars sat lounging in driveways, kids played on front lawns, and lights glowed dimly from kitchens, living rooms, and bedrooms in the early evening twilight.

He wanted to call someone, tell someone the news. But Hawkins was right. He didn't have anyone. Not a soul.

That's why I got the job, he thought.

Hunter loosened his tie and tried to banish the negative thoughts from his head. Wishing wouldn't do him any good. He had chosen this life. The assignment is what he had wanted. The rest was all an inconvenience. He turned the car stereo on and allowed himself to drive just a few miles over the speed limit as he passed through the quiet street. He never sped. He never did anything illegal. His career in the bureau would be over if he did. But tonight was different. Tonight he pushed his foot gently down on the accelerator just to prove that he was still alive.

When the red ball rolled out into the street he should have braked more quickly. He had been distracted and the driveway was partially hidden by flowering bushes, but it was just a ball. His foot was just pressing down on the brake when the child appeared out of nowhere. Seeing the motion in his periphery vision,

Hunter's training and reflexes instantly went into action and he slammed down hard on the pedal. Up until the last second, he thought he would miss her and everything would be okay. But then there was a sound, a horrible sickening thud and the momentary glimpse of a little girl, short-sleeves and yellow shorts. He caught a blur of a freckled face and Twins baseball cap, disappearing beneath the hood of his agency car. Then everything stopped. Just stopped. Sitting in the vehicle with his hands on the steering wheel, the car stereo still blaring *When the Levee Breaks* by Led Zeppelin, he kept thinking over and over again, *Oh God. Oh God. Oh God. I have to do something.* But he couldn't move. He sat paralyzed in fear and horror until the EMT, a young woman, opened the door and put her hand on his shoulder.

"Kind of late for a nap isn't it?" a woman's voice said breaking his troubled slumber.

Hunter opened his eyes and bolted upright.

Where was he?

For a moment he was speechless, still lost in his nightmare. Then he regained a portion of his wits.

Blinking his eyes, he could make out a uniform, dull green, and a name badge reading Sabah. The middle-aged woman wore a cap with the word **Security** spelled out in tree-like letters. Dark, curly hair speckled with gray peeked out from underneath her hat. She wasn't smiling.

"Guess I must have fallen asleep," he said. "What time is it?"

"About five hours past the Arboretum's closing time. I've got to ask you to leave." Then she softened unexpectedly. "Hope I didn't scare you."

"Just a little bit jumpy," Hunter said, getting to his feet. "Probably time I got home."

Hunter started walking, hoping he was going in the right direction.

The arboretum employee gave him a long look as if sizing up his potential for trouble.

"You looking for something?" she asked.

Hunter stopped in his tracks, but said nothing.

"Others have come out. You're not the first. There are strange things going on here," she almost whispered. "I've been here sixteen years, ever since I came from Egypt, and I haven't seen anything like it. Black shapes. Animals. Maybe they're panthers or cougars. Maybe they're not. Maybe," she began, and then caught herself. "Maybe I've been on the job too long."

Hunter turned around to face her.

"When were they first seen in the Arboretum?" Hunter asked.

"Couple weeks ago," Sabah answered. Her outline was silhouetted in moonlight making her appear like a ghost. "Everybody's talkin' about it."

"Any animals killed?"

"That's the funny thing. On my rounds I haven't seen any carcasses. Whatever they are, they don't seem interested in deer or anything like that. People, though, that's another thing."

Hunter took a deep breath and then let it out.

"What do you mean?"

The guard moved a step closer and leaned in. "Late last Wednesday I was driving through the grounds doing my rounds. It was raining so I was in a security vehicle. Warm and dry suits me just fine. Anyway, the moon was almost full so I could see beyond the road right into the forest. There was a shape in there, moving among the trees next to the road shadowing me. I've never seen anything like it. When I slowed and turned my flashlight on the creature, it vanished."

She stopped and fixed Hunter with a look of desperation.

"Don't tell anyone," she said. "I could lose my job."

Hunter nodded. "Here's my card," he said, handing one over from his wallet. "I'm a detective. If you see anything strange, give me a call."

"I hope I don't," Holly said. "Stay safe."

Then she walked off to resume her rounds.

"Well, good night," Hunter called after her. "And thanks."

As soon as the security guard left the grounds seemed ominous again. Even the moonlight couldn't dispel the growing sense of foreboding that Hunter felt. Something was watching him. He could sense it. Goosebumps rose on his arms. Something ancient and hungry walked the woods. It had been waiting for the guard to leave until he was alone.

Hunter shook his head and laughed, but it came off as a strangled sound.

Easy does it, he thought.

Paranoia wouldn't get him anywhere. What he needed to do was control his emotions and think logically. This wasn't the African savannah, after all. If only he could clear his head. But he felt groggy from his interrupted nap. Looking around he tried to imagine the arboretum bathed in sunlight with row upon row of flowers bordered by trees filled with birdsong. He had been here once before as a small child on a class field trip. He had always felt a connection to the place. Something nagged at the back of his mind. There was something he should know, something he needed to remember. Above him the stars shone brightly in the sky. Hunter gazed around the grounds again, but this time he no longer felt so alone or ill at ease. Surrounding him were the comforting and familiar outlines of dusky gardens and blacker woods. They gave him peace.

Relaxed and refocused he revisited the job he had to do. After leaving his office and the scene of the crime, he had driven his aging Ford Thunderbird to the Minnesota Landscape Arboretum near Chaska.

To find a phantom, he thought. *To try and find Ashmore's kids.*

A cloud passed over the moon and the world grew less distinct. Hunter shivered.

Someone or something was watching him.

That's when the shadow came out of the trees, a dark hole somehow sharper than the night. He felt it more than he saw it. A primal fear rose up inside him, enveloped him. But there was something else hidden deeper. Something buried in him that wasn't afraid.

The creature moved silently, almost invisibly on all fours. When it was about a hundred feet away from him, it stopped in front of a gnarled oak tree. Hunter blinked, imagining the horror would vanish. But there was no mistaking the red eyes which stared back at him or the glistening white teeth which shone starkly in the moonlight. It was other-worldly, a nightmare-made flesh. Spikes rose across the creature's back in tortured angles as if hope itself could be impaled on them.

Slowly, Hunter turned his head to weigh his available options. He wanted to run. Hide. But somehow he knew if he did, he would die just as surely if he stood here and did nothing. He had to fight, had to do something before it was too late. With careful precision he reached for the gun holstered at his hip. All the while the thing remained gargoyle still, its visage unflinching, its body a black hole of primal flesh, never moving, just waiting for the perfect moment to strike.

Hunter's lips curled into a snarl, revealing a fang shaped tooth. Despite his fear a raw wildness was building inside him. He tasted blood in his mouth.

He must have blinked. When the moon came out from behind the clouds, the space in front of the oak tree was empty. The creature was gone.

Hunter found he was breathing heavy, almost panting. His forehead was wet with perspiration. It felt as if he had just run as hard as he could and then stopped himself just before going over a precipice.

What the hell just happened?

Shaken, he turned and made his way through the wooded landscape, keeping to the open gardens and paths whenever possible, but still feeling more like Little Red Riding Hood than he wanted to. Over the next hill was the arboretum road and civilization. He had never been more thankful.

The next day he went back to the arboretum to talk to the security guard only to discover that she had called in sick. No one else around the place wanted to talk. He followed several improbable leads to dead ends and that night, he spent eight uneventful hours traipsing around the grounds again. When he returned to his aging car, he noticed that one of his tires had been slashed. Stifling a curse Hunter walked around to the trunk and put his key into the lock. A moment later he groaned. The feeble interior light illuminated what he had just remembered. There was no spare and at this late hour no garage would be open. With no other option he left the derelict vehicle and began walking. It was about 8 miles to Chaska. He could pick up a cab or an Uber in the suburb and take it back into Minneapolis. Walking on the darkened shoulder, he had plenty of time to plan his next move.

He couldn't return to his ramshackle office and apartment in the city. That would be suicide. The goons would be staking it out waiting for him to return so they could finish the job and the police would be hunting him down as a prime suspect. Rockwood at over three hours away was no longer an option, not unless he found some alternative transportation. The small town was the next place he had wanted to investigate since that's where the kids' disappearance had occurred. A little more distance between him and those murderous thugs wouldn't be a bad thing either. The bus it was then, he decided.

An hour later he wandered bleary-eyed down big city streets, past darkened shop-fronts and checker board apartment buildings. The Hawthorne Avenue bus station wasn't far off, but he was tired now, exhausted beyond measure. If only he could lie down for a few minutes and close his eyes. Too much had happened in the last 48 hours. He felt beyond himself, unable to cope with his debt to David Ashmore and his new-found homelessness. Passing underneath a brightly lit bar sign he paused, looking longingly into the opaque front door glass. He needed a drink, badly.

Just one, he told himself stepping forward. Then he froze as a bartender flipped the Open sign to Closed and locked the door. A moment later the sign went dark.

Unbelievable, he thought. *What else could go wrong tonight?*

Rounding the next corner, he came upon a short, gnarled tree surrounded on three sides by a rusted wrought iron fence. Over time the tree's trunk had grown into the protective metal bars encasing many of them within its woody flesh. A small bed of grass grew up from beneath. Somehow he felt drawn to the little oasis. It felt like he belonged here. He had felt something similar at the arboretum. Nature always comforted him. Living in the city he had forgotten. Now he was starting to remember.

A bone-weary tiredness weighed him down and the thought of slogging on in search of a cheap motel seemed a herculean task. After a last look to make sure no one was nearby and checking to make sure he still had his gun, he curled up inside the fence. The bus wouldn't arrive until the morning and so he decided to take his chances out on the street and get some rest. Laying on the soft grass, it felt as if he was coming to the end of something. Or perhaps a beginning. Hunter closed his eyes and within moments fell fast asleep.

Early morning light filtered through the leaves above him as Hunter Greenwold opened his eyes. He felt far from rested but the brief respite allowed him the ability to entertain the notion that he might just make it to the bus station. Before he could get to his feet, however, a businessman walked by, paused awkwardly, and then reached into his wallet. Drawing out a five-dollar bill, he dropped it through the bars at Hunter's feet. Keeping his eyes averted, the man quickly continued on his way.

"Who do you think I am?" an unshaven Greenwold yelled after he had recovered from his shock.

The act of charity stung him to his core. He felt like crap. How had he ever become this lost? Everyone around him seemed so normal, and if not happy, then they at least still had the possibility of something better. To a passerby on the street he looked pitiful, a soul beyond redemption, with haunted eyes that daylight only accentuated. A foul stench on the air caught his attention and after a moment's confusion, realized that the source was him. But there was nothing to be done about it. Any delay now could be fatal. He had to keep moving.

Standing up he stepped through the opening in the metal bars and looked around. Traffic passed him, oblivious to his plight. Turning around like a compass needle gone haywire, he noticed a set of narrow stone stairs cut into the side of a three-story building nearby. At the top was a small door which huddled under a torn metal awning. Above it loomed a billboard for Fortune Investments. It showed a smartly dressed woman, beautiful and alluring. Her hands were folded around a smoky blue crystal ball that was filled with glittering dollar signs. In a trick of the light it appeared that the contents of the globe were moving. A memory flickered in Hunter. There was a spark of recognition as he continued to gaze at the billboard, remembering back to a day seventeen years earlier.

How Talley had convinced him to go to the Minnesota Renaissance Festival was still a mystery. She always had a way of getting him to try new things. It's what he had always secretly liked about her. Talley had been his girlfriend in college. She had green eyes with short brown hair and a smile that never seemed to waver. In his mind's eye, standing on the sidewalk, he pictured her again in her favorite jeans and paisley shirt that she had worn that September autumn day.

Dappled sunshine hung in the air with a hint of coolness as he and Talley had walked, crunching through fallen leaves. They didn't talk much as they wound their way through the crowd past shops and jugglers and bards with outrageous English accents. The festive atmosphere carried them along as if it could make them forget what tomorrow would bring. Talley was leaving for graduate school. He was getting ready to follow his dream.

"I toldest thee it would be fun," she chided, whacking him on the shoulder playfully with a wooden sword.

"You call this fun?" Hunter retorted trying to be funny but failing miserably.

On Sunday she was leaving for San Francisco. He was flying to Quantico, Virginia soon after for FBI training. *They would be on separate coasts,* he thought bitterly. A familiar emptiness grew and filled him with a foreboding that deepened with every step he took.

Would they ever see each other again?

Suddenly Talley grabbed his arm and steered him to a ragged little tent apart from the other pavilions. The few people that walked by it seemed to take no notice of the lonely structure. A small, wooden sign over the entrance read simply: *Madame Frija's Fortune Telling.*

He followed Talley up to the entrance, and then with a renewed tug on his arm, through the musty smelling cloth to the other side.

For a moment, Hunter was blinded by the inky darkness. It seemed distinctly out of place in the cheery, sunshine of the festival. Even the air was different. Instead of autumn leaves and food stands, the heavy smell of incense choked his throat and nose. Then, as if an unseen spell had been cast, his eyes began to adjust.

Recognizable shapes coalesced out of the feeble light. A simple table stood in the middle of the room covered in a royal blue cloth inlaid with swirls. A candle burned on each end of the table, providing the only illumination in the pavilion. At the very center of the table sat a crystal ball that glittered like a sphere of ice. A woman sat directly behind it, her two gnarled hands playing around the globe as if they were warming themselves.

To say she was old would be like calling the desert dry. Masses of skin around her face and arms hung limp and pallid while the rest was nearly transparent, offering unpleasant glimpses of ancient blue-black rivers winding just beneath the surface. Even the downy robe she wore was mottled and stained.

"Come in," she said in a spidery voice. "Come closer. My sight isn't what it used to be."

Talley pulled gently on Hunter's hand and he stepped with her to the front of the table. Even this close, however, the old woman didn't seem to be quite in focus. It was as if an invisible screen were pulled down in front of them that made the details of her form waver and blur. Hunter blinked. Surely the light was sufficient. More likely it was the King's Finest Ale he had sampled repeatedly against Talley's half-hearted objections.

"We'd like our fortunes told," Talley said, still holding his hand to ensure he wouldn't run off.

For an uncomfortable amount of time, the crone said nothing. She simply sat and stared with the bluest eyes he'd ever seen, as deep and dark as a Scottish lake, holding secrets he couldn't begin to fathom. Although she looked at them both, Hunter got the uncomfortable feeling the fortune teller was studying him.

The prolonged scrutiny was worse than all the bad English accents, jugglers, and overpriced turkey legs he had weathered so far.

Let's get on with it, he thought staring back. *C'mon, entertain us with your mystical charms.*

The old woman's gaze unnerved him. She certainly didn't look like an actress. Her eyes did not flinch nor did she begin an exotic performance on cue. As he waited, Hunter got the feeling that she was curious or surprised about something.

"Look into the Eye," she breathed at last, speaking to both of them but lingering on Hunter. "Remember, what you see is not fixed and may yet change."

Hunter Greenwold leaned forward and peered into the shimmering orb. For a few long moments nothing happened. He almost looked away when it abruptly changed. Cumulous clouds as seen from above floated lazily by inside the crystal.

Flash.

A red ball rolled across a quiet street. A freckle-faced girl, no older than seven or eight, ran after it, her blonde hair waving in the slight breeze from beneath her baseball cap. The ball bumped the curb on the opposite side and then came to a rolling halt but the little girl never reached it. A car that was going too fast down the neighborhood street struck her before she was halfway across the road. He wanted to close his eyes, but he stared straight ahead transfixed.

Flash.

Another scene appeared. A little boy, perhaps five or six years-of-age, stood on a great wooden deck under the shadow of a towering wooden mast. A horde of animals of every size and description surrounded him from the lowliest snake to a spindly giraffe. As Hunter Greenwold watched, a lion began licking the child's hand affectionately. Showing no fear, he stroked the animal's bushy mane distractedly before getting up and meandering through the zoo of beasts to the empty stern of the vessel. Gazing out over the railing from his lofty perch he took in the desolate valley of rock and sand like a sailor who has been at sea too long and no longer remembered where home was.

Flash.

A young woman was running, running as fast as she could down a rough staircase of winding bark and branches wearing an expression of pure terror. Every few strides she cast a sharp glance behind her as if expecting the worst. Pools of light shone on the steep shadowy path like glittering jewels. Although the strange path was wide, her feet slipped over the raised edge more and more frequently causing her to nearly lose her balance. And still she ran faster, an invisible threat nipping at her heels.

Then he saw them. An army of animals beyond description moved down the path after her from the heights above like thunder incarnate. Buffalo and leopards, elk and hippos, horses and alligators all surged forward, a force of nature beyond description. Some creatures flew, others slithered or crawled. Hunter caught only momentary glimpses of individual species. They were all one mass of primal anger, a stampede of fury and reckoning that had no limit. He could not begin to count them and still they kept coming. It would not take them long to reach her.

The path's slope grew steeper now as it widened out near the bottom. Shafts of light fell more strongly here and Hunter spied snatches of meadow not far below. Taking the last curve, the woman lost her footing and could not recover. She fell off the limb in a flurry of shaking branches and was gone from sight as an army of darkness swarmed down the massive trunk toward the unsuspecting Earth below.

Flash!

Then the crystal ball clouded over.

Hunter shook his head as if trying to free himself from a nightmare. Everything had seemed so real. Only Talley's presence steadied him.

"What did you see?" asked the gypsy slowly turning away from him.

Talley hesitated, embarrassed.

"I'm sorry," she said blushing slightly. "I didn't see anything except some flashes. Was I supposed to see shapes in the vapors?"

The old woman shook her head and smiled slightly. Then she looked at Hunter.

"Did you see something?" she asked, but it wasn't really a question.

Hunter Greenwold still stared at the crystal ball. With an effort he tore his eyes away from its shifting depths. He couldn't bear to look at the old woman so he looked at Talley as if she could save him.

"I saw a vision that we'll soon be poorer," he quipped, trying to mask how unsettled he felt. "What do we owe you?"

The old woman spread her lips wide in a Jack-O-Lantern caricature of a smile revealing broken and missing teeth.

"Let me work the crystal ball for you again," she suggested as if it were a revelation, "and tell you all I can divine of your future. You need only give what you wish."

In slow dramatic fashion she told Hunter and Talley what fortune awaited them, but always in the vaguest possible of terms. Regarding their relationship, the gypsy was surprisingly silent except to say, "Love is a bridge spanning from heart to heart. We cross, often at our own peril. I see troubles ahead but also happiness on the other side for those that make the journey.

"Of course, I could be wrong," she said wryly. "The future, as I mentioned, is not set in ice. The clouds I spin sometimes obscure."

"Well, I for one believe you," said Talley politely.

Fishing through her purse she pulled out a twenty-dollar bill and handed it the old woman. "Is that enough?"

"You are very gracious, my dear," the fortune teller replied taking the money. "Your belief sustains me."

A wave of her gnarled hand told them it was time to go. The telling was done.

Talley and Hunter turned to leave.

"There is one more thing," she added ominously. Now she made no attempt at subtlety and looked right at Hunter. "Beware the trickster."

A minute later, they were outside in the autumn sunshine walking down the noisy promenade. Everything seemed too bright and crowded. Suddenly, Talley turned to him clutching at her side.

"Oh no!" she cried. "I must have left my purse in the fortune telling tent."

"I'll go back and get it," he offered. "Why don't you get us some seats for Puke & Snot. They probably fill up fast. I'll catch up with you."

Talley looked at him intently trying to gauge his newfound chivalry.

"All right. But don't dawdle. And no making any passes at Ms. Methuselah in there."

"Knight's honor," he toned in mock seriousness and then started walking back the short distance to the grubby little pavilion.

Hunter Greenwold needed time. His mind spun with what he'd just seen in the crystal ball. None of it made any sense. Why had he seen something, but Talley hadn't? Maybe it was some kind of illusion randomly projected for dopes like him. It was tempting to believe that the scenes he'd witnessed were just parlor tricks, ingenious holograms, or hallucinations. But they felt too real. Try as he might he could not easily dismiss them. The more Hunter thought about the scenes, the more the lines between what was real and what was illusion seemed to blur.

The little pavilion lay just around the bend now. Hunter Greenwold started to run as he thought belatedly of Talley's credit cards and cash; a tempting prize for an unscrupulous fairgoer or fortune-telling charlatan. He hardly wanted them to spend their last day together filing a police report.

Moments later he stood in front of the squalid tent. Pulling aside the fraying fabric, Hunter stepped inside the entrance. The light shown better now, spilling in through scattered holes and rents. Nothing prevented him from seeing immediately that the tent was empty. Gone were the covered table and candles. Gone too were the old woman and the crystal ball. Even the musty smell of incense was absent.

No, more than absent, Hunter Greenwold thought, looking around wildly. *It was as if none of it had ever existed.*

For a moment he stood frozen as his brain attempted to process this impossibility. Then he remembered his mission. With a start he stepped forward and nearly tripped over Talley's purse. Bending down he picked it up and strode from the pavilion like a madman grasping his only evidence of sanity.

Confused and out-of-sorts, he turned left instead of right and found himself entering a little copse of oak trees. Their branches were gnarled and oddly threatening like the old woman's appearance. Sudden pounding assaulted his ears like an erratic war drum. Turning around he saw two festival workers at the edge of the underbrush. They were hammering a large sign into the root-veined earth on the far side of the fortune teller's tent. It read: "**Attention Ye. Space for Rent. Inquire with the King's Administration**."

Hunter Greenwold stared at the sign in disbelief and then walked toward the employees.

"You guys work fast. I was just in there five minutes ago. Did they fire the old lady?"

"Who'd that be, squire?" inquired one of the workers raising an eyebrow.

Hunter scowled at the totally unnecessary accent.

"The fortune teller," he said with impatience. "I think her name was Frija."

"That would be a trick," the other worker replied. "This tent has been vacant for over two years. Something about its location, I reckon'."

"The shop name is right out front. Over here," Hunter insisted.

He ran around to the pavilion, his face dropping as he looked up.

There was no fortune telling sign hanging from the entrance. Instead, there a weathered placard hung from its place reading CLOSED FOR REPAIR.

The two Renaissance Festival workers rounded the corner and then shook their heads in bemusement. After a few moments of awkward silence, they raised their hammers again. They had a job to do.

The sound of pounding, of metal on stone, grew incessantly louder and drove Hunter back to his unpleasant reality. The memory frayed and fell apart. Hunter Greenwold became aware that he was still standing on the sidewalk in Minneapolis as morning traffic sped by oblivious to his confusion. The staccato noise stopped and then started again as a construction worker with a jackhammer tore open the asphalt nearby.

To Hunter it felt as if his soul was being pulverized. It was he who had been at the wheel that day. It was he who had taken that little girl from the world. But now he knew that he had seen the terrible event, years before, and not even known his part, of what was to come. It was maddening. Why had the old woman shown him something he couldn't change? The memory of what he had done haunted him every day. He would never forget her and he could never forgive himself. Her name had been Emma Jean.

The boy and the young woman from the crystal ball had been strangers to him. They had meant nothing at the time he had visited the fortune teller. Only their need had pulled him in. Now, however, he saw certain connections. The second scene had clearly shone Dustin, David Ashmore's missing son. Where the boy was, he still had no idea. Hunter silently cursed himself. He should have remembered that as soon as Ashmore had shown him the picture, but he had been in poor shape that evening. It had been the anniversary of Emma's death. After all this time, he was still picking up the pieces and trying to put them back together. The final tableau depicting a young woman racing for her life was a mystery to him as she was much too old to be Jackie.

As if proving that it would never stop, the jack-hammering resumed again, somehow managing to be even louder than before. Hunter raised his hands to cover his ears and felt something scurry lightly across his feet. He looked down.

A large black-nosed, albino squirrel looked up at him and chattered impatiently as if to say, *Well, what are you waiting for, loser?* People streamed by on the city sidewalk but Hunter Greenwold hardly noticed.

The creature held his startled gaze for a moment and then bounded off of his tennis shoes, scurrying several yards down the sidewalk before turning around. It chattered again, more insistently. It almost sounded like an insult.

Hunter took a step forward and then stopped himself.

There were certain lines that couldn't be crossed. One of them included chasing a squirrel down a crowded street like a lunatic. He must be losing it to even consider such a thing.

The events of the last week caught up with him then and he slumped heavily to the curb. Too many things swirled in his head: Baland's thugs, David Ashmore's stupid heroics, the missing kids, the strange creature sightings, dear little Emma Jean, and his ex-wife Rebecca. They had been married seven years when she told him that she wanted a divorce. He had been late coming home again from work, his breath smelling of alcohol, but he didn't try to hide it anymore. It just didn't seem important. Nothing seemed important. Caring brought too much baggage.

"I can't take this anymore," she said simply. "I love you, but I want a divorce."

He hadn't said anything. He hadn't even tried to change her mind or explain why he had been so absent. There was nothing to say because there was too much to say. She was right anyway. He just stood there in the kitchen of their comfortable suburban house holding flowers like a frozen statue thinking of the little girl he had run over nine years earlier and the dreams that had died that day. Truthfully, he had already lost long before that. He didn't blame Rebecca for leaving. In fact, he thought he deserved it.

That had been six months ago. Now he sat on a curb in Minneapolis wearing yesterday's clothes, washed-up, divorced, and on the run.

Taking out his wallet, he leafed past the crisp green bills he had taken from David Ashmore and took out the picture of Dustin and Jackie. Hunter looked at the small crinkled portrait.

His mind spun back to the fortune teller and he wondered again how they were all connected. The old woman must have had a reason for showing those images to him. It was almost as if she had known that David would come and ask for help. Looking down at Ashmore's photo again, he thought of the little girl as she ran across the street and made a silent promise to himself. Although he didn't know Ashmore's kids, they felt like the most precious thing that he had left in the world.

Hunter couldn't have said how long he sat on the curb staring at the image of the missing children in his hands. Was it five minutes or five hours? Eventually, though, a soft padding on his shoe and then his leg caught his attention and he looked down.

The white squirrel sat perched on top of his knee.

"Oh, it's you again," he said sighing. "Go away. I don't have any food."

In response, the animal just stared back at him as if it was the most natural thing in the world to do.

"Get lost, you ugly rodent." He lifted his hand threateningly.

That's when Hunter saw it, a silver coin attached to a gold chain dangling from the animal's neck. It caught the sun and flared in sudden brilliance.

"Are you someone's pet?"

In a white blur the creature lunged forward and grabbed the photo out of his fingertips with its teeth and then scampered off down the sidewalk.

For a long moment Hunter Greenwold just sat there in shock. Then he jumped up and ran headlong after the creature. It sprinted around the corner of a building. Block after block he raced after the furry thief, weaving between oncoming pedestrians like a madman. Soon the buildings became more and more dilapidated. There were fewer people now. Those that he saw looked beaten-down with a sense of hopelessness that couldn't be hidden. They hardly gave him a second glance.

Although he didn't gain on the creature, it was almost impossible to lose sight of its chalky color in the trashy surroundings. It turned another corner and a few heartbeats later, Hunter Greenwold found himself running down a narrow alleyway.

"Have a good trip," a voice rattled in his ear.

He looked around and saw a man dressed in rags slouched against the wall. The stranger held a bottle in a paper bag to his lips.

Hunter Greenwold ran to the end of the alleyway and out into a courtyard surrounded by crumbling one and two-story buildings. In its dirt-filled center was a perfect circle of great tree stumps. Nothing grew in the soil, not even weeds.

As Hunter watched, an animal appeared from behind each stump. Rabbit, raccoon, chipmunk, sparrow, dragonfly, rat, spider, mouse, snake, and sightless mole, all took their place, one after another, atop a weathered base. Then they sat completely still.

In the center of the circle sat the white squirrel, still holding the picture in its mouth like an improbable oracle.

Hunter Greenwold crept forward. When none of the creatures reacted, he moved more confidently into the strange gathering, passing between two of the squat monoliths that rose to his waist. He had just entered the circle and was thinking about making a running lunge at his quarry when the mammoth tree stumps started glow. As they increased in brightness, they formed a ring of blinding light blending one into another. Hunter could feel the growing heat and wondered how the animals could stand it. Yet they did, never flinching or moving in their gargoyle-like pose. Then the whole circle began to spin and the detective with it, faster and faster like a woodcutter's nightmare carousel.

Unable to find his balance he lurched one way and then another as a feeling of dizziness and then nausea overcame him. At the very moment when Hunter's hold on consciousness frayed, he found himself surrounded by a comforting stillness, a glowing eye of tranquility, calm and deep. Slowly, as if in a dream, he fell to the ground. The last memory Hunter had was of something white leaping up on him and gently placing the picture on his chest.

CHAPTER 25

Jackie awoke stiff, but well rested. Overhead, the sun chariot climbed the sky casting a pale glow on the land below. What had been hidden in the failing light yesterday was clearly visible now. Their rescue party had camped on the edge of a steep ravine that ran down towards a barren landscape.

"We must negotiate the descent," Nimbus said. "Then we will have nourishment."

Jackie looked longingly back at the wispy clouds of Treetops, but there was no going back, only forward. Yawning, she helped ready the animals until they were in single file. Then she looked down the line at her Chosen and felt a swell of pride. Each one had agreed to help her. Perhaps she could give them something as well. Her Chosen deserved proper names that matched their personality. One at a time she stepped in front of each animal and christened it while Nimbus looked on curiously. "Harry," she said to the wooly mammoth, reaching up to pat its thick fur. "Peanut," she continued stepping in front of the elephant. In response, the creature twined its trunk around her wrist. "I think I'll call you Quake," she said to the seismosaurus, and to the cougar, she said,

"You must be Striker." She paused, taking in the rhino's solid bulk. "And you must be...Rocco." Next up was the downy unicorn. "I will call you Wintra, if that's alright." The mythical creature's intelligent eyes stared back. The blind river dolphin hovered nearby, thrashing its tail from side to side in barely contained excitement. When Jackie stepped in front of it, the mammal sped off, racing through the air above her. "I will call you Speedo," she said laughing. Last up was the red-bellied monkey and the sea eagle. "I name you Flambeau, and you, my feathery friend, I think I will just call you Iggy."

She scanned the group and prepared to give the call to move out when something struck her. Urgently she counted the animals and then counted them again.

"Nine!" she exclaimed. "Where's Pence?"

She looked at every paw, hoof, and three-toed foot, and peered into the shadow of Speedo the hovering dolphin, but saw no flash of white, no scurrying movement.

"Pence!" She called. "Come out! Where are you?"

"He is not here," Nimbus sighed.

"What do you mean?" asked Jackie.

The thought of Pence gone robbed her of some vital comfort and security.

"I noticed his absence last night. I had hoped he would have returned by now."

"Where did he go?" she demanded. "I chose him."

"Yes, you did," said Nimbus gently. "If Pence left us, he must have had a good reason. Unfortunately, that reason is beyond me. Pence has his own mysteries. He is more than what he seems."

The Keeper paused as if searching for an elusive memory.

Jackie stared back at him, unable to comprehend how Pence could have just left or how Nimbus could be so unhelpful. Swallowing hard, she found her voice.

"Don't we need ten creatures? That's how many I had to choose. Maybe we should wait until Pence comes back. He might have some important information that will make a difference."

"No," replied Nimbus without hesitation as if eager to let go of the effort required in remembering. "Pence will return if he is able. We must continue to the Arkanum and Flood. Hesitation will not save your brother or bring to light his abductor's full purpose."

"I feel like there are too many questions," began Jackie, "and not enough answers. What does my brother have to with the First Call? Where has Pence run off to?"

She felt irritated and didn't try to hide it.

"You must know something. You're the Keeper."

"I am a Keeper, that is true," said Nimbus. "But I am not a seer. And I am but a shadow of what I once was. Still, there is always hope. We must never give up."

Her anger and frustration, mixed with fear, suddenly rose to the surface. She couldn't contain it. It was obvious he didn't know what was going on. More and more animals from Treetops were wandering away and Nimbus didn't even know why. First at the Grove of Earth Trees and now with Pence. On top of everything else, the Keeper could barely walk and didn't even know how to get to the Arkanum. The whole situation was beyond ridiculous.

Jackie opened her mouth to tell the Keeper all that and more, but then she saw Nimbus, so tenuous and fragile, his leaf and bark figure swaying slightly like a tree clinging to life at the edge of a windswept cliff. The words cooled and died on her lips.

"Listen, I don't mean to be telling you what to do," she said instead. "I just got here. We'll figure something out. Somehow."

At this Nimbus smiled morosely as if she had just said something sad and funny at the same time.

"You are older than your years," he observed. "There is much I should tell you, if I can. But not here, exposed as we are. Come."

Walking together, the Keeper and Jackie led the Chosen down the rough, winding path. Their progress was slow and treacherous, in part because of the steepness of the trail and partly because the loose ground shifted as they walked. The seismosaurus, in particular, had great difficulty in coming down and only succeeded with the low lullaby coaxing of Nimbus, for Jackie could not bear to command the creature when it was so fearful.

After reaching the bottom, the Keeper had the group rest so they could eat and plan a marching strategy to the Arkanum. In front of them stretched a vast desert valley. Nothing living could be seen in any direction. The landscape was tinged with what Jackie could only describe as a Martian red hue. The ground was littered with rocks, from apple-sized ankle turners to house-sized boulders. Cracking the desert in two was an ancient riverbed, although no water could be seen in its shadowy depths. Following its meandering progression, Jackie saw where it disappeared into the mountains on the opposite side, many leagues in the distance.

The vast emptiness in front of her mirrored Jackie's rumbling stomach. She was hungry and wondered if her Chosen animals were too. Thankfully, Nimbus was already at work.

For the animals and humans alike, the Keeper grew berries from his branches until they hung red and swollen. Jackie had never eaten fruit that tasted so fresh and vital. She held each precious morsel to savor it. Before her first bite, she briefly marveled at the length of her fingernails. Soon all the creatures, even the meat-eaters, were sated. But the group also needed water so Nimbus cupped his hands on the ground and whistled a song like a high mountain stream. Eventually beads of moisture appeared between his leafy digits and then the beads became rivulets of water until the ground on which he knelt was covered in the reflection of his success. Sighing, Nimbus stood and straightened. More than a few of his leaves had yellowed or browned and his balance seemed unsteady.

"It is what it is," was all he said when Jackie asked if he was alright.

When all had their fill, it was time to leave. A snarl curled from the sharp-toothed jaw of the cougar and the eagle cawed impatiently.

"Yes, yes, I know," Jackie soothed into the Orchlea. "We must go find my brother."

Her words quieted the great cat, but the eagle shrieked again, louder.

"Sorry," she told the eagle. "Of course, you can fly now. The way is clear. Go and see what you can see."

At the utterance of these words the sea eagle spread its great wings and flew up into the heat-wavering sky. It was a beautiful sight. The bird's white body and dark wings climbed until it was nearly lost in the light of the strange sun.

A trickle of sweat ran down her forehead and she wiped it away.

"Our rest is coming to an end," announced Nimbus with an air of increasing weariness. He leaned heavily on his staff. "We must cross the Desert of Sorrows. That much I know. But which direction I am unsure."

Jackie looked at him in disbelief.

"What do you mean you don't know?"

"I have never been outside my domain of Treetops. Why should I? The Outer Realms do not concern me or my duties. I have no time or inclination to be an explorer. Legends hold, however, that the Outer Realms encircle Treetops and contain mysteries as ancient as the Earth. That is where Flood abides, brooding in his great ship, marooned by time. I am too weary to retrieve the map. How to get there must be by your choice."

"Mine?" Jackie started in disbelief and then controlled herself. Getting upset would solve nothing and only waste precious minutes that could better be spent trying to save Dustin.

"I don't see a path," Jackie said began. "This desert seems to go on forever. Unless..."

Nimbus's leafy vines above his eyes rose expectantly.

Jackie forged ahead.

"...unless we follow the way that is already here," she finished.

Had Regnal been there Jackie might not have said anything at all. The dodo's scathing criticism would have silenced her and his sarcasm would have robbed her of even a sliver of certainty. But now, despite her fears of being a leader, she felt emboldened by what she was about to say.

"We should take the riverbed. It should be freer of obstacles and will take us out of the desert."

Nimbus looked at her for a long moment, shrouded in thought.

"Why yes!" he cried suddenly, all signs of feebleness temporarily banished. "That will do nicely. Yes, well done!"

He patted her on the shoulder.

"Let's get going then," said Jackie. Her face flushed with pride.

Minutes later she sat perched atop the wooly mammoth again, leading her small rescue party across the desert toward the river channel.

"Thanks for your help with the seismosaurus before," she said to Nimbus after they had traveled across the rocky sands for some hours in silence. It seemed important for her to acknowledge that she couldn't do it all herself.

When he didn't answer, she turned around and found that Nimbus had fallen behind. His breath came out loud and wheezing, his face strained.

"Halt!" called Jackie raising a hand.

After a moment Nimbus shambled to a stop and the animals all looked to her, waiting expectantly.

But she didn't speak immediately. Her mind raced. Jackie didn't feel comfortable ordering Nimbus to do anything, yet it was clear that he could not keep up the pace.

He's worn out, she thought looking over at his haggard form. *I should have done something before now. It should have been him riding, not me!*

Jackie descended from her perch so she could face and address the gathered animals.

"Iggy," she began, "is scouting for us, looking for signs of trouble, but we can make ourselves useful too by traveling faster."

Jackie paused, looking at the Keeper, before continuing. "Nimbus will also ride. He can't be expected to walk all the way to the Arkanum. We will make better time since the animals won't have to slow down and wait."

Nimbus nodded his head in approval and gave her the slightest of smiles. Jackie felt her confidence grow. "Peanut," she said, "Nimbus will ride on your back." The Keeper threw down his staff as if he would no longer need it and ambled over to Peanut.

After helping the Keeper up to his perch, she clambered up Harry's back and using the Orchlea, politely asked the mammoth to rise. In deference, she turned to Nimbus to start them on their way.

The Keeper shook his head at such formalities. "Enough," he said. "Time is not our friend and I am thirsty for this journey to end. But you must lead. Down into the DreamsEnd riverbed we must go."

"Catchy name," Jackie muttered under her breath.

From her perch high atop Harry, she wished that Nimbus would reconsider and take charge. The world seemed so much larger and scarier from where she sat. After a moment's hesitation, biting her lower lip in nervousness, she made her decision. Squaring her shoulders, she gave her mammoth mount a tap with her tennis shoes.

"Let's go," she said, speaking clearly into the Orchlea, feeling like the least prepared general in history leading the strangest army imaginable.

They covered the broken dusty ground in silence inching toward the meandering riverbed in the distance. Even riding, Jackie's breath became ragged as if the desert itself was sucking the life from her. The air was hot and stale. Soon her lungs were laboring like a bellows. But it was more than the oppressive climate. It seemed to Jackie that a weight had been placed on her, one that she wasn't ready to carry.

Behind her, the echoing footfalls and exotic sounds of her chosen rescuers only reinforced her feelings of inadequacy. Each had talents and grace that set them apart from any other. With a sigh she glanced up at Iggy as she soared high overhead scouting for trouble or unseen paths. Her movement seemed so effortless. When Jackie thought of what she was doing, her mind spun with the impossibility of it all. Worst of all, she was filled with guilt. Dustin deserved better. Her father deserved more. The person she had been, the girl closed off to the world, seemed a lifetime away. Who she was becoming, though, wasn't clear. Only the thought of her kidnapped brother, all alone, forced her to continue on.

The DreamsEnd appeared to be only a short distance away when they started walking, but this proved deceptive. The desert landscape offered up the illusion of closeness, but they were still trudging towards the riverbed when the golden sun reached high in the sky. Jackie felt as though they were on a treadmill since their destination remained remote despite their best efforts. Suffuse light and red caked ground were constant companions, causing Jackie to wonder if they had entered some kind of limbo. It reminded her of the last day of school before summer vacation when the minute-hand, she was quite sure, did not move at all.

There were a few curiosities along the way. From time to time, giant boulders seemed to gaze at them from a distance, their features grotesque or oddly comical, only to drop away or diminish as they carried on. At other times Jackie noticed strange artifacts sticking out of the ground. They seemed to resemble the crumbling remains of ancient buildings, although most of the architecture appeared alien to her. Fragmented columns, splintered domes, and windowless walls peeked through the sand and rocks like unexpected visitors from another time. Once she thought she saw movement in one patch of ruins and a glimmer of metal, but when she asked Nimbus about it, he told her they were only memories or mirages of the world down Below, and to pay them no heed.

Time passed. Eventually they made headway, finally crossing the desert valley floor to the meandering riverbed that cut across their path like a welcoming shadow. Jackie led them cautiously to the lip of it, afraid it would cave in under their combined weight, but it proved to be unusually solid and with a more graceful slope than the cliff they had negotiated earlier. The bottom of the riverbed was only a short distance away. Gazing down at it, the ancient waterway had a bone-hue to it as it stretched out before curving away like a fossilized snake. It looked to be free of obstacles, including any trace of water.

"We reach the DreamsEnd at last," said Nimbus wearily from atop Peanut. "I never thought I'd be so glad to see such a waterless blight."

Slowly, the Keeper dismounted from the elephant.

"It is enough for one day," he said. "Helios will soon be in the west and the Chosen will need to conserve their strength. We have a long way to go."

Once again they made camp and the Keeper provided what sustenance he could. Afterward, Jackie lay down on the dry dusty ground and dreamed of water.

The next morning dawned without a trace of coolness. Jackie awoke with a parched mouth and her bones ached as if they had been stretched while she slumbered. Trudging over to the top of the riverbed she looked down.

What had seemed like a good idea yesterday now seemed less so. They could easily become trapped within the walls of the riverbed should someone or something to decide to attack from the riverbank above, she realized. It would do little good to bring this matter up, however, since it had been her idea.

A rustle of leaves told her that the Keeper approached.

"Today will be hot," he remarked. "We would do well to get an early start."

Jackie nodded and stood, eager to get moving.

The animals, rising from their slumber, shook of the reddish caked dust which still clung to them and chorused their approval. After more nourishment provided by an ever-weakening Nimbus, they were ready.

Jackie looked across the desert, noticing for the first time a dark shadowy smudge on the horizon where the riverbed finally disappeared. *Mountains,* she realized. Swallowing her trepidation, she led Harry and the rest of their force down the side of the embankment toward the white channel below. They negotiated the descent without issue and soon all the Chosen were following the bleached winding path, all save Iggy, who soared above, still scouting.

As leader, Jackie led the march single file since the channel was too narrow to accommodate side-by-side travel by most of her companions. The only exception was Striker, who padded soundlessly next to Wintra, who tolerated the intrusion with a haughty air. Directly behind Jackie came Nimbus, perched atop his mount and looking for all the world like a tree growing in a mound of mud. Next in line was Flambeau, riding atop Rocco like a skillful jockey. Quake brought up the rear. Wriggling through the air a few feet above the entourage was Speedo, a playful smile curled on his face as if the mere memory of water was enough to sustain him.

They made good progress. Even the heat was less severe due to the depth of the channel and shadows cast by the sides of the riverbank. Despite her growing confidence as a rider, Jackie still braced herself on Harry by grabbing great tufts of brown hair on the mammoth's neck as they traveled. She wasn't so much afraid of falling, but rather felt exposed to unseen dangers. As time went on, Jackie found herself glancing up at the edge more and more frequently.

Turning her gaze even higher, she scanned the sky until she found the familiar dark form of the Madagascan sea eagle. Iggy glided directly overhead, turning in gentle arcs against the pale, blue sky.

"Iggy," she began tentatively, speaking into the base of the Orchlea. "Iggy, I need your help. I need to know if the way ahead is safe for us. Does anyone wait on top of the banks?" A shudder ran through as she thought of someone lurking unseen. "Do you see any danger? Fly down and take a look, please. If you see something dip your wing once and let us know."

Iggy screeched in response. Within a heartbeat the eagle dove through the air, descending in a steep trajectory towards the line of the riverbed. Faster and faster Iggy flew, angling up at the last moment to rocket overhead. Instinctively, Jackie put her hands over her head as the avian missile rocketed past just inches above them. A powerful rush of wind blew through Jackie's long unkempt hair as Iggy swept by. Straightening up again Jackie brushed the veil of hair from her eyes and watched as the sea eagle climbed above the riverbank, flapping its wings for higher altitude, before settling into a more leisurely reconnaissance. The eagle's wings remained level.

"Show off!" she laughed into the Orchlea. "It's good to know we're safe for the time being. Fly up ahead, to the mountains if you can. If you see something suspicious, if you see people or other creatures, remember to dip your once wing to let us know. Do you understand?"

Iggy screeched in response and continued her scouting. The rest of the Chosen resumed their riverbed march.

Time seemed to drag as Jackie rode along waiting for the eagle's return. Trying to forestall worries she turned the Orchlea over in her hands, taking comfort from the connection it represented. Part of her felt glad for the increasing distance Iggy flew because that meant that the area ahead was clear of danger. Little by little she relaxed as she watched the bird's progress.

The bird was halfway to the mountains now and there had been no sign of trouble or frantic return. Even so, they had further to go and anything could happen along the way. There was so much she didn't know.

Dustin and the Arkanum might be a hundred miles away. He could be surrounded by a legion of ferocious warriors or held in a high tower by only a single guard. Perhaps her brother was alone, forgotten by his captor, starving in an unlit room as some terrible game played itself out. Perhaps he was already...

But Jackie couldn't finish that thought. If Flood hurt Dustin, she was going to make him pay.

Almost immediately Jackie realized the folly of that emotion. She was only a kid. What could she do? But that's why she had her Chosen and Nimbus to help her. Together they would find a way. She had to believe that. The alternative was too terrible to contemplate. Everything felt like her fault. Dustin had been kidnapped by Gaylon and brought to the Arkanum, but it was her brother's love for her that had propelled him up that tree in the first place. Jackie's own actions had driven him away. She had wasted countless opportunities to give him the attention he deserved. Now she led a rescue party, the likes of which she still couldn't quite believe, hoping and praying that she wasn't too late.

"Look! The scout tries to return," Nimbus called from behind.

It took Jackie a moment to register that the words were directed at her. Clearing her head, she looked up and glanced around wildly. It didn't take her long to see what the Keeper had shouted.

Above the horizon line of the riverbank, two birds wheeled in the air off in the distance. One, small and brown with a white head and bronze chest, was unquestionably Iggy. The other was black and much larger, with wings that beat the air with darkened malice. As she watched, the eagle flew with breathtaking speed, moving and dodging with acrobatic precision. But even from her remote perspective Jackie could see that Iggy was in trouble. No matter how fast she flew or how expertly she evaded, the attacker always remained within striking distance. Only Iggy's unexpected movements prevented the great raven from driving home its stabbing beak.

"Do something!" Jackie cried, halting Peanut with a shout. "That thing is going to kill her!"

"We are too far away," Nimbus sighed. "Even in the realm of Treetops the distance would be too great for me. Here, in this desolate and forsaken land, I am further diminished. Alas, I cannot stop Gaylon."

Silently, she berated herself for not recognizing the Keeper's former shape-shifting apprentice. For several heartbeats, Jackie could only watch helplessly as the giant raven pursued Iggy more and more savagely. Soon the eagle's efforts became more labored, her speed and altitude slipping. It was terrible to watch. Then Jackie remembered herself.

Lifting the Orchlea from her chest, she pointed the end of the twisting wood toward Iggy and spoke into it urgently.

“Come back,” she commanded the Madagascan eagle. “Come back right now!”

Almost at once she recognized the uselessness of the gesture. The sea eagle was already attempting to do that. The raven, however, prevented Iggy’s return, forcing her to wheel and dive in ever more desperate circles.

As Jackie watched, a sudden blow from the raven almost tore the eagle from the sky. Iggy faltered even further, rapidly losing height and almost disappearing behind the riverbank. The assault jarred Jackie to action.

"Speedo!" she yelled behind her urgently. "Go help Iggy!"

Immediately the flat-nosed dolphin obeyed and began swimming off through the air, its large grey tail twisting back and forth.

Still clutching the smooth Orchlea, Jackie pointed it at the rest of the Chosen and shouted, "We ride!"

She barely had time to twist back in place as Harry thundered forward.

Fly home, Iggy, she thought as the wind tore through her long hair. *You can do it! We're coming!*

There was nothing else she could do. Speedo wasn't even a third of the way there and the rest of the Chosen were hopelessly too slow. No matter how much she urged Harry on, it wasn't enough. They weren't going to make it in time. Somehow the eagle remained airborne despite the punishment being inflicted. The rest of the Chosen made ground, no matter how tedious it seemed. Soon they had covered more than half the distance, with Speedo nearly three quarters of the way there, when unexpectedly, Iggy wheeled around desperately and attacked. The maneuver caught the raven off guard, allowing the smaller bird to score a tearing hit with her beak on Gaylon's right flank as she passed. But the raven adjusted quickly, turned, and dove at his struggling prey with renewed ferocity. One of Iggy's wings was already badly damaged, causing her to tilt slightly as she flew. Most of the eagle's remaining strength had been used up in her attack gambit. There was little she could do as the raven swooped in, sinking its beak first in Iggy's back and then, like a final nail, into her head.

Jackie watched in horror as one of her Chosen fell like a stone into the twisting gap of the riverbed up ahead. Without thinking, she halted her mount and stared at the empty sky where Iggy had been.

"There was nothing you could do," Nimbus said gently behind her.

Silently she watched Gaylon's dark, murderous shape disappear over the horizon.

"I never should have sent Iggy up there. Gaylon killed her. Now Flood knows we're coming."

"I would have done the same," Nimbus said. "We were in need of a scout. It was only logical. There is no one to blame."

Jackie cringed as if the Keeper's words had harmed her. "Will they all end up like that?" she asked turning around in her mount to see him. "All the creatures I chose. Will they give everything just to serve me no matter what? Because I'm not sure I can take that."

Nimbus struggled to speak, perhaps trying to find an answer that would suffice. When he finally found his voice, it had an air of resignation.

"It may well be that everything we do is not enough. Yet what else can we do except try? The world and your brother need our help."

If Jackie heard, she gave no sign. Turning away she started her mount forward slowly. The group followed behind like a funeral procession with Quake's footfalls the only sound breaking the silence. It was then that the cramps hit her suddenly, almost doubling her over. She felt as if an earthquake were tearing apart her insides. The pain was excruciating, radiating out from between her legs. Jackie didn't think she could take another moment. Then as quickly as it had come the attack vanished. For a long time, she simply breathed in and out, afraid to believe the agony had really passed, and braced for the spasm's return. But after minutes of dread with no relapse she started to relax.

What was that? She wondered into the clear blue sky. Gaylon, it would seem, could not be blamed for *this*.

In front of her, the DreamsEnd riverbed unraveled like a parched tongue from one unremarkable bend to another, narrowing in nearly invisible fashion. Even Speedo's rejoining of the group could not break the spell of monotony and her own rattled uneasiness.

Iggy's death had unsettled her. Now that she knew what was at stake, she doubted all over again if she could handle the challenges that lay ahead. There was so much she was ignorant of and the Keeper either couldn't remember or he refused to tell her. Part of her just wanted to keep riding atop Harry down the dry riverbed and never stop.

A fatal sameness crept into the company's movements. Bereft of weather and natural wind, the humans and animals alike succumbed to the changelessness of the environment. Although it was cooler in the channel, lack of water and food took their toll as well. Soon the mammoth's strides became more labored. It did not help that the ground itself had become more treacherous.

The smooth sand and pebbles were largely gone, replaced by rough rocks and scattered fossils. The remains sparked an ember of curiosity in Jackie. Around each bend she would look forward to the next half-buried surprise. In the beginning, they were usually small, resembling a fern or trilobite. Eventually these changed into fish, which grew larger and larger with every turn of the riverbed. Soon their mouths filled with teeth and their bodies lengthened until the party could no longer walk around the fossilized skeletons but instead had to pass directly through them. The current specimen was more sea monster than fish, with razor-sharp teeth as long as her hand, paddle-like flippers, and a tail that twisted in serpentine fashion into the very rocks at her feet. Watching Harry step around its cavernous ribs, Jackie felt a bit like Jonah and felt glad when she was finally free of the ancient leviathan. As they approached the next curve in the riverbed, however, her sense of trepidation rose again.

What new evolutionary horror would she encounter? *Maybe,* she thought irrationally, *it will still be alive and rise from a deep, watery passage to swallow us whole.*

To her relief, no monstrous aquatic beast appeared as they continued on. There was no fossil at all. Instead of chalky-white ground, a bluish tinge radiated from the scattering of stones which lay around and ahead of them. Beyond that sat a small pool of tranquil water. Next to it laid Iggy.

Jackie swung off her mount and began walking at a brisk pace towards the fallen eagle.

"Hold!" Nimbus warned, both to her and the thirsty animals who were already eyeing the pool. "Do not move! This is a place of power. I can feel it. Something resides here."

Jackie froze and then looked around, wide-eyed and alert, but could see no danger. Further away the riverbed turned again like it had done dozens of time before. Following Nimbus's gaze onwards, she saw the once-distant mountains rising majestically on either side of the riverbank. They towered above the company, their slopes barren and their peaks crystal tinged.

"There," the Keeper whispered, pointing up ahead.

At first all Jackie saw was the lifeless tail of the DreamsEnd disappearing from sight between the mountains, but then she shifted her gaze lower. Lost in a pile of stones nearby and obscured by a tangle of emerald vines lay a pear-shaped object, white in color and smooth as perfection. It was the size of a soccer ball. Jackie walked toward it, drawn by the sign of life after so much desolation.

"This?" she asked. It looked sort of like a prehistoric egg. "It's just some dumb old stone. I'm gonna get Iggy."

"There is energy here," warned Nimbus. "Stay where you are! I sense great danger. An ancient magic dwells in this place."

Jackie stopped and turned around. "I can't just leave her," she argued. "We have to help her if we can."

The Keeper nodded sadly. "I would assist her if I could. Yet I can't bring back the dead. Iggy is past saving now. She will not suffer the wait. Her form has departed Treetops, never to return. All we can do is honor her sacrifice."

For a moment Jackie wrestled with indecision. Then she turned back around and looked at the crumpled bird lying on the ground.

"I'll be careful," she told Nimbus. Then she ran toward the pool and Iggy.

Behind her Nimbus raised his right arm and pointed his mossy fingertips at Jackie's running figure. Slowly, he sung a sad, but powerful melody. The Keeper's eyes closed and a stream of sparkling leaves ushered forth from his cupped hand, filling the air. With each note of his song, the tang of sweet decay increased as leaf upon glittering leaf joined together and then swirled around before speeding on. Jackie felt the pull before the manifestation hit her. It slowed her movements as if she were deep underwater fighting against the weight of water. When the full force of the leaves enveloped her, it was as if the hand of Nature herself took hold. She could not move. With both feet frozen, Jackie watched as the swirling, mass of vibrant leaves lifted her off the ground and began carrying her back.

No! She cried soundlessly as the roaring vortex tore her protest away. Feebly, she tried to raise her arm to protect her face. But the whirlwind was too strong and kept her arms pinned. Slowly, the force pulled her away from the sea eagle and back towards the Keeper. In that moment of failure, as the rustle of swirling leaves filled her senses with death and decay, Jackie could no longer think clearly. Her destination was no longer Iggy. In her panic and desperation, her minds-eye now fixed itself on Dustin. All her guilt and shame were focused on reaching him. He couldn't be gone. She couldn't bear it.

Lifting her arms through the tumult, she spoke the words that rose from within her like a seed pushing through black earth.

"*Sunaria Folium. Mortalis Arwolaeth Nahla!*"

They were her mother's words, forgotten from her childhood until the moment of need. With a flash of light, the vortex of leaves shredded to dust and Jackie found herself on her feet again, free to move of her own free will.

Jackie swayed, feeling seasick, and then ran the remaining distance to the pool and knelt next to Iggy. Blood covered its feathers but the bird's eyes were still clear and shining as if even death could not deprive her of that one small beauty. Picking the eagle up gently, Jackie cradled it to her chest. The pool nearby cast a somber reflection. Leaning forward, she peered down. Not surprisingly she looked like a mess. Her makeup had long ago worn off and her face was smeared with dust and dirt. Dark circles bloomed under her eyes from worry and lack of sleep. But Jackie also noticed that her clothes appeared too small, as if they had somehow shrunk, causing a tightness that bordered on the uncomfortable. There was something else out of place, and it frightened her; she didn't altogether recognize the person staring back at her.

Somehow the girl in the reflection didn't quite match up to the picture in her head. Things had changed. The glassy surface was like a photograph showing her future. Defensively, she put her hand over her face, exploring each feature for clues. Her fingertips twirled around hair that had grown too long. Her nails were longer too, much more than before.

"And my chest is bigger," she thought. *"My face looks..."*

Jackie didn't complete the thought. Sudden warmth was spreading outward from inside her. It was warm and overpowering in its intensity. Looking down, she noticed for the first time the darkening on her shorts and felt blood trickle down her thigh. Her face reddened in embarrassment though she didn't know why. Quickly, she checked herself for cuts and bruises but didn't find any. She didn't really expect to. There was only one thing it could be.

From somewhere nearby she heard cries. Someone, perhaps Nimbus, called out, but the words did not reach her. With a shudder she lashed out at the watery image with her free hand. At once the reflection on the surface of the water changed to the outline of a man lying on his back. As Jackie watched, the figure opened his eyes. Deep dark blue orbs stared up at her. Time seemed to stop. When the stranger finally blinked, Jackie felt as if she could breathe again. When the water stilled, the pool only held her reflection. A moment later, a shimmering translucent figure appeared before her, hanging in the air above the still water. His form shifted between solidity and transparency as if the wind itself might trouble it. Even so, the man was redolent in autumnal glory. Red, green, and orange raiments hung from him in a blaze of color. His head was crowned with a band of light and in his hand was a staff of burning fire.

"I am the Sentinel of the Elementals," the man spoke like the sound of distant thunder. "Crafted by Xylum, the second Keeper in his victorious image, I mark the spot where the Elementals were met in battle and finally contained."

As these last words were spoken the apparition flared brighter, becoming more substantial.

“Being part of the living world, the Elementals could not be defeated, merely tricked into slumbering,” the Sentinel continued. “I am a warning and a riddle for only I have the key for the soul who wishes to try and awaken them. There are four: Air, Water, Fire, and Light. Their power is unmatched in all of creation, harkening back to a time when wild and world were young. Unlock their prison with wisdom if your need is true."

From behind Jackie heard the unmistakable rustle of the Keeper as he came to stand beside her.

Having stated its purpose, the Sentinel closed its eyes and fell silent. The figure hovered in the air before them waiting.

Nimbus took an involuntary step back as if the mere sight of the figure filled him with dread. “I thought it a bedtime story, a fairy tale,” he mumbled. “I read of it upon my arrival in Treetops like every other apprentice. Xylum I could perhaps believe, but the Elementals were beyond me. How could I know it was all true?”

Jackie barely heard him. All she could think of was that this might be a chance to gain more allies. Surely, Nimbus could find a way to control them. He was a Keeper just like Xylum had been, only a bit more forgetful.

"What does one have to do to free the Elementals?" she asked the Sentinel, feeling very smart and brave.

The figure opened its cobalt eyes and gazed at Jackie with a sudden coldness that made her shiver.

"Answer this riddle correctly," the Sentinel replied. "I will say it only once."

"Wait!" Jackie interrupted. "What happens if I answer incorrectly?

"Then the Orb of the Elementals will remain sealed and their dread powers will not be released upon the world," the Sentinel answered.

"Child, you know not what game you play," Nimbus interjected. He turned gravelly toward the Sentinel. "Why allow for a way to free the Elementals at all? Surely, they are better off imprisoned forever."

The shimmering figure smiled faintly. "You are a Keeper. The answer is known to you. Part of the bargain resulting in their containment required a way to also let them out. There is no death without life and no life without death. Such an agreement has been in place since the stars were first born."

"I am old and the wisdom your master found was lost ages ago," Nimbus replied. "Even then the Elementals could not be commanded. There is no way to control the uncontrollable."

The Sentinel dimmed at those words as sadness passed over his golden face. "Has so much been forgotten and so little knowledge gained? No matter. There are two who have been foretold with the power of communion or command. The KeyStone is one, of course, but even in my time that was only a legend, a binder of the dispossessed and harbinger of doom. The other is Wildness incarnate from when the world was new, elusive as the water running through your fingers. Many names have been written in the dust or heard in the wind moving through the trees. Jack in the Sage is one. What is your name girl?"

"Jack—ee," she said slowly as if solving a puzzle.

"A coincidence, nothing more," the Keeper said quickly.

"Perhaps," the figure said. "The girl's power is hidden from me, if she has any. Yet she is here in Treetops with an army of animals at her call."

With an effort, Jackie met the Sentinel's stare. "I don't know if I'm anything special or not. This is all new to me, but if there's a chance we can command these Elementals then it might be worth the risk. My brother's life is at stake."

Nimbus shook his head. "More than that, the world above will be lost if you fail. I will be of little use afterward should the four elementals ravage Treetops once more. This is madness. Lead your Chosen away from here."

Jackie looked from the Keeper to the Sentinel and back again. She didn't know what to do. A lump grew in her throat.

"The decision is yours alone," the Sentinel declared. "Ask or be silent."

Turning around she looked to her animals for guidance. Each stared back, waiting and expectant. The only way to communicate with them was through the Orchlea that hung around her neck. Suddenly that felt like a heavy burden. One of her Chosen had already perished. How many more would meet the same fate? But what if not trying to control the Sentinels meant her brother might die? Despite some flashes of power, the Keeper's strength was failing and her Chosen were untested. If there was a chance she had the power to command, shouldn't she at least try?

Her voice shook as she made her decision. "I will answer."

Nimbus cringed and tried to speak, but Xylum's servant was quicker.

"Here is your riddle," the Sentinel began. "This thing devours all. Birds, beasts, trees, and flowers. Gnaws iron, bites steel.

Grinds hard stones to meal. Slays king and ruins town and beats high mountains down. What is it?"

Possibilities swirled in her head. She was so nervous that she could hardly think. The answer had to be obvious. She was sure of it. Every time Jackie opened her mouth to speak, she reconsidered, sudden doubt overpowering her. Nimbus looked away as if she had already sealed the fate of his world. Sweat trickled down her temple and behind her ear, flowing over her birthmark.

"How much time do I have?" she asked.

"That is correct," the Sentinel toned. Then it closed its eyes momentarily as if remembering what the taste of death and oblivion were like. "Time *is* the answer. The Elementals will be freed from their aura as the magic that binds them sputters and dies."

"Root and leaf!" the Keeper exclaimed. "You can't count that. She was merely asking a question."

"Yet she said the word at the right moment," reasoned the Sentinel. "Nothing else is required."

"How long do we have before the orb gives way?" Nimbus asked gravelly.

"By tomorrow's sunrise," the figure replied.

Nimbus sighed and looked fleetingly toward the mountains.

"I must advise you. Make no attempt to flee," warned the Sentinel. "Remaining here you still have the chance of commanding. If you try and escape through the Pass you will find it barred. The Elementals will simply track you down and sate their ancient hunger."

In the gap between the snow-capped peaks, a shimmering wall appeared. It towered nearly fifty feet high. The magical barrier hung in the air like a potent mirage, shifting in shades of silver and ochre.

"This is madness," rumbled the Keeper. "Are we your prisoners now?"

"Of your own choosing have the Elementals been awakened,"

countered the Sentinel. "If you cannot harness the creatures in the Orb then a price must be paid. Your destiny waits."

Nimbus turned to Jackie. "I urge flight, while there is still time. If not to the plains, then back to HeartWood or across the wastes. There is nothing I can do against Xylum's defenses and the brute strength of the Chosen will be rendered naught."

"I'm not abandoning my brother. We've come too far," protested Jackie. "If I'm our only hope then I'll just have to do my best. Perhaps I am the KeyStone or the Sage."

The Keeper scowled. "And what if you are but a well-meaning child? Xylum's best was barely enough to stop the ferociousness of the four Elementals."

"I am the leader of the Chosen!" Jackie bristled, her cheeks flushing red with anger. Nimbus' words had hurt her deep, exposing a raw nerve of inadequacy. "We will stay and find a way out of this. It's our only option."

"Listen to the riddle solver," advised the Sentinel with a smile. "She speaks wisdom and foolishness all at the same time."

Nimbus let out his breath and with it his last remaining resistance. "It is decided then. We await our doom."

"You will not have long to wait," remarked the figure. "Look! The Elementals stir from their slumber."

From its resting place nestled amidst the twisting vines, a small crack appeared in the surface of the egg-like orb that Jackie had briefly examined earlier. A moment later a prism of color erupted. Even as Jackie watched the fissure grew wider spilling a kaleidoscope of color in all directions.

"It has begun," the Keeper toned.

Another crack appeared in the prison and the Sentinel dimmed in response.

"You're disappearing," Jackie said.

"Of course," the figure observed becoming less substantial before her eyes. Already his colorful robe had faded to a ghostly grey and he hung in the air like a dying star. "My time and purpose here are done. As the magic that binds the Elementals fails, I also diminish in kind. I am part of the orb and the legacy of Xylum."

He flickered once as if in prophecy of what was to come.

"Help us," the Keeper said, his voice a mere whisper.

The Sentinel smiled sadly, nothing more than an outline with a face now. "There is no time. They are almost upon me."

Then the ghostly image winked out of existence. A moment later a voice met them across a great distance.

"Remember when all is lost, give up what you can't bear to lose."

A heavy silence descended.

"Another riddle," Nimbus grumbled, "to while away the hours as we await the end of days."

Jackie looked over at the pool. The water was still, but it contained a troubled image. Reflected in its surface now was the eerie glow from the Orb of the Elementals.

CHAPTER 26

The first thing Hunter Greenwold saw when he opened his eyes were stars. They twinkled at him from above in cold profusion mocking his life and actions.

I must have fallen asleep, he thought wearily. *Where am I?*

He couldn't quite remember. The last thing he remembered was sitting on the curb near a tree. Then it came back to him in disconnected pieces.

The white squirrel. The picture of Ashmore's children, he recalled with growing agitation. *The rodent stole it!*

Hunter tried to sit up as if expecting to still catch a glimpse of the albino thief, but feeling weary, he fell back.

He had chased the little thief all the way through a strange back alley to a circle of stumps. There had been other animals. Everything had started to glow and spin around. Now his head ached at the memory of it.

Gathering his strength again he managed to prop himself up into a sitting position. As he did so the photo fell from his chest and landed on the ground between his legs.

Jackie and Dustin. The kids he was hired to find.

Finding new resolve Hunter stood up on shaky legs and put

the picture carefully back in his wallet. His head spun in protest, but he ignored it. It was no worse than one of a countless number of hangovers he'd weathered over the last few years. Steadying himself he looked around.

The sight nearly knocked him over. Hunter gazed about, bewildered. Instead of the expected city scene, he found himself in the center of a small dirt circle bordered by a knee-high ring of gray mossy rock. Beyond this sat a living enclosure of leaves and branches. Strangest of all, he couldn't detect a ceiling. The walls simply arced high above him until they gently faded away into the inky blackness and twinkling constellations of light. As beautiful as the sight was, it did little to illuminate his surroundings or make him feel at ease. If anything, it made him very jumpy.

"Excuse me," a voice said.

Hunter wheeled toward the sound and managed to take two steps forward before tripping in surprise over the stone barrier at his feet. Looking up he blinked in disbelief as his faculties struggled to process what his eyes were clearly showing him. His mouth moved in fitful starts, but no words came out. Finally, he managed three syllables, torn loose from the depths of his throat.

"...a—dodo?"

"Yes, yes, a dodo," said the overstuffed bird dryly through its long beak. "Congratulations my dear birder, you've successfully identified me. What was the giveaway? Was it my limp and ineffectual wings? My rotund mass? Quite possibly my disarming look of innocent fatalism and humorous stupidity clued you in. I'm sure that was it."

Hunter Greenwold looked up at the avian apparition and nodded weakly.

"No need to bow down before me, however," the dodo continued sarcastically as it waddled closer. "I believe the usual reaction will suffice. Just shoot me. I'm told we make wonderful hats."

The mention of shooting something steadied Hunter as his

mind reeled back to the events of yesterday. Images came in rapid fire succession. David Ashmore pleading for his help, the hired thug, a fatal-sounding gunshot as the father took the bullet meant for him.

Nothing else mattered now, he reminded himself, except finding the missing kids. No one else was going to get hurt. He had lived his life and made his mistakes. There was nothing left to do now except one last job.

Getting to his feet, he blinked his eyes in the hopes that the creature would go away but it stubbornly persisted in remaining real. He needed facts. Already his newfound sense of equilibrium was fading. His hands began to shake with fear and confusion. Rushing to fill the opening void, he blurted out the first question that came to his mind.

"Where the hell am I?"

"That will be difficult to explain," the dodo began as if addressing a child. "You are in HeartWood, the home of Nimbus, the Keeper of Treetops. My name is Regnal. I help where I am needed here and keep an eye on the Portal."

The bird tipped its wing toward the miniature stone wall Hunter had just fallen over.

"Most Earth Walkers who accidentally stumble through the gateway never make it to the other side," the creature explained. "At least not in one piece."

"Portal," mused Hunter. "Is that how I came here? Through some kind of hole?"

"Nothing quite so crude. You will find no Cheshire cats here or playing card royalty. This is not a wonderland, although you *will* find wonders here. The only game is staying alive."

The dodo looked him over with a critical eye. "I'm not sure you're quite up to the task."

Hunter Greenwold shook his head and dug his hand into his pocket until he felt the cold metal of his gun.

"I don't care about your riddles," Hunter spat. "None of this is real, anyway. It can't be. Dodos are extinct. Birds don't talk. Hallucinating or not, I need some answers, and I need them fast."

"Ask away, Mr. Greenwold. Consider me your personal oracle."

Hunter's original question died on his lips replaced by sudden alarm.

"How do you know my name?"

"A little squirrel told me. I hope for all of our sake's it wasn't a white lie."

As if on cue a familiar sight scampered into view. The rodent circled twice around Regnal nervously before finally climbing atop one of the extinct creature's three-toed feet. The squirrel sat back on its hind legs as if enjoying a brief respite.

"There it is!" Hunter erupted. "That's the thing that lured me here. That thing stole my picture and then ran down the street like a pint-sized pick-pocket."

"Yes, yes, I know," consoled Regnal, patting the squirrel gently on its head with a wing, and paying Hunter absently no mind at all. "It's a very dangerous business going down Below. But I'm sure you had your reasons."

Pence chattered back.

"Excuse me," fumed Hunter, all the more upset for being ignored. "What *reasons* could a squirrel possibly have?"

The dodo turned toward him now, but slowly, as if it were facing some unpleasant task.

"That is no concern of yours," Regnal said disdainfully. "What you need to do is eat and drink. Your body will be weak from its journey."

After a moment Regnal added pointedly, "You look dreadful."

Hunter knew he must look like a wreck, but he certainly wasn't going to stand around and let some portly extinct bird take cheap shots at him. A tyrannosaurus rex would get no argument from him, scavenger or not, but a dodo was a different story! Yet, the mere mention of food awakened in him a forgotten hunger.

When was the last time he had eaten a full meal? It seemed like a lifetime ago. And a drink! It was only with considerable effort that he was able to banish the thought of an ice-cold beer.

"Help yourself," Regnal said, glancing over its downy shoulder. Then it turned back to Hunter and cast a withering stare. "You should be grateful there is no dress code."

As the dodo and the white squirrel moved off to the side, Hunter saw what the infuriating bird had been squawking about. A broad stone table stood a few yards away. A wide variety of fruits and breads and cheese were arrayed on its surface. Here, finally, was an illusion he could sink his teeth into.

"Do I need to ring a bell?" chided his ill-mannered host, but Hunter was already moving toward the feast.

The taste and texture of the food as it met his lips and tongue felt intoxicating and soon he was putting as much in his mouth as he could get his hands on. Within minutes it was gone. Hunter looked down at the empty plates and was filled not with disgust for his near barbaric behavior but intense contentment. It felt good, really good, to be full.

"There is water at the fountain if you'd like to cleanse your palette," Regnal remarked scornfully.

Ignoring the bird, Hunter walked over to the fountain which sat in the center of a round pool. The leafy walls surrounding it made an exotic backdrop and the gently rising and falling water soothed his still jumbled nerves. Unexpectedly at peace, he closed his eyes, gladly dipping his hands into its glassy surface for a drink. At first contact, a rush of icy chill swept through his fingers and up his arm as if he'd just claimed the heart of a glacier. Quickly he tore his cupped hands free and with a shiver, placed the blue-tinged water to his lips.

Life!

Cool refreshing water flooded his senses and he opened his eyes, for the first time looking *into* the water. Instead of a shallow bottom, an immense black void opened beneath him, much like the sky that he had awoken to when he first arrived except this scene had no stars. In its place swirled a giant blue-green world wrapped scantily in a shifting cloak of cloud.

The Earth!

His hands still dripping, Hunter whirled around. There, standing directly before him was Regnal, but now the avian creature took on more sinister possibilities. Looking down at the dodo bird, he became painfully aware of an out-of-this-world prospect.

"Are you some kind of alien?" he asked, very much aware of how stupid he sounded. "Have I been abducted or something?"

"What you saw *is* Earth but this is not a spaceship and you need not fear an imminent anal probe," drawled the dodo. "Treetops is here because the world still abides. The Keeper labors to ensure that beauty should not be forgotten. It has always been this way. Treetops is a place of remembrance. It's a photo album endlessly filling up with pretty pictures of what was."

A little alarm went off in Hunter Greenwold's brain.

Pictures, he thought.

Nothing the dodo bird said made any sense, but it didn't matter. He remembered again what he had to do.

"I have to find someone," he stammered. "Two kids named Dustin and Jackie."

He reached for his wallet and pulled out the photo.

"Have you seen them?" He asked.

Regnal rustled his feathers.

"You're late. The girl was here. She is with Nimbus and the Chosen. They are marching to the Arkanum on the Forgotten Plains where Samuel Flood holds her brother captive."

The information, confusing as it was, sent a shockwave of action through Hunter.

"I have to go. How do I get out of here?"

"Yes, you must leave and find them," Regnal advised. "But first you must learn things and understand your purpose. If you'll just humor me for a moment, we can..."

"I don't need to have a moment and I don't need to understand anything!" Hunter exploded taking out his gun and pointing it at the bird. "There's no time to argue. None of this is happening. None of this is real. I took a case to find two missing kids and that's what I'm going to do. I made a promise. You're not stopping me. No one is. Got it? So, I'll ask you again, nicely: where's the door to this funky place?"

~

Despite his better judgment, Regnal told him where he could find the exit and then lifted a wing in the direction of the distant Arkanum. Later, he would chalk it up to a misplaced survival instinct. The man called Hunter Greenwold would not allow him to say anything more and only became more agitated when he saw Pence dart out ahead of him. Moments later Regnal watched as the detective ran through the thick brambles of HeartWood toward the light, a gun still gripped tightly in his hand.

There was no way Regnal could keep up with the private investigator even if he was allowed to leave the Keeper's abode. Hunter would spot his ungainly attempt at pursuit in any event. Luckily, Pence was small and fast and very clever. Oh yes, and practically invisible atop the clouds. There might be one small hope left after all. But Regnal, never one to wager, wasn't betting on it.

CHAPTER 27

Jackie sat huddled next to the fire that Nimbus had conjured hoping its heat could somehow restore a measure of her self-confidence. Instead the dancing flames only seemed to mock her, reinforcing how unstable and fragile everything seemed to be. Because of her, the Elementals would soon be free. There was no place to run to. She would either be able to control them or she wouldn't. Sitting in the half-light in her stained clothing, it was hard to imagine that she could command anything, and certainly not the mysterious creatures that inhabited the nearby Orb. Risking a glance, she saw that multi-hued light still poured from the failing prison. The cracks were widening, alarmingly so. It looked as if a jail break would soon be in full swing. Even more disturbing were the earthquakes that had begun to shake the ground beneath their feet. Something big was coming. She shuddered in spite of the blazing fire nearby.

Too late she realized that she had taken the coward's way out. By not believing that she and the Chosen were enough, the Orb was about to hatch and the things inside would run rampant. When they did, the quest would be over. The Elementals weren't going to save Dustin. They were probably going to end any slim chance they had of succeeding. There was nothing special about her. The Sentinel had been right when he said he could not sense her power. She had been a fool to think otherwise.

Once again, she looked over at Nimbus. He still sat in silence, lost in his own thoughts, barely saying a word since starting the fire. Part of her needed someone to talk to, someone to tell her everything would be all right. The other part basked in the solitude.

Jackie still felt deeply shaken by what she had seen in the pool of water by the Orb. It had been her and not her at the same time. A stranger, of sorts, had stared back. True, her hair was much longer, but what really disturbed her was her face and chest. Her features looked more refined, more grown up; older. She had always hated being treated like a kid and longed to be a teenager, and someday a woman who could make her own decisions. Now she wasn't sure if she liked what she saw.

Where before only two small bumps had sat meekly under her shirt, now a pair of breasts curved unmistakably like rising mountains. She looked down at them with a mixture of wonder and terror unable to fathom how they had grown so quickly.

What is going on? Jackie wondered staring into the crackling flames. *What is happening to me? Why am I growing up overnight?*

Perhaps Nimbus had sensed that she needed her personal space. After bringing forth water so she could cleanse herself and conjuring a comforting fire with a few alien sounding words, he had sensibly retreated from the wood-eating flames and let her be. Beyond the Keeper were her Chosen.

For a moment the protective circle of animals comforted her. Speedo danced in the air as if any delay could be borne happily. Peanut and Harry trumpeted to each other like the long-lost cousins they were. Striker patrolled his section nervously, padding a path in the riverbed. Flambeau still rode atop Rocco like an ungainly jockey and Wintra and Quake faced the orb in an unblinking stare. When Jackie cast her eyes upward, the sky was empty. Iggy was dead. And Pence, who should have been curled beside her foot or asleep in her hand, had disappeared.

Maybe Gaylon got him too, she thought morosely.

Already two of her ten Chosen had been lost. She didn't think she could bear to lose any more.

Such was the state of her worries that when Nimbus put a leafy hand on her shoulder she nearly jumped into the fire.

"My pardon," the Keeper apologized. "It was not my intent to startle. I should have announced myself."

An angry retort simmered on Jackie's lips but then burned away. Without speaking she settled herself woodenly in front of the fire again and wrapped her arms around her knees.

The Keeper looked at her, opened his mouth to speak, and then hesitated, as if the task before him was too much.

"Jackie," he said finally. "I erred earlier when I called you a child. Such was my fear of facing the Elementals. No longer a child, you are also not yet a woman. Instead you are somewhere in between, and your gifts remain elusive. We need to talk. There are things," his eyes shifted away for a moment, "concerning you which we can no longer safely ignore. Time is short."

From inside her mental cocoon, Jackie looked at the Keeper.

"I was afraid you were going to say something like that."

Jackie clasped her hands together as if she were steadying herself against an onslaught of revelations. The Keeper, not able to sit because of his tree-like form, laid down his staff and extended roots onto the ground. They spread all around him, thick pale tubers that in their turn let out a filigree of rootlets. With a sigh Nimbus let go of his aging muscles and let his living anchors carry his burden. But still he did not speak. The remnants of his face glimpsed through the shroud of leaves seemed twisted in pain as if his whole countenance reflected some kind of inner battle. Finally, the Keeper mastered himself and scrutinized Jackie.

"Do you know who you are?" he asked plainly.

Jackie glanced at the Keeper in surprise.

"What do you mean? Of course, I know who I am. I thought you were going to tell me something important."

"I'm trying," Nimbus said. "What I mean is, are you familiar with your family history? Did your mother ever tell you any stories, ones that weren't in any book?"

Jackie shook her head.

"Did she tell you what she did before she met your father?"

"Yes," Jackie said.

Nimbus smiled hopefully.

"She told me she worked in a garden nursery somewhere in Maine. I don't know where exactly."

The Keeper's face fell back into disappointment. "True, after a fashion," he managed. "Surely, you've wondered about your birthmark. Did your mother ever talk to you about that?"

Jackie touched her neck gently, as if the mottled skin there were a tender bruise, and concentrated.

"Yes," she said. "My mom told me once that I should be very proud of my birthmark. That it was special."

"And?" the Keeper asked with rising excitement. "Do you remember anything unusual about your mother? Think hard. It is very important."

"I kind of remember her making things grow. I know that sounds weird, but she was really good at that. If I had a cut when I was a kid, she could heal that too. At least I thought she could. One time I imagined I saw her controlling the wind, but I was really little and didn't know any better."

"What about the Amarantha? Surely your mother had time to explain *that* to you."

"You mean that big vine I climbed up? No, not really. She left the seed as a birthday present, after she died. There was a note, but it didn't really say much, other than the Amarantha would take me far. She said there were secrets I would have to discover for myself. What did she mean by that?"

Nimbus sighed.

"Try harder," The Keeper urged. "Can you remember anything else?"

"No," Jackie said, feeling deflated. "That's about it I guess."

Nimbus bowed his head. "Then you know nothing. It falls upon me."

Taking a deep breath, the Keeper began.

"Your mother would have told you on your thirteenth birthday the things I am about to reveal, if she would have been able. You are ill-equipped. It's hard to explain and harder still for you to believe, but Jillian had a gift. A wonderful gift."

For a moment Nimbus seemed to look past her and off into the distance.

"Have you ever listened to the birds sing or sat by a waterfall and almost thought you could make sense of it? That the birds and the water and the autumn leaves in the wind and the buzzing of invisible insects in the orchestral grass were somehow all speaking a common language? That they were linked voices in the same chorus speaking to you, comforting you, urging you, revealing to you alone?"

"I'm not sure what you mean," Jackie began.

Nimbus sighed. "The point is they all try to speak with us, but few can hear. All of them are part of the planet. The living Earth."

A bemused smile grew on Jackie's face.

"Oh, I don't mean some faerie notion where the world can play checkers with you," the Keeper continued. "No, it's much more wonderful than that. But alive, it is. Several times in the long history of this blue-green sphere, disasters have befallen her. Such an event occurred some 65 million years ago. Death from the blackness of space helped wipe the dinosaurs out and most other species as well. It could have been much worse were it not for our planet's ability to heal itself. She has acted at other times as well through the eons. These calamities caused the world great pain, but she weathered them, and life continued.

Now human beings, the voice of the Earth, are poisoning the air and water. Nature can no longer renew the planet on her own. She needs help to stem the losses that humankind inflicts. Thousands of years ago, about the time when man first built crude cities and put seeds in the deathless ground, the Earth planted a seed of her own so hope might be sown. That's where the Keeper and Treetops come in. And Flood to, I suppose, although he is closed off to me in darkness. Treetops helps to heal and protect, safeguarding precious memories so regeneration can occur. It reminds us what has been lost even as life goes on."

Jackie thought of her mother and how she would never see her again.

"In this way," Nimbus was saying, "nothing is ever truly lost. We are fast approaching, however, a crisis that may at last trigger an ancient planetary response, a last attempt at survival that entirely bypasses my power. I have been sensing its approach over the last few decades and have only become certain of its existence recently."

"What is it?" Jackie asked.

"That is not yet clear to me. Yet it must somehow involve your brother. Why else would Flood go to the trouble of kidnapping him?"

Jackie frowned.

"But what does this Flood want with my brother? He's just a kid."

"I'm not sure," Nimbus said. It seemed to Jackie that he had other things to say on the matter, but he hesitated, and the words wilted on his moss-covered lips. "Your presence is a force in this story as well," he offered instead. "You were granted a great honor in the Grove of the Earth Trees. You chose from all the animals assembled. They listen to you. There is no mystery there. You may have other talents as well. Surely you have noticed something different about you, something your friends didn't share. For me, when I was even a very small boy, I could predict storms days before they swept over our coastal home in England."

Jackie hesitated.

"I've never done anything like that," she said self-consciously. "I guess that would have been pretty cool. I don't know. I guess I feel almost at home here, like I have the space to become something I'm supposed to be."

"That feeling may get stronger," the Keeper said. "Then again, it may not. When your mother was much younger than you, she was already talking to owls and laying hands on trees to determine what ailed them. The mark you wear is your birthright. It guarantees your entry into Treetops. Whether or not you have the ability and talent to serve are another matter. Your mother did."

The Keeper paused.

"When you first arrived, I told you that Jillian was one of my best students. That was not an exaggeration. Such were her gifts and dedication. While she was here, Treetops was transformed. I could not have rebuilt HeartWood nor protected the Grove from Flood without your mother. With her assistance the animals flourished. In time, she could have taken my place as a Keeper. Yet she left, as many have in the past, to reclaim her former life, and to bring forth life of her own. It is only natural, after all."

"My mom gave all of this up, so she could have me?" stammered Jackie.

"Of course," answered Nimbus. "Many do, while others choose to remain. Serving here is entirely voluntary, I assure you. Anyone can refuse, although most do not. Length of time varies. A few, like me, have served their entire adult life. There were many that came before your mother. They've all had a calling. Each had a gift. From the Seven Families they climbed, each carrying their special mark and their own surname. Yours is one. Gardner."

"That's not my last name. It's Ashmore."

"But your mother's surname wasn't," the Nimbus explained evenly. "It was Gardner. That is why she kept her last name when she married your father. Dozens of your ancestors served Treetops as a special helper or *noventice* through the centuries. Some may have even become Keepers. Your roots are deep here."

Jackie stared back at the Keeper. "You're from a different family then?" she asked.

"There are seven lineages: the Leaf, the Flame, the Wind, the Water, Earth, the Sun, and Shadow. I come from a different family tree, but I find it strange to think of myself in those human terms after so long."

Jackie looked at Nimbus covered in leaves and bark and tried to imagine him as an ordinary person. She couldn't.

"What is my talent?" she asked tentatively. "Will I be like my mom?"

The Keeper paused as if he were searching for some truth.

"It is perhaps still too early to say for sure. If you have abilities, Treetops will bring them out. One thing is for certain, you have your mother's temper and tendency towards self-doubt."

Jackie thought she understood what Nimbus was trying to say and she appreciated it. Perhaps she was more like her mother than she thought. Yet she couldn't help but dwell on how unfair it all felt. Her mother had served Treetops only to get sick when Jackie needed her most.

"Why did my mom have to die, if she was so powerful and everything?" Jackie demanded. "It doesn't make any sense."

The Keeper met her fierce stare and then bowed his head in silence. When he finally raised his leafy bough again the bright green had faded from his leaves replaced by autumnal colors.

"Ah, no one is that powerful. Not even Xylum. But you are right, of course, it is not fair. Disease and death take beauty and never ask forgiveness. But keep this in mind: it was her choice to return Below. We all must live our own lives under our own terms and accept the consequences. Life brings beauty and goodness again. You are proof of that."

Just like that Jackie's anger was extinguished, replaced by something else she couldn't quite describe.

The Keeper reached out and patted her shoulder with a leafy hand. The sensation did not feel comforting; instead of being warm and firm, Nimbus's touch was pallid and alien. Suddenly, Jackie felt terribly alone. Without her mother, father, or brother, who did she have? She tried to tell herself that everything would be okay, but it didn't seem like it would. Everyone in her family was now alone or worse. To distract her from things that had no answers, she asked Nimbus the question she had been avoiding since their talk began.

"What is happening to me, Nimbus?"

"It must have been a shock to see yourself in the pool, and to have gotten..." the Keeper said quietly.

Nimbus faltered.

"My period? Yeah, it freaked me out even more than the Sentinel. I guess that's not unusual but what about *these*?" she demanded motioning to her chest. "I certainly didn't have them when I climbed up here. Believe me, I would remember."

Nimbus exhaled like the last leaf falling in a winter wind.

"There's no easy way to say this Jackie. You're not supposed to be here. It is not your time. For Jillian, your mother," he continued, "time moved much slower here than Below. That is why she could stay nearly ten years and still return virtually unchanged."

Jackie's mouth gaped open, but no words would come. *Ten years!* It didn't make any sense.

"Time moves differently in Treetops," the Keeper explained. "The clock ticks slower, only a third as fast. For those that belong here and are strong in spirit, the ravages of time are eased, preserving our choice to serve. That is how I have remained here since the reign of mad King George III and your American revolution. I have served as Keeper longer than any other. That is why my appearance is so strange. In a sense, I am becoming part of Treetops. Your mother only aged a few years while here. Twelve months in the clouds, however, equals two years in the world beneath. Everything adds up. Until they take their Vow, young *noventices* can visit their homes if they choose, but such excursions can only accomplish so much. In the end each person must decide. But it can't work the same for you."

A silence grew between them.

"Tell me," she asked, her voice only a whisper. "How does it work for me?"

"The reverse," the Keeper said at last. "Time moves much faster for you. Without a calling, unable as yet to tap a vital power of your own, you have no protection here. You are literally aging before your eyes. I estimate that you are now at least 16 years old. By the time we reach the Arkanum you will be at least seventeen, maybe more. A day in Treetops is a year for you. It is imperative that we rescue your brother and get you down the Portal Tree as fast as possible. There can be no delays. What you lose cannot be regained."

Jackie wrapped her arms around herself tighter as if to somehow slow the transformation. She stared at her hand half-expecting to see the molecules change before her eyes. Her world had shrunk, collapsing in on itself. Instead of having all the time in the world, it felt like she had none. Standing there, she could almost imagine her blood being replaced by sand as her hourglass body ran out.

"There is one more thing," added the Keeper. "No matter what happens tomorrow when we face the Elementals, no matter what you may see at the Arkanum, you must remember that your brother Dustin is not entirely himself. Flood will bend the boy to his will, corrupt the child with half-truths until he is a merely tool, and a dangerous one at that."

CHAPTER 28

Dustin sat on the deck of the great ship, his eyes unfocused, as the lion licked the salt off his hand, its hot pink tongue as coarse as sandpaper. His other hand lay buried deep in the animal's thick mane as if the beast were nothing but a stuffed toy he'd grown tired of. Animals of every size and description lay prostrated before him or stood solemnly at attention. They formed multiple rings of devotion, great orbits of attraction with Dustin at the center. In the beginning, he had marveled at the display of affection. Now he hardly noticed. Overhead the sun chariot made its lazy way across the sky as if it had nothing better to do.

"What is wrong, my boy?" asked Flood, putting a firm hand on Dustin's small shoulder. "You don't seem yourself lately. Perhaps playing fetch again with all of creation will help raise your spirits."

All of creation wasn't *quite* true, mused the Master of the Arkanum to himself. Treetops held only those Earth animals extinct or close to extinction. Even so, that was the vast majority of species. Flood frowned as he looked closer, surveying the animals assembled. He couldn't yet even boast that he had all of the Keeper's denizens aboard the Arkanum. Hundreds of species had yet to respond to the summons. Each took their own path here, independent of terrain or distance. Some had appeared almost immediately following the summons, clambering over the gunwales or alighting atop the mastheads. Others had trickled in days later with hides scratched and scales battered as if the very air had sported thorns to block their way. But come they did. None could refuse the Horn of Calling.

It mattered not that they had never heard its sound before. All obeyed, as was the law. Soon nearly every creature that had ever walked, swam, flew or burrowed in the Earth would be here, under his control while down Below, the Cyclix were doing their work. Even those borne of humankind's imagination were here: the dragon, basilisk, griffin, gorgon, minotaur, satyr, chimera, and cyclops. All but the unicorn, Flood mused absently, tousling the boy's wavy hair. Treetops was slowly emptying of its inhabitants until it sagged like a balloon with a gaping hole. It mattered not that Nimbus was aware of the depletion, as he must have been the instant the Callixar sounded. In fact, over time the Keeper would have doubtless become aware of the animals Flood had maneuvered away from Treetops even before Dustin blew the horn for the first time. But such tactics were too strenuous and too time-consuming. The planet could not wait while he stole an animal here and there from the failing Keeper. Bolder action was required.

Flood had little doubt that the Keeper, despite his weakness, was also aware of the reverberations that resulted from the sounding, and the dire warning it represented. There was no way he could have hidden such an event from the Keeper, even if he had wanted to. Nimbus, like he, was attuned to the world, in a way no mere human being could be. Yet he did not require secrecy. Having the old caretaker aware of his actions was a necessary risk. Carefully, he let his breath out, relaxing his chest and mind as a feeling of calm spread through him.

"What do you say?" he asked Dustin. "I'm sure the t-rex would be happy to play fetch with you."

In response, Dustin pulled his hand away from the lion's soft mane and turned toward the Master.

"Can *you* play with me?" he asked.

Flood smiled. "Later. I promise. Until then the animals will do anything you like."

Before he could react, the boy stood up and strode through the throng of creatures. Immediately they parted for him, musk ox and blue whale alike, gently genuflecting at his feet as he passed through the open space they made for him.

Dustin walked all the way across the deck, finally coming to a stop at the foot of a wooden crate pressed against the side of the ship. Despondently, he stepped up on the perch and looked over the railing to the desolate landscape below. He felt utterly alone.

"Come find me," he whispered to the empty air. Tears flooded his eyes. "Please. I don't wanna play hide and seek anymore."

CHAPTER 29

Within minutes of leaving the Keeper's home, Hunter Greenwold realized the difficulty that lay before him. The vast landscape of white blurred his vision, obscuring his senses. Without any landmarks, the featureless vista was worse than a maze. Any direction he went could be leading him astray, wasting valuable time. He didn't even know where or what this damn Arkanum was.

Movement in the valley below caught his eye and he paused. A pair of giraffes, their long necks bobbing, trotted towards the edge of the cloudscape. Stepping into a bank of floating clouds, they vanished from sight. Two Bactrian camels gamboled along in their own fashion, and then they too disappeared as they crossed the wispy wall boundary. Dozens of other animals dotted the terrain, oblivious to their shrinking numbers. Even as he watched, another species joined its brethren, and flew, swum or walked, seemingly out of existence, into the land beyond the cloud vale.

Everything around him seemed insubstantial and unbelievable. Even the milky ground beneath his feet was little more than spongy contradiction. He kept expecting to fall through the cloud-top at any moment. Instead the sky held him up like a miracle. Hunter took a few more wavering steps and then sunk to his knees, overwhelmed by impossibility. Grasping for the only thing that felt real anymore, he took out the picture of Jackie and Dustin and gazed at their faces as if he could glean inspiration from them. But their smiles held no answers and only left him with the disquieting feeling that they had disappeared like the animals below, never to be seen again. He kept telling himself how far he had come and that he must be close now. That only made it worse, of course. Everything in his life had been a series of missed opportunities and tragic occurrences.

Memories of Talley, the girl he almost married, welled up in him along with the career he had chosen over her. Even that job was not to be, obliterated in a moment's carelessness on a quiet city street. He could still see the little girl, her baseball cap pulled on backwards as she chased the ball across the street. A familiar emptiness rose up and enveloped him as he remembered braking too late, being unable to stop.

Thinking about it, reliving it again, was almost too much to bear. A shudder passed through him, like a precursor to death as an icy coldness seeped into his bones. How could he ever overcome what he had done and forgive himself? He knew the answer to that. He never could. He had tried to make some kind of restitution to the girl's family. Tell them how sorry he was, but they wouldn't speak to him. Each time he had called, they had hung up. Out of desperation he went to their house and knocked, his hands trembling. The door opened a crack. Through the sliver of light, he was just able to see a graying middle-aged man, his eyes hard and red.

"Stay away," he said in a tight, deep voice. "My wife can't take it. None of us can. Have you no mercy?"

Hunter's mouth opened around the words he had practiced for long months, but nothing would come. He was mute with grief and inadequacy.

"Is that *him*?" a female voice cried. "You killed my Emma Jean. *Murderer!*"

Then the door slammed shut. He never returned.

Somehow the years went by. Unable to work for the FBI or law enforcement, he turned to private investigating to pay the bills. It was ugly, boring work, but he did it, because he didn't know what else to do.

He met a woman, ten years younger, and in his own damaged way, fell in love. Sorrow was never far away. He didn't know how to heal. Guilt consumed him. It poisoned his marriage, drew him to alcohol, and cast a shadow over everything he did. Although his wife wanted children desperately, he always resisted, never giving a specific reason. How could he tell her? That changed a few short weeks ago. They had been fighting again. In a drunken rage, his secret had come pouring out. There were tears, angry words, and awkward embraces.

"I love you," Hannah told him. "But I can't go on like this. I'm not even sure who you are anymore."

The next day she packed up her stuff and left. He never said a word to stop her. What could he say? He deserved no less. He had nothing left. His punishment was complete.

When David Ashmore unexpectedly stumbled into his office, he had given him something. Not absolution, that was impossible, nor even restitution, but a chance to make himself useful, to really make a difference.

Racing off across the clouds, however, seemed a fool's errand. Every direction looked the same. Instinctively he patted his shirt pocket for the cigarettes that weren't there. Cursing, he began walking again. Soon he made his way down into the valley. The cloud terrain sloped gently until he finally arrived at the bottom. A myriad of animals congregated defensively in the center, as if by staying together they could somehow keep themselves safe. Many were solid, while others were ghostly and nearly transparent. Hunter marched across the valley floor like he knew where he was going. Nearby he saw a small group of animals break-off from the others. Curious, Hunter followed a pair of strange reddish-brown kangaroos as they made their way towards a bank of vapors that hung like a shifting wall in the distance. The two marsupials had white bellies and striped tails. They moved effortlessly across the landscape. After a short while, Hunter tired. He lost the animals as they hopped through the wall of mist and he was hesitant to follow.

He tried again with two small bears. They were black with cream-colored chests and had dark rings around each eye. This time he steeled himself and followed into the vapors. Soon he again struggled to keep up as the creatures increased their speed, pulled along as if by some nameless force. Finally, he lost them amidst the thickening veil. With each step the clouds grew more opaque. Soon his pace slowed, not from tiredness, but from simple confusion. He could no longer ignore the fact that he had no idea where he was going or even where he was. If this a fevered dream he would eventually wake up on the sidewalk grate. If Treetops was somehow real, then he was indeed a stranger in a strange land. Either way he would need help.

Looking back, the other animals were nowhere to be seen. A cocoon of white encased his vision. Even the sky was obscured by a milky film as if the sun could not quite reach here. He felt lost. Slowly, he began to turn in a circle as panic welled up in him. Faster and faster he spun but every direction looked the same. Inside he faded away until he felt as insubstantial as the clouds.

"Don't disappear," Talley had said to him once as they were sitting in her apartment. He had been silent, nervous about something.

He looked at her, really looked at her, and after a moment said, "I'm not going anywhere."

But he had of course, and so had she. That was just how the world worked. There was nothing you could do about it.

He sat down on the wispy ground then and put his hands over

his face. Slowly at first, Hunter cried for the first time since he was a child. He shed tears for Talley, for his ex-wife, for the little girl he had killed that twilight evening, for David Ashmore and his children. Sitting alone atop clouds heavy with rain he cried because he couldn't change any of it.

That's when he heard the faint metallic tinkling sound.

CHAPTER 30

"It's time," Flood said. "Are you ready for your second blow of the Callixar?"

Dustin stood at his usual perch on the lip of the Arkanum and looked out across the lifeless valley. There were no clouds here, only barren unbroken ground that stretched to the horizon. His scraggly hair blew like tumbleweed tossed in the hot wind.

"I don't know," he replied without turning around.

"Would you like to play games again inside first?" Flood suggested. "Lancelot loves to play checkers with you, even when he loses."

Dustin shook his head.

"Perhaps you would enjoy another ride atop the triceratops. You have to watch out for his horns, though."

"I just wanna go home," Dustin said with a small sigh.

With these words the boy's body sagged against the railing.

"But you are home, my boy. At least for now. Where you are loved and cared for and no one ever forgets about you or is too busy." Flood paused and spread his arms out wide as if to encompass all the gathered animals. "Every one of these noble creatures would lay down its life for you. And do you know why?"

Dustin shook his head again.

"Because you will set them free and save their world. That is a very brave and wonderful thing for a little boy to do. They will never forget you."

Flood reached out and put his hand on Dustin's shoulder, and turned the boy gently around to face him.

"I know it's hard," he whispered in the boy's ear, his voice hinting at secrets and buried pain. "It's hard to be alone. Always apart." Suddenly he gripped Dustin's shoulders, raised him up with careful strength. "If there was any other way, I'd have Gaylon carry you down the portal of the Earth Tree this very moment. But there isn't. I'm counting on you. We're all counting on you, Dustin. Just one good blow. That's all it takes."

Dustin trembled in quiet fear, but said nothing.

"All right," Flood said at last, putting Dustin's feet back on the deck and stepping back. Immediately the boy collapsed again against the railing and buried his face in the hollow of his arms. "If this is how it must be."

A silence grew between them. Earth's creatures sat assembled around them and made not a single sound.

"Go home, then. Leave," Flood began. "You've always been able to you know. No one will stop you."

Slowly, the boy raised his tousled head.

"I can go?"

"Of course. You are my guest, and a very special one at that."

"But you stole me."

Flood smiled and patted Dustin's shoulder.

"Have you ever found a frog, lost and alone, hopping in the middle of nowhere? Did you feel sorry for it and then put it gently in your pocket and taken it home? Perhaps you filled a jar with grass and sticks, something it would like, and then kept it for a while, until it was better. That is what I did with you. We rescued you. If Gaylon had not been watching that day, who knows what could have happened. All I've tried to do is take care of you until your family returns."

Bending down on one knee Flood touched the boy's cheek with his great hand. Dustin didn't shrink away. Instead, a fragile smile grew on his face.

"I can see you are better now. Still, it is a long walk and Gaylon is away and unable to take you. I need Lancelot to help with things around the Arkanum. Better if someone came and got you. They must be coming for you now. Your family is looking for you. Blow the horn so they will know where you are."

"I blew before and they didn't come," Dustin said sadly.

"No, but they are coming," Flood explained rising up to his full stature. "That much is certain. They just have lost their way. The world can be a very big place. You want them to find you, don't you?"

Dustin nodded and sniffed his nose, holding back tears.

"Blow louder then," Flood suggested. "Lancelot," he called. "Bring the Callixar!"

Without delay the gorilla lumbered through the wall of animals, his tortoise shell glistening like armor in the bright sunlight, a red baseball cap still perched precariously atop its hairy head. In his bulging arms he cradled the great horn.

"Set it down there," Flood commanded, motioning to a curved depression in the deck railing.

Lancelot set the golden horn down in its ancient resting place, bowed slightly, and then moved away to make room for the boy. Flood dragged a wooden step-stool over so it lay directly beneath the artifact.

Dustin approached and then climbed the steps slowly, as if his footsteps could set off a sudden eruption of noise. When his lips were nearly touching the horn, he stopped and held his breath, making a silent wish.

"Go on," said Flood. "It will only take a moment. What are you waiting for? Let em' know you're here."

This time, Flood covered the boy's ears with his massive hands. Dustin leaned forward, placed his lips on the cold metal of the Callixar's golden mouthpiece and, for the second time, blew. A thin, high sound capable of shattering worlds erupted. In the sky to the west, a vein-like crack appeared, bleeding red, like sap from a mortally wounded tree. As if expelled from the growing fissure a sudden gust of wind swept across the Arkanum and nearly tore Dustin off the step and over the railing before Flood steadied him.

"There!" the great robed man yelled pointing to a black spot on the horizon. "Another good sign. Gaylon returns. You have done well, my boy. It has begun!"

All around them the animals made for the exits disappearing into the bowels of the great vessel.

CHAPTER 31

As the echo of the second sounding of the Callixar faded and as the sky reddened high above Treetops, there appeared on every earthly continent creatures of shadow, passing from the depths of the Arkanum into the living world like a nightmare incarnate. With each passing moment they grew more substantial, yet their purpose remained unchanged. Daylight was not a barrier, but the Cyclix preferred the night to do their work. In many ways they *were* the night, encompassing all the primal fears and instincts from ages gone by. And like any creature they wanted only to survive. This trait, more than anything else, is what they were designed to pass on.

The Cyclix were conscious of none of this, of course. They existed to do but one thing, a simple task that each had been waiting for since the world began. Oblivious to the towering buildings, the Cyclix crept unseen down darkened streets, claws and fangs glistening in the moonlight, evoking a nameless shiver from those in its wake. They passed through walls into living rooms and dreaming cats stirred. In backyards and alleyways, dogs sensed their presence, remembered, and howled in recognition.

The Cyclix never lingered, but kept moving on, out into the countryside, under the cold starlight in stark fields, and taught even the animals there where they came from. Finally, they returned to the sacred forests, to the unforgiving desert, to the beginning waters, and, like a homecoming, sang the Song of Awakening.

All except one, that is. One shadow darker than any of the others stood at the foot of a great tree in the heart of a dark wood like a sentinel of doom waiting for the final sounding that would bring the army from above the clouds to the unsuspecting world below.

CHAPTER 32

Jackie lay on the hard, barren ground in the pale twilight and tried in vain to sleep. Her head spun with worries. The Orb of the Elementals was failing. Her body had been fast-forwarded to have its first period. Even now she imagined time stealing the days from her, transforming her in ways she couldn't imagine. She had learned secrets about herself and her family. It was little wonder that long after Nimbus had finished talking and the fire had dwindled to glowing embers, Jackie was still wide awake.

Much had been lost along the way. She thought of Iggy and how she would never see her again in the sky, her wings beating in graceful flight. Even the information she had gleaned from Nimbus had been hard won. There were so many things she still didn't understand. A whole new world had been opened up to her but she hadn't the faintest idea what it meant.

When the first glimmer of Helios touched the eastern horizon, Jackie sat up and hugged her knees to her chest. Rocking back and forth she tried vainly to banish her fears.

Nearby stood Nimbus, rooted to the spot with his vine-covered back toward her as he faced the orb. The object was now nearly split in half by a crack that ran down its middle. Potent light of every hue emanated from it as the earth trembled again. Beyond the bend in the river rose the mountain pass off in the distance. A chill ran down her spine. The high towers of stone on either side reminded her of colossal guards.

What if we become trapped, she wondered? *How can we escape?* Suddenly the riverbed which had offered a degree of protection now seemed fraught with danger.

Shaking her head free of another mystery she couldn't solve, Jackie rose tiredly to her feet and looked around. There, still spread out all around in a protective circle were her Chosen. The sight of Peanut and Harry reassured her, as did the solidity of Rocco Striker, who silently stalked his portion of the perimeter like a half-visible shadow, seemed a match for anything. Nearby, Flambeau seemed to have found a new climbing partner as the red monkey scampered along the great back of Quake and then hung upside down on the dinosaur's serpentine tail. In the air above Speedo wheeled in great arcs as if the sky were his dance floor. For a nervous heartbeat, Jackie could not locate the unicorn. Then she spotted a snowy white outline where the dry riverbed meandered into the open desert behind them. Wintra was guarding the rear.

Before she could catch herself, Jackie glanced above for a glimpse of Iggy. An empty gray sky stared back at her. Her Chosen golden eagle was gone. The memory only reinforced her desire to save her brother and get him back before anything else terrible happened. Behind her she heard the familiar rustling footfalls of Nimbus. Gaining confidence from the remaining Chosen, her resolve returned and Jackie turned to face whatever the Keeper had to say.

"You did not sleep well," the Nimbus observed. "You will need your strength."

"I'll be fine. How much time do we have," Jackie asked, "before the Elementals are free?"

"It will not be long now," the Keeper replied.

As if to reinforce this observation, a brilliant rod of light shot up suddenly from the stricken orb reaching high to the heavens as another tremor wracked the ground beneath their feet.

"The last of Xylum's power is fading away," the Keeper breathed. "Listen carefully. Your brother's life and more may depend on it. Once through the Giant's Pass your brother and the Arkanum lie just beyond the Forgotten Plains. Two days march if you are not delayed. Be wary of Flood. He will be waiting for you."

"Why are you telling me this? You're coming with us."

The Keeper opened his mossy lips to explain when a sudden thunderous noise rolled over the encampment, eclipsing all other sound. The tone was deep as if it originated from the bowels of the lifeless ground, yet it also contained another range, this one of fury, of sharp-tooth and raw survival. The sound drove all thought away, burrowing down into bone and tissue, freezing all action before passing on and fading away.

Jackie could only mouth the words *what was that?* Her voice had fled. Her ears rang like a bell in protest and her vision clouded over with a sudden dancing constellation of stars. She felt shell-shocked by what had just happened. It was worse than before. They had heard the previous call only yesterday, but this sounding felt stronger.

As her eyesight cleared, she looked up to see a blood-red crack open and spread itself across the northwestern portion of the sky. Slowly, the hazy blue heavens above her head were becoming bruised. Jackie felt the bile rise in her throat.

What could do something like this?

In panic she glanced back down at the orb. It still spewed forth the ancient magic which had held its elemental prisoners at bay for so long, and the rod of light still reached ever higher for the damaged heavens. The Elementals were not yet free.

Movement in the sky her caught her attention. Turning her head, she glimpsed a winged black bird flit nervously in front of the gash before disappearing over the horizon.

Gaylon! she thought bitterly.

As she watched, the crack grew like a great and bloody maw bent on devouring worlds.

"Oh my God," she heard herself saying out loud. "What is it?"

Nimbus looked away from the spectacle, as though unable to bear the sight of it.

"It is the Second Call, the Call of Blood" explained the Keeper, his voice ragged with dismay. "So soon. Only the Call of Command remains."

Jackie listened, trying hard to convince herself that all wasn't lost. The Keeper's words made no sense to her. Everything was happening at once. The orb had been too much. The bloody omen in the sky had loosened a fraying knot and now all of her fragile hopes were coming apart.

"Tell me in English," Jackie said. "I don't know what any of that means."

"I should have remembered," Flood continued as if he hadn't heard her. "I should have noticed. The animals that Flood has stolen have gathered at the Arkanum…" His voice dropped as if telling a terrible secret. "Now they will begin the exodus to the Portal Tree. There they will wait."

Jackie frowned in dismay. "Wait for what?"

Suddenly the ground beneath their feet shook again, this time violently.

Jackie looked at the Keeper. He looked adrift as if recent events had rendered him obsolete.

"What's going on?" she asked. "I'm getting scared."

"There is something else. Something worse," Nimbus said as if he had discovered a memory that the eruption of noise had jarred loose. "The Second Call awakens."

Jackie waited, but the Keeper did not continue. The rumbling of the ground grew louder and she fought to keep her balance.

"Awakens what?" Jackie shouted.

"I don't remember," the Keeper said, his voice sounding hollow and forlorn. There were tears in his eyes. "Wait!" he shrieked. "How could I forget? Even after all these years. Nightmares. Terrible shadows that walk the Earth. They turn the creatures down Below, inspire bloodshed. I knew more once. I knew so much more. But there is a Third Call," he continued with a visible shudder. "A final sounding. That is the worst of all."

Jackie reached out as if to steady his thoughts. "What does it do?" she whispered.

The Keeper paused and Jackie thought the moment had passed. Then his eyes widened as his face contorted in dismay. "It commands the creatures of Treetops to invade the world below. Then the Earth itself will rise up."

A sudden shower of fireworks erupted from the orb. They both glanced over in surprise.

"The Second Call, the Blood Call has accelerated the Elementals escape," the Keeper breathed, leaning on his staff as if his life depended on it. "May the gods help us."

Just then four distinct concussions rocked the air and riverbed around them as the light of Xylum's orb finally flickered out. In the distance, the shimmering barrier in the Pass sputtered and disappeared. A terrible stillness grew. Jackie looked over at Nimbus.

"Remember what I told you," he said.

Then the first Elemental rose from the shattered husk of the orb. A great pillar of fire burned before their unbelieving eyes. Two great rocky legs emerged from the flames and anchored themselves on either side of the mountain pass. From each side, the creature grew a cracked and creviced arm ending in mighty metamorphic hands. On top of the tectonic torso, perched like a giant boulder, towered the creature's head, with a gaping cave for a mouth and two glittering rubies for eyes. A smoldering sphere of molten lava burned in its smoking palm. Even from this distance Jackie could feel the terrible heat press down upon her.

Next a great ring of light materialized above their heads, growing in fearsome intensity until it was blinding. From the center of the circle, two slits stared down mercilessly. Jackie shrunk away from the baleful presence, her spirit withering and watched in horror as the other Elementals materialized.

Nearby, a transparent winged creature coalesced out of the very air itself and formed into a writhing serpentine body, dark as tempest storm clouds high above them. Finally, much too close at their feet, the dry riverbed began to undulate like a fevered mirage, causing first rivulets and then small cobalt waves to gather from the ancient sediment and merge together into a great seething watery mass. From this grotesque form grew an immense eyeless creature with rows of sharp dripping teeth.

Jackie forced herself to take a step forward. Her hands were shaking. The Orchlea hung around her neck, but she somehow knew it would not serve her needs with these beings of chaos.

"Elementals," she called in a small voice. "I set you free. Now I command you to obey me. Follow me to the Arkanum to rescue my brother and defeat the one called Samuel Flood."

For a moment the Elementals stilled as if spellbound. Then the Fire Elemental drew back its mighty arm and hurled the great fireball. The blazing mass streaked like a comet over Jackie's ducked head, searing her face and hair, and exploded in the river-bank nearby. Black tendrils of smoke snaked skyward from the crater. The other Elementals began to move as if this act of violence had now completely severed Xylum's hold. Another globe of molten lava formed in the fiery creature's hand. Sounds of fury erupted from the freed monstrosities.

Jackie stood, cowering. Her failure was complete.

Nimbus said something, but his voice was lost amidst the Elemental din.

"What should I do?" Jackie screamed. Tears formed in her eyes.

The Keeper looked at her, concern tugging at his aged features. For once he appeared lucid and capable of miracles.

"Go!" he told her, finding the strength in his voice. "While there is still time. Take the Chosen. Go through the Pass. Remember what I told you. Rescue your brother." Nimbus paused. "I have a gift for you," he said. "I don't know if it will help, but..."

Without hesitation he gripped his pinky in his right hand and in one violent motion snapped it free. There was a sickening crack, but no blood. The digit looked more like a stick than flesh. The Keeper grimaced, but did not cry out.

"Have no fear," he explained. "I am lessened a little, but the pain is manageable. You may need some extra help in the days to come. It will also prove useful in finding you again, should I somehow survive."

Jackie stepped back in fright. "Why would I want your finger? That's just gross."

"Because it is imbued with my power as a living Keeper," Nimbus told her. "We have no time for squeamishness. If nothing else," he smiled briefly, "it may bring you luck."

Jackie reached out and took the wooden digit, stuffing it quickly into her jeans pocket.

"Be brave," the Keeper soothed. "I will do what I can. Perhaps I still have one final trick up my sleeve."

Nimbus turned away and Jackie felt something within her break. What would she do without him? Suddenly, she felt very much alone. She watched him walk away toward the Elementals as quickly as his leaf-encrusted limbs would carry him. Jackie stared in disbelief. Whatever the Keeper was going to do seemed a futile gesture. The Fire Elemental's face was contorted into deep crevices of rage and glee, a molten boulder burning ever hotter in the palm of its hand. The creature's entire rocky surface was aflame now as if it intended to set fire to the world.

The three other creatures, its brethren Elementals, were

finishing forming around it, awakened from their long slumber. The hovering ring of light to her left shone like a true sun now, blinding and radiant. In size the Light Elemental was smaller than HeartWood, yet there was a malevolent quality about it as if the creature meant to swallow them up in a brilliant embrace. Its eyes were slashes of darkness. As Jackie watched, the glowing ring began to pulse. Tendrils of luminescence snaked out in all directions.

Directly above, the Storm Elemental had finished its terrible transformation. In the ominous swirling clouds Jackie could make out a giant reptilian head tapering to a snake-like body. Two great wings beat the air in easy magnificence. Extending from its vast open maw was a multitude of smaller heads set on wispy, wriggling necks. Each time the creature's jaws closed they severed any of the interior heads unlucky enough to have been caught. A clap of thunder resulted. In dismay, Jackie watched as each head grew back like a cloud-hydra. Along its entire surface the Storm Elemental crackled with electricity amid the supercharged air. Only its many faceted eyes, tinted like stained-glass windows, seemed to have any real solidity. With each flap of its luminescent wings, great gusts of terrible wind ushered forth as if the creature were calling upon the very sky to do battle.

In desperation, Jackie clung to the image of the Keeper, who had rooted himself to the ground in the shadow of the Elementals. He stood precariously upright, like a weather-beaten pine tree on a desolate cliff edge.

Suddenly, a giant mass of steaming water shot skyward and Jackie took an involuntarily step backward as a spray of scalding hot water soaked her clothing and burned her skin. The Water Elemental surged ever upwards again, trying to forsake the dry riverbed to rise above the cliff walls like a tsunami. Each time it fell back only to rise higher. Overhead the Storm Elemental spun black storm clouds from its wings into the bruised sky. From its serpent's mouth a lightning bolt issued forth, striking downward into its watery brother in a shower of sparks. Out of the smoke, a colossal quivering mass emerged. As Jackie watched it seemed on the verge of taking on human characteristics, before becoming something wholly alien and unrecognizable again. From sunken primordial eyes it looked down at her.

Jackie stared dumbstruck. The small, primitive part of her brain was trying to tell her something, trying to get through so she could survive, but Jackie existed in the eye of the storm. Nothing touched her. She noticed that Nimbus was moving again, making his way toward the mountain pass with fervent strides. He held aloft his walking staff and it blazed the bright blue of a new day. As one, the Elementals moved toward him like moths to a flame.

A terrible golden beam flared and then shot out of the Light Elemental's pulsating ring. Jackie watched as it erupted close to where Nimbus walked, the blast throwing him to the ground and scorching his leaves. She held her breath. Slowly, the Keeper rose. With a wave of his aged hand a glistening shield of ice arced over his head, suspended in midair. When the blinding beam came again there was a shower of crystals from the attack, but for now his defenses held.

Jackie shook her head as if waking from a dream. Spurred to action by the attack and the Keeper's narrow escape, she looked around in sudden panic, half-expecting her animals to have fled or worse. Instead they all congregated behind her, patiently waiting for her command.

Urgently she grabbed the Orchlea which hung around her neck. "Chosen!" Jackie called into the howling wind. "Follow me!"

She leapt onto Wintra's back and then spurred the unicorn into motion. Behind her the other Chosen thundered and flew, straining for the mountain pass. With a final burst of speed, they rounded the verge of the riverbed where the Fire Elemental waited. The creature rose above them, twin slabs of flaming stone wedded to the bedrock of the twin mountains. She caught a leafy blur to her left that could only have been Nimbus. Then he was gone. On either side, the towering cliffs jutted out as if threatening to close the gap on tectonic hinges. They had no choice. They would have to go underneath the fiery Elemental to escape.

Jackie tightened her grip on Wintra's mane as they entered the great shadow thrown by the creature. Peering up she could see the animated rock of the elemental, its legs and arms twisting as the being shifted around like an earthquake, suffocating heat radiating off of it in fiery profusion. The world closed in and she tried to make herself small, insignificant. The air grew heavy. Jackie held her breath, afraid to even breathe. A moment later they were through the pass just as a fiery boulder crashed into the gap. Before them a new openness stretched out like an exaltation. Yet there was no relief. Looking back Jackie saw the Keeper before the scene was obscured by the mountain walls. On the other side of the Pass, Nimbus was spinning slowly in a circle, wrapping himself in a filament of fire, then copper blue, followed by the purest white she had ever seen, and finally shimmering gold. His scorched ice-shield was nearly melted now, and the four Elementals converged on him, damage raining down on all sides. Slowly, he stilled himself. Somehow he managed to raise his arms, alone in their midst like a sacrifice, his staff burnt down like a candle. Jackie watched in horror as the Elementals fell upon the Keeper. Then he was gone from sight, stolen from her, as she was borne away on Wintra.

"Oh Nimbus!" she sighed.

She was too dumbstruck for tears. It felt inconceivable that the Keeper was gone. Suddenly she felt very alone.

The unicorn galloped on. In time she steadied herself, reminding herself of the gift that the Keeper had given her. Ahead the Forgotten Plains beckoned, a vast rolling landscape that seemed to whisper secrets on the wind. She had no time for mysteries, only impossible tasks. Her brother needed her. Together with the Chosen she would have to find a way to get

Dustin back. She would have to do it without the help of the Keeper. Jackie knew it had been a mistake to release the Elementals. She had chosen not to listen to reason and instead gambled with all their lives. Nimbus had paid the price.

Gritting her teeth, Jackie dug her fingers into the unicorn's silky mane and watched the horizon with impatience, hardly noticing the flowers erupting like an epiphany from the barren ground with each strike of Wintra's hooves as they raced on.

CHAPTER 33

There it was again. A tinkling sound like running water or the distant peal of bells tickled his ears. Then it disappeared.

Hunter Greenwold wiped the tears from his eyes and turned slowly around. All he saw was the endless white of the cumulous cloudscape broken only by irregular dark lesions. There was no movement anywhere on the surface. Overhead the faint outline of a strange golden chariot carrying an orb of light made its way across the pale blue sky.

That's great, he thought. *Now I'm hearing AND seeing things.*

Hunter Greenwold ran a hand through his hair and reviewed his options. He was lost, without food or water, and probably hallucinating as the result of a nervous breakdown. His only grasp of reality involved finding the two missing children but he had no idea what the Arkanum was or where it might be. On top of everything else, he felt very, very tired. It felt as if he had been running forever and all his mistakes had finally caught up with him. Still, he had to keep moving. Running across the strange cloudscape had at first reminded him of childhood playing, an endless day's freedom with his friends playing games on a field of snow or across freshly mowed lawns. Now, however, the clouds swirled at his feet like quicksand as he stood still, waiting to be sucked in. It was dangerous, he reminded himself, to remain in any one place for too long. You could get lost in your dreams. Armed with this fragile new resolve, he trudged on.

That's when he heard the sound again, both strange and familiar. It came from the opposite direction he was heading. He spun around and strode toward it like a sun-beaten man who had just spotted an oasis. Wisps of cloud vapor tore past his face, obscuring his vision as he sought the source of the elusive sound. There was something about the bells or their nature that suggested he ought to remember, but the memory would not come clear. Surely, at any moment, he would catch a glimpse of whatever it was.

Driven on by panic and desperation he ran as fast as he had when he was a boy, through woods and backyards, across frozen lakes and long summer grass. He had been so wild then, so full of emotion, he remembered, even his fingernails had grown like vines and the wind had whispered things he didn't understand, until he learned to control it, to shut out the voices so he could be normal.

The clouds around him were a blur as he ran towards the fading sound. Slowly, however, his legs began to tire and the elation left him. His lungs were on fire from too many years of smoking. With one final panting step he stopped and listened.

The bells had disappeared as if they had never been.

Cursing the silence, he caught his breath and then forced himself forward. A milky veil parted before his eyes and he found himself standing on a patch of solid ground. In front of him, just out of reach, was a small white squirrel, the bane of his existence. Small blue eyes regarded him curiously. A leather cord was tied around its neck. An ancient looking silver coin dangled from it. As if on cue the animal shook its head and a tiny peal of metallic laughter issued forth.

"Damn you," Hunter snarled. "I'll show you for whom the bell tolls."

With that he pulled out his gun and pointed it at the little creature sitting peacefully in front of him. Then he squeezed the trigger.

Nothing happened.

Hunter Greenwold looked down at his weapon. Somehow it had been transformed into a harmless olive branch. There was a hole in the wood where the trigger should be.

"How did you do that, you furry freak?" he demanded.

In frustration the detective stripped away the leaves and then lobbed the stick at the creature. For one mad, hopeful second, he thought it might actually strike. Just before impact, however, the projectile became a harmless flutter of butterflies.

"What are you?" he demanded, but the fight had left him. His body sagged in defeat.

Taking this as an invitation Pence scurried closer and then sat up on his hind-legs. Hunter Greenwold stared into creature's blue eyes and considered his odds at a lunge. They weren't good. Instead he asked, almost pleaded "Where can I find the kids? Tell me."

In response Pence simply stared back like an ordinary squirrel. Almost imperceptibly, the animal tilted its head to one side and Hunter Greenwold crumpled to the ground.

CHAPTER 34

With fatherly pride, Flood watched Gaylon the Black approach across the sky as Lancelot stood at his side. There had been so many setbacks, so many doubts, but Gaylon had weathered every challenge, proving groundless any lingering concern.

When the Keeper's apprentice had shown up at the Arkanum's gate angry and confused nearly two years ago with a small bag of belongings slung over one shoulder, his arrival had not been totally unexpected. If Flood were not so cautious, he might have even called it inevitable.

From the beginning he had sensed darkness about the young man as well as a passion that went unfulfilled. It had taken only a few parlor tricks to manipulate those feelings so that a schism between Gaylon and the Keeper resulted. There had been the risky but necessary "chance" meeting in one of the cloud top valleys as well as the later secret tour of the Arkanum. But the reasons for success, as it so often happened, were more the result of luck than design. How could he have predicted that the old fool Nimbus would begin to lose his mind and wilt to inaction? All Flood did was put himself in a position to take advantage of these occurrences and steel himself for the smaller failures along the way. There had been far fewer of those than he had feared. Even the unexpected arrival of the teenage girl and small boy were now pieces of a puzzle falling into place. Of course, he had to admit, it helped to have a spy in the very heart of your enemy's kingdom.

The great black bird glided down from the sky and blew past him and his small entourage, wings spread wide, landing with a graceful flourish. Samuel Flood smiled and watched as the sleek feathers slowly metamorphosed into pale arms, talons shrunk to harmless toes, and the midnight beak became a slightly crooked nose. When the transformation was done, Gaylon stood on deck, naked as the day he arrived in the world. His bowed his head, not from shame of his appearance, but from fatigue. Each transformation drained him of some fundamental essence. He had flown a long way as well, part of it through the savagery of the Second Call. Suddenly, his legs buckled and he fell forward. Moving in a blur, Lancelot deftly caught him with one powerful arm before the assistant hit the ground. Then he carried Gaylon, as if a child, over to Flood and a wide-eyed Dustin.

"That will do," ordered Flood softly. "Put him down please."

The genetically altered ape snorted, but obeyed immediately.

Gaylon's vision swam and then steadied as he forced himself to remain upright. Passing a hand in front of his face as if brushing away invisible cobwebs, he muttered the ancient word of servitude and fealty.

"Ankra Strazatria," replied Flood dutifully. "Welcome home."

With formalities out of the way, Gaylon dressed from the pile of clothes at his feet and then eagerly began devouring the tray of bread and cheese that Lancelot gave him, thrusting his head forward with each bite as if lunging at the food.

"So this is the KeyStone," Gaylon observed once he eaten his fill. "I had almost forgotten." Flood's servant eyed the boy as if for the first time. "He seems rather...small."

When Gaylon turned away to take a final swig of berry wine, Dustin stuck his tongue out.

The Master of the Arkanum watched this exchange with apprehension. This was a dangerous time. There was always the chance that Dustin would recognize Gaylon as the hooded rider atop the clouds who had carried him away. For once there could be no mistakes. Nothing could interfere with his shaping of the boy.

"What have you seen?" he asked his servant. "What has the wind whispered in your ear?"

Gaylon wiped a hand across his mouth.

"They are coming," he said. "The girl is leading a group of the remaining Chosen across the Forgotten Plains as we speak."

"And what of the Keeper?" asked Flood quickly. *Why did the idiot mention Jackie? He would wreck everything.* "Where is he at this critical hour?"

"Lost," replied Gaylon. "I saw him surrounded by the Elementals; overwhelmed by their fury." He swallowed, visibly shaken, and then continued. "No one of flesh and blood could have survived."

Flood put a hand on Gaylon's shoulder. "Your feelings of sorrow are misplaced. The fool had his chances tenfold." Slowly his fingers tightened their grip. "But why did you not stay and see that it was finished? Even old and feeble, he is still a Keeper. Much more than mere flesh and blood."

"I returned when I saw the Blood Call as were your instructions."

"Yes, of course," conceded Flood. "You have done well. What of the Chosen?"

A smile crept along Gaylon's face. "I dispatched the sea eagle above the DreamsEnd riverbed."

"What of the others?" Flood inquired. There was an edge to his voice that was not lost on his servant. "Do they still trouble us?"

Gaylon took a deep breath and chose his words carefully.

"As you know, the girl chose well. She picked not only might but speed and intelligence as well. Even so, her small band has no chance of breaching the Arkanum's defenses, let alone of liberating the KeyStone. There's nothing—"

"The KeyStone has a name," interrupted Flood with a flash of impatience. "He is called Dustin."

In response, Dustin hugged the leg of the Master of the Arkanum and then stuck his tongue out again at the bird man.

"I meant no disrespect," Gaylon replied in surprise. "Allow me to explain…"

"Tell me. It is as simple as that. Enough of your snake tongue," warned Flood, turning the conversation back to the reconnaissance report. "How many of their party remain?"

All gamesmanship and bravado drained away from Gaylon's face. "Eight. The last of their Chosen was our eyes and ears. When I flew over, he was absent. I know not where he has gone. He does his own bidding."

Flood let this news sink in. Cold water realities flooded his grand designs before he saw things more clearly.

"It is no matter," he said at last. "He serves no one for long; he is rightfully called the Last Byzantine. But his short service was not without benefit. Now the time has nearly come. Look at the walls that surround us. Our mighty vessel would seem to be impenetrable. The ancient city of Constantinople was as elaborately defended but it fell to the Turks just the same. So I went ahead and made a few upgrades just to be on the safe side. There's nothing like going on the offensive."

Flood swept his arm down the railing of the Arkanum. What Gaylon saw left him dumbstruck. Sitting like technological gargoyles along the top of the bulwark at regular intervals were ten alabaster weapons, glistening and deadly. Each had a long-tapered barrel with silver metal rings surrounding it. A small turret mounted on the deck allowed each gun to tilt as well as rotate back and forth.

"Do you like the new modifications? It's a little something I borrowed from the late-21st Century by dipping into the time stream. They called them pulse laser cannons but we can just refer to them as our insurance policy."

Gaylon still stood speechless, a frown hiding on his face.

"I know what you're thinking," Flood told him. "If we're successful in taking back the Earth, how can this technology exist in the future? The short answer is: the normal laws don't apply in Treetops. How could they and still have this place exist? The longer answer is somewhat more complicated. Let me put it to you another way. Our great invasion hasn't happened yet. When we are victorious then the weapons will simply disappear the moment we make them impossible. Consider it a form of recycling."

The Master of the Arkanum paused.

"Of course, I couldn't have managed it without Lancelot. He did most of the heavy lifting and secured the weapons in place. They've been tested thoroughly. When our visitors arrive, we'll be ready."

Gaylon frowned with barely veiled dismay. "They seem unnecessary."

"Why the sudden interest, my pupil?" Flood growled. "Second thoughts do not become you."

"I meant only that your power is adequate enough. When they are in the shadow of the Arkanum and look up, fear will grip them and the fight will leave. They will realize it is impossible to breach your throne. If any of the Earth's Chosen happen to be spared then all the better."

"It is too late for sentimentality," Flood said taking a step toward his apprentice. "We are starting over now. You must accept this."

An uncomfortable silence fell between them. Gaylon bowed his head.

"Who will fire them all?" he asked at last. "There is only you, me, and Lancelot. With respect, I don't think your experiments in the strongholds will be much use in this capacity. They'd just as likely kill us then help defend the Arkanum."

Flood gave his pupil an icy stare but made no retort. The memory was still too recent; the failure still too painful. Instead he said simply, "There will be no need for anyone to fire the weapons. They are automated. Once activated, the weapons will fire on anything that comes within a half-mile of the ship. Nothing will stop what has already begun. Even now the hour of Earth's salvation approaches."

"Are we really that close?" Gaylon asked, his voice catching.

"Come look," Flood said not bothering to suppress a growing smile. "You too, Dustin. This is all because of you."

Gaylon walked across the deck and joined the Master of the Arkanum in gazing out over the ship's railing. Looking down, he was surprised to see the hangar-sized doors open along the length of the vessel. Animals of every size, color, and description congregated there in a state of restless agitation, but something kept the creatures from leaving and unleashing their growing fury. Surveying the animal armada, he saw that nearly every period of Earth's history was represented from the amphibious Devonian through the warming Permian, the dinosaur evolving Triassic to the asteroid-ending Cretaceous, and finally through the mammal-rich Tertiary and habitat dwindling Quaternary. Tiny creature and gigantic beast, insect and two-ton mammal, untold numbers, all pressed themselves toward the opening, straining to be released from the bowels of the Arkanum and out into the desolate landscape which surrounded the great bone-encrusted vessel.

"They've been straining ever since the Second Call," Flood explained with pride. "Soon they will be free. Only the Call of Command remains. Then I will lead our soldiers to the Portal Tree at HeartWood and down to the world below."

Gaylon looked down at Flood's Army and then out at the horizon. His hand shook slightly.

"It's too bad our troops can only have one mission," stated Flood matter-of-factly. "Then we could have taken care of the troublesome girl and her Chosen at the same time. Ah well, you can't have everything."

Flood tore his prideful gaze away from the spectacle below and reconsidered his words. He must watch what he said. Children hear things. They remember. He glanced over to where the boy stood only to find that he was gone.

"Dustin?" Flood called looking around the deck.

A quick check of the boy's room inside the Arkanum only confirmed what he already knew.

"Our careless words have betrayed us. Lancelot," directed Flood, trying to contain the urgency and frustration in his voice. "Find our guest, please, and bring him back to me unharmed."

The great ape pondered these words for a moment or two longer than a human would have. Then its enhanced neurons unlocked the meaning.

"YES," Lancelot toned and walked down the hallway, his red baseball cap nearly brushing the high ceiling. Outside, in the forever twilight sky, the terrible gash continued to widen.

CHAPTER 35

Sitting on the back of Wintra, Jackie hung on, digging her fingers into the unicorn's hoary mane as the wind whistled in her ears and the landscape rushed past. Here and there in the distance, sticking up from the ruddy ground like discarded toys of the gods, were the tops of minarets, crumbling castle walls, ruined cathedrals, and odd geometric fragments of mosaics whose pattern was lost long ago.

A cylindrical shape, metallic and alien-looking, lay partially buried in a depression they skirted. A more familiar sight appeared a short while later in the form of a metropolitan skyscraper, its art deco peak struggling to rise above the landscape. Jackie barely noticed any of it. The strangeness did not touch her. Speed was her primary concern and putting as much distance between her and what had happened. She still couldn't believe Nimbus was gone. Numbness covered her body like a shroud, filtered her perceptions and filled her reeling mind with disbelief. Even so, she couldn't escape the image of the Keeper as they rode into the Pass, leaving him behind. Surrounded by the Elementals he had looked so lost and insignificant, but also incredibly brave. Jackie wondered if she would ever have had the courage to act like that.

Despite his maddening secrecy and never-ending forgetfulness, the Keeper had also been kind. He had taken her in when she first arrived in Treetops and helped her select the Chosen so she could rescue her brother. If she hadn't appeared on his doorstep, the Keeper never would have set off for the Arkanum or gone into battle only to be... she couldn't finish the thought. If she did, it would freeze her into inaction. Harder than she intended, Jackie slapped the unicorn's side, prodding the mythical beast into an even greater gallop.

Behind her the rest of the Chosen struggled to keep pace. The terrain became more challenging, with the flat plain blending into gently rolling hills. They were on a gentle rise racing to the top. She was just about to use the *Orchlea* and tell Wintra to slow down when Jackie finally noticed the flowers. With each footfall, at the very spot of contact, an eruption of color took place, blossoming and growing before her eyes. With amazing speed, the plants spread into the gaps between the hoof-prints and covered them with vibrancy. Tendrils shot up in a vain attempt to latch onto a hoof. It was as if a new species came into being with each step. Maybe it was.

"They're beautiful!" Jackie exclaimed, too excited to use the *Orchlea*. "Even my dad could grow those."

Yes, but be careful, a bright strong voice said in her head. *They are more than they seem.*

Before she could make sense of how the unicorn had spoken to her, Jackie felt Wintra stiffen in surprise.

Hang on! The unicorn exclaimed.

Jackie barely had time to notice the crest of the hill as it suddenly fell away into splendor. Wintra dug in her hooves so they didn't tumble down the slope. With only tufts of Wintra's silky mane to grab on to and no saddle to keep her in place Jackie lurched violently forward and then left her seat, flying through the air over the unicorn's head, landing in a heap a short distance away. Immediately upon impact flowers began growing around her, covering her sore and stunned body with petals as if the Earth itself were trying to heal her.

As Jackie lay there the flowers and vegetation twined and darkened around her until they blotted out the light. It felt as if she were in a cocoon. Despite the throbbing ache in her arm and the burning sensation running down her leg, a wave of tiredness washed over her. Suddenly, nothing in the world seemed as important as closing her eyes and sleeping. Just for a little while. It would feel so good. She could forget all the pain, all the regrets, and all the fear. She could forget everything. It would be so easy. With each passing moment, her discomforts became less important. Jackie yawned and her eyelids begin to flutter and close.

Just a one little nap, she thought lazily.

Jackie sunk deeper and deeper into slumber. One by one all the things that mattered to her floated away. Even Dustin. In the midst of a wonderful dream, she felt something furry touch her cheek. It shook and prodded her. With mild irritation, she ignored it and slipped back into slumber. Then something wet and abrasive invaded her sanctuary. She felt a warm, wet tongue slide across her face like damp sandpaper. Again and again it lashed out, each time more insistent until she could take it anymore. Infuriated, Jackie opened her eyes to a blinding shaft of light. Wintra's muzzle stuck through the flowers and the unicorn looked at her quizzically. She stared back and Wintra nudged her hard.

"Okay, okay. I get the idea," Jackie said in irritation. "I'm getting up."

You fell asleep, the unicorn informed her. *Flambeau and I had much difficulty rousing you.*

"I was tired," Jackie managed.

You were in danger, Wintra replied. *These plants induce sleep so they can feed on the living. We have been here for nearly an hour trying to wake you.*

Jackie stared back not comprehending. "That can't be possible," she countered.

Then she noticed the vines that wrapped around her ankles and arms. Small suckers attached themselves to her skin. Jackie began to panic.

Don't move, the unicorn warned. *You will do harm to yourself. Allow me.*

Tipping her head down, Wintra cut the base of the vines with her horn.

You are free, but get up slowly, she cautioned.

Yawning, Jackie rose awkwardly to her feet. She felt light-headed. All of her Chosen encircled her, but they spun in blurry profusion. She reached out a hand and steadied herself against Wintra's soft flank. As the world slowed its rotation, her friends came into clearer focus. There was Rocco, and Peanut, standing over her like two colossal parents as Striker and Speedo patrolled nearby--one going clockwise and the other counterclockwise. Both stopped when she waved at them, and Speedo turned on his side and playfully greeted her. Flambeau scrambled over and poked her again, before brushing Jackie's long chestnut-colored hair out of her eyes. Then he chattered once, and gamboled off. Close by the long snake-like neck of Quake came into view. She patted his speckled head once when he lowered it. It felt vaguely like silly putty. Finally, Harry lumbered over and Jackie wrapped her arms as far as she could around the wooly mammoth's hairy leg, burying her face in its musty richness for a long intoxicating moment.

"I'm okay," she said to the gathered. "Nothing broken, I don't think. Just bruised and—"

Jackie stopped mid-sentence and grabbed self-consciously for the *Orchlea* at her neck. It wasn't there.

She scanned the ground frantically. At first, she didn't see it.

Then she spotted the horn-shaped object on the ground, partially obscured by a patch of lavender flowers. The ancient wood was broken in two. Kneeling down she cupped the remains in her hands. The fall from Wintra had robbed Jackie of her numbness. Now she became fully aware of her predicament. Nimbus was lost. She was on her own with no way to communicate with her Chosen. The battle for the Arkanum could be over the next rise for all she knew. How would she give them orders? Panic started to rise within her. Then it hit her.

Jackie stared at the unicorn in disbelief.

"You talked to me," Jackie exclaimed leveling her gaze at Wintra. "In my head. Without the *Orchlea*. I heard you!"

The unicorn did not move its mouth, but held perfectly still for several long moments. It seemed to be thinking.

An effect of the Sleep Catchers, I believe, the creature said in her mind. *The flowers can sometimes make the sleeper more sensitive to the thoughts and feelings of others. It is usually temporary. In addition, you still carry a piece of a living Keeper. For a time, it may provide some benefit. That was his hope. Then again, you may be discovering your own gifts.*

Jackie wanted to believe that was true, but she didn't have the luxury to dwell on things out of her control. She had to get Dustin back. Too much time had already been wasted. They had to get moving. Her whole body ached from her tumble, but she ignored it as best she could and swung up the side of Wintra.

From her perch atop the unicorn, Jackie and her Chosen resumed their journey, this time more cautiously. At the bottom of the slope nestled a small patch of flowers. A second glance revealed the grisly figure of a skeleton covered in vines. The unfortunate victim lay on his back in restful repose, bony fingers entwined, lost in a sleep eternal.

Jackie tore her gaze away. That could have been her if not for her Chosen. Ahead of them stretched a rolling terrain. Jackie steeled herself as they climbed a series of gently rising hills. On the last ascent she noticed that the lush grass thinned beneath their feet and then disappeared as they crested the top. Looking out across the landscape she stopped cold. She had been expecting the Arkanum, forbidding and ominous, crackling with power, defended with legions of midnight warriors. This felt worse. Down below stretched a great stone wall straight out of China's Middle Kingdom. It rose perhaps five times her height into the air, not counting the watchtowers that broke its symmetry at regular intervals. In the distance past the bulwark rose a lonely lifeless hillock, the counterpart to the green rise she stood upon.

The massive structure zigzagged across the undulating terrain like a colossal stony centipede without a beginning or an end. There would be no going around it. The rescue mission that had come so far was now effectively at a dead-end.

"Why is it *here*?" she asked Wintra in frustration.

The mythological beast pondered the question.

The Earth's memory is deep and dark, it said at last. *Who can say what it remembers and why? Perhaps the Keeper knew of such mysteries. I do not.*

Jackie gazed at the imposing structure and tried not to feel defeated.

"Let's go take a closer look," she told her Chosen.

Together they made their way to the barrier. It soon became apparent that there were no gaps or gates in the structure the closer they got. Jackie stood in front of the Great Wall, her hand close enough to touch the weathered stone, the Chosen fanning out behind her. Looking up at the towering battlement she didn't feel like a conquering hero, the head of a liberating army or an unspeakable horde. Suddenly she felt very small and helpless and far from home. She needed desperately to keep moving so she could make herself believe that hope still existed. Even so, she was nearing what she could do without rest. Her whole being was exhausted from escaping the Elementals, riding across the plains and nearly becoming plant food. With her last bit of energy, she dismounted from Wintra and then half-crumpled, half-laid down on the ground well away from the wall. The last thing she saw before closing her eyes was another glimpse of the barren hillock that rose over the barrier.

Atop the lonely knoll stooped a copse of gnarled trees, their bare branches deformed and twisted as if something had driven them mad. From the center of the small tangled wood, a black snake of smoke wound its way slowly into the stricken sky. Deep in his throat Striker growled once as the sun chariot made its way in the western sky, but Jackie was already asleep.

Perhaps the bleakness of the nearby hill prompted troubled slumber for she dreamed of something the Keeper had only mentioned in passing when she had first arrived in Treetops—the fabled city of the dead, Necrowane. Never the same twice, the elusive town appeared and then disappeared again moving across the vast landscape of Treetops in random fashion. It shone in various guises: colorful towers and minarets, squalid tenements, sandy cliff dwellings, sleepy suburbs, red-roofed medieval houses, lofty glass buildings reflecting the sun, and teepees huddled on open plains. The lucky traveler who spied Necrowane would be reunited with vanished friends and relatives. The dead would live again, if only for a moment.

In her dream, Jackie roamed both near and far in her quest to find the fabled city. Always she was a half-step too late. On a windswept highland wet with rain she finally found Necrowane. It glittered on a nearby rise as a small and oddly familiar Midwestern town. The houses had no yards. Instead they were stacked on top of each other. Every color of the rainbow shimmered in the dwellings that stood like boxes of light. She ran toward the strange city. Faces peered out of windows, motionless as statues. Desperately, Jackie dashed from one aperture to another looking at each stranger in turn. Details grew clearer. A curtain blew open and then another.

Jackie stopped. She was floating in midair.

Her mother looked out at her from a seventh floor living room window. She gazed at Jackie, a sad sweet smile and waved. Jackie couldn't tell whether it was in greeting or farewell.

"Mother!" she cried.

In an adjacent window her father stood. He looked at her with worry and concern, his emotions unguarded. A pang of guilt seized her. He put his hand to the glass and spoke urgently, but she couldn't hear what he said.

"I can't hear you," she yelled. "What is it?"

She watched his mouth move. There were only two words. She didn't need to hear to understand. He was saying the same thing over and over again.

"Come home. Come home. Come home."

It felt overwhelming to see her father and mother together again. She wanted to remember this scene forever so she closed her eyes. When she opened them, the window was empty and the curtain closed. Her father was gone. In the next room her mother stood looking out, a smile spreading across her features, an outstretched hand frozen in place.

An unbelievable sadness rose up inside Jackie to be so close and yet so far away. She felt a heaviness take root. It pushed her down and tipped her over an invisible edge. She was falling through the clouds. There was nothing she could do.

Still screaming, Jackie watched as the city winked away.

CHAPTER 36

Hunter Greenwold lay on a soft bed of clouds and wondered what had happened.

Whatever the squirrel had done, it had not robbed him of his senses or rendered him unconscious. There had been no pain, only a momentary tingling sensation. He still had awareness of himself and the world.

Lying on the ground, still stunned, he could see the little white-haired rodent looking over at him with feigned innocence.

With a wrinkle of its nose, the squirrel scampered closer to him, its movements cautious, and sat up. Its blue eyes did not blink. The creature seemed to be waiting as if it had all the time in the world.

Rage flared within the detective. He wanted nothing more than to choke the rodent with his bare hands. But when he reached out nothing happened. His arm would not move. His fingers would not clench. Panic and confusion coursed through his veins. He stood there immobile, effectively helpless. A scream rose in his throat and then died away unuttered.

Now the little rodent moved more boldly and without hesitation. With a speed that shocked Hunter, it bounded on top of him and then sat on his chest peering down just inches from his face. An involuntary gasp hissed past Hunter's lips as he waited for the animal to lunge. The creature was far heavier and more powerful than he would have imagined.

The moments passed and a premonition that Hunter couldn't name grew within him. Something waited to be shared. He continued to stare into the creature's deep azure eyes, unable to turn his head or look away.

Without warning, the world suddenly shifted and reality spun. He felt sick and unmoored. As if in response, a warm glow flooded his mind. A hidden door opened and his vertigo subsided like a fire doused by a healing rain. Later Hunter wouldn't be able to tell if he peered through the opening or the contents of the other place reached out to him. In the end, it didn't really matter. Suddenly, he was immersed in a memory not his own, an overlay to the cloud-top world that still surrounded him, and he watched in unmoving amazement as a chaotic scene unfolded.

People dressed in strange garb ran through an ancient street. There was no order to their movements. They fled in all directions in blind panic. Men, women, and children sought shelter that Hunter somehow knew was no longer possible. Mighty walls ran along the perimeter of the cobblestone avenue and then swept out of sight. They seemed impervious to time.

Standing in complete contrast to the disorder raging around him, the wall exuded a reassuring permanence; fortifications of this magnitude could never fail. They would never fall. Then he noticed the gaping holes, small in comparison to the structure itself, but openings nonetheless. Defenders valiantly tried to plug them with debris, but there were too many. As he watched, another thundering cannonball rocked the great wall, opening new wounds. Through these gaps, colorfully clad soldiers of the Sultan swept inside, hacking to pieces the screaming citizens of Constantinople. Imperial troops fell back in disarray, the surviving members regrouping and making a stand at a narrow bend in the road. Swords on both sides flashed and Hunter watched in horror as human beings fell like cut wheat. The invaders were greater in number but the defenders had the strategic advantage and had the added benefit of necessity. If they didn't hold here, the so-called City of God, already over one thousand years old, would be lost. Desperation drove them to do the impossible. They held back the Sultan's soldiers, killing them to the last man in the name of their Lord with an inhuman vengeance. Winded, spent to the marrow of their bones, the bloodied survivors stood over the carnage and watched in dismay as five thousand more of the Sultan's elite soldiers, scimitar-wielding Janissaries, bloodlust burning in their eyes, poured through the inner wall. None of the imperial soldiers had any illusions that they would prevail this time or that reinforcements were on their way. The sound of the Sultan's great cannons continued to echo throughout the city, and what little remained of the Emperor's guard was occupied elsewhere trying to stay alive. There would be no help today. Any ordinary person would have given up. After a siege of more than five weeks, the defenders were weak beyond endurance. Solemnly they raised their swords and donned their helmets one last time as the equally fatigued Ottoman troops approached. Only the nearness of victory invigorated the Turks. Behind them a bearded man, adorned in golden mail with phrases from the Koran stitched across his outer vest, strode proudly.

"Allahu Akbar!" he shouted to his army. "God is great. Go on my falcons, march on my lions!"

Within moments the first line of Christian defenders had fallen. The remaining members faltered, and fell back in fear and confusion. It was at that moment, when Byzantium's flame flickered weakly, soon to be gutted, that the Emperor Constantine XI and his retinue appeared on the steep streets above, attempting to get to the Horn and escape from the city. The Emperor was dressed in palace white, but his crown and jewelry were noticeably absent so as not to attract attention. When Constantine saw the battle below, however, he turned his mount, and ignoring the protestations of his court, galloped down the uneven stone, holding an already bloodied blade in his grasp. A cry went up from the Ottoman soldiers when they saw the Emperor approach. Reaching his beleaguered men ahead of the attacking soldiers, Constantine clasped the shoulder of the nearest guard and raised his sword higher. His thin lips twisted into a grim smile as he urged his horse forward. The slanting uneven stone was slick with blood from both sides, however, and his faithful mount lost its footing, and before any blows could be dealt, Constantine was thrown from his falling horse.

That he didn't hit the ground was somewhat of a surprise to the watching Hunter who had quite reasonably assumed that gravity worked the same in the fifteenth century as it did the twenty-first. It took the detective a moment to spot the unexpected. In mid-air the last Emperor of Byzantium's body shifted and wavered. Then in the blink of an eye it simply disappeared, forgotten amid the confusion of the battle.

When the last sword had been swung and the defenders of the city lay dead, no one immediately realized that Constantine was not among them. The conquering Ottoman army (like many armies before and since) was too full of pent-up violence and plunder. In frenzy, the Sultan's soldiers swept through the Gate of Charisius towards the Emperor's palace. Like a wave of history, they washed over the statue of Justinian and then approached the Column of Constantine, near the great church of St. Sophia. According to legend, an enemy would penetrate the city only to this point and no farther. An avenging angel, it was said, would descend, fiery sword in a milky-white hand, and drive the attackers out.

There were no miracles on this day of May 29, 1453. The Byzantine Empire, continuing the legacy of ancient Rome, had endured for more than 1,000 years, but now that story was finally finished. Many of its people were killed or enslaved. Its remaining treasures were taken or destroyed.

Later that afternoon, the twenty-one-year-old Sultan Mehmet entered the city again, this time accompanied by a formal contingent of his viziers and ulemas as yellow and green banners flew in pageantry.

In front of the procession Mehmet's crack commander held a spear aloft and skewered on the end of it was a prized bloodied head. The Turks would have been surprised to learn that it wasn't Constantine's. Amid the shell of the broken city, crawling among the fallen, a small white squirrel emerged from under the Emperor's horse unnoticed and scurried away, his new instincts leading him to a hidden world.

Hunter looked on, trying vainly to follow the fleeing creature but the scene dimmed and faded before his eyes. Soon Byzantium vanished completely and only Treetops remained. The white squirrel was gone from his chest. Without thinking he rubbed his eyes and stretched his arms, realizing with a start that his body was his own again. Slowly, he picked himself from off the ground.

"So now you understand, perhaps at least a little," said a dignified voice from behind him.

There, standing in a bejeweled robe and gazing at Hunter with bold blue eyes was the Emperor Constantine XI.

CHAPTER 37

Dustin ran down into the depths of the Arkanum.

His heart beat wildly as fear and anger coursed through his veins. Flood had talked as if he had meant to hurt his sister. How could that be? It made no sense. Panic and confusion all battled each other in his head as he descended the great stone steps. After all this time Jackie was finally coming, but now he was scared for her and he didn't know what to do about it except run away. The narrow staircase wound ever downwards into the deepening shadows. Hallways split off from open archways of stone, but none of them looked familiar. He had long since left behind the areas of the ship that he knew. With each spiraling revolution the torches that burned in the walls sputtered and shrank until they were little more than dying embers. The coldness crept into him as the light retreated.

Dustin slowed his descent, afraid he would fall in the growing darkness. He took another step. He stood on flat stone in front of a grand archway. The stairs had ended. He was at the bottom. Goosebumps radiated down his arms and legs. When he exhaled, his breath clouded the air. In front of him stood a tall wooden door outlined in the fading light. It was plain except for the intricately carved flower adorning the center panel. The bud was closed, its petals pressed tightly together. It took Dustin a moment to realize there wasn't a knob or handle.

"I know you are there. I can hear you. Can smell you," said a deep simian voice echoing from above. "Bad boy to run away. Don't be afraid. I am coming."

Dustin looked up at the stairs he had just come down. Already he heard the heavy footsteps of Flood's servant Lancelot coming towards him. They were still a long way off but getting closer.

Standing there alone, Dustin very much wished that there was someone he could go to and wrap his arms around, and they would in turn hold him tight, keeping him safe. He thought of his mother, smiling as she gently tucked him to bed every night. He loved his mother and missed her very much. It made him sad to think that she was gone and wasn't coming back.

"I am al-most down," toned Lancelot in primitive syllables. Dustin saw the great ape's shadow slice across the torch-lit stairs above him and heard the heavy padded steps as they worked their way closer to where he stood.

Dustin thought of his father and their tickle fights and all the games that they played. He smiled as he remembered rising up on his dad's shoulders each evening before bedtime and being carried around the house like royalty, his father bowing low beneath each doorway. If only his father were here. He would protect him.

The torch in the nearby wall was nearly out now, but enough light still shone that Dustin could see the massive form of Lancelot as he descended the last steps. He shuddered and then turned away.

Finally, he thought of his sister and how she used to hold his hand before crossing the street together and would play tag with him in the back yard. Sometimes Jackie would read him a bedtime story. His favorite was called *The Fisherman and the Genie*.

Staring at the closed door, he thought of the most magical words that he knew.

"Open sesame," he whispered.

The door remained stubbornly closed.

"There you are," Lancelot said coming into full view. Flood's servant looked frightful in the failing light. "You bad. Should be punished."

"Abracadabra," pleaded Dustin banging on the door. "Pretty, pretty please with sugar on top?"

His sister would have told him to ask once and not to beg. "Just say please," she would say when he demanded something. "Ask nicely, okay?" All he wanted was to go home. And so he reached out his hand and touched the center of the carved flower. "*Please*," he thought.

"Got you!" bellowed Lancelot, grabbing Dustin by the arm.

The creature's grip was like a vise squeezing pain out of Dustin's thin soft arm. He felt himself being pulled away as effortlessly as his father had lifted him up on his shoulders, having only a moment to notice the inlaid flower petals in the door slowly unfolding. From each side and from the top and bottom the door retracted. Bright sunlight grew from a speck in the center to a brilliant golden shaft.

Lancelot released his hold on Dustin. "What did you do?" exclaimed the ape in surprise.

Where the door had been now yawned an open portal. Warm sunlight spilled out onto the cold stone, inviting him in. Dustin gazed into a room so vast the walls were obscured by hanging vines and the ceiling was lost in shadow. Instead of a floor a lush meadow grew underfoot with a sparkling stream meandering across. He could hear birdsong in the trees and smell the wildflowers that grew with abundance everywhere he looked. From the threshold green grass grew. He took a step forward.

"No," commanded Lancelot, but Dustin barely heard, he was so mesmerized. Then he raced into the dazzling world.

Flood's servant appeared to fight down a quiver of conflicting emotions before finding its purpose. After a moment's hesitation the ape leaped across the threshold, his great arms extended to snatch Dustin back. But Dustin was one step ahead. He had already escaped into the green world beyond. The door shut behind him just as Lancelot thundered against it.

CHAPTER 38

It is time. Awake, an insistent voice in her head demanded. *Meet the day and the destiny you make.*

Slowly, Jackie opened her eyes. To her surprise, she found herself staring up into the impatient face of Flambeau. The monkey jumped up and down making shrieking noises that brought her fully conscious in record time. Wintra stood next to him.

It is good to see you finally up, the unicorn continued telepathically.

About time! About time! About time! Flambeau exclaimed over and over again in her head.

Bewildered, Jackie got to her feet. The rest of her Chosen crowded around her and soon their combined voices rang in her skull.

NOWWWW, urged Peanut, Rocco, Harry, and Quake, in a slow and deep cadence. *We---must---go.*

Yes, Yes. Time to swim, to fly, to walk, to run, clicked Speedo circling overhead like a slippery trapeze artist.

Wintra's crystalline voice joined the chorus. *It is high time. The sun chariot races ahead of us.*

A hot breath steamed in her ear as Striker pressed close. *I am hungry,* the cougar growled between her ears. *I need to eat.*

Still the voices of her Chosen came, crowding out her own thoughts until she fell to her knees with her hands over her head. Too much information rained down on her. There was no way to sort it all out. She began to flounder.

Enough! she screamed to the inside ruckus. *Be quiet. You can't all speak at the same time.*

At once her Chosen obeyed. Silence filled her being and she drank it in as if it were precious water. Another minute passed. Slowly, she let down her defenses and stood up. Behind her was the wall and beyond that the lonely hill.

Is this better? Like this? Speedo quipped. *I don't have to talk. Not at all. If you wish for silence than silence you shall have. I can stop if you want me to. If that's what you really want, I can do that.*

But even as the dolphin spoke, the thought faded from Jackie's mind until one by one the presence of the Chosen dropped away and her mind became her own again. Jackie breathed in the tranquility. Despite her relief, she couldn't help but feel a bit cut-off. What if they never returned or she didn't learn how to control it?

It has still not taken root, murmured Wintra as if an echo from far away. Then the fragment dissolved into nothing.

Alone again, Jackie took a step toward the massive wall.

"We march," she told Wintra.

The unicorn closed its eyes momentarily and the rest of the Chosen fell in line.

Taking the lead, Jackie walked up to the towering barrier with her animal entourage trailing behind. Even Quake was dwarfed by the size of the fortification. Somewhere, at the back of her memory, Jackie remembered hearing that the Great Wall could be seen by astronauts from space. She wasn't surprised. Looking up at it she had no idea how they would get through. Speedo could probably swim over it, of course, and Flambeau might be able to climb over, but what about the rest? Then she saw the cracks that ran down the length of the stone like varicose veins. No light spilled through them but many were deep, the result of earthquakes or perhaps ancient attacks. If only she had a bulldozer or a battering ram. Then it hit her. *I do!* An elephant, a black rhino, and a wooly mammoth were perfect for the job. Out of the corner of her eye, she saw Quake's long serpentine tail. It was ready-made for knocking big things down.

Turning to face Wintra and the rest of the animals, she felt a smile spread across her face.

"Chosen," she said. "You are now a wrecking crew. Here's what we're going to do."

When Jackie had finished explaining and when all the animals were in their places, she took one final look around. The first wave of attackers was ready. Harry, Rocco, and Peanut snorted and bellowed in anticipation. Behind them Quake looked on, oblivious to the commotion.

Jackie felt a lump grow in her throat. This was it. If they failed here, the mission died with them. They had to get through.

"Okay then," she began. "Let's see how great this wall really is."

The trio of animals on the front line began stamping their feet in unison. The elephant lifted his trunk and trumpeted.

"Rocco, Harry, Peanut," Jackie commanded. "Knock it down!"

In one thundering wave of destruction the three great beasts charged across the open expanse toward the barrier. Jackie held her breath. Even Flambeau the monkey stopped his incessant chattering. Speedo hovered in hopeful silence. Then the three animals smashed into the wall. The world shuddered. Stony debris flew everywhere. Through the cloud of dust Jackie tried in vain to see whether the effort had been a success. Finally, the scene cleared and she spied the wall. It still stood. No hole marred its surface. Jackie fought back tears and the growing fears that rose within her like a fluttering of dark wings. Looking closer, however, she realized that the crack running down the wall had widened considerably and new fissures spread out across the ancient surface. She almost allowed herself to hope.

"Again," she instructed her four-legged warriors who still stamped their feet in front of the stubborn obstacle. "Take it down!"

Once more the beasts charged and once more the Earth shook with the violent collision. This time the cracks resulting were larger, almost the width of a man's hand, and where several of them met, there was a hole perhaps three feet across.

"Again!" she commanded.

More slowly this time the animals obeyed as they shrugged off the effects of their violent encounter. Within a few minutes they were in place.

"Break through!" she called as they erupted from the starting line.

For a third time Rocco, Peanut, and Harry ran into the impregnable wall. A third time the air split in a concussion of sound and Jackie waited impatiently for the results. This time she was not disappointed. They had indeed broken through, but stony debris littered the approach to the hole and piled up at the mouth. When cleared, she hoped the ragged archway would accommodate all of the Chosen. Until then, there was work to be done. She looked at her Chosen for ideas and let out a small cry. Harry still stood solidly in front of the wall and bobbed his head as if taking pride in his work, but Peanut and Rocco both stumbled around as if drunk. Suddenly, Peanut toppled over and landed heavily on his side.

Jackie rushed to his side.

"What's wrong?" Jackie asked putting a hand on the elephant's thick skin.

For a few long moments the elephant did not answer. Jackie could only watch the creature's labored breathing and listen to his trumpeting shrills of pain. Then Peanut spoke directly in her mind.

Need rest, the great creature told her. *Need...* Then the thoughts fragmented like static from a fading radio signal.

Looking at the elephant Jackie shuddered as she noticed the bruises blossoming across the animal's mottled skin. Ribbons of red from the impacts glistened wet on his knees and head.

"Oh Peanut," she moaned. "I'm so sorry I hurt you," Jackie said out loud. "I should have had you kick with your hind legs instead. I don't know what I was thinking."

Nearby, Rocco seemed as if he was doing better. No longer so unsteady on his feet, the creature had come over to check on his friend.

"He's going to be okay," Jackie told the rhino, but there was a pleading quality to it that she couldn't mask.

Not your fault, Rocco told her unexpectedly. *That was a tough nut to crack.*

When Jackie finally got the double meaning she smiled in spite of herself. Peanut was indeed tough, but only up to a point. Everything has its limits. The last push through the wall would need reinforcements. Without hesitation she made the call like a football coach on the sidelines facing fourth down and inches.

Get in there, she instructed Quake. *We need to clear that debris. Use that tail of yours and give it a few good whacks.* But be careful.

Untroubled, the seismosaurus continued chewing whatever was in its mouth as if nothing else existed. If it had heard her the dinosaur gave no indication. Jackie was about to have Wintra relay her command when slowly, like the gears of some rusted contraption, the dinosaur moved its tree-trunk-like legs. Ponderously, Quake walked towards the barrier. Each time it took a step the ground shook beneath Jackie's feet. Even the wall seemed to tremble at the creature's approach. When Quake was finally in position, Jackie made ready to give the instruction again, thinking the dim-witted beast would need a reminder, but there was no need. Without warning Quake's great tail snapped back and then smashed into the fallen debris. Many of the pieces shattered, tumbling away to reveal a clear opening through the wall. A spiderweb of cracks ran through the archway above, but for the time being it seemed stable. Even Quake, she reasoned, should be able to squeeze through underneath.

"Great job!" Jackie exclaimed. "I knew you could do it".

I'm slow, but I get the job done, Quake replied with a touch of pride in her head.

A guilty pang shot through Jackie and she looked away.

"Chosen," she called to her animals. "There is no time to waste. We can't rest yet. We must go through the wall now."

Leading the way, she stepped around and then over the ancient rocks and stones that littered the approach. In front of her, the gaping hole in the wall beckoned with a vision of what awaited. The copse of dead trees she had seen earlier was framed in the rough stone window. Now Jackie could make out greater detail. In the center of the lifeless forest was a bare patch, glowing faintly. From a point at the top of the hill, black smoke still rose, but it was thicker now, as if the recent violence at the barrier had somehow awakened a sleeping fire. Passing through the archway on foot she felt her heart quicken with excitement and dread. Above her head a dark bridge of stone was all that remained of that section of the wall. Moments later she emerged into the open air on the other side. The ground here sloped gradually upwards toward the blight of trees above. Spotty vegetation littered the landscape around them, but the plants looked like they were clinging to life rather than thriving. Closer to the dead woods, Jackie could see nothing growing at all.

Each of the Chosen made it through the opening in turn. Jackie watched with trepidation as Peanut labored over the rocks. She could see by the tentative way he moved that the elephant was in pain. When he finally made it through, Jackie breathed a sigh of relief. Only Quake remained. The dinosaur approached the wall and began slowly moving through the debris field. The shattered edges of the wall loomed on either side. It would be a very tight fit.

"You can do it," Jackie said encouragingly.

Halfway through the archway, however, the colossal creature got stuck. The sauropod, perhaps the biggest creature ever to walk the Earth, began shaking its body and moving its tail frantically from side to side. Soon ominous cracks appeared in the barrier and large chunks of stone began to break away. Free, but still fearful, Quake stampeded through the tight opening with more speed than Jackie would have thought possible, bringing more sections of the wall, including the bridge above, toppling down.

"Look out!" Jackie yelled to the rest of the animals who were gathered next to the wall. "*Get clear!*"

Each creature obeyed her command, distancing themselves from the falling chunks of wall and the runaway dinosaur. Everyone made it to safety, or so she thought. Then she saw Peanut. Jackie watched in dismay as the elephant, still ailing, tried to save himself. He was turning slowly, attempting to follow the others, when a huge slab of wall came crashing down. Jackie saw it all in terrible slow-motion, helpless to do anything. One moment he was there and the next he disappeared in a thunderous clap. Jackie stood transfixed, staring at the spot. There was no sign of Peanut beneath the stony rubble, now an unexpected grave. She listened for his cries of help, for anything, but there was only a fatal silence.

Alone in her shock and grief Jackie felt the tug of the others, pulling her into a mental embrace. Hurting, suffering, sad beyond words, the rest of her Chosen opened themselves to her and she took strength from the union. Each creature reached out to one another and was comforted in return. Quake was especially grieved, his usually dim intelligence now afire with primal guilt. For the first time, Jackie became aware of the mental signature that made each of her Chosen unique and precious. In that moment she knew she would do anything for them. They were all in this together. If only there was a way to undo such losses. *If only,* she thought. Amidst the communion of shared anguish, she felt the absence of Peanut like a missing tooth. Her heart ached.

Eventually the sharing came to an end and she found herself in a circle with her Chosen. They formed a ring around their fallen comrade. Unsure of what to do, Jackie walked over to Peanut's resting place and laid her hand upon the stone. The promise she made resonated in the remaining Chosen. "Thank you for your service. I'm sorry. I'm so sorry. I will do better. I will never forget you."

What more could she say? It was her fault that Peanut was dead. If he hadn't been injured ramming the wall, the elephant would have made it through. Feeling awkward, Jackie turned and trudged up the slope toward the copse of trees as if she were going to her own execution. Peanut wasn't the first of her Chosen to die since the rescue mission began, of course. Iggy had perished high above the riverbed scouting for danger, but the injured elephant had been the first since she had truly taken over leadership from Nimbus, the first since she had been on her own with the Chosen. It was her decision, and no one else's. She had ordered the repeated battering of the Great Wall. That action had weakened the barrier, but it had also injured Peanut so that he could not react quickly enough.

How many more? she wondered.

At the edge of the dead woods, Jackie stopped as if balancing on a precipice. Ahead of her, only a few steps away, she felt a presence she could not explain. A visceral dread seeped into her bones as if blown from the assemblage of skeletal branches. The chill sapped her strength and numbed her mind, extinguishing what remained of her wavering courage. Still, she paused only a moment, looking back over her shoulder to make sure that her remaining Chosen were following. The action was unnecessary. The echoes of the communion still lingered in her mind, and although she couldn't hear their individual thoughts, Jackie could tell without seeing that they were all waiting for her. That connection, that tenuous support, was all that enabled her to carry on.

Purposefully, Jackie stepped into the forest. Immediately the wind howled at her with increased ferocity as if she had inadvertently opened a door to a frozen landscape. She staggered forward another step or two, brushing the hair from her eyes before she realized that something fundamental had changed. For the first time since she arrived in Treetops, there was something close to darkness.

All around her, the great black trees stood engulfed in shadows. Feeble light fell through the branches, but it did little more than highlight the eeriness of the place. Cautiously she stepped forward, leading her animal entourage. Ahead of them, a narrow path wound through the threatening trees like a lifeline, climbing ever higher, out of reach. A thin mist snaked around her feet. Several times as she walked through the dim forest, Jackie tripped on hidden roots that twisted across the desolate forest floor. Everything about the place reminded Jackie of death or impending doom. She felt certain with a sudden chill that if they wandered from the path, they would be lost. The Chosen made their way through the dead grove, with the smaller creatures nimbly finding their way while the larger ones did the best they could. A crash sounded behind her and she turned to see another lifeless tree, ancient beyond measure, tumbling down in Quake's wake.

If someone is here, we will not be surprising them, she thought.

Although the forest did not seem expansive from the outside, once inside it seemed much bigger. The effect reminded Jackie of Highveil Park. Distance, as well as time, had worked differently there. Yet this was not quite the same. Here she needed an imagination to see the beauty. Looking up at the leafless branches she imagined what it must have been like long ago. It appeared as if this had once been a young grove of Earth Trees, but for some reason had fallen into decay. Perhaps the life-giving magic had left, replaced with something darker.

A familiar landmark came into view through the mottled trunks. A column of dark smoke wound its way up into the sky growing more massive as they approached.

To Jackie, it reminded her of a spectral tree, rootless and without form, the spirit of the forest finally passing on. The trees ahead thinned and the wind died as if the world was holding its breath. The air grew colder. Her breath came out in ghostly bursts. Pushing through the last of the lifeless sentinels she emerged into a clearing ringed by deadwood the color of bone. She half-expected to find a wizard's humble dwelling or a ruined castle. Instead she saw a high slab of exposed rock the color of magma. Lying on it was a dragon. Thick sooty clouds emanated from its terrible nostrils like smoke from a bellows.

Jackie stood transfixed and terrified.

The creature's eyes were closed, thank goodness. The great beast appeared to be sleeping, lost in dreams ancient and dark, a twisted grimace curled on its lips.

Jackie exhaled quietly, trying to calm herself.

Stay here, Jackie communicated to her Chosen. *I'm going to take a closer look.* Then she crept across the barren rise until she was in the shadow of the rocks above.

The dragon's scales were differing hues of red. Each glittered with a dazzling fire all their own, a treasure unto itself, somehow magically transformed from hoard to hide by some devilish alchemy. Rows of deadly teeth, worn but still sharp, lined the beast's gaping maw and its talons were as large as scimitars. Black leathery wings draped over the rock like a demon's bed sheets. The air in the dead grove reeked of sulfur. Pungent and acidic, the stench burned Jackie's lungs until she could no longer stifle her cough. The broken sound cracked the silence and Jackie held a hand up to her mouth in horror, looking at the dragon in dismay.

In response the great beast snorted once and shifted menacingly before resuming its uneasy slumbering.

When she had made certain she wasn't going to become a human s'more, Jackie inched forward just far enough to see beyond the rocky outcropping atop which the dragon lay. Down below, a faint path cut through the deadwoods and out onto a vast plain. Fighting was out of the question. To get to the path they would all have to sneak past the scaly creature. Her larger Chosen could not pass undetected. Nervously, Jackie looked around for another way. Next to the slab was a thin spindle of a tower with crude steps much too small for a dragon ever to use, but they seemed ideal for humans.

Carefully, Jackie made her way back to her Chosen. She was already reconsidering the plan she had made. It was dangerous and reckless, but it also seemed to be the only way to keep them all moving toward the Arkanum and out of harm's way. Come what may, the animals that had pledged themselves would not suffer. Sensing that Jackie needed them, the Chosen came and gathered around her in the lifeless woods. When they were all present, she spoke to them through her mind, telling them what she would do.

It is madness! the Chosen protested in a chorus of disagreement. *Never! All for one and one for all. Couldn't we simply go around? A dragon is not a sleeping child one can awaken and comfort. Have you lost all sense? Death and pain will be the result. Let us fight!*

I know, Jackie admitted. *It seems a terrible thing to do. But the path out of these woods is right behind that dragon. There is no other way. Even Quake is no match for the beast and these woods won't let us pass. You know it as well as I. If we leave the path we're lost. I can feel it. These woods will never let us go. But if we can get past this guardian, the plains Nimbus spoke of are in sight. The Arkanum must be near!*

You know we will serve you as you bid us, Wintra said silencing a rising wave of protests. *Yet this task you have set before yourself is fraught with danger beyond life and limb. This dragon guards no mortal treasure of glittering gold. Before you can pass you must surely give something up. Have you considered what that might be?*

I have little to give and much to lose, Jackie replied.

That is the dilemma, the unicorn said. *Better if it was the other way around.*

"I have to try," Jackie whispered.

And with that she left the protective circle and walked through the dismal trees and out onto the hilltop where the dragon still slept atop its high stone slab. More slowly now, she climbed the weathered stone steps that were cut into the side of the natural spire. Upwards she went one foot after the other, sweat dripping from her brow, until she finally made it to up to the top. Luminescent scales littered the rough stone floor. Swallowing her fear, Jackie stepped cautiously around them so she wouldn't waken the creature. When she was close to the edge, Jackie allowed herself one glance back at her Chosen. How fragile they seemed to her from this vantage point, surrounded by deathly trees, and yet they also seemed so brave, so impervious to doubt or betrayal. Seeking comfort, she reached out to them, but was met with silence. She felt cut-off and alone in this strange place. Whatever she had to do, she would have to do it by herself. Turning around she faced the dragon from her own rocky precipice.

Jackie stood unbearably close. The creature lay perhaps ten yards away on a slab of stone scattered with bones. Jackie watched the terrible rhythm of the rise and fall of its scales culminating in a great blast of air from the sleeping dragon that swept across the open face of the tower. When the exhalation first touched Jackie, she steeled herself for a burning heat, expecting her clothing to char and hair to ignite. Instead an icy coldness touched her like an early frost. She shivered. Smoke tendrils snaked upward from the beast's nostrils into the sunless sky like the memory of fire. Jackie tried very hard not to look at its teeth.

"Hello," Jackie choked in greeting.

Even before she had finished speaking, however, the great

head of the dragon snapped upright and its terrible eyes opened, settling upon her small and insignificant frame. If she had wanted, which she certainly did not, Jackie could have reached out and touched one of the long whiskers that dangled from the creature's armored chin.

"Sleeping I was, but not unaware," the dragon rumbled. "I have been waiting. To pass you must pay the price."

Jackie froze in complete terror waiting for a searing blast of fire to envelope her. When it didn't come and when she realized that her heart was still beating, Jackie decided to say something back.

"Tell me the price and I will pay it," she said, her voice a mere whisper.

The dragon smiled. Jackie did not like it.

"I exist to dream," the great creature explained. "When the world was still new, my brothers and sisters dreamed of the fire of creation. We did not yet know death and the dreaming was without end. When the first stars finally cooled, we found new dreams, alive with the kindled potency of passion and possibilities. The heavens were open to us, limitless and inexhaustible. Slowly, however, the darkness grew and time claimed us one by one. I am the only one that remains. You cannot imagine what that is like. For untold millennia I have slept upon this primordial bedrock and dreamed the dreams of those who have come before you. But humans are such small, short-lived things. Nothing you do or desire lasts long. When these feeble offerings grow faint, my dreams quickly turn to nightmares that no one will come, and that the dreaming will end. Without dreams I am like the space between the stars; cold, dark, alone and forgotten. My flames have grown cold. I have been too long without nourishment. To pass you must give me a gift."

"What kind of gift?" Jackie asked.

"A dream, of course," said the dragon, its black wings unfurling behind it ominously. "A wish. But it must be one of your most precious and powerful. Not just any old one will do. It must be your secret heart's desire. The gift must be a dream that once given, leaves a hollow hole of emptiness in your soul. It must be one that you will regret giving away every day for the rest of your life."

Jackie thought about what the dragon was asking.

"What if I refuse?"

"Then I will eat you and your friends," the dragon said almost sadly, "devouring your flesh, sucking out your marrow and spitting out your bones. It will sustain me for a short time, for even dreaming dragons need to eat. I'll feast, but it would be a poor substitute."

"So you'd rather have one of my dreams," Jackie ventured.

"Much more," agreed the dragon amiably. "Do we have a deal then?"

"Do I have a choice?"

"One always has a choice", the dragon replied.

"Tell me what to do."

"Think of the dream, your secret wish, clearly in your mind and when the time comes let it go. That is very important. Do not resist or fight. Give it to me freely."

Jackie closed her eyes until she found the dream she wanted, the one that was dearer to her than any other. It was one she had never chosen, but now could not imagine living without. Despite her dire need, it seemed inconceivable that she had to give it away. Jackie became increasingly aware of the dragon and the bargain they had made. Time seemed precious to her now as she shivered on the rocky tower. Everything seemed so fragile and worthy of protection.

"Will it hurt?"

"Only later," the creature told her truthfully. "And then I'm afraid it will hurt quite a lot."

But these were words, slippery and hard to hold on to in the present and so they slid off her.

"Okay, I guess I'm ready," Jackie said.

Without warning, the dragon lunged out with jaws wide open straight toward her. There was no way for Jackie to avoid seeing the rows of sharp teeth that lined the dragon's terrible mouth. In one horrible instant her head was engulfed by the scaly guardian. Suffocating darkness pressed down upon her and Jackie could see tiny ice-blue flames flickering at the bottom of the dragon's throat. Yet the creature did not bite down. She was still alive! The creature was waiting. Then Jackie remembered. She thought desperately of her dream. In her mind's eye, her mother lived and breathed again. She smiled and said something to Jackie, but the words didn't matter. What mattered was that her mother was fine and always would be. Then she forced herself to do what she had promised and it was even harder than in the stinky hospital room with her mom. She had to say goodbye. With tears flowing down her cheeks she did as the dragon had instructed and offered up her gift.

True to the creature's word it didn't hurt. There was no pain, only a moment of tearing like a stubborn tooth that won't quite come free. Then a wave of cold chilling blandness washed over her. Jackie opened her eyes. She was standing on top of the tower, her hands clenching the rock as if it were the last thing in the world she owned. In front of her the dragon lay sleeping again, a smile of complete contentment spreading across its serpentine features. Heat radiated from the dragon now and bright yellow flames flickered in its nostrils. The whole slab of stone where the dragon lay began to glow red like a pyre. Slowly, as if she were stumbling from an accident scene, Jackie made her way through the graveyard of beautiful gems.

"Take a souvenir," the dragon sighed, one great eye fluttering open before falling closed once more.

Pretty, Jackie thought numbly, and picked a scale up, cradling it in her arms like a baby. Then she went back down the tower steps to her Chosen.

The unicorn was the only one to see her return; all the others were fast asleep. Dimly, Jackie wondered how long she had been gone.

You are safe, Wintra said, the relief evident in his voice. *And you come bearing a gift. This is most fortuitous and rare. Dragons, as you can well imagine, are loathe to part with anything. This one must have been suitably impressed or grateful. What did you give in return?*

Jackie stared back, her brow creasing in concentration. "I don't remember. Must not have been a big deal."

Still in a haze, Jackie glanced down at the object in her arms. Each irregular facet sparkled with the color of fire, sunsets, and blood drenched battlefields. The scale was light, but tougher than diamonds to the touch.

It is dragon mail, Wintra breathed. *You have done well. Try it on.*

After a moment of confusion Jackie pressed the scale to her chest. After a bit of adjusting she took her hands away. It felt snug to her body, but not uncomfortable.

Nearly a perfect fit, the unicorn observed. *It will serve you well in the battle to come.*

Jackie nodded and then removed the shining scale, cradling it her arms. For the longest time Jackie said nothing, only stared blankly ahead as if something in the surrounding trees captivated her.

Do you need to rest? the unicorn asked.

"I don't know. Does it matter?" she said. But Wintra deserved better so she added, "It's like I'm not really here."

The unicorn studied her with concern, gauging her fitness for travel.

Dealing with dragons comes at a high cost. You may be melancholy for a while, but it will pass. If you can manage, we need to keep moving. Time grows short. With your assent I can send out a call rousing the rest of the Chosen.

Weary beyond measure Jackie mumbled, "Thanks," and then led her sleepy Chosen around the slab and onto the overgrown path. Like a zombie, she stumbled onward through the deadwood, leaving the heat behind. One by one the Chosen tried to console her, but she closed herself to them. In silence the group continued on until the path widened and the wind blew hard. Finally, a space ahead opened out onto a wide dry basin, leaving the last of the trees behind. A vast landscape beckoned in front of them as large as any ocean. Yet the geography was overshadowed by a foreboding shape, an unlikely ship that lay marooned amid the dry desolation as if some ancient sea had retreated from its very presence. It was, without a doubt, the Arkanum. It glittered bone white in the distance like an apparition.

Jackie stared at the sight, the goal that had kept her going when all seemed lost. Across Treetops and beyond she had traveled, braving Elementals, deadly sleep-inducing vegetation, mighty walls, and now dragons. Iggy and Peanut had paid the ultimate price, she thought guiltily. Here at last was the place where her brother was being held. She should be nervously making plans. But the vessel did not excite her the way that it should. In fact, she felt nothing at all. Deep inside her there was an empty space, a place where she had safeguarded a hidden treasure for her alone. Now she was aware that dream was gone forever as if it had never existed. Never before had anything, not even her brother being taken away, hurt so much. Jackie looked down at the Arkanum and, though she willed otherwise, found that she did not care. Her mother's face was fading from her memory. Details were blurring. She knew this was just something that happened with time, but she was caught up in the emotion of it. What troubled her more was the realization that she would never see her mother's smile or be held in her arms again, not even in her dreams.

CHAPTER 39

Hunter Greenwold stared at the white-robed emperor that until recently had been a squirrel, his jaw agape.

"This will not do," the Byzantine ruler chided. "There is too much to be done for you to be lost in amazement."

This was true. But in the last twenty-four hours Hunter Greenwold had witnessed more impossible things than he had dreamed of in all his inebriated existence during the last four years. Since being led to this strange place high above the clouds he had seen many crazy things. Now a man that used to be a rodent stood in front of him and asked him, rather unfairly thought Hunter, to just get on with it.

"What did you put in my head?" demanded Hunter. "What the hell are you? Tell me, you goddamned shapeshifter."

The austere-looking Emperor scowled, but then bit back a scathing reply. Constantine then sighed. "The squirrel you know as Pence and the true form you see before you now are one and the same, intertwined somehow in the magic which lies in my bones, and was passed down to me, passed down to all of us who have the gift. That rodent," Constantine emphasized the word with distaste, "is my embodiment, my animal avatar if you will. When I fell in battle on Constantinople's walls, all those many years ago, the magic within me was awakened and I changed, involuntarily, to survive. Over time I learned how to control the transformation. Yet when I climbed to Treetops I was soon, how shall I say it, disposed of this freedom and my avatar form was thrust upon me by way of this cursed medallion. It is my punishment for reckless behavior, hubris run amok. Appearing before you in this way is a Herculean task and one that I am bound to lose, although the power that holds me wanes. I am still not strong enough to remain. Look! Even now I fade."

Hunter Greenwold blinked his eyes in amazement. It was true. The Emperor's form was receding, becoming more transparent by the moment. Hands, chest, feet and face all faded in solidity, breaking down and transforming slowly into something else.

"What are you, some kind of criminal?" the detective asked.

Constantine or what remained of him, looked abashed, but then he found a secret reservoir of indignation. "I am guilty, it is true, of warping the Keeper's Vow; to preserving the memory of the Earth's creatures. But I thought I should do more than simply safeguard or wait quietly behind walls and so I attempted to organize the valley's denizens to attack the Arkanum. Against all odds," he swelled, "I finally succeeded in creating a sentient servant, Regnal, using lost magic from the time of Nwyfregal, the third Keeper."

He paused, overcome with the memory. When he spoke again his voice seemed deflated. There was little that remained of him now. Once a ruler of an ancient kingdom and a Keeper above the clouds, Constantine had become little more than a specter.

"Alas, I failed to sway the valley's denizens. In my desperation and foolishness, I marched on Flood and the Arkanum myself, before finally being stopped at the DreamsEnd by my two apprentices, Nimbus and Oriana. They drew on the magic of the first

Keepers and sang songs of binding. The animals themselves helped corral me. Fearing my continued disobedience and revolt, the next Keeper, Oriana, magicked an English coin from her First Apprentice. Using this as a talisman she confined me to my animal state. Who could blame them?"

Little remained of the former emperor now. It was as if the act of speaking drained him of substance.

"Listen to me," Constantine continued, fighting for every word, his voice begging now. "You must follow. There is no more time to explain and you would not believe me anyway. There are things you do not understand. That which you seek depends on it."

Constantine shimmered and then let out a voiceless cry. Then the last vestiges of his human form faded away to the point of oblivion.

The detective stared back.

The spectral smile of Constantine hung in the air Cheshire Cat-like, and then, for a moment so short Hunter thought later that he had only imagined it, there was something strange. He thought he saw the frantic blur of a bee and then a flash of red hair and a crooked nose. An outline of Constantine's features reemerged, overlaying the stranger's face, but they were contorted in dismay and anguish.

"Get out!" the Emperor hissed.

A moment later they both were gone, replaced at Hunter Greenwold's feet by

Pence once again.

"Ah, hell," the detective muttered, wishing he at least still had his gun.

The little white squirrel stared up at him with beady black eyes, its tail twitching playfully, as if it were enjoying a secret joke or trick.

"Well, get on with it," Hunter said, looking out across the desolate cloudscape spotted with dark lesions. The sight seemed to suck his remaining hope away. "Lead the way."

When he looked back, however, Pence was already far ahead, an almost invisible movement of white and flashing silver coin. Hunter Greenwold's hurried footfalls made no sound as he labored across the soft and slightly spongy clouds beneath his feet.

CHAPTER 40

Dustin walked away from the closed doorway and into a meadow surrounded by forest. He was standing in a green world conjured up out of thin air. Verdant and luscious life filled the vast room that gently sloped away from him. The tall trees sang to him; their scent-filled boughs and branches charged the air with abundance. Between their solid trunks shafts of golden sunlight fell, illuminating a profusion of groundcover and sky-pointing saplings. Small creatures, chipmunks and rabbits, scurried through the long grass. Overhead, high birdsong echoed.

The sudden pounding of Lancelot intruded on the peaceful setting. Dustin jumped and saw a flutter of wings take flight in the treetops above. A tension-filled silence descended. Moving away from the portal, Dustin ventured into the woodland, the hard-stone floor at his feet giving away to moss-covered ground. A glowing path of sunlight stretched ahead of him and he followed it, cautiously at first, but soon with a relaxed comfort. He could not have described why, but Dustin felt at home here amid the green growing things, and especially the animals that he sensed all around him. To his relief none of the creatures in this place felt sad as they often did at home, nor were they filled with a barely-contained anger as the Arkanum animals were. Here, they just *were.*

Before long he was skipping down the long avenue of light pretending it to be the Yellow Brick Road. He paused when a doe stuck her nose out of a clump of trees and then wandered over to him. Dustin held out his hand. The young doe's fur felt warm as he stroked her side. Soon the rest of her family came near. Then the birds descended, followed by chipmunks, squirrels, plump rabbits, and long-nosed foxes. They made a circle around him, waiting their turn with uncanny patience as if such a gathering were the most natural thing in the world.

"Perhaps I should rename you Francis of Assisi," a booming voice said as a familiar robed figure stepped out of the wooded shadows. "I have been worried, yet you are clearly at home here."

Dustin's smile turned into a frown while around him the animals tensed but did not flee. A fox next to Dustin bared her teeth and growled low and dangerous.

Flood strode to the very edge of the ring and then stopped, just out of reach. The smile on his face did not waver. "Do you know what this place is?" he asked. "I call it Eridu. That's a very, very old word. Everything that you can touch in this place was made by me from the bosom of the Earth, from the hidden material that the naked eye cannot see. I won't bore you with the technical details, including the artificial sky and sun, but it really is incredible, and ultimately so very simple. My original idea was to *improve* the natural world so it would be more powerful in the coming struggle. You saw my greatest failure in the depths of the Arkanum. Pitiful creatures I call the Lost Ones."

Now Flood's face fell and his mouth twisted up in pain.

"That was all a mistake, full of the same self-serving hubris that pollutes humankind's thinking in the world below. The Earth has existed for four and a half billion years, did you know that? That's a lot of birthdays. All through time it has been changing and evolving, giving birth to untold wonders of life, none of them more important or deserving that any other. How could I possibly improve on that? It is a nearly perfect system and yet it is failing. You see, one species sees itself as special, above everything else. By taking and rarely giving, human beings threaten life itself. That is why I, the Changer, and Master of the Arkanum, have finally acted, before it is too late. It is why you are here, my boy, and why this splendid little garden exists, a preview of things to come."

Dustin stared back.

"Ah," said Flood with a sigh. "You don't understand what I'm saying, do you? It matters not. The time for words is over."

Flood took a step forward into the ring of animals and Dustin flinched. From the boy's side the fox lunged, its teeth bared as it shot through the air toward Flood's fleshy neck. At almost the same moment several birds erupted in flight amid a flurry of wings. Wide-eyed, Dustin watched as a surprised Flood managed to stick out a thick arm and grab the long-nosed animal just before it tore open his throat. Overhead two hawks stopped their circling and then plunged through the sky at the Master.

"Call them off," Flood commanded. "Call them all off!"

He shook the fox like a rag doll in his grip and then raised his other hand into a fist, aiming it at the avian dive-bombers.

"Don't make me hurt them," he cried, his voice breaking. "Is this what you want?"

Dustin felt the anger and fear radiating from the animals around him. It nearly broke his heart. He missed the peace and curiosity he had felt only minutes before. Somehow the change must be his fault. Flood's eyes filled up with tears as he prepared to strike.

"Okay," Dustin said.

That was all it took. The hawks aborted their attack and leveled off above their heads, flashing by in a feathery whoosh, their talons glittering like fatal jewels.

"Thank you," the Master of the Arkanum said, letting the fox slip from his grip and fall to the ground below. The creature lay limp for a long moment before crawling off to the shelter of the forest. Taking this as a cue, the rest of the animals dispersed and soon disappeared into the shadows. The two remaining beings faced each other in comic fashion, a giant and a small boy, one in shadow, the other in bright sunlight. Now it was Dustin's turn to speak.

"I wanna go home," he said simply.

"I know," Flood admitted. "I have good news for you. Your sister is close by."

Dustin's face lit up in a smile, but then darkened. "Really? She is?"

"I told you she would come, didn't I? I know I've said some things you don't understand, but I never wanted to hurt you or the ones you love. You believe that, don't you?"

Dustin nodded his head slowly, but truly he did not know what to think.

"I have done everything I could to make you happy and comfortable until help arrived," Flood continued walking up to him.

He put his hand, the same hand that had grabbed the fox, reassuringly on his shoulder. "Gaylon has spent countless hours searching for your sister and then leading her here. But he is too tired to fly. There is just one more thing you have to do. From far away, our little boat can look like just another rock so we have to get her attention. To make sure she doesn't miss us, you have to blow the horn again. That's all. Do you think you can do that?"

Dustin nodded again, this time with more enthusiasm.

"That's good. You know I'm really impressed with how you made friends with the animals in here. They like you. You're the first person they've ever seen. Even I try not to come in. No one's supposed to ever come in here. It's a very important rule. Do you understand?"

Flood squeezed the boy's shoulder hard enough to make Dustin wince.

"Let's go and greet your sister," the Arkanum's master said with a smile. Then he led the boy deeper into the forest, away from the entrance Dustin had come from and the light.

"The door is the other way," Dustin said as he was hurried along.

"I know a short cut," Flood replied. "Lancelot waits for us there."

The forest grew ever more tangled and dismal until they entered a grove of young oaks with one conspicuous ancient sentinel near the center. Flood led them directly to the colossal tree and then reached out to the knotted bark, tapping a quick rhythm. The sound came back hollow and metallic. A moment later a door swung open, letting in flickering torchlight. Dustin immediately recognized the hulking mass of the great ape standing in front of a wide winding staircase. Lancelot snorted his displeasure at seeing the runaway boy.

"Ready the Callixar and the Lost Ones," commanded Flood.

The ape servant turned obediently and mounted the high steps, disappearing from sight.

Dustin followed wearily behind.

"Here, let me help you," Flood suggested, and after closing the door behind him, scooped the boy up in his arms and ascended the giant steps two at a time.

"When will I see Jackie?" Dustin whispered as they rose through the dim stairwell to the waiting world above.

"Let's give her a welcome she won't soon forget."

CHAPTER 41

Jackie forced herself to take another step onto the bleached scrubland that separated the Arkanum from the dragon's forest. Wintra had offered to carry her but Jackie refused, wanting to be by herself. The warm open air of the plains was a welcome relief after the cold and claustrophobic trees, but Jackie barely registered it. Each footfall she took only made her more aware that she was further away from what she had lost. The dragon's scale in her arms felt more and more like a terrible burden. After a short while her stride faltered.

What have I done? she wondered.

Once more Jackie closed her eyes and tried to imagine her mother alive again. With all the magic in Treetops there must be a way. She needed her mother now more than ever. And yet the more she wished for a miracle, the clearer it became that her mother was gone for good. It had been foolish to think otherwise. She was no longer a child. For comfort she tried to visualize her mother's face or the sound of her gentle laughter. For a brief time the memories held her, but then the smoky visage of the dragon rose up in her mind telling her that she was alone. That her mother was dead.

Why have we stopped again? Wintra asked in frustration, appearing in her thoughts. *Time grows short.*

It took Jackie a moment to find herself. When she finally did, she saw the unicorn standing beside her, an unusual look of concern stretched across its equine face.

Do you not hear me? We must march. The Arkanum and your brother are near.

I can't, she thought simply.

What ails you? I sense a hurt that was not there before.

The other Chosen animals came up around her. She felt their confusion and concern reach out. All that support made her feel even worse for being so weak. To help distance herself, she spoke out loud.

"The dragon took something from me. Something I really miss. I can't expect you to understand. Right now, I just need to rest a little while. Try and get my strength back. Then maybe—"

No! said Wintra with an air of finality. *I am sorry for your loss, but there can be no delay. No excuses. Have you forgotten your brother is in the Arkanum? Have you forgotten that the Horn has already sounded twice? A third time will unleash the animals of Treetops upon the world, creatures that Flood stole from the failing Keeper, creatures who ready in his fortress. So too will the animals of the Earth below rise up, turned by the shadowy Cyclix. Any denizen of the clouds knows the signs. Now that the Keeper is gone, we are the only hope. Get on my back. Use the scale as a saddle if you must. We ride!*

Jackie stared back as the other animals murmured their agreement in her mind. It felt to her a lot like mutiny.

"I'm the leader here, aren't I? I make the decisions."

Then lead, Wintra said sternly in her head. *Tell us your plan and we will follow it. Life only has one direction—forward.*

The unicorn's words hit her like a slap. Staring past the pointed horn of the unicorn, her eyes fell upon the mirage-like shape of the Arkanum glistening bone-white in the distance. Swallowing her fear, Jackie realized how wholly unprepared she was for what lay directly ahead. Everything had always been about the journey, of getting through, and finding their way here. Now they had finally made it, and she had no idea what to do next.

"How long will it take us to get there?" Jackie asked.

One, perhaps two hours of hard riding, Wintra responded. *And we will be observed the whole way. There is nothing to give us cover.*

Jackie put the down the scale and then twirled her fingers nervously through her hip-length hair. "We'll have to give each other cover then. Striker, Flambeau, and Speedo," she called, "position yourself so you are safely behind Rocco, Harry, and Quake." Then she turned back to Wintra. "What kind of defenses can we expect?"

The unicorn closed its deep blue eyes and pondered the question. To Jackie it appeared that the creature was trying to access some hidden lore.

I do not know, the unicorn finally admitted. *Samuel Flood the Master of the Arkanum is not bound as a Keeper is bound. Even time can be bent to his will if the need is great enough, or so the legends say.*

"What else do the legends say?"

The unicorn ground a hoof with impatience.

Very little. There haven't been any masters before Flood and there will be none after. Flood simply is. The being called Flood has abided the ages preparing for the day when the world below will need saving. That day is here.

New mutterings rose among the gathered animals, thoughts too skittish and quick for her to get completely. Jackie thought it might be fear.

"So what is this Flood?" Jackie asked with a nervous laugh. "Some kind of god?"

No, of course not, chided the unicorn. *That is a human invention.*

"Then what is he?" Jackie pressed.

The unicorn whinnied. *So many questions and there are few answers. This much is known. Everything in life must be kept in balance. Light has its dark. Spring has its winter. And so Keepers have their counterpart as well. In this way the living Earth is complete.*

"What are you saying? That Flood and the Keepers are somehow connected?"

Perhaps, Wintra replied. *Nimbus knew more, but he is gone. Keepers provide shelter and Flood delivers justice. Beyond them there are others, lost fragments that sing their own song.*

Unable to fathom the information she had just been given, Jackie covered her face with her hands and let an audible sigh escape through her fingers. So much was beyond her. She tried not to think about what the dragon had taken. There was a hole and nothing to fill it with.

What would your mother tell you? the mythological creature asked unexpectedly.

"What?"

I mean no disrespect. What would the human female that gave you life tell you to do now?

Jackie stared back in incomprehension.

"Can you read my mind?"

No. I cannot read thoughts that do not want to be heard, nor would I want to. Your pain is elemental, as visible as the scar of a dried up river or the stumps of once proud trees. All things are born, live and die. That which has given life, as I have, can tell when it is missing from another. You grieve.

Nodding her head slowly, Jackie cleared a tangle of hair from her misting eyes and straightened her back slightly.

"I suppose she'd tell me to do my best and that she loves me."

As do we all, the noble beast said with a nicker. Her other Chosen responded in their own fashion.

A warm glow spread over Jackie, and though she still felt the emptiness where the dream of her mother had been, it didn't seem quite so deep or quite so dark.

"Okay. Here's our plan. We need to hit that ark with everything we have as fast we can," Jackie began, gaining confidence.

Turning, she addressed her Chosen. "Since we don't know what'll get thrown at us, we'd better have multiple moving targets. When we get closer to the Arkanum, Rocco, Quake, and Harry will split up and each come at the target from different paths. The goal is to get close and bust a hole. Be careful," she added. "Don't hurt yourself, but we need to break through that ship."

Now Jackie looked at the smaller Chosen.

"Your job is to find a way in. Either through a created breach or some other way, by climbing,"—Flambeau let out an excited shriek—"or by swimming up to the deck. Think you can get that far up, Speedo?"

In response the river dolphin clicked and nodded its flat nose energetically.

"And I know you'll think of something Striker," she added, patting the cougar's head gently. "No matter what happens we keep going. I'll ride Wintra and communicate any changes directly to you. We can make adjustments on the fly."

Taking a deep breath, Jackie stroked the unicorn's silky mane as Wintra nodded her regal head.

"I guess that's it."

Without being asked, and without a word being spoken or communicated, the Chosen and Jackie came together, flipper pressing against fang and hairy digits, paws to horns and tusks, great sauropod head dipping down to Jackie's slender shoulder. Silently they all entered a shared communion where each thanked each other for their service and gave their support for the battle at hand.

When they finally disengaged Jackie swept the hair out of her eyes and asked Wintra a final favor before they rode. The unicorn bowed her head. Jackie laid the length of her tawny hair, from the neck down, across the gleaming surface of the creature's horn. Then Wintra raised her head and sliced upward. Truer than any man-made blade the spiraling horn cut the hair. It fell to the ground at Jackie's feet. Feeling a weight had been lifted she reached down and pressed the dragon's scale to her chest. It curved around her like a glistening glove. She felt like a gladiator.

"We ride!" Jackie shouted. "For my brother!"

At her command, the Chosen swept across the dry ocean bed with Wintra and Jackie leading the charge. Ahead of them, still far off, but growing bigger with every passing minute, was the Arkanum, seat of Samuel Flood and the world's fury.

CHAPTER 42

The Cyclix were almost done with their mission. Across every landmass and through every ocean each had traveled, slipping like a silent nightmare into the sleeping subconscious of animals everywhere. It had taken time. Precious time. Avoiding the scrutiny of humans had complicated matters, and even with the dwindling number of animal species, there still remained a lot of ground to cover. Yet the Cyclix felt no frustration or impatience. For untold millions of years, they had waited in darkness, lost in dreams of death, wondering, if they had been forgotten. Finally released to their fatal purpose, they wasted not a moment, neither resting nor eating, though the urge to feast on their foe was strong. They existed only to ready the animal multitudes for the coming battle cry and there was much to be done before their black light burned out. Memories had grown dim in the world and blood was long to boil. The Cyclix were good teachers, though. Slowly, almost imperceptibly, a change in the Earth's creatures began. There was no sudden attack. An unlucky person might witness a surprising flash of fangs or a dangerous snarl that would disappear almost before it began. If you were walking down a quiet city street or strolling through a park, you probably wouldn't notice anything. One by one, though, even as the dogs and cats and the multitude of wild creatures continued to act in their ordinary everyday ways, the animals of the Earth were also doing something else.

They were waiting.

CHAPTER 43

"Here we are," Flood beamed, putting Dustin down on the wooden step by the railing's edge. The armored ape stood nearby casting a watchful eye. "And there your sister is," he added pointing across the desolate landscape.

Dustin looked out across the dry seabed, past the rocks and scrub bushes, past the scattered bones and timbers of forgotten ships and sea monsters, wanting to see Jackie more than anything else in the whole world.

"Do you see them?" Flood asked.

And then he saw the smudges, because that's all they really were, halfway across the plain, not human looking at all. A short line of shapes, some big, others small, moved slowly across the terrain toward the Arkanum. He could feel their thoughts, some intelligent, others muddy, but all strangely focused. One after the other, he lingered on presence of each mind until there were none left. Then his little head hung down in disappointment. His sister was not among them.

"Not there," he said. Tears filled his eyes.

Flood leaned in next to him and, taking Dustin's hand, pointed gently at a spot perhaps a short distance away from the parade of animals. "Look again."

The figure was too far away to make out clearly, but it was definitely a person, a girl perhaps, riding some sort of creature. He closed his eyes and reached out with his mind.

"Jackie!" Dustin screamed. "It's Jackie!"

"Yes, I believe so, but she can't hear you. The time has come. Let her know you are here, and that you are waiting. Blow the Callixar one final time. Make it a good one. It's important that it be long and without pauses. Can you do that for me?"

Dustin nodded happily, but still he hesitated.

"Will it be loud?" he asked.

"Not like last time," Flood said.

Dustin leaned in. It felt effortless and right. He put his lips to the ancient instrument, took a deep breath, and blew.

From the end of the Callixar, a lonely sound grew. It began as a faraway cry and then rose into a chorus of moans. A deep rumbling filled the air like a great beast growing near. Overhead the crimson tear in the sky grew wider as if meant to swallow the world in blood. The light of Helios flickered. Down below water gurgled up darkly from the ground, spreading across the dry seabed like a harbinger of doom.

"That's it," he heard Flood say as if from far away. "Just a little bit longer."

Then another voice, this time inside his head, spoke unexpectedly. Its tone was silky and intelligent yet tenuous as if the attempt strained to reach him. Dustin knew immediately that it was a unicorn. He even knew the creature's secret name. It was the most beautiful thing he had ever heard.

Jackie knows where you are. She is coming. There is no need to make such noise.

The request seemed a reasonable one. When Dustin stopped blowing, a great wind ushered in as if filling a vacuum. It shook the Arkanum and sent ripples scurrying across the spreading pools of water. Then unexpectedly, the bubbling slowed. In the sudden silence that followed all Dustin could hear was Flood's scream of frustration and his own ringing ears.

CHAPTER 44

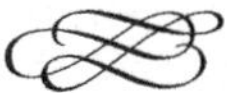

Across the Earth's vast surface, the Cyclix heard the third and final sounding from the Callixar, sensed the sacred reverberations and did as their purpose demanded. Gathering together at the foot of the Portal Tree they encircled the great trunk, a black band of power shimmering in the pale moonlight. Their dark natures probed for any missing element to their mission, any flaw to their efforts. In the stillness the Cyclix hesitated, sensing a momentary incompleteness. Then it was gone. The final intonation receded away into oblivion. It was only then that the Cyclix deemed their mission ended. Yet they did not depart, at least not right away. Instead, they tarried a moment longer, the briefest of delays, measured in the blur of a killing stroke, and breathed in the fragrant air of the Earth. Then one by one they bowed their head in dissolution.

CHAPTER 45

Across the dry sea bottom, the Chosen sped like a wedge of hope and fury toward the growing bone-encrusted mass of the Arkanum. They had made good time, their progress unhindered save for strange bubbling pools and the skeletal remains of watery denizens. Their prize loomed directly ahead. Perched on a gently sloping rise, the Arkanum seemed utterly alien and grotesque like a cancerous growth. Jackie shuddered as she looked up at the vessel from the back of Wintra as the unicorn jumped another pool of water. The ship was bigger than she imagined and defied any attempt to scale it. She was reminded of the time her mother and father had taken her to see the giant sequoias and redwoods of California before Dustin was born. The only basis of comparison had been other trees nearby. There was clearly only one Arkanum.

All manner of bone covered its massive hull. The skeletal remains of countless animals glittered white. Taken together and seen from a distance, the vessel resembled a gravestone, marking the place where some ancient titan once fell. At key junctures high in the hull what looked to be human skulls were placed, their twisted visages peering down like anguished gargoyles. Above them, ringing the now visible deck were the long slender barrels of futuristic-looking guns that pointed down ominously. They didn't look like any naval cannons Jackie had ever seen. Above the deck she spied the great masts standing stark and unadorned like fleshless spines. No people were visible.

They were close enough now, Jackie knew. Maybe too close. They had entered the shadow of the great vessel. She called a halt. With the Chosen gathered around she went over the plan again. Rocco, Quake, and Henry would take up their positions in the front while the others waited in the rear. Each knew what they had to do. All she had to do was give the order and wish her Chosen good luck, but she felt paralyzed. It was as if the specter of the Arkanum held her spellbound. Next to it she seemed so small. Even her Chosen seemed ill-equipped in the face of such power. Jackie felt utterly afraid. The great bone gate of the ship had already lifted to over half her height before Wintra's alarm finally reached her.

A door opens! Do you not see it?

"I don't like the look of this," she answered back, embarrassed by her fear. "Something pretty big could come through that."

Or a lot of something, Wintra answered back.

Jackie opened her mouth to speak, but the words died on her lips. Pouring out of the opening from the bowels of the Arkanum was a wave of abomination, a deviltry beyond words. In madness and fury, they crashed through the still-rising gate as if it were straw, leaving a jagged opening in their former prison. The horror came in all shapes and sizes, warped almost beyond recognition. Bits and pieces of species were welded to one another in nightmare fashion as if their creator had been blind or mad or both. There was something covered in scales with the head of a cow and the fangs of a snake. Next to it came a shambling mound of hair and bone and a shell-covered creature with bloody raw flesh visible in the cracks in-between. A feathery thing doomed never to fly flapped its flippers as it ran in broken strides baring its long row of razor-sharp teeth. Other ghoulish images remained half unseen, lost in the rush of the onslaught, a blur of too-bright color, a flash of teeth or a claw a bit too long.

At their lead was the most gruesome and alien of all. It rocked forward on two legs, bear-like and massive, but instead of arms only a slithering mass of tentacles reached out in frantic helplessness. From its jaws issued forth a hideous forlorn cry that was echoed by all the others. As a whole, the creatures were not unnaturally fast or graceful. Their bizarre breeding had robbed most of them of any great degree of dexterity or coordination. Unexpected freedom, however, gave the creatures a frantic energy and they launched themselves through the opening, spurred on by a rage that lay coded in their genetic manipulation.

In fury they came down the slope, some snapping at each other, but most drawn to Jackie's entourage at the bottom as if they could not bear the normalcy the Chosen represented. All bore down on her. At least that's how it seemed to Jackie. Of course, she and Wintra were just convenient targets riding ahead of the others. There was no time to send orders. Each of her Chosen would have to react and fight as well as they were able. Jackie fought down a swell of rising panic as a terrible desperation seized her. She did a quick check to make sure her dragon scale was still in place—though there was little good would it do her against such ferocity. Then the first creature was upon them. The unicorn dodged violently, almost unseating Jackie. A tentacle slapped against Jackie's face as they galloped past, but the suckers did not stick. More were coming now—*too many,* Jackie thought in the pit of her stomach.

Hold on! Wintra commanded in her mind.

She only had time to grab onto an extra tuft of mane before the unicorn took off. It felt to Jackie as if the mythological steed had only been sauntering before, conserving its strength. Now Wintra exploded like a rocket, its hoofs chasing the ground toward the horizon as it zigzagged through the charging beasts.

Countless times Jackie was certain they would not make it and a mutation would smash into them. Each time she would close her eyes and wait for the deadly impact only to find that she was still very much alive facing another horror.

Directly ahead came a creature covered in quills. It moved ponderously, but with purpose. For an instant it seemed they might escape unscathed. Then their paths converged and its long sloth-like arms shot out, raking across Wintra's pearly-white flank. The unicorn shuddered but kept moving, shifting to the right to avoid another lunge.

Jackie saw the final collision a moment before it happened. The last creature looked almost normal, at least from the neck down. It was a familiar black and white striped zebra in almost every way except for one. Instead of an equine head it labored with the massive jaws of a shark nearly dragging on the ground. One eye was black and soulless. The other was big and brown. Undeveloped gills blended into black and white fur that tapered down to legs unable to support the unnatural weight. It was a killing machine unable to kill. Jackie sensed that it just wanted to die. At the sight of a meal it made a half-hearted attempt to lift its head and bite. That's when Wintra slammed into it, the unicorn's momentum preventing any change in course. The collision tore Jackie from her perch atop Wintra and sent her sailing over the zebrark, hitting the ground hard. She lay on the dusty ground in a crumpled heap. When Jackie finally managed to pick herself up, the sight took her breath away. Wintra and the zebrark were locked together in mortal struggle, jaws and horn flashing. Wintra lunged again impaling the patchwork abomination. A trail of blood oozed from the point of entry. The strange, poor creature shuddered and then collapsed on the ground.

There is no joy in killing, the unicorn said slowly, *but this creature thanked me before it died. There is some comfort in that.*

You're bleeding! Jackie thought back with her mind. Bright rivulets of blood ran down the unicorn's flank collecting in a small pool on the ancient sea bed.

It is nothing to be concerned about, Wintra responded. *Take care of the others.*

With a start Jackie looked at the field of battle. The marauding creatures were converging on the Chosen. Suddenly Rocco went down amidst an onslaught of tentacles and teeth. Even from a distance, she could see that the rhino fought bravely, jabbing with its horn as he tried to squirm away but then a spiny creature blundered into the struggle and overwhelmed him. Jackie watched as he went down. She felt his fear and pain as his life ebbed and went out. He was gone.

"No!" Jackie screamed.

She made ready to leap onto Wintra's back, but the creature backed away.

I cannot carry you. I cannot fight, the unicorn said in her mind as it limped along and then finally stopped. *You must help them.*

This was the moment she had dreaded. Still reeling from the death of Rocco, Jackie began to panic. What could they do against such destruction? They had marched all the way here only to be slaughtered. With every moment she delayed, the situation only grew worse. The Chosen were outnumbered. They could survive for a while on account of their attackers being unorganized and random, but this only postponed the inevitable. Without blind fury or surprise on their side, the Chosen's only hope was to work together. Each animal waited for instructions from Jackie. More attackers were coming and they already had more than they could handle.

Her friends were counting on her. She had to do something. Focusing her mind on Quake but letting the others hear as well, Jackie let the urgent instructions tumble out of her. *Use your tail and try to take down as many as you can. The rest of you come around from each side afterward and finish off what's left.*

The giant sauropod flexed its tail impatiently as the rest of the

Chosen took up their positions in back, making sure to keep a safe distance. A moment later the second wave of Arkanum creatures came rampaging through. Quake swept his tail around striking all three of the attackers down. There was barely time for the seismosaurus to ready his tail again as three more mutations came storming in. Another sweep of his tail and two more went down. The third abomination, however, got through unscathed and made for the exposed flank of its prehistoric prey. It had the body of a ravenous dog and the head and legs of a bird. The creature dug its claws into the tender flesh of the dinosaur and then began ripping, its beak stabbing forward in violent thrusts. Quake shuddered in pain and shook his massive body, but the thing grimly held on.

"Striker, get in there!" Jackie commanded as Quake's injuries coursed through her psyche.

In two quick strides, the cougar launched itself in the air and landed on the attacker. Surprised, the hideous beast released its hold as the cougar tore open its jugular.

Okay, five left, coming fast, Jackie thought in rapid-fire. *I want Quake and Harry to charge, with Striker close behind. The rest of you wait in the rear for instructions.*

The wooly mammoth moved first, with Quake following more slowly because of the gash in his side. Striker followed, his lips dripping blood. With every step, Harry and Quake picked up speed as they thundered toward their smaller opponents. When they made contact, the effect was immediate. Two of the mutations, a cow-snake-like thing and something resembling an alligator with flippers went down immediately beneath Harry's furry feet. The first lay still, while the second quivered and shook on the ground spasmodically. Another two attackers disappeared under Quake's gigantic weight and were splattered flat into unrecognizable blobs. The final abomination, covered in quills, went between them both. Striker landed amidst the barbs, his paws impaled, as the creature ran mindlessly on. Lunging for the only exposed skin he could find, the cougar tore open the creature's face until it spilled over in a cloud of dust.

"Striker, are you okay? Jackie thought anxiously, unable to pierce the veil of dust which had arisen around the battle.

"Full," said the cougar emerging into view, his muzzle now completely covered in fresh blood. His gait was no longer sleek and effortless. Each step was tentative and faltering as if the cat walked across broken glass. Jackie could feel the barbs as they dug into his paws. Finally, the cat stopped and lay down, gingerly pulling each jagged piece from the bottoms of his feet with his teeth. When he was finished the great cat resumed his walk slowly back toward her, following Harry and Quake.

Jackie took stock of the situation. Rocco had been lost. His death stung her to the core. She blamed herself for not acting fast enough. Quake was hurt and Wintra wasn't in much better shape. Striker would need time to heal before traveling far. Yet they lived, somehow, against incredible odds. Beside her, Flambeau chattered nervously while Speedo weaved circles in the air above like a magician's trick. Perhaps there was still hope. Jackie looked at them all and felt immensely lucky to be alive.

"Fire!" a voice yelled from high atop the Arkanum.

That's when everything went wrong.

CHAPTER 46

The air crackled and a bright bolt of energy, blue as a summer sky, rained down on Quake. It was over almost before it begun. For a moment the giant sauropod cried out in anguish as skin burned and then bone dissolved away. Jackie sunk to her knees as her friend's cries eclipsed her heart. Then the assault ended. Quake was gone. Nothing remained except a smoking patch of ground. Sickened and startled Jackie turned away just as the air erupted with more deadly blasts. They came from the lip of the vessel's starboard side and crackled through the air like super-charged lightning. Focused beams as hot as a sun's core sliced through the air, covering the distance in a heartbeat. With searing precision each found their mark. Harry was incinerated so quickly that his cry remained curled in his great trunk, never to be uttered. A violent blast tore through Flambeau in midair as he leapt, leaving behind only a fine rain of reddish hair. Striker hugged close to the ground snarling, the closest to fear that Jackie had ever seen. Several times a bright blue beam shot over the great cat before a final adjustment was made, and then he too burned away into nothing. Speedo had better luck weaving through the air. Blast after blast just missed him, yet he tired and his slow movements made him an easier target.

Get to the shelter of the Arkanum! Jackie thought desperately to the dolphin. *Do what you can there. Go through the hole in the gate or look for Dustin on deck.*

Speedo's reply reached out to her, but she could not make sense of it. Pieces were missing and others were garbled and incomprehensible. Communication she had taken for granted slipped away from signal to noise. Her gift, or that of the Dream Catchers and Nimbus was fading. She threw herself flat to the ground looking wildly for somewhere to hide. The nearest cover, a pile of rocks, was perhaps twenty yards away. It might as well have been a mile.

She looked up. With a final burst of speed, the dolphin reached the safety of the Arkanum, free from the deadly guns. The next moment a cerulean blast rocketed over Jackie's head searing the air with its inconceivable heat. Relief turned to terror. Another beam had found its target.

"Wintra!" Jackie exclaimed. The unicorn's pearly body glowed red for one agonizing moment. Her friend bowed her horned head and then was gone. Jackie gaped at where the unicorn had been. A tendril of smoke curled into the empty sky. Jackie felt bereft and in shock. Her mouth hung open in disbelief. The wonderful creature had been her friend, but there was no time for mourning as laser blasts kept streaking down. She was too stunned to move or think and no longer had the will to overcome the carnage she had seen. A multitude of deadly beams crackled around her, burning the ground. Out of options she remained frozen in place, lying in clear sight as death rained down from the great bony ship. Jackie's world collapsed. No voices comforted her. No gift or companion remained. She was alone. They had come so far, but it wasn't enough. Eventually she realized that the attack had ceased and that someone was calling her name.

"Jackie! Up here!" an achingly recognizable voice called, almost too far away to be heard.

Dazed, Jackie rose to her feet cautiously and looked up at the source high above on the Arkanum. A small boy stood at the railing. Small hands cupped around his mouth as he shouted her name over and over again. His voice was racked with sobs and soft, but it somehow made its way to her. It was her brother.

"I'm here, Dustin! I came for you!" she shouted as tears filled her eyes. With a start she realized that her brother must have seen the battle. He would have seen the animals burned away. The thought was too much to bear, but somehow she got to her feet. "Don't move. Don't worry. I'm going to take you home and away from all this."

Even as she said the words, she nearly regretted them. How could she get Dustin out of that technological fortress with no wings and no army? Then she spied Speedo hovering impossibly against the Arkanum wall, still out of sight as he inched his way closer to the boy. There would have to be a distraction, she thought desperately, if the dolphin had any chance of success. Swallowing her fear Jackie stepped forward.

"Is there someone else up there with you Dustin? Show yourself Flood! Do you hear me? Give me back my brother!"

Silence fell over the great ark and the plain below as deep and absolute as the grave. Then Jackie saw a giant figure of a man step forward and put an arm protectively around Dustin.

"You must be the long-awaited Jackie, beloved sister and selector of the Treetops denizen. Your Chosen fought bravely. I am saddened by their demise, but they were sacrificed for the greater good. Some know me as Cernunnos or Samain, but you can call me Samuel Flood."

"I don't care what names you go by. I want my brother," Jackie called back. "You had no right to take him!"

"I think there has been a misunderstanding," Flood retorted. "I've merely helped a lost child. Still, let us not spend more time fighting and arguing. Believe me," he called down in a voice that rolled like distant thunder. "This is not how I wanted it to be. At the very least I planned on Dustin going with you upon your arrival. But the situation has changed. Things are, shall we say, literally up in the air."

At this he spread his arms to the sky above where the giant crack bled and grew like a wound that would never heal. Over half the horizon was already corrupted, with more overtaken every minute.

"I can hardly just hand over such a special little boy while things are still nearing completion. So close, yet better to err on the side of caution. He'll be safer here in any event."

While Flood talked like a showman with all the time in the world, Jackie kept wondering why he didn't just blast her and be done with it. Then a chill went through her. He needs me alive because of Dustin. Things are still unfinished. Then he'll kill me.

"How is old Nimbus doing by the way?" Flood asked conversationally as if he were talking about the weather. "My scout saw him earlier, but he seems to be missing now. I hope everything is all right."

Anger flared deep within Jackie, molten emotion breaking through the numbing ice that had formed around her senses.

"I'm sure you know how he's doing!" she shouted back to the top of the Arkanum. "He was lost fighting the Elementals at DreamsEnd. It was the bravest thing I ever saw. But you wouldn't know anything about being a hero hiding out here in your creepy bone ship."

"It's all a matter of perspective," Flood replied. "This vessel used to be covered in dead man's nails, but I redecorated."

She imagined the Master of the Arkanum smiling and silently calculating how the Keeper's death would help his dark designs. When he spoke again, however, his voice had an air of uncharacteristic reverence.

"I am truly sorry for your loss," Flood said from his lofty perch.

"It was none of my doing, I promise you that. He was a worthy counterpart in his day and an upholder of the richness of Life. I will not soon forget him. Yet his time has passed as it has for all Keepers. Nimbus will be the last."

"How can you say that?" Jackie asked her voice shaking with grief.

"There is a time for words and then there is a time to act," Flood called down, his voice gathering momentum like a storm coming ashore. "Memories and good intentions no longer suffice. Too long have the innocent suffered at the hands of creatures with brains big enough to know better. The world you come from, my dear, is dying. Humankind, for all its cleverness, is killing something precious in the universe. It cannot be allowed to succeed."

"What gives you the right to play God? What gives you the right to decide who lives and who dies?"

"I might ask you the same question," Flood responded from high atop his fortress. "Did you not pick and lead ten creatures on a journey of daring rescue across the realm of Treetops and beyond? No doubt they obeyed you at every turn and put themselves in danger without hesitation, all to fix what you have broken. How many still live?"

Jackie flinched as Flood stabbed down at the battlefield.

"For me, though, the answer is simple. It is my purpose. It is what I was created for."

Jackie's eyes burned as she remembered the Chosen. She could not disown the guilt Flood laid at her feet, but it was not that simple.

"They came," she stammered, "they came all this way, to stop you. Finding and rescuing Dustin was my idea. For Nimbus and the Chosen there was something bigger, something beyond themselves worth fighting for and holding on to. It's called hope." Her voice broke as she continued. "I'll never forget what they did. I'm not perfect, but at least I'm trying. There are people down there in the world that are trying too. That's more than you are doing. You've given up."

"Enough philosophizing," proclaimed Flood. "Enough rationalizing. The time of the Final Battle for the fate of the world approaches." He raised his arms to the reddening sky. To Jackie, he looked like a biblical figure. "I have no quarrel with you. Go if you wish, but your brother remains until the end is certain."

Jackie saw Flood pull her brother closer even as he tried to squirm away.

"No!" screamed Dustin. "You do bad things. I wanna go home!"

Flood turned toward him, but Jackie couldn't hear what he said.

"Not later. Now!" Dustin demanded, trying in vain to wiggle free. "Let me go!"

Jackie could only look on helplessly as Flood carried her thrashing brother back from the railing and out of sight.

CHAPTER 47

"Stop," commanded Flood just inches from Dustin's face. Vise-like hands dug into the boy's arms and he grimaced in pain. "Be silent! I cannot tolerate this behavior. Not when we're so close."

Hot tears welled up in Dustin's eyes. "You're hurting me."

"Only a little. Lessons must be learned so the greater good can be served." The Master of the Arkanum squeezed ever tighter.

Unable to free himself Dustin sent out a desperate call for help to the only thing he could see; the misshapen simian giant who only an hour before had terrified him in the bowels of the Arkanum. He had no desire to harm Flood's servant, but a five year-old's temper can be hot, especially when they have no other choice and so he instructed the altered ape to save him. Lancelot was not like the forest animal from the strange oasis at the bottom of the boat, however. He had been changed and warped from his natural state. At first Flood's servant resisted him and threw up his arms in fury, baring his teeth and grabbing his head violently.

"Must not! Must not!"

"What's gotten into you?" Flood said sternly. "Be still. Have you all gone crazy?!"

His master's rebuke silenced Lancelot, but only for a moment. Dustin did not relent. Again and again he silently asked the creature to help him. Tears streamed down the boy's face with the effort, which prompted Flood to ease his grip, but not his hold.

Please! Dustin pleaded.

Finally, his thoughts burrowed through to the still-beating animal heart; a core left untouched by all of Flood's genetic manipulation. The result was instantaneous and unstoppable. With lightning speed Lancelot shot out and grabbed Flood's arm twisting it free of Dustin.

"Lancelot! This will not be tolerated. Bad behavior is punished."

Flood raised his free hand up high to strike his servant. But the blow never came. Hesitating, he mastered himself and then twisted free of Lancelot. His servant cowered. For precious seconds, the Master of the Arkanum towered over the mutineer before realizing his error. Flood glanced madly around for the boy before launching himself in pursuit. At first, Dustin ran toward the cabin door, but then he veered toward the railing as a gray streak flew into view. Speedo accelerated and then came to a stop hovering by his knees. The dolphin nudged him once and Dustin climbed aboard.

Hang on! The dolphin warned.

A heartbeat later they took off and sped away from the great bone ship.

Flood could not believe what had happened. He leaned heavily over the railing and stared as the last of the Chosen and the KeyStone wobbled away in the cracked sky. Every moment they grew more out of reach. Shaking himself out of his bewilderment he ran to one of the cannons mounted at the side of the Arkanum. Pushing buttons madly, he released the unit to manual control and swung the nozzle in the direction of Speedo. The light turned green. Then he fired. Bright laser beams sliced through the air on either side of their target. Flood fired again, but these were even further off the mark. He could not bring himself to shoot the boy. The next instant the dolphin arced around the ship and vanished from sight.

"Terminate!" Flood commanded in frustration.

Immediately the weapon powered down, its red eye dimming to black.

"The danger is too great. The boy cannot be harmed," he mused to himself. Flood paused and looked around. His simian servant Lancelot stood behind him cowering. "Gaylon!" he shouted in the direction of the cabins. "Awake! Your services are needed!"

With increasing frustration Flood waited, ready to order Lancelot to retrieve the shape-shifter. Transformations exerted a heavy toll. Sometimes Gaylon would sleep a full day or more after returning, but there was no time now. "For Earth's sake wake up!" he bellowed.

"What is it?" Gaylon mumbled as he stumbled out onto the deck rubbing his eyes.

"Get ready, my young apprentice," Flood directed, impatiently pointing at the sky where Dustin had disappeared. "I have a mission for you."

Quickly, he described what had happened.

"I know you are still weak, but there can be no delay. The fate of the natural world depends on it."

Gaylon hesitated.

"Hasn't it already begun? I heard the Third Call."

"Perhaps," Flood admitted. "But the Call of Command was flawed. The boy did not finish it. There is still some doubt."

Yet even he had to admit that with every passing moment the signs were becoming clearer. Overhead the sky bled, the dome of Treetops flooded from the wound that hung in the heavens like a prophecy of doom. Water gurgled up from the ground once more in the valley as the ancient prophecies foretold. It was unfortunate that the seabed filled too slowly to wait and ride the Arkanum on a wave of glory as he had planned. Grand entrances only came along once. Flood was a showman, but he was also a pragmatist. There was still that nasty hole in the ship caused when the Lost were released.

Most distressing was the boy's escape. If only the KeyStone had blown the Callixar for a few more seconds. Hopefully it no longer mattered. Things were looking up. The Cyclix had returned to the ship's hold briefly, before going on to their secret caves until called again. He had felt their dark presence alight as he conversed with Dustin's sister. That meant all was ready down in the world Below.

Still, one should never take unnecessary chances.

"Bring him back," barked Flood grabbing the horn from its fastenings and ripping it free. "Kill the flying mammal if you must. Meet me at the gathering point by the Portal Tree. The time of vengeance against the humans is at hand. I lead our army to victory!"

Off in the far distance thunder crackled.

"What about the girl?" Gaylon asked looking out over the railing.

Jackie was stumbling around below, a lonely figure on the seabed, water collecting around her in ever growing pools.

Flood didn't try to contain his anger now.

"She is no concern of yours," he bellowed "I gave you an order. Carry it out! I will take care of her myself."

Pressing a series of buttons Flood manually powered up the laser nearest to him. Adjusting it slightly he looked through the targeting sight. The button at his fingertip pulsed yellow and then orange, finally blinking green, signaling dwindling power reserves. It would have to be enough. Flood pressed it. A bolt of cobalt light shot out striking Jackie full in the chest. She crumpled to the ground and did not move.

"There, that's done," Flood remarked. "She was entirely too much trouble. A trespasser in realms best left for others."

He turned to Lancelot. "Hold the Arkanum while I'm away. Do not let me down again."

The ape shuddered at the threat in its master's voice.

"Time is ticking Gaylon. Are you in need of encouragement?"

Flood took a step toward his apprentice.

"No, Master," Gaylon replied. "I am here only to serve."

The Arkanum's commander smiled.

Gaylon tore his gaze away from Jackie's still form as dangerous emotions flickered across his face. Then he bowed to Flood and dutifully initiated the change that sent black feathers erupting through his still sore skin. His eyes shrunk and narrowed from human to avian, watching as Flood disappeared into the Arkanum. Alone, Gaylon bore the pain, and clenched his fists.

CHAPTER 48

Something was happening to Treetops. All around Hunter the cloudscape was changing. Dark lesions grew more numerous like patches of amnesia over the once unbroken pearly landscape. Hunter's footfalls in these areas felt less spongy as if the surface of Treetops was drying out.

He paused in horror as the ground around his feet blackened like an illness taking hold.

Up ahead, Pence still raced ahead through the patchwork cloudscape as if nothing had happened. Mumbling another curse Hunter started forward as the squirrel turned around on cue. Clicking its teeth impatiently the rodent waited there, imperious on its hind legs, looking away as the detective shambled forward.

"What's happening to this place?" Hunter demanded as he approached the blue-eyed rodent.

Lightning flashed somewhere far below his feet, and Hunter flinched. He took a deep breath and steadied himself. If the Last Byzantine understood the question, he gave no sign.

"Well, lead on then," he muttered to his guide.

In response Pence lifted his furry head and stared up at the sky.

Biting back harsh words, Hunter followed the Emperor's gaze to the west. That's when he saw it. A red gash bled across the hemisphere as if the world had been dealt a killing stroke. As he watched, it soaked across his field of vision, its rosy tendrils reaching into the final unblemished arc above his head.

When he looked back down Pence was gone. Propelled by fear, both for himself and for David's children, Hunter Greenwold tore across the mottled ground without caution, blindly following the only thing he had left, the lonely metallic sound from the Last Emperor that tolled hope and despair with equal measure.

Before too long he regained sight of Pence. Hunter's breathing came in ragged gasps and he barely managed to remain on his feet. Years of drinking and smoking had done little to prepare him for this marathon. Every muscle and nerve of his body screamed at him to stop but he kept going, refusing to give up, to fold and quit. He didn't deserve a rest, and there wasn't time even if he did. The apocalyptic sky still burned, searing his conscience with the shame of failure. For a moment he left his body and seemed to float above the ground, the agony of the exertion dropping from him, as a new elevation took over. Was this what runners experienced? Without any warning, he tripped over a hidden obstacle. The next thing he knew he was laying on a stretch of unblemished ground, twisted in a motionless heap like a derailed train. When he opened his eyes, Pence was sitting next to him, still as a statue.

As quick as his aching legs would oblige, Hunter got to his feet, upset that he had fallen and wasted valuable time. His shins were bruised and scratched, but they were only superficial injuries and nothing to worry about. The pain anchored him. The ground here was white and gently rolling, free of the troubling lesions that had plagued their recent travels. Here and there a column of unblemished cloud rose into the air gently taking on the shape of a castle tower or minaret.

"Tell me this isn't the end of the line," he said. "I've come too far."

In response, Pence tipped his head slightly and narrowed his azure eyes.

Immediately the vapors at their feet shifted and cleared, revealing a ring of low mossy stones dripping with water as if they had all been submerged deep beneath some hidden sea. As one they rose from the ground until they towered over him. Looking around Hunter swallowed nervously. He couldn't help but notice that the monoliths completely encircled them. The Last Byzantine had led him to another doorway and Hunter had no idea what waited on the other side.

CHAPTER 49

A great black bird rose from the deck of the Arkanum in a flutter of wings and then flew slowly over the battlefield. There were no animal carcasses littering the area surrounding the great bone ship. Flood's lasers had burnt away even the slightest trace of flesh, but ash-colored stains dark as sin lay scattered on the ground. The human part of Gaylon fought down a sudden urge to be sick when he realized what must have happened. The fact that he had slept through it only made him feel worse. Only the body of the girl remained. That was surprising. Her molecules should have been vaporized like those of her animal companions. Against his better judgment Gaylon circled ever lower above her still form trying to figure out the mystery. Finally, he made his decision.

Landing a few feet away he walked over to her on his spindly legs and peered down with his unblinking beady black eyes. She looked different, changed in some way. Each time he saw her, Jackie appeared older. Where before—only a smattering of days ago—near the verge of the Earth Trees, she had been little more than a troublesome girl, now she was a woman, and a beautiful one at that, he had to admit. They could have been the same age. Too bad he wouldn't get the chance to know her.

Then he saw her chest rise and fall beneath the strange plate she wore. The revelation sent a wave of unexpected relief coursing through his avian form. For a moment Gaylon hesitated, caught between hope and fear. She was too big for him to carry in his bird-form. Even a child of Dustin's size would have been presented difficulties. Gaylon had limited options and none of them were good. He had no clothes, only the feathers he wore. Somehow that didn't seem to matter or he hoped it wouldn't. Swallowing and cursing under his breath he initiated the command to change back.

Her eyes were fluttering now as her body shifted in discomfort or pain. Somehow it felt important that she not see him like this. With his remaining strength he sped the transformation from feather to finger and then waited a short distance away for her to awaken.

When she awoke lying on her back the first thing Jackie realized was that she was alive. The dragon's scale had been a deadly gamble that had paid off. Serpentine armor had overcome the futuristic technology. She was really alive and Dustin was hopefully far away in HeartWood after his daring escape. There had been a terrible cost, one she could never fully repay, but at least she hadn't failed. Her brother was free, but still in grave danger with no Keeper to protect him. She tried to sit up. A stab of pain tore through her and she cried out before falling back down.

That's when she noticed the stranger. He sat cross-legged with his hands in his lap nearby. A residue of sweat clung to his brow and a look of trepidation kept sabotaging the fragile smile that played across his face. He was, without a doubt, completely naked.

"Who are you?" she breathed, fear rising within her.

The man swallowed. He looked up at her and then bowed his head again in embarrassment. "Gaylon. My name's Gaylon," he stammered. "We've never formally met. I know my appearance is alarming. I just changed back."

Jackie frowned.

"What does that mean?"

Gaylon looked around as if help might arrive out of thin air.

"I transformed back from raven form." He paused. "I came from the Arkanum."

Realization hit Jackie.

"You! You took my brother!" she screamed despite the pain. "You took him and gave him to that monster, Flood. And you killed Iggy! I watched her fall from the sky. Have you come to finish me off?"

Gaylon looked back at Jackie and attempted to meet her fierce gaze.

"That's all true," he said. "I don't expect your forgiveness or for you to understand. I saw what Flood did up on the Arkanum. What he was. I came down to see how you were. To see if I could help. When I saw that you were still alive, I changed back so I could take you to a healer."

"Liar!" Jackie wailed, tears streaming down her cheeks. "I bet you were just making sure I was really dead. Get away from me."

She tried to get up, to run away, but the pain enveloped her again and she fell back down exhausted.

"You're too late," Jackie whispered, a defiant smile on her lips. "Dustin got away. He's free."

Gaylon sat speechless as if he was out of excuses. His fingers twitched in his lap nervously.

"Listen, I'm sorry," he said finally, speaking the words slowly as if he had never used them before. "But you need healing. You're hurt."

Blood soaked through her ripped shirt and the cracked dragon shell bit into her skin, but Jackie took no notice. Using the last of her strength she knotted her hands into fists.

"Let me remove the carapace," Gaylon told her. "Your injury may be severe."

He reached out.

Jackie jerked away as if he had struck her. "Don't touch me!" She needed the dragon's protection now more than ever. It made her feel safe. Part of her didn't want to know how messed up she was. Pain tore through her chest again and she moaned through her clenched teeth.

"Clearly you are in distress," he said, his voice betraying frustration. "Please, let me help you."

"How kind and observant you are," she replied after the worse of the pain had subsided. "Aren't you supposed to be looking for my brother? Flood will be mad. Your prize has gotten away. He might stick you in a bird cage and ground you for life."

Gaylon laughed nervously. "He's leading the army. What he doesn't know won't hurt him."

"Go to hell," she continued brokenly. "Why don't you just finish me off?"

Anger blossomed on his face.

"I could," he spat. "It's what Flood wants."

Gaylon took a menacing step forward and despite her resolve, Jackie flinched. Then the emotion broke over him like a wave.

"But it's not what *I* want. You are hurt," the young man continued, his rage dissipating into something close to tenderness.

"So you keep saying," Jackie sighed. "You're a doctor then?"

"No," Gaylon said. "But I know someone who can heal you."

Jackie didn't have any warning. More quickly than a fluttering of wings, he covered the short distance between them. "Don't move," he advised. "Unless you want this to hurt."

Gingerly he removed the dragon scale. Before he could set it on the ground, the weakened shield fell apart in his hands.

"Hopefully the same won't happen to you," he remarked. The

next instant he lifted her up off the ground, cradling Jackie awkwardly in his arms as she struggled to resist him. Then he marched off across the plain like a naked madman.

For a time, Jackie howled that she be put down. Weakly she pounded her fists into his chest calling him all the names she could think of. Insults were hurled. Vengeance was promised. He was a servant of Flood, someone to be detested and never to be trusted.

Yet eventually she tired, exhausted from her injuries and the effort to resist.

"Why did you do it?" she asked finally. "How could you help someone like Flood?"

Gaylon said nothing. Nothing he could tell her would make any difference. He simply walked on, avoiding the bubbling pools of water that dotted the landscape. Finally, she descended into a deep, but troubled sleep leaving Gaylon with nothing but his own demons for company.

Before long, Gaylon began staggering. He had already been tired from his transformation. The effort of carrying Jackie across the uneven terrain brought him to the brink of exhaustion. His legs and arms burned in agony, but he ignored it.

Gaylon felt the dampness of her blood seeping into his skin, warm and alive, from an invisible wound in her chest. He walked on with her in his arms as if each stride he took would take her further away from hurt. From time to time when the burden grew too great he put her gently down, careful not to disturb her, and then after a moment's rest made sure the bleeding was in control. Then he continued on.

Her earlier question hung over him like an unwanted visitor and so he squirmed away from it, trying to shut the door on his own awareness. Why had he changed sides? The truth was that

Flood's answers turned out to be no better than the Keeper's. Worse, they terrified him. Caught between Flood's manipulations and the Keeper's disengagement, he struggled to make sense of his life as he carried Jackie in his arms. If there was another way to save the world from itself, Gaylon could not see it.

Over a corner of the great plain he trod wearily, leaving the pools of gurgling water behind, until he finally came to a series of rising, twisting hills that folded in on themselves. The way was rocky and unstable, but he knew a clear path from years before. The memory made him wince. Soon the winding path took him into the shadow of the highlands where the late afternoon light danced across the distant rolling hills. At the end of his strength he followed the trail as it thinned and faded, finally ending at the foot of a small cave. Eager now to release his burden, he set Jackie down roughly on the ground and stood back up, looking around expectedly. A knot of fear gripped him.

"Nexra," he called. "I'm here. I need your help."

The black of the cave remained unbroken.

"Do you not remember me? I'm Gaylon."

A shambling shape appeared suddenly in the doorway. Gaylon flinched, and fought an impulse to recoil, even though he had met her before. All new Apprentices were Initiated by the Nexra. The woman was old beyond measure and extremely ugly. Her clothes were in tatters. A multitude of pockets, all in varying sizes, covered a faded gray blouse littered with holes. On her swollen feet were a pair of sandals while her long thinning grey hair failed to hide the patches of mottled skin beneath. One eye was half-closed and her teeth were mostly gone. She stood there like a ghastly apparition guarding the entrance as contorted expressions flickered across her misshapen face.

"Bring her in," she rattled finally.

Then she disappeared into the darkness with an unexpected quickness, not caring if he followed or not.

Entering the old woman's demesne, Gaylon felt a chill pass

through him. The damp shadows called to him, tugging at memories. Shaking his head as if to rid himself of a bad dream he walked through the twisting passageways, always careful with his burden. Eventually they passed under a wide archway limned in silver and entered into a cavernous room that rose to a lofty ceiling. High in its center gaped a small, crude hole. Below it, suspended in midair by dried sinews, was a large eye-shaped mirror. Pure unadulterated light spilled through the opening and then was transformed by the glass facets into a dazzling spectrum of light that illuminated the smooth rock floor below. The Nexra stood at the edge of the luminous glow, waiting, her arms cradling what looked to be rags. Entering that colorful bright beam for the second time in his life, Gaylon put Jackie gently down and then withdrew into darkness as if his nakedness or choices shamed him.

"Put these on," the woman's voice commanded.

Abjectly he took the white robe from her aged fingers and began dressing. It felt strange to put the garb of an initiate on again.

When he had finished, the Nexra turned away as if he no longer mattered. "You've done well. Leave us before we lose the light. I will call when you are needed."

"She's hurt," he said quickly. "She needs help. The dragon's scale saved her life, but Flood's weapon was very powerful. There is bleeding…"

The old woman gripped his shoulders and spun him toward her with sudden ferocity.

"Do you forget who I am?" she demanded. "I am the Nexra. My purpose is clear. I do as I see fit."

Gaylon bowed his head.

"You are the Nexra," he said abashed. "I do not forget."

For a moment they stood in silence. Then she released her grip. Risking a look at Jackie who still lay golden on the floor like a princess encased in amber, Gaylon obeyed the Nexra's command and disappeared into the shadows beyond as if he had been banished.

The Nexra took a deep breath and then entered the dancing light. For a long moment she stared at the young woman and her mouth twisted and puckered until a hideous smile spread across her face. Caught in the harsh light, the girl's life was laid bare and exposed to the old woman's gift of percipience. She saw the struggles, the fears, and the adolescent dreams that were so typical. Yet there was more. This Planet Walker had knowledge that she shouldn't have. There was a hidden connection that linked her to Treetops. The Nexra followed the blood path and for the first time in many years was surprised at where it led. This child's mother had gone through the eight initiation rites, of which the light of the *Aperionus* and the cave were but the first. She had guided the woman herself. The revealing light determined whether a candidate was fit for service in Treetops and bestowed certain healing properties that helped with the ease of transition and discomfort. This latter quality was the reason the Nexra had brought this stranger to the *Aperionus*. For an individual to be in Treetops, it was always assumed, and had always been the case, that they *could* be here, that they had a gift and only needed help in developing it. True, on rare occasions, for various reasons, a person could not complete the rites or upon reaching the end, decided to return to their formal life, uninitiated and bereft of service. Even rarer were the individuals who passed through and took their charge only to turn away down a dark road. Gaylon was one of only two such cases that the Nexra could remember in her millennia here. The young woman's mother, Jillian, had been strong and full of promise. She remembered that now. Jillian might have become a Keeper if she hadn't left for root and family.

The Nexra turned the woman's face so it was fully in the power of the light.

More answers revealed themselves. Here was Jillian's child full of guilt over her lost brother, newly rescued from Flood's clutches. Would surprises never cease? Yet Jackie, for all her passion and commitment, was lacking an essential quality. The Nexra searched within the sacred light again and again, but to no avail. The only source of power detected, weak and failing, was clearly not her own. Gently she removed the Keeper's woody finger from Jackie's pocket and stuffed it into one of her own. Yes, there could be no doubt. None at all. This young woman, the daughter of a Keeper's First Assistant, had not a single scrap of talent or gift. She was, the old woman realized in horror, completely rooted to the Earth. Her presence in Treetops as a wayfarer left her exposed to the ravages of the cloud realm's own time machinations. Although the Nexra could see the physical telltale signs of aging, her heightened percipience felt the acceleration throughout Jackie's body as atoms and corpuscles, skin and bone expanded and multiplied at a feverish rate. Another week or two here and she would leave her youth behind. A few months and she would be an old woman. Yet that was not the most immediate danger, she realized in disbelief. Even now her mortal flesh burned and deteriorated under the harsh light of the *Aperionus* for she had no natural protection. Oblivious to her plight, Jackie slumbered on. The Nexra chuckled darkly. The two of them were not dissimilar. Although spared physical pain, each ray that struck the Nexra laid another twisted layer of madness upon her already addled brain.

With undisguised relief, the Nexra stepped out of the light and into the psychic coolness of the surrounding cave.

"Come Gaylon! Now!" she shouted.

She was about to call again when he finally appeared and moved to her side in reluctant attention. A yawn spread across his features and he seemed to only remain standing with conscious effort as if his earlier transformations and exertions had cost him too dearly.

"Don't just stand there, boy," she said. "Get her out of there! She's burning up."

For a moment her former pupil didn't react. He seemed to be struggling with incomprehension. The *Aperionus* was a place of healing, after all. It could not harm. The fact that it did meant something had gone terribly wrong. The painful pink of Jackie's bare skin reddened and a slight but growing acrid odor filled the subterranean cavity. Launching himself into the light, Gaylon scooped her in his arms and carried her back into the waiting darkness.

Jackie's eyes fluttered and her body writhed as the painful burns penetrated her unconsciousness. She was waking up. Holding her out to the old woman expectantly as if he were presenting an unwanted sacrifice, Gaylon waited for the Nexra to speak. Without a word, however, the hunched old woman turned and strode off down a side passage.

Muttering under his breath, Gaylon followed behind cradling the still fervid body of Jackie. Away from the *Aperionus,* the cave system was engulfed in darkness. The only sources of illumination came from Jackie herself who glowed faintly from the immersion in the discerning light, as well as the occasional wax-eaten candle that flickered sadly in the stones above. Gaylon was forced to track the old woman by the shuffling sound she made traversing the uneven terrain. Once or twice he nearly lost his footing as an unexpected rock or turn caught him off-guard, nearly causing him to drop his precious cargo. Finally, the tunnel opened out into a small room that he had never seen before. By the standards of the *Aperionus* cavern, this space was much smaller. Although thrice as wide as the passage they had just come through, the ceiling arced just a hand's length above Gaylon's head. In the sputtering light cast by a wax-dripped candle, he could discern the stubs of stalactites broken off from their imperceptible geologic plunge. On the far side of the space an ancient-looking bed, its wooden frame falling apart, sat covered in a rotting blanket. With a start, Gaylon realized that he stood in the old woman's bed chamber.

Several crudely built and warping shelves stood on the far side of the room. They were packed full of bizarre-looking knick-knacks, books, and bones. It was a hoarder's paradise. The Nexra crouched nearby, digging through a strange assortment of objects that littered the floor. Holding them briefly in her wrinkled hands she scrutinized each mystery before tossing it aside with increasing anxiety. Gaylon spied earthen bowls, intricately carved figurines, sea-polished rocks, slender golden rods, a filigree of many colors and jeweled daggers, some caked with dried blood. A mirror carved in amber caught her attention briefly. As she held it up in the flickering light, Gaylon caught a glimpse in the glass of a young, fair face framed by brown locks and freckles. Casting it aside with a bemused smile, she continued her frantic search. Suddenly the Nexra froze. There under a pile of faded scarves sat an unexpected prize: a worn leather book. She looked at it lovingly, her mouth agape in the act of remembering. With one arthritic finger she traced an undecipherable pattern across its faded cover. Trembling, she reached out to open the pages, but then stayed her hand. A moment later the Nexra shook her head as if waking from a dream and tossed the book over her shoulder, resuming her search with increased desperation. Gaylon saw flashes of gems and strange runes written across faded parchment. One series of letters on a crumbling fragment scrap of vellum seemed to be written in a language Gaylon could read. He leaned closer, just making out the words, Dawn Thistle.

"So that's my true name," the Nexra chuckled, gazing down at the writing. "I had forgotten."

Then she cast it away as if it no longer mattered and frantically began digging again through the confusion of her belongings.

"It must be here!" she wailed.

Gaylon could only look on with growing impatience. The weight in his arms, however slight to begin with, was growing heavier in his weakened state and there was no place to lay his burden down. Jackie let out a low moan and opened her eyes, but he had little attention to spare at the moment. The stone walls of the Initiator's room seemed to close and shrink around him. His breathing became shallow as if there wasn't enough air in the cave to sustain even his meager needs. It was no coincidence that his animal transformation was that of a bird. He longed for open skies and flight unencumbered. Instead he now felt as if he were suffocating.

"Yes, yes!" the Nexra exclaimed. "Here it is. Yes. I knew I still had some."

In her hand she held aloft a small vial. In the candlelight, the substance glowed. Her mouth gaped to form a hideous jack-o-lantern rictus.

"Don't just stand there," the old woman snapped. "Put her down."

With relief Gaylon bent over and set Jackie on the cold, rough floor.

"Not there!" the Nexra commanded. "On the bed."

Grunting with exertion and displeasure, Gaylon heaved his charge up again and trudged over to the crude bedding. There he laid Jackie down as gently as his quivering arms could manage.

"Where am I?" Jackie asked opening her eyes. "God I hurt. My skin, it feels like it's on fire." She tried to say more, but only a long moan emerged from her throat.

Gaylon paused. He didn't know how to answer her without causing more confusion.

"I know," he began. "Don't try to talk. You're going to be okay".

"Only if the young and foolish get out of the way," the Nexra retorted, moving him roughly aside. The old woman bent down with a supreme effort so that she was on the same level as her patient.

"You're in the Cave of the Nexra," she said. One eye was closed and the other was swimming with cataracts. "I'm the Initiator of the Eight Rites. I was consort to Xylum, greatest of the Keepers. That was eons ago."

Jackie glanced nervously at Gaylon, but he gave no reaction.

"He left me with his signet, a source of power which has sustained me."

Beaming like a new bride, her face broadened into a gap-toothed smile as she extended her hand. On her finger glittered a metal ring the color of a new spring leaf dipped in morning dew. It wrapped around her finger like a twining vine.

"Together we cared for Treetops," the Nexra went on. "Before I assumed my calling, many were lost or unguided. With the light of the *Aperionus,* I see where talents lie. I heal that which I can, using the ancient knowledge that has been preserved. I also bury the dead."

The Nexra paused as she lathered her hands with something that looked like congealed blood. Then she reached out for Jackie's burned flesh, noticing a familiar birthmark on the girl's neck. "This may sting a trifle."

At the first moment of contact, a series of spasms gripped her body and Jackie's fists knotted in sudden agony. As soon as it began, however, the reaction died away, replaced with a coolness that enveloped her entire being. One by one the hot spots on her body were put out and she breathed a little easier.

"What did you do?" she asked in wonder.

"A touch of some very old healing ointment," the Nexra replied. "Made from mastodon grass or so I was told." She placed a gnarled thumb on Jackie's forehead. "It knows how to do the rest and where to go."

"Thank you," Jackie said, trying to smile through her weariness. "You too," she added turning her head to where Gaylon stood breathing softly.

"You must stand now. Lying can do no more good. There is nothing else can I accomplish."

Jackie groaned and rose slowly from the pungent bedding. The world wobbled a bit, and then steadied.

With the tip of a long, yellowed nail, the Nexra lifted the

corner of Jackie's shirt, which was soaked with dry, crusted blood, until the milky underside of her left breast was visible. In sudden embarrassment, Jackie tried to tug down her shirt but the old woman stayed her hand. A long and oozing cut ran down from the gentle slope of her breast to the middle of her stomach where Flood's laser weapon had broken through the serpentine defense. Without a word of warning, the Nexra plunged her nail into the bloody crevice. Jackie screamed before she realized that there was no accompanying pain. Instead a feeling of warmth spread as the old woman ran her finger down her body. The injury faded by degrees as Jackie looked on until it was only a faint scar, nothing more. Grunting her approval, the Nexra nodded and smoothed down the young woman's t-shirt.

"I recommend," the old woman began with a note of finality, "that as a trespasser and interloper to the land of Treetops, you leave immediately. There is no time for hesitation. Your brother is free. With each step you cast away days of your life never to be recovered."

Surprise jolted Jackie. Thoughts spun in her head. She had just been healed. Surely, she could not suddenly be an outcast. Before she could ask even one question, Gaylon filled the silence of the chamber.

"The Nexra was my teacher," he began, doing nothing to mask the shock that was etched across his face. "She is everyone's first teacher who arrives in Treetops. I brought you here because you were hurt in the battle at the Arkanum."

Jackie tried to interrupt him but Gaylon continued on. "The Nexra healed your injuries with the light of the Aperionus. All who come here are healed and tested by it. How could she know —," he began and almost faltered, "what would be revealed?"

Jackie turned from Gaylon to the Nexra. A look of exasperation crossed her face.

"Would someone please tell me what's going on?"

"Child," the Nexra began with a hint of compassion. "You

know that time runs differently here. Surely you must have realized that you are not immune to its ravages as others are. Have you not wondered why? Has no one told you?"

Jackie nodded her head. "Nimbus tried."

"You do not belong here," she said quietly. "That is the sad fact. Every day in Treetops you age by one year. You are not protected because you are not supposed to be here."

"But the animals at the Grove of the Earth Trees let me Choose them," she sputtered. "And I communicated with them, even without the Orchlea."

The Nexra shook her head as if trying to remember forgotten words of consolation. Gaylon ran his pale slender fingers through his straight black hair as if trying to free a secret word or insight. He walked over to Jackie, but her growing anxiety stopped him from reaching out and comforting her.

"You don't understand," Jackie cried. "My mother was a Keeper's Assistant. She helped Nimbus. Before I came here, she gave me a seed from an Earth Tree. How could she have done all that if I don't have the gift? You don't know what you're talking about."

Hot tears fell down Jackie's face and she wiped them away fiercely. When she spoke again, however, it was in mere whisper, chocked with sobs. She felt drained.

"It's the only thing I have left."

"My dear," the Nexra began as gently as her rattling voice would allow. "Let me try to explain. You could no doubt communicate with your wonderful animal companions because the Sleep Catchers in the Forgotten Plains aided you with their well-known effects. The Keeper's gift to you may also have helped, until the magick ran dry."

She plunged a hand into the largest of her pockets and held up Nimbus's woody finger. Jackie opened up her mouth to protest, but the Nexra barreled on.

"You were only able to choose your companions at the Grove because Nimbus and necessity required it. As for your tree-shaped birthmark—it is leafless and lifeless compared to others, and is merely a sign of the long lineage you are part of. Your particular line is not broken, however. Given time you may still pass on the dormant gift to your child someday."

Everything the old woman said made a terrible kind of sense. She felt the world closing in. Then a final hope appeared to her.

"I broke the Keeper's magic near the pool with Iggy by uttering some words that my mother once said. How could I do that if I don't have any power?"

Her protest hung in the air demanding an answer. For a time even the Nexra seemed hesitant to counter it. Finally, she gave Jackie a response.

"At a time of great need, any member of the seven families, even a leafless one such as yourself, can do a small magick, if the words are known and the connection is a strong one. I have no doubt you could do other trivial acts, provided they were taught by your mother and the need was dire, but you can never truly practice the natural arts for you haven't a gift residing within you. I'm sorry, but you are hardly the first family member to be without a talent."

Jackie stared back in disbelief. Arguments flowered and died on her lips as she crumpled forward.

Arms circled her now and the pungent smell of the Nexra filled her nostrils. But she didn't care. For the first time since she had arrived in Treetops, time moved slowly and she let the small act of human kindness envelope her. Finally, the old woman stepped away. Although she wasn't ready, Jackie forced herself to face whatever the Nexra said next. Defensively, she folded her arms across her chest and watched as the Initiator of Treetops turned and walked out of the chamber.

"Follow me," she called as an afterthought. "I know a shortcut back to HeartWood."

CHAPTER 50

Dustin gripped the slick dorsal flipper of Speedo and hung on tightly as the dolphin flew through the air in frantic arcs and dips. Bright beams sliced through the air above and below them. Then they rounded the corner of the great bone ship and he allowed himself to breathe. Any joy he felt at escaping from the Arkanum was immediately snuffed as the world continued turning around him in a sickening blur. The dolphin was taking no chances and continued to weave through the sky until the bone ship was far off in the distance. Only then did his mount level out and their flight became steady as they glided through the open spaces.

Dustin worked up the courage to look around. Nervously he glanced behind him, still expecting to see one of Flood's minions or a blast of energy. Dustin stared in relief. Empty sky stretched as far as he could see. No hooded riders or great birds beat the air to bring him back to the Arkanum. Yet it wasn't true that he was free of danger. Even he could sense that. Half the sky was red. From a great gash down the middle seeped the life blood of the Earth. Dustin could feel its ancient power as it spread across the horizon, violent tendrils of hatred and primitive rage straining for release. In fury the rupture reached ever eastward, towards the fleeing speck of Dustin and the distant intolerable presence of HeartWood.

With a shudder Dustin turned around and buried his face in the cool skin of his mammalian savior.

"Thanks," he breathed.

You are very welcome, clicked the dolphin. *It was my pleasure. I'll have you back safe in no time.*

"Speedo," he said, reading the creature's mind and seeing the name that Jackie had used. "I'm scared."

There was the briefest of pauses before the dolphin replied in its usual rapid-fire manner. *The Earth prepares. War is coming. I feel the urge to join, to strike, to reclaim. It is hard to resist. Only my oath in the Grove holds me to my purpose. I will not fail. It will suffice.*

Dustin blinked as the wind whipped through his hair.

Hang on.

Suddenly Dustin found himself pressed flat as the dolphin dove through the air. Wind whistled in his ears as they descended at a frightful speed. By slow increments they leveled off until a giant vaporous mountain loomed directly ahead of them. As they flew closer, the peak's true shape became clearer; a crumbling fortress with one misty tower pointing like an accusation at the damaged sky. With each second its size increased until they were almost upon it. Dustin closed his eyes and gripped the dorsal fin with all his might as he burrowed his head against Speedo's flank.

Do not fear, the dolphin said playfully.

When Dustin opened his eyes again, he found himself passing through a luminous landscape like the inside of cotton candy. All around bright jewels of color shone from the depths of hidden cloud chambers. Then it all vanished as they emerged into the open air again.

Wow! Dustin exclaimed. That was bee-uuu-tiful.

Speedo clicked in laughter.

There is so much more. I wish I had time to show you.

They flew on and Dustin took it all in wide-eyed until finally Speedo began a slow descent to a wide empty cloud valley.

Down there, chattered the dolphin waving a flipper. *HeartWood.*

Dustin looked at the almost limitless expanse of cloudscape that hung beneath them. Some of it shone pearly white, but a multitude of dark spots covered the surface in ever growing numbers. Only around a small dwelling made of what looked like sticks and moss was the ground clean and pure. Speedo circled down to the structure in a lazy fashion, finally coming to a smooth landing near a wall of tall bracken ripe with berries. An impossible bird stood in the arched doorway formed from twisting vines. It flapped its small useless wings impatiently. As Dustin slid down from the hovering dolphin, the bird's preposterous beak opened and closed several times as if it were so vexed that it couldn't decide where to begin.

"About time you got here," the dodo complained. "What did you do, walk?"

Speedo ignored this affront and Dustin was too stunned at the bird's speech to make any sort of reply.

"Listen, we don't have much time," the creature continued, turning toward the boy. "So let's skip the formalities. My name's Regnal. I'm a servant of the Keeper. And this is," he made an attempt to spread his wings in a majestic manner, but then folded them with a look of frustration, "HeartWood. You must be the Wayfarer's brother. Where is that sister of yours anyway? Couldn't she catch a ride on a manatee or something?"

Dustin swallowed nervously.

"I dunno," he managed in a small voice. He hoped she was alright, but he didn't know.

"Hey, it's okay, kid," Regnal began. "I bet Flipper here can go back for her."

The dolphin shook his head sadly.

"He's too tired," Dustin said. "Needs rest first."

Regnal sneered at the flying mammal.

“Stupendous. Sensational,” he said with rising sarcasm. “No Wayfarer. No Keeper. Only one Chosen left. Even Pence is gone missing—not a great surprise, mind you. Portents of doom abound underfoot and overhead. It looks like you’re just in time for the End of the World.”

CHAPTER 51

Hunter Greenwold stared at the ring of stones. Unlike the circle of stumps that had brought him here, these were taller, nearly up to his shoulders. Each dais measured about five feet in diameter and sat atop a squat monolith. At the center of each base a symbol was carved into the granite surface. Hunter squinted and strained trying to make them out. They were weathered almost beyond the point of recognition. Slowly, as if remembering a dream just after waking, Hunter walked over to the nearest one to take a closer look.

Following the faded lines, he managed to piece together the body of a great bear with razor sharp claws and a beak where its mouth should be. Some kind of owl-bear, he realized with growing alarm. He stumbled on to the next pedestal and traced the grooves and etchings with his finger until the image of a griffin, half lion and half eagle appeared in the living rock. From one to the other he shambled with growing apprehension. A cockatrice, a chimera, a baby dragon with long whiskers dripping water from its smiling mouth stared back at him. There was a pegasus, a great stag, a basilisk, a snake with a head on each end, and a manticore with leathery wings. Across the circle was etched a fiery bird with wings outstretched rising from flames, a silent cry of rebirth resounding from its beak. On the last monolith Hunter discerned a Kraken, its tentacles reaching out as if to encompass the world.

At the center of the circle the clouds had retreated, replaced by long, wet grass. A flat, rectangular object caught Hunter's eye and he went to investigate, his footsteps making a squishing sound. The stone marker was covered in dripping vegetation as if it had come from deep beneath the sea. Hunter cleared the surface to reveal a face of leaves and grotesque, twisted branches. A faded hand with thorny talons reached out with wild intent.

Hunter took a step backward. The image disturbed him. Something seemed familiar about it, something he should know. Mesmerized by the engraving, Hunter didn't notice the movement happening all around him. The platforms were filling with their respective occupants. One creature after the other took their place and then waited in patient stillness, seemingly as lifeless as their carvings. Hunter spun around in a desperate attempt to ward off an attack. Pence skittered over and looked up at him, chattering a warning.

The next moment the stone circle started to rotate slowly, as if on some invisible track. Faster and faster it turned until the animals and the pedestals upon which they sat were a speeding blur. For the second time Hunter felt his body shift as he fell forward. Only this time he didn't lose himself. There was no blackness of forgotten time, only a harmless blink. When the detective opened his eyes, he found himself immersed in a wintry slipstream of glowing matter. On either side of him were temples, some grand and made of marble or vaulted stone, while others were simply sacred groves or half-hidden springs in which secrets dwelled. In each special place there stood an entity, arms outstretched calling to him in the frigid air like a forlorn carnie at a midway. Hunter stood transfixed by the spectacle. At his feet, the ground shook slightly, like the echoes of giants.

"Wisdom is mine to give," growled the one-eyed Norse god Odin. He wore a dark cloak and broad-brimmed hat. "I have hung on the World Tree and plumbed life's secret depths. Stop and let me feel the warmth of your breath for a while and I will tell you things not even dreamed about by gods or man."

Hunter caught the scent of sweet perfume in the air. A woman, the most beautiful he had ever seen, stood nearby, beckoning him.

"Desire is all there is. Only I can fulfill the hunger that's inside you. Come closer," invited Aphrodite with her siren song. The thin fabric of her dress allowed her milky white breasts to show through before flowing over her shoulders all the way down to her slender, thighs. Hunter could not look away. "Let me feel the beat of your heart and I will show you ecstasy for a lifetime."

A man with a jackal head stood next to a scale, beckoning him with the silence of the tomb. Hunter felt the weight of his conscience at the sight and had no doubt what the verdict would be. Even after he passed, Anubis kept motioning to him with long bony fingers that seemed to say, "We will meet again."

Above a lush carpet of spreading ferns, a colorful winged serpent hovered, its forked tongue darting in and out. A warm wind blew and the shadow of four other suns appeared in the sky overhead. When Hunter walked to the other side and looked back, the divine feathered creature became a man adorned in a bright headdress with a conch shell draped around his neck.

Many of the gods that Hunter saw, however, were achingly unfamiliar to him. It was as if their names were hidden by a veil.

A woman with a dragon's tail smiled at him as he passed. Further on there was a bearded man holding a great eight-pronged war club. An oaken harp with strings made from the seasons stood next to him. Nearby stood a young man in a Roman tunic and cap, a sword in his hand and a face that shone like an unconquered sun. Nearby a great horned serpent glistened with the water of the ocean's salty vastness. Ravens and coyotes, chameleons and spiders competed for his attentions with smooth-tongued offers. A solitary black jaguar paced back and forth in the dark water of his own making while across the causeway an antlered figure sat in the lotus position. From an invisible source, thunder boomed loudly and lightning crackled in the distance.

Hunter walked on feeling very small as Pence led the way. The rodent's pace quickened as if it were anxious to show him something. With relief, Hunter hurried along, half running past a menagerie of deities and monsters that seemed to stretch without end, their calls and gestures now bordering on the obscene. Finally, the glowing air around him began to dwindle. On his left was a giant slab of weathered stone. A set of thick metal chains were broken across its surface, their purpose defeated.

"He escaped," a beautiful girl said. She stood next to the empty prison in a meadow of flowers. The sweet scent of April filled Hunter's nostrils. "Shapeshifters are hard to hold. Now it begins," she said with a touch of winter sadness.

He knew who she was. It came to him like the name of a long-lost friend. Eostre. The goddess of spring stood looking at him, priceless as a new day, with tears streaming down her face.

Hunter wanted to ask what she meant and who had escaped, but her countenance held him speechless. A dim memory stirred within him. He had heard those words before. They were important. They held a clue. Something he read in a book or heard someone say, but it would not come to him. The more he struggled to remember the more it slipped out of reach.

He walked on. It was all he could do. Some part of him noticed Pence up ahead. The air was almost clear now. The glittering magic reduced to dying embers that sputtered and faded away. The line of deities was nearly at an end. A young woman in a white flowing robe sat at a spinning wheel pulling a wispy thread. Long dark braids hung down her back. A winged helmet rested atop her head.

"Beware the trickster," she said pausing in her work and looking up at him. Then the goddess smiled. "I am Frigg, but you may know me by a different form." With the twirl of a slender finger she changed into an old fortune teller. The only thing missing was the crystal ball. "In the clouds of Treetops," she told him again, "is woven your destiny."

Hunter stumbled backward with a start. He recognized her from the Renaissance Festival pavilion. Memories of another time flashed through his mind. When he looked up the Norse goddess was young again, but she was no longer smiling.

"Stop him," Frigg pleaded. "He will doom us all."

She started spinning again.

"I don't know what you want me to do," Hunter said.

As he watched , the spun wool obscured the Queen of Asgard's face.

At his feet Pence chattered for his attention before scrambling on. Shaking his head Hunter followed. Directly ahead lay the last sacred space: a grove of trees. An ancient hickory tree stood near the center, its twisted branches forming a canopy. A figure stood obscured in a patch of sunlight and shade underneath. Hunter found himself walking between the trunks to where he sensed a deity waited like a kindred spirit.

"My name is Tane," the god said in a voice that was not entirely masculine nor feminine. Rather the sound of his words reminded Hunter of a breeze rustling through leaves.

"I'm Hunter Greenwold," he said awkwardly.

The god stared back intently. Something flickered in his eyes.

"In only the most insignificant of ways," replied Tane with playful certainty. "Do you not know your true name, lost one?"

Hunter felt a brief wave of unease pass through him as the woodland deity stepped silently toward a shaft of sunlight.

"All of us here are forgotten or un-worshiped. Yet all retain a sense of their once grand nature."

"What are you talking about?" Hunter asked in irritation.

Tane smiled and all around him an invisible chorus of birds broke out into song.

"I may not speak of it. You must discover that for yourself."

As Hunter looked on, the forgotten immortal waved his hand in a magician's flourish and stepped back into the tree's knotty trunk, dissolving from sight. For several heartbeats Hunter stood rooted to the spot. A flicker of movement up ahead caught his attention. Pence. The rodent was leaving without him. Hunter took off running. Through the rarefied air he sped, past crumbling statues and fading light until he finally passed, like a specter, through an invisible curtain separating worlds and stepped into a vast woodland, dark and ancient.

Instinctively he sensed that no human being had ever seen this. It was a primordial place, impossible and glorious. Moss carpeted the ground like the accumulation of time, rendering his footfalls harmless and inconsequential. Great columns of living wood and twisting branches rose around him in silent epiphany. Oak, ash, and gingko, redwood, monkey tree, and baobab, bristlecone, cypress, and banyan, and a forest of others grew magnificently around him. Hunter knew them all without knowing why. Berry bushes and bracken, ferns and deadly nightshade all spoke to him with their chlorophyll tongues in a language strange and yet familiar. It wasn't just woods, he realized with a start. This was *the* archetypal Forest, wild and untamed. A light shone from above, but the rays did not touch the earth below. Instead the illumination was captured in the web of leaves above as if the forest were protecting a secret essence, harboring something sacred.

Hunter took another step and spied Pence. The magicked rodent was nearly invisible perched as he was on a low-hanging branch of a bone-white birch tree that rose like a skeletal hand into the pristine sky, the tips of its reach breaking into sun-dappled splendor. In the center of the great mottled trunk arced an opening, natural and unassuming. For the briefest moment he could have sworn he saw a smudge of red as a short, shadowy figure disappeared into the blackness. Then it disappeared from sight.

Pence scampered down the tree in pursuit. He chattered once at Hunter before disappearing through the gap, the bell around his neck chiming softly in his wake. Hunter walked to the portal and peered in. Impenetrable darkness stared back. Looking behind him at the garden of green, he let the verdant majesty wash over him until his skin tingled with anticipation. Finally, he turned back to the bark-lined aperture and stepped into the heart of the tree, letting the mystery swallow him whole. It felt like going home.

CHAPTER 52

Jackie followed hurriedly as the Nexra, torch in hand, led them through a maze of twisting passageways. Her mind still spun from the Initiator's revelation. Nothing felt real. Each hollow footfall merely confirmed her insignificance and status as an outsider. She could almost feel the weight of days descend upon her out of the inky blackness. It felt as if time mocked her, giving her more life than she could enjoy because the moments happened so fast. Like the subterranean scene before her, Jackie's life was a blur. No longer a teenager, she grieved for what she had lost. Most of all, however, Jackie felt betrayed. Her mother had given her a gift she didn't deserve. More than anything else, that hurt the most.

Gaylon crept like a shadow behind her. The torch in his pale hand guttered like a soul in limbo. Earlier he had edged up next to her and asked if she was all right. When she had made no reply, he had retreated into his own doubts.

Up ahead the passage twisted again and the Nexra disappeared around the bend taking most of the light with her. Jackie found herself in nearly complete darkness as Gaylon's torch dwindled to a burning ember. The walls were narrower here and after bumping into the unforgiving rock, she had to turn sideways to squeeze through so she could continue her progress. With increasing anxiety Jackie shuffled around the claustrophobic bend, afraid that any moment the passage would come to dead-end. It became hard to breathe and a different kind of weight pressed down on her. No longer moving, she floundered in panic and fear. Somewhere in the darkness she felt a presence behind her. Then Gaylon grasped her hand, leading her out of the stifling nothingness and into a world of air and light.

The cave exit was little more than a splinter of space in a lonely outcropping of rock surrounded by a vast sea of green. A forest of trees stretched as far as the distant horizon. Jackie blinked at the light of Helios as the celestial chariot made its way toward the western horizon.

Something was wrong. Black smoke rose from the chariot up into the heavens. The god himself fanned the smoke, directing it with strange motions of his arms. As the vapor snaked their way skyward letters formed.

Loptr undan.

Then the message dissolved into twilight.

"What does that mean?" Jackie asked.

The Nexra let out a heavy sigh. "Believe it or not my ancient Norse is a bit rusty, but it can't be good, whatever it is."

From the slight vantage point that the rocky hillock afforded, Jackie attempted to get her bearings. No landmarks met her gaze. Nothing familiar dotted the landscape. The more she took in the forest's details, the more they seemed like strangers from another world, almost alien. Tall spindly sentinels with drooping spatula-like branches stood closest to the cave opening. To Jackie they looked like a coat rack designed by Dr. Seuss. Smaller versions grew further away, their trunks rising from a dark marshland. The most bizarre trees had long tapering limbs ending in large milky orbs. Others species had glossy fan-shaped leaves. A variety of ferns grew in clumps here and there. Some were quite short and grew out of a root ball while others were stately and tall resembling palm trees or cacti with bright green tips. Taken together the scene was a comic profusion of natural oddities, as if they were all placed there by a divine gardener with a good sense of humor.

"It's not just animals that Treetops remembers," the Nexra told Jackie in a sudden burst of lucidity. "We remember our namesake as well. Almost everything you see here is extinct down Below. Gone for good. Cures for cancer and poisons alike. Only here do they live on."

Gaylon looked as if he'd heard the lecture before, but in Jackie her words found a tender spot.

"My mother loved to plant things," Jackie said. "I think she would have liked this place."

The Nexra smiled fondly. "If memory serves me right, she did, child. Perhaps even more than she cared to admit."

Questions spun in Jackie's mind, but she didn't get the chance to utter them.

"Follow me," the old woman urged. Her brusque manner was back. "Time dwindles. It will not be much further."

With those words she ambled off down the slope and entered the profusion of trees following an invisible path that only she could see. Jackie moved after her with Gaylon beside and for the first time realized that their hands were still clasped. Jackie let go. Her cheeks blushed in embarrassment. Something had happened in the cave both tenuous and fragile. Together they hurried after the old woman into the maze of vegetation.

True to the Initiator's word, their travel was brief. After half-running through a grove of cyads, they fell in behind the Nexra as she led them to the edge of a perfectly round clearing. There the Initiator stopped. Jackie kept waiting for them to continue, but the old woman simply stood as if HeartWood were in the empty field and her guiding was done.

"How many doors do you see Gaylon?"

"Two," he answered swallowing thickly. "They are unchanged as before."

"Ah," the Nexra smiled showing her broken teeth. "Yet not all is the same," she observed glancing at Jackie. "What door do you pick servant of Flood, former assistant to Nimbus? Arkanum or HeartWood? One leads to the Ship of Bones. The other leads to the Keeper's sanctuary. What way will you go? The portal must be answered and the Doors of Choice reckoned."

Try as she might Jackie could see nothing and the emptiness in the meadow only mirrored the emptiness she felt inside, a growing sense of inadequacy and conviction that she was an outsider in a world of hidden magic.

"Do you mock me? I have already made my choice!" Gaylon exclaimed. "I completed my Initiation long ago. My deeds in Treetops altered that choice. If there was a way to change my path or pick a new one I would. Nothing can be done now. It is too late."

The Nexra looked at him with hard eyes, but her voice was gentle. "I think not. Choose again. It will do you good."

For a moment Gaylon the Black hesitated. Then he looked over at Jackie. She smiled, trying to reassure him the same way he had helped her in the catacombs. A moment later he strode across the field. At the halfway point he stopped and looked from his right to his left. Then he turned back and with a strong voice that broke the forestall stillness said, "I choose HeartWood." Reaching his hand out to the left he turned an invisible knob. Immediately a small door swung into view at the center of the clearing. A landscape of clouds with the Keeper's cottage was framed in the opening.

Jackie stood with her mouth agape.

"Go," the old woman said roughly pushing her toward the impossible gateway. "There is little enough hope to waste it here."

"I don't understand. How did we get here?"

"Talking. Always talking. There is no time," the Nexra spat.

"There are shortcuts, portals that open for those that have an honest desire to serve what waits on the other side."

The Nexra stepped forward and made ready to shove her again, but Jackie put out her hands.

"Aren't you coming with?"

"I cannot go through a Door except in death. Only the Initiated may pass. I must remain in my cave with my secrets."

"But I haven't been initiated. I failed," Jackie managed.

"It's time you were leaving then," the Nexra told her.

"Hurry," Gaylon called. "Take my hand."

She looked up at him in surprise.

"You need a connection," he explained, "or you won't be able to cross over safely."

"Right," she said quickly. *Because I don't belong here.* "Let's go."

Before she could grab hold of Gaylon, the old woman shoved Jackie across the empty ground and through the Doorway. She stumbled and fell. When she stood up, she found herself transported alone to a barren landscape. In front of her lay a pool of water, ringed with flowers. Curious, she peered over the edge and looked inside. The water seemed very deep, so deep that she couldn't see the bottom.

A ripple moved across the clear surface and then a face slowly appeared, as if arriving from a great distance. Her mother smiled as she had always smiled, but with a touch of sadness at the corners.

"You have grown up," she said.

Tears filled Jackie's eyes, but she didn't wipe them away.

"We don't have much time," her mother said gently. "You are only between, in flux, in the space between portals."

The water wavered and for a moment the image in the pool faded.

"I don't understand," Jackie said, afraid she would lose her mother again. "I thought you were gone for good. The dragon said so."

A shadow passed over the loving face in the water.

"The dream that you had of me is gone. That is true," she said. "I cannot return and be with you. You know that. I wish it were not so. But you can still think of me anytime you wish." Her mother's smile returned. "I will always love you."

Jackie leaned over the pool until her face nearly touched the surface. The sweet smell of fragrant flowers filled her senses.

"I miss you, Mom," she whispered.

In response, the image of her mother clouded over and nearly disappeared.

"Walk back through the Doorway," her mother said as if from very far away. "Your friend still waits beyond this portal. Be brave. You are stronger than you think."

Fighting back tears Jackie stepped through the shimmering frame.

"There you are!" Gaylon exclaimed. "Where did you go? I couldn't find you."

"Somewhere I needed to visit one last time," she answered. "The next time you see the Nexra, thank her for me."

Gaylon gave her a look that said she must be crazy, but he nodded. Without further delay Jackie took Gaylon's hand and they stepped through the doorway together.

CHAPTER 53

Jackie blinked in momentary confusion. She stood in the middle of the Keeper's humble residence. Interior vines and autumnal leaves covered the walls. The Earth window still ringed the floor like a giant blue watery eye but the room seemed somber and charged with an air of foreboding instead of its usual peacefulness. There was an empty space, of course; an absent presence where Nimbus should have been. That was to be expected. There was also something else. Releasing Gaylon's grip, she spun around wildly looking in all directions. No one was there. No one was here at all. Panic rose in her throat.

"Dustin!" she called. "Dustin, where are you!"

She ran through the main entrance and down the thorny walkway heedless of the branches that scratched and tore at her skin. When she burst into the open cloudscape in front of the Keeper's dwelling, Dustin ran toward her. The sight took her breath away. Without even realizing it, she stopped in her tracks. All the recent struggles melted away and tears streamed down her face. When he ran into her arms, Jackie lifted him up like he was the lightest, most precious thing in the world. Then she hugged him close, never wanting to let him go. Dustin buried his face in her shoulder and sobbed.

"I was so worried," she finally said as she put him down. Jackie dried her eyes. Then her hands gripped his shoulders and her voice shook frustration. "I thought I'd lost you. That was such a stupid thing to do."

Dustin looked up at her, tears pooling in his big blue eyes.

"It doesn't matter now," she said quickly, wrapping her arms around him again. "I guess I would have run away from me too. Everything's okay now."

"I missed you," her brother said.

"Missed you too, squirt," she told him.

Sniffling, Dustin buried his wet face against her side. When he spoke, his voice sounded faint and fragile as a robin's egg. "I miss mom. I really miss her a lot."

"I know," she said. "I do too. I think about her every day."

Jackie squeezed him tight and then released her grip. Dustin stepped away and looked up at her. A quizzical expression formed on his face.

"You look different. Older," he said.

"It's a long story. Guess I had some growing up to do."

Her brother smiled as if that explained everything.

"Thanks for coming to get me," Dustin said wiping his eyes. "I'm sorry I ran away. Are you back now? Are you back for good? I wanna have fun again. I want it to be like it was before."

The words nearly broke her heart.

"I'm back," she breathed. "I'm not going anywhere. We're a family. But don't do that again, okay? You have to promise. No more running away. I love you. You know that, right?"

Dustin nodded. "Uh huh."

A smile grew between them. Overhead Speedo spun in a lazy circle. Eventually Jackie became aware of Gaylon standing nearby.

She turned to him. Now it was her turn to feel naked and exposed.

"Thank you," she said, and she meant it. "You may have taken him, but you also brought me back here. I never would have made it without you."

The apprentice to both Nimbus and Flood held her gaze for a heartbeat before looking away.

"It was bad of you to steal me, but I forgive you," Dustin told Gaylon, but the words seemed lost on the tall, brooding young man.

Gaylon looked down and shuffled his feet self-consciously. Then he straightened and seemed to come to a decision. "Your gratitude and compassion are misplaced," he said looking Jackie with a sudden fierceness. "The world is on the brink of destruction because of my actions. If I hadn't delivered your brother to Flood, none of this would be happening."

A flurry of feathers rounded the corner of HeartWood.

"The turncoat is right," Regnal said. "But he was just a tool delivering an even greater tool. Now if you're all done assigning blame and clemency, we need to get busy. I hate to break up this touching little reunion," said the dodo, "but we have company fast approaching."

Looking out across the darkening cloudscape Jackie's hopes all but died. Fanning out across the valley came a vast army of every conceivable animal the world had ever known. They swarmed and flew hungrily over the dying ground from one edge of the horizon to the other in numbers that could not be counted. Overhead of the advancing horde, the sky an almost uniform blood red. The fatal gash was an even darker crimson running down the middle. It still seeped into the surrounding heavens like a wound that would never stop.

Teeth and claw thundered nearer, and with every footfall any remaining whiteness in the clouds turned black. The mass of Earth's Army was shaped like a colossal wedge as it swept ever onwards like an unstoppable wave. In front of the leading edge, striding like a giant, was Flood himself.

Jackie had only seen the Master from a distance looking up at the Arkanum as she huddled next to Wintra. He had seemed big then, with his voice booming out across the plain like a commandment. What he had become was nothing less than mythical. Flood loomed larger than life, adorned from head to toe in armor the color of dried blood. A gilded helmet sat atop his head with a plume of real fire dancing at its peak. Even from this distance she could see his eyes smoldering scarlet as well as the strange glow which radiated around him. Flood had somehow become infused with power from the wave of animals flowing like anger incarnate all around him.

The Master of the Arkanum seemed oblivious to HeartWood and did not veer from his path to the Portal Tree, whose uppermost branches were just visible above the cloud tops. It was as if the penultimate moment, the purpose for which he had existed for untold millennia, made him exalted and blind to anything other than the battle that threatened to begin. So massive was his animal army that it soon became clear to Jackie that they all were in danger of being trampled as the creatures swept across the landscape. Intended or not, the Keeper's sanctuary would soon be reduced to dust, with humanity to follow.

"What a shame," Regnal lamented. "Here am I, the most intelligent bird in existence, a product of both Keeper lore and Earth wisdom, and yet I am completely doomed once again on account of these."

With a dramatic flourish the dodo raised its pathetic wings and let them drop to his side.

Jackie hardly noticed him. Her eyes were still fixed on Flood's Army that thundered towards them. "My god," she breathed. Almost unconsciously she wrapped her arm around Dustin and pulled him close.

"They're hungry," her brother whispered in a voice almost too small to be heard. "I called and they came. I did a bad thing."

Gently, she lifted Dustin's chin.

"Listen to me. This isn't your fault." Jackie told him. Concern was etched on her face. Her brother was safe now. None of this should be happening.

"Flood told me to blow a horn," Dustin explained. "The Cal-lix-ar. He said I was special. He promised it would help you find me. I wanted you to find me. The animals could it hear it too. I liked that. They were my friends. But then they changed."

Her brother paused and looked at the animals as if they were not something to be feared. "Maybe they will listen to me."

Dustin closed his eyes and concentrated. His features screwed up as if he were battling some internal enemy. Beats of sweat broke out on his forehead. Through clenched teeth, he pleaded, *"Please stop, please stop, please stop."* Then his features relaxed and he opened his tear-filled eyes.

"They won't listen to me anymore," he told her in a voice tinged by sadness beyond his years.

"It's okay, squirt. Flood tricked you. We'll figure something out."

But what that might be she had no idea. She had spent all of her energy and willpower to get Dustin back. Through a long, arduous journey she had made it to the Arkanum. Though the losses at the bone ship still grieved her, Dustin had been rescued. Seeing him again was a dream that had come true. Somehow she had persevered and found a way to do the impossible. Now, however, it seemed as if it had all been in vain. She had simply ensured that they would die together.

"She's right, you know," Gaylon said sliding up next to Dustin. "Don't feel bad. He tells people what they want to hear. Flood's really good at making people do things they want to do."

"Indeed," sneered Regnal. "That is why he is known as the

Changer. The boy did not know any better. You, on the other hand, had been warned."

Gaylon winced. Turning toward the dodo, he addressed the group as a whole. "That is true. I left the service of Nimbus, Keeper of Treetops, out of anger to do the bidding of Flood. I was foolish. I know I don't deserve it, but I would give anything to make amends to the Keeper. Perhaps there is a chance he still lives."

Jackie felt momentarily at a loss.

"Nimbus is gone, Gaylon. He fought the Elementals and was lost. He sacrificed himself so we could escape."

Gaylon bowed his head. "That's what I thought, but I needed to be sure."

"Are you certain, girl?" Regnal asked.

"Of course I'm sure," Jackie said. "I saw him surrounded. No one could have escaped that."

For once the bird seemed stricken. "It is as I feared. I sensed his power consumed days ago. What can we do now? A girl with no power, a little boy, a flightless bird, and a traitor are no match for the Earth's Army. Treetops will be swept away by its own inhabitants and the World Below will soon follow."

Regnal turned to Gaylon in desperation. "Help us stop him. Surely you must know some secret, spied some weakness in Flood's plan."

The former servant looked pained. "Once the Callixar has been blown a third time, there is nothing that can stop Flood's Army. Nothing that I know of anyway."

"Very helpful indeed," remarked Regnal. "Glad to hear that your time with the Master of the Arkanum was not wasted."

"Flood did mention something, though," continued Gaylon slowly. "It's a small thing. I was tired from my transformation, but I remember him saying that he was worried about the Third Call, that Dustin may not have blown long enough."

"Looks like it worked to me," quipped the dodo casting a glance at the army of animals that thundered ever closer.

"Maybe Flood's hold isn't as strong as he wants it to be," Jackie ventured. "Dustin, can you try again to slow up the animals? I know you tried before, but it's worth a shot. I don't understand your power, but right now it's all we've got."

She turned to the Keeper's servant. "Regnal, is there some force that we can tap into here in HeartWood?"

Regnal shook his feathered head. "Since you are an interloper here you can't be expected to know. All the power of HeartWood and Treetops comes from the Earth. Connecting to it requires a connection, a Keeper or someone else potent with gifts. It has become clear, my dear, that you have none. The traitor can change his shape, but not our fate, and I am merely a servant. Only the boy as the KeyStone has any measure of hope."

Jackie looked over to Dustin. He closed his eyes and concentrated, reaching out to the animals that stampeded in the valley below. Beads of perspiration appeared on his forehead. His forehead wrinkled with effort.

"I can't," her brother said weakly opening his eyes. "They hear me, but they won't listen."

"We must face facts, Earth girl" Regnal said gently without ridicule. "You have done much more than I thought possible for a person of your station. Yet the day is all but done. All we can do is meet the end with a measure of grace. What would you have me do?"

Jackie felt outrage boiling up inside of her. Hadn't she proved herself time after time? In spite of everything this extinct bird kept putting her down while the world hung in the balance. Before she could tell Regnal to shut his fatalistic beak, a hole formed in the clouds nearby. She watched spellbound as a figure climbed out. The scent of damp leaves wafted through the air. The man crawled a few feet and then teetered as if spent from a long journey. A heartbeat later a small white squirrel appeared in the gap amid the thinning wisps before scampering away as if nothing had happened. Then the passageway sealed itself closed.

Jackie stood protectively in front of her brother with one arm resting squarely on his chest. Regnal flapped his wings nervously as the figure dressed in jeans and an unfortunate tropical t-shirt struggled to stand, his face still hidden. Finally, the man gained his feet and stood before them.

"Oh, it's *you* again," drawled the dodo. "Aren't you a little late?"

Hunter barely acknowledged the annoying bird's presence. There before him were Ashmore's children, their backs to the crude enclosure he had ran out of earlier. With shaking fingers, he took out the crumpled picture from his pocket and held it up as he looked back and forth at their faces. The girl was older, but there could be no doubt. Maybe he wasn't crazy, after all. He smiled now, despite himself, even though he didn't have anything to do with their being safe. He stuffed the photo back in his jeans.

"Your father hired me. I'm a private detective," he said. For the first time Hunter felt proud saying what he did for a living. "He wanted me to find you. Guess it's all about ignoring the red herrings and following the white squirrels."

Jackie's eyes lit up.

"You've seen our dad?"

Hunter' smile evaporated. He didn't know what to say. Finding the missing children had been his only goal, his all-encompassing obsession. It had been his last chance to make things right. He had let nothing else intrude upon his thinking, of what he had to do. Somewhere in the back of his mind, however, he had known that this moment might come. If he was lucky enough to find the kids alive, he had always known that he would have to answer for his actions.

The truth was harsh. It always was. Hunter had left David Ashmore dying on his office floor. Yes, he had called 911 and tried to staunch the bleeding the best he could, but that was little comfort. He could rationalize his exit and argue that staying would have meant endless police questioning and suspicion. In all probability he would have already been dead from one of Baland's thugs. What did all his posturing matter, though? His intentions and best efforts came to nothing or close to nothing. He hadn't really tracked them down so much as stumbled upon them. Even if he knew how to get back there was nowhere to go. Ashmore had taken a bullet meant for him. His wife, if Hunter remembered correctly, had passed away recently when they were still out east. There was no home left for them in Rockwood. All Jackie and Dustin had was a defective detective.

He swallowed thickly. "My name's Hunter Greenwold," he said and then coughed, as if hoping to expel the truth lodged in his throat. "Your father saved my life. He was very brave. You need to know that."

"What do you mean *he was*?" Jackie asked. "What's happened to him?"

Hunter put his hands together on his chest as if he were praying.

"Listen," he pleaded. "There will be time to explain things later. Right now, we have to figure out a way to get you out of here."

Even as he said the words, however, he knew something was wrong. Ashmore's children seemed hesitant, as if something held them back or stole their focus. They gazed behind him as if his offer of freedom and safety was meaningless.

"Perhaps your keen powers of observation have deserted you detective," remarked Regnal. "It would seem you are not Heart-Wood's only visitor."

Hunter turned around slowly and then tried in vain to make sense of what he saw.

Unbelievably, the valley landscape was moving, rising and falling towards the place where he now stood with his mouth agape. Details came slowly and his brain refused to believe what his eyes showed him, but eventually he registered the shapes and the teeming mass of animals that moved across the clouds like a plague. Only the first few rows were discernible with the vast army melding together into a million-legged nightmarish creature. Yet it was the creatures he recognized that terrified him the most for although known to him, they had lost some unnamable essence. Each had been transformed from the inside and warped into mindless killing flesh. At the front of this hellish army strode a giant figure of a man who acted like a conquering hero on a path to some invisible goal. With his florid armor the color of an open vein, the man lifted his arms and the multitude of animals behind him cried out in a cacophony of blood lust and frenzy. The ground under Hunter's feet trembled.

Jesus, he thought.

Hunter was utterly speechless. What he could do in the face of such unimaginable violence? For a moment he found himself back on that quiet suburban street, music still blaring from his car speakers, as the little girl disappeared under the wheels of his SUV. His hands were clenched now with shock just as they had dug mercilessly into that long-ago steering wheel. They would all be trampled underfoot. Suddenly he needed a drink, anything to numb him out. He felt his pockets for a cigarette, but they were empty. He didn't even have his gun. Eventually, he realized that Dustin and Jackie were looking at him.

Ashmore's daughter should have looked disgusted at what she saw. Instead her eyes pleaded with him.

"What are we gonna do?" she asked.

Hunter knew that she was looking at him for answers. He didn't have any. How could he? A desperate part of himself wanted to scream at her. *What do you think I can do against something like that?* His mouth opened and closed but he didn't know what to tell her. It all seemed hopeless. Still, he had to try. He was still here. He was still alive. He wanted his life to count for something. The rusted gears of his FBI training sputtered into motion. Perhaps he might be good for something after all.

"Listen, we need to get away from here," he began. "Try and put as much distance from us and that goddamn animal army before were trampled. I suggest we start moving. Now!"

Jackie shook her head sadly. She stood there with her arm still wrapped around Dustin.

"You don't understand. Those animals aren't really after us. They're going to wipe out everyone in the world below. A being called Samuel Flood is controlling them. They have to be stopped."

Hunter looked at her and tried not to laugh. What she was asking was impossible. Something like that couldn't be stopped. It couldn't be survived.

"There's a tree Dustin and I climbed up," she continued more forcefully. "That's how we got here. That's how Flood's army is going to invade the world. We have to *do* something. Escaping isn't good enough."

The animals were close enough now that Hunter thought they resembled an ocean wave about to break over them. Like a rising tide across the valley, they swept closer to the little hill on which HeartWood sat. Closing his eyes, the detective tried to block them out, but the sound of their approach overwhelmed his senses.

"You can't go away. Not now," he heard her say. "You're better than this. My father trusted you."

Opening his eyes again Hunter saw Jackie standing defiantly, waiting for an answer that would satisfy her. *Where in the hell does she get such guts?* He wondered.

"If running isn't an option and fighting isn't possible then I'm not sure what we can do," Hunter said. "I'm guessing this luxurious shack doesn't have a basement."

The bird turned its head toward him menacingly. Before Regnal could answer, a flash of light rippled across the dome of the sky, leaving the air glowing in its wake. A muffled concussion of sound followed that reverberated across the valley, a harbinger of stranger things to come.

The source of the disturbance came from behind the advancing army. At first it appeared to be little more than a glowing speck on the horizon. The object began to take shape as it sped across the cloudscape like a comet at unbelievable speed. As Hunter looked on the figure shifted before his eyes, turning in a kaleidoscope of color from one state of being to another. One moment the entity was liquid blue with a body undulating in watery profusion, the next it turned into a storm-darkened cloud in the figure of a man crackling with lightning. Then it changed to a figure of molten fire, a conflagration with feet of stone who transformed finally into the glorious, blinding form of a man made of light, a star gone supernova.

Hunter shielded his eyes from the brilliance. When he looked again the detective saw a powerful figure of leaf and bark. On top of the being's head sat a leafy crown. An aged human face looked out in anguish as if trying to contain the other aspects. Then it changed, continuing the terrible cycle.

"It's Nimbus!" Jackie exclaimed in disbelief. She hardly recognized the Keeper.

Regnal's sarcasm left him. He whispered, "How can it be?"

Even Pence chattered in agitation or surprise at this unexpected homecoming.

Dustin stood wide-eyed and overwhelmed at what he saw. He seemed on the verge of crying as if Nimbus were a strange and frightening apparition, something that should never be.

"What is it?" Dustin asked.

"I'm not sure," Jackie said stroking his hair. "He used to be the Keeper of this place."

Hunter looked on, a look of worry spreading across his unshaven face. He recognized something about himself in the strange being that Nimbus had become.

"Friend or foe," the detective asked, not sure he wanted to

know the answer. There was too much to deal with and none of it made any sense.

Jackie stared at the approaching spectacle.

"A friend, I think," she said at last to the detective. "At least he used to be. When we escaped, he was surrounded by Elementals, four really powerful creatures that are connected to different parts of the Earth."

She paused and wiped a tear from her eye.

"I'm not sure what he is now. I thought he was lost. I don't know how he survived or what he's been turned into."

"Listen," replied Hunter. "I've never met this Nimbus, but I think I can safely say that he's a changed man. No one goes near him until we find out what he's up to."

Only Gaylon seemed undisturbed by Nimbus's sudden return and bizarre transformation. In contrast to the others, he seemed almost giddy with excitement as he stood watching his former mentor streak across the landscape.

"The old fool is craftier than any of us thought," the former apprentice murmured. "He's been here so long that he's part of Treetops now. Somehow, he was able to merge with the Elementals. Absorb their essence."

Within moments it became apparent where Nimbus was heading. Giving the charging animal mass a wide berth, he looped around like a blazing comet and then came to a shuddering stop. Standing there, a menagerie all to himself, he faced the Master of the Arkanum for the first time.

"Get out of my way, you imbecile!" roared Flood as he thundered toward the Keeper with his massive fists clenched and the power of a million animals thundering at his heels. His eyes burned red. "Your time has passed. I don't know how you survived, but you're too late."

Nimbus did not speak. Perhaps he had moved beyond mere speech or simply chose to ignore the command. Sparks shot out from his fiery manifestation into the air around him like dying constellations. Reaching deep within his molten core he withdrew a red-hot ball of magma. Holding it in his burning hand, the former Keeper cocked his arm back defiantly and launched the flaming orb at the Master of the Arkanum. Caught by surprise, Flood had no chance to evade the strike or defend himself. The attack struck him squarely in the chest, bursting into violent incandescence and stopping his forward momentum. For a moment the Master was ablaze, his whole being consumed in elemental fury. Then the maelstrom passed over him, leaving behind wisps of smoke that curled from his unharmed body.

"Is that the best you can do?" taunted Flood taking a step forward. "My army makes me stronger. Do you not see?"

The fiery plume atop Flood's helmet grew bigger and brighter as his legion approached.

As if in response, the Keeper changed his form again, this time becoming a dark tempest. Storms flashed in his eyes and a wind ushered forth that would have toppled leafy forest kings. Flood grinned with effort and took several steps towards him before faltering.

Animals streamed around them now as if their battle had no significance. Onwards the creatures sped towards the Portal Tree and a meeting with the world below. In another minute they would be at HeartWood's doorstep where Jackie and the others looked on in disbelief.

Raising his arms high into the air Flood let out a primal roar of rage. Earth's Army echoed his outcry in a show of camaraderie. Taking on their strength the Master of the Arkanum grew visibly taller and more massive, dwarfing his ancient enemy. His teeth tapered into vicious points and the nails of his hands extended until they were shimmering talons. His lips curled into a snarl. With renewed confidence he strode toward the Keeper, and into the teeth of the gale. Nimbus shifted again, transforming into a being of light. He was radiant. Brilliance pulsated from him with each measure of his labored breathing. Raising his hands, the former Keeper took aim. Bright beams of luminescence shot out from his palms toward the Master and then were deflected, bouncing off his crimson armor.

"I have the power of Creation on my side," echoed Flood. "What do you have but the dying embers of the Elementals? It is unfortunate that you survived their onslaught only to die here."

Now the Master of the Arkanum drew himself even higher until he had the stature of a god. The steady glow around him became incandescent until it eclipsed the Keeper's light.

Then Nimbus changed again, this time unexpectedly into his mundane human form. Vines and leaves still covered his body, but there was no hiding the anguish which wracked his visage. He seemed spent, exhausted by the Elemental transformations which consumed his being. It was as if his being burned away from the inside. Defenseless, he stood beneath the colossal Flood as his former creatures thundered around him, oblivious to his presence.

"Oh, Nimbus," Jackie whispered.

She felt helpless.

"This is the day I have waited for," Flood proclaimed. "This is the moment that's sustained me through the long eons as you and your fellow Keepers scurried around Treetops casting a deaf ear to the cries below. Thinking yourself sages, you ignored the living while you tended the dead. No more. Today it changes! The Earth shall be reborn. Even if I should fall, my army will carry on. But I will not fail. Beauty is worth fighting for!"

Clenching a mighty fist Flood swung it at the spot where the bent figure of Nimbus stood. Straining to see the action between the never-ending stampede of animals, Jackie let out a cry. The Keeper remained fatally still as the death blow descended. At the last moment, Nimbus changed his form again, his eyes flashing a brilliant cerulean blue as his body dissolved around him. When Flood's devastating punch came there was no impact at all. Instead, his mighty blow passed harmlessly through the air. Where only a moment before Nimbus had stood helpless, now he was a liquid elemental, a shifting figure of permutable water. Unable to stop his forward momentum Flood toppled over, rolling over onto his back and into the path of his ravenous army. The weight of his armor held him down for precious seconds as he struggled to regain his feet. The Master of the Arkanum had just enough time to raise one steely arm in defense before a lumbering triceratops crushed him underfoot.

Even then, however, Flood still lived, although his body was broken. Soon the damage would be repaired. The former Keeper had only a brief time before his elemental-fused form changed again. Still he hesitated, or at least Jackie thought he did, before covering his foe in a drowning embrace. Through Flood's mouth and nose he poured himself as the crash of animals blocked the intimate scene from view.

"No!" the Master of the Arkanum gurgled. His body writhed on the ground while his hands clutched weakly at the elemental's elusive substance.

Further words and desperate commands directed at his animal army were lost amidst choking incoherence. Flood grew weaker and weaker. With every second he shrank in stature.

Nimbus looked at his nemesis with a sad, watery countenance, his fluid form resembling a massive human tear.

"Your army is an abomination," the Keeper reasoned. "They care for nothing except the hate you've sown within them. You are not their champion. They need no one. Not even me. Their destruction will have no end."

Flood tried to respond but only succeeded in coughing instead. His eyes were wide with panic, but slowly he began to let go.

"Don't fight it," the former Keeper told him with a touch of melancholy. "You and I, we don't really die. The Elementals helped me see. Treetops is only part of it. There's so much more."

A smile played across his aqueous face. Then, like the tide returning, the expression vanished.

"We're one, don't you see?" he continued. "We're part of the Earth."

Nimbus released his hold on the Master of the Arkanum. With a shimmer he coalesced into the shape of a pillar of water.

With the last of his strength Flood raised his head to look at Nimbus. A wave of anguish passed over his face.

"The Earth is dying. The world will pass away as if it were nothing but a dream. It needs saving."

"But not like this," the Keeper responded, his voice as gentle as a ripple on a mountain lake.

"Then how?" asked the Master of the Arkanum.

The former guardian of Treetops did not answer for a long while. "People are part of the Earth." he said at last. "They are beginning to remember. Perhaps it isn't too late."

Flood shivered. "I'm scared."

"I know," Nimbus replied.

Then, for the first time in a million years of existence Samuel Flood closed his eyes, and then he was no more.

A great tremor passed through the animal army. They slowed to a crawl, but did not stop their trek towards the Portal Tree.

Nimbus looked down at the lifeless body on the wispy ground. With each passing moment it became less substantial until it became transparent and then, finally, nothing at all.

"If only there had been another way," he thought. *"Yet you wouldn't have listened and too much was at stake."*

Suddenly his watery form convulsed. Something was wrong. For a moment he felt his human form reemerge, but it couldn't hold. He braced himself for another transformation. They came in rapid succession, fluctuating wildly between different elemental states. Faster and faster they erupted, each eclipsing the other in a dizzying carousel of being. It was a chain reaction, building to some cataclysmic end.

Then suddenly it stopped.

Nimbus stood, teetering on the edge of existence. A leafy crown adorned his mossy head just as it always had. Only now his autumn leaves were nearly black, as if the transformations had burned away his essence. The slightest wind might blow him to dust. He had given too much of himself. His face looked drained and sallow. Tremors wracked his body and his eyesight was veiled like the end of days.

Slowly the vast animal army came back into focus. They were still moving toward the Portal Tree, but something distracted them, slowing their advance to a crawl. Those closest to the Keeper came to a halt. Too fragile for hope, he spied Jackie across the distance. A shadow passed through him.

"Oh no," he mouthed.

Then Nimbus crumpled to the darkened ground and was lost amidst the sea of animals.

As one, Flood's Army came to a complete stop and stood transfixed upon the darkened cloudscape. Even Helios paused, a glowing chariot in a darkening sky.

"Keeper!" Jackie screamed.

Racing down into the valley, she dodged between the motionless creatures, nearly colliding with a polar bear that stood like an iceberg of frozen fury. The tension holding Flood's army in place was palpable. Tooth and claw barely kept in check. Soon, she feared, the desire for blood lust would reawaken. She didn't have much time. Finally, she spotted Nimbus up ahead, just past a pair of Siberian tigers and bony ankylosaurs. He lay on the ground, small and frail, surrounded by the animals he had cared for all those many years. His eyes were open and his breathing faint. Kneeling beside him she scanned his flesh and bark and bones for signs of injury but could find none.

"What's wrong?" she asked. "What can I do?"

"Do?" questioned Nimbus. "There's nothing to be done. No point in holding on when the holding is gone."

As if to prove his point a section of leafy growth on each arm fell off revealing frail human skin underneath.

"You're changing again," Jackie said with growing panic. "Tell me how to save you."

"No. This is who I am or was. I don't remember anymore."

"I don't understand. Tell me what to do."

The former Keeper shook his head in anger. "Can you give me back my memories?" he demanded with sudden viciousness. "Can you make all those whom I loved and left alive again?"

Jackie sat speechless. His words and outrage made no sense to her.

Just as quickly as his ire had risen, it collapsed upon itself. Nimbus studied her face intently as if finding faults or a newly discovered mystery.

"Who are you?" he asked slowly with the voice of a frightened child. "Do I know you?"

Shock and disbelief buffeted Jackie. How could he not recognize her? After all they had been through. It was too much.

"Keeper," she said, trying to keep her voice calm. "Please. Don't leave me again. I'm Jackie. Remember?"

Faster and faster now leaves and twigs disappeared from his form, replaced by mundane skin and hand-spun clothing. Nimbus watched the transformation taking place as if it were a game, a childish smile playing across his almost bare face. It felt as if she wasn't even there.

"Look at me!" Jackie shouted.

Immediately she regretted her outburst.

At once his innocent reverie was broken and the former Keeper looked up at her, fear etched across his features as if the ruler of the cloudy kingdom was nothing more than a boy caught making mischief.

"I'm sorry," she began. "I didn't mean to yell. I'm just scared. Help me understand."

Nimbus stared at her. Then a smile of recognition swept

across his aged face. For a moment the old Keeper returned. Yet he appeared different. Jackie had never seen him like this. Gone was the covering of leaves and living vine that had adorned him for so long. In their place was ordinary skin, wrinkled and fragile. Wisps of grey hair swept across his balding head like the remnants of a once beautiful garden.

"Jackie, it is good to see you again," the old man began as if awaking from a dream. "I'm sorry I had to leave you."

She glanced nervously back at HeartWood. Dustin's small form stood motionless, his head bowed in concentration as he tried again to turn the vast animal armada. Beside him, Gaylon gesticulated wildly with his arms creating a shimmering band of energy at the leading edge of the creatures that sputtered and then died out. Regnal hopped from foot to foot in a silent tirade. The creatures around them were still in check, held by the Keeper's unlikely return, but his power was fading fast. Soon their fury would be unleashed again.

"Help us," Jackie told him, her voice raw. "I don't know how to stop Flood's Army. None of us do. We don't have much time. They're trying to get to the Portal Tree so they can exact some kind of revenge on the world below. They've only stopped because of you. It won't last."

Nimbus sighed. "If only I could, my dear." Then he started to close his eyes. All around them the animals grew more restless.

"What happened to you?" she blurted out, trying to find a way to keep him present. "How did you survive?"

The Keeper steadied himself.

"Always questions," he smiled faintly. "I surrendered to them. What else could I do? It was a terrible gamble, but it worked. I fused with their essence. It was like dying and being reborn over and over again." A tremor passed through him. "Reading the signs in the sky, I made my way here as quickly as my new form would allow."

"Is that why you were shifting back and forth?" she asked. "Are the Elementals trying to get out?"

Nimbus coughed. "My transformation is the cost that must be borne. The price paid to try and contain that which has no limit. In a sense, I used my aging body like a wick to a flame. I've burned out or will in short order. But I will take them with me."

Jackie nodded, feeling like a student who nodded in class, but had little idea what was actually being said. Even so, she decided to risk one more question.

"What's happening to you?" she asked hesitantly. "You look —different."

Once again, a shadow of a smile passed over his face as if he were remembering something bittersweet.

"My name is Arwel," he told her. "I wasn't always a Keeper, you know. I was born a very long time ago in a village in Wales. I grew up, fell in love, and even learned a trade before I found my true calling. I've been here ever since living out these centuries atop the world, safeguarding its beauty. All things must come to an end, however. Treetops cannot sustain me forever. Even now the world grows dark."

"But time runs differently here..." Jackie protested.

"Yes," interjected Arwel with an air of impatience. "Still it passes. I am old. The centuries have unwound me. Would it be unreasonable to assume that my mind and body are not what they were?"

Jackie flinched as if being scolded. The Keeper was right, of course. He couldn't help the way things were, and he'd done so much for her, for all of them. Heck, he'd even given the last of himself to stand against Flood.

Tentatively, Jackie reached out and took Arwel's wrinkled hand. It felt warm.

She felt as if she should say something, thank Nimbus—Arwel —for everything he had done or tell him everything would be all right, but she just sat there with him in silence instead.

The former Keeper gazed at her as something close to joy slowly spread across his face. Color blossomed on his cheeks and his eyes twinkled like the promise of spring.

"I've had a good life, my dear. Don't worry about me. My only regret is not being able to help you in the final battle to come."

A chorus of growls reminded her that the animals were returning to their ferocious state. A myriad of eyes looked at her hungrily.

Nimbus lay dying, helpless as a newborn, but the pain she felt was overshadowed by the realization that they were all in grave danger. The world was about to be thrown into chaos and she had no idea what to do. She didn't think she could bear anymore. At that moment when she felt most alone her companions appeared at her side, much as her Chosen had. Regnal the dodo bird, Hunter Greenwold the detective, and her brother Dustin all gathered around at the place where she knelt. Only Gaylon stood apart, still dressed in the Nexra's white garments, as if he found some reason to doubt himself again. Pence was nowhere to be seen.

"Who do we have here" breathed Arwel. "Friends, I hope."

"You know Regnal, of course," Jackie managed, "as well as your former apprentice." Gaylon nodded stiffly. "This is my brother Dustin," she continued, "—back at last from Flood's clutches, and a private investigator named Hunter Greenwold that my father hired. Of the Chosen, only Speedo the Dolphin survives. He is resting nearby."

Nimbus closed his eyes as if in prayer for a long moment. Upon opening them the former Keeper looked stricken.

"What of Flood's army?" he finally managed. "My vision grows dim."

Now Gaylon stepped forward.

"They still remain in the valley Keeper. They are— waiting."

"Is that really you Gaylon?" he asked.

Before Gaylon could respond, a fit of coughing seized Arwel.

When he spoke again it came out as little more than a whisper. "We have a short reprieve. That is all," the former Keeper told them. "The animals, they are only pausing until I am gone."

As if in response, a chorus of ravenous sounds erupted. Jackie flinched, wanting to make herself even smaller.

Arwel ignored the distraction. "Someone else is here," he began. "Someone you have not named. Oh my," mused the Keeper in surprise. "There is power here great enough to crack the Arkanum in half and split the Earth Trees asunder. Somehow the name eludes me. How can that be?"

"We need to depart Keeper," Regnal implored. "The animals, they are stirring."

All around, the creatures eyed them with increasing interest as their bloodlust returned. Hunger and hatred Mouths opened to reveal sharp teeth and claws extended on the wispy ground.

Arwel nodded his head in dismay and let go of Jackie's hand as if it were the last link to life itself.

"Go," he commanded, somehow finding a hidden reservoir of strength. To Jackie he sounded like the Keeper he must have been in his glorious youth. "My time is nigh and the world hangs in the balance. No long goodbyes. With my passing so too does Treetops with no clear successor to pass the seed. Keep the memory of all you have seen alive in your hearts and in your head. In that way Treetops will never truly die."

"Die?" Jackie murmured. Shock and disbelief rocked her to the core as she stood up unsteadily.

Regnal flapped his wings in protest as Gaylon moved in front to stand by Arwel.

"What is your wish Keeper?" the former servant asked bending over him.

Arwel stared in surprise at his apprentice. The Keeper's blue eyes searched the young man's face for a long moment. Finally, he spoke.

"For you to find peace. The world below needs you. There is always hope."

"But as Keeper I could turn the animals," pleaded Gaylon. "Slow them down at least."

"You do not have the training," Arwel replied flatly. "And even if you did, is it your desire, your *heart's* desire to reside over this domain?"

Gaylon glanced over at Jackie and his cheeks flushed like a schoolboy.

"Maybe," Gaylon managed weakly. "I'm not sure," he managed at last. "I'm not sure of anything anymore. Everything has changed."

Arwel sighed. "Time grows short. Only one thing remains, and it is, perhaps, the most important of all. Where," he asked looking around, "is Pence?"

Jackie was taken aback by the question. The unassuming world below was about to be overrun by an army of ravenous creatures. Millions, perhaps billions would drown in blood from injuries inflicted by Creation itself and yet Nimbus worried himself over a harmless white squirrel. Who cares where Pence was? And then it made sense. He was having another episode, slipping away into a sea of dementia.

"It's okay," she consoled him like a mother would to a frightened child. "I'm sure he'll turn up sooner or later."

The look he shot her convinced her immediately that her diagnosis had been mistaken. "My wits, at present, are fully intact. The matter is grave if he is not with us. Who has seen Pence the Traitor?"

"I have," Hunter growled. He stepped closer so Arwel could see him. Leaves speckled his hair from where he had crawled through the ancient tree. "I followed him here. Think he wants me to find something other than Ashmore's kids."

Arwel turned his head and looked at the disheveled middle-aged man. Then he put his hand over his mouth in shock. "Of course," be breathed in amazement. "I *am* losing my mind if I don't recognize you."

Hunter glared at the old man. "I've never met you before in my life. Do you want to tell what's going on, please?"

"How can it be?" Arwel asked in dismay, "that you don't know yourself when all around the Earth sings your name?"

"No offense, but what the hell are you talking about?" demanded the detective.

In response, another collective growl like a murderous symphony warming up, rose from the throng as the assembled creatures remembered their killing instincts. Whatever power Nimbus still had on Flood's Army was failing fast as his life dwindled away. And without the Keeper to protect them they would be torn to shreds in moments. Their death would only be a footnote to the greater horror that awaited the world below. Jackie knew they must flee. Yet none of them made a move. They were still spellbound, much like the animals around them, waiting for one final truth to be revealed.

Arwel looked lost searching for words that wouldn't come.

"Keeper," Regnal began gently, "if story time is over then we really need to get going."

The animals were being released from their stunned bereavement. The passing of Flood and the return of the Keeper had confused and soothed the horde, but the effect wore off with each passing moment. Hungry jaws snapped the empty air as a final deafening roar rivaling the Callixar split the air. Jackie felt a growing unease that they were prey.

"He's right," she agreed. "Let's get out of here."

"Too late," Arwel croaked as his eyes clouded over. His final words were nothing more than a whisper. "They awaken."

As Jackie looked down the Keeper closed his eyes and his body went terribly still. Flood's Army shook as one as they threw off the vestiges of restraint. In unison all the assembled creatures bared teeth or claw and inched towards the small defenseless group. All that is, she noticed, except a lone wolf the color of freshly spilled blood. It was unusually large with cunning eyes. Unlike the other animals it did not have a partner and seemed to act on its own volition, periodically nipping at docile beasts or herding members of the horde forward. The great wolf paused, sensing something beyond the gathered army, then tipped its back and let loose a primal howl.

Into this strange scene darted Pence. Ignoring all common survival instincts, he raced toward the wolf and then circled it chattering loudly. The wolf lunged viciously at the white squirrel while all around the animals of Flood's Army closed in. Jackie steeled herself for an attack reaching out protectively for Dustin, but the creatures seemed momentarily distracted. Although they still teetered on the edge of blood rage a subtle curiosity seemed to hold them, a presence greater than their own tricking them into forgetting. Instead of lunging toward their prey, the army turned as one toward the fiery wolf in their midst and bowed.

"Can you help him?" Jackie mouthed to her brother. "No matter what Pence has done, he doesn't deserve this."

"I'll try," he replied closing his eyes.

She could tell the moment Dustin reached out and made the connection. Suddenly he opened his eyes wide as if what he experienced could not be contained. For several heartbeats he seemed unaware of anything around him. Beads of perspiration dotted his face. His hands clenched in some invisible struggle. Then his awareness returned. His knees wobbled from the effort, but he stayed standing. Jackie put out her hands to steady her brother.

"I'm okay," he told her. "Just tired."

Whatever he had done must have been enough. The wolf yelped as if burned by an invisible flame and then slowed its attack allowing Pence to approach the group. As Jackie looked on in amazement the alabaster rodent shifted and faded before her eyes. In its place a new form took shape. A robed man, tall with a proud face and piercing eyes gazed out at them.

Regnal stared, caught between revolt and trepidation, but it was the detective who spoke first.

"Hello again, Emperor" Hunter said. "You're just like a bad penny."

The stranger bowed fractionally, and then turned to Dustin. "Thank you for your help, young friend," the figure said. "That was very kind of you." He smiled, but a tremor in his voice betrayed what the ordeal had cost him. Then he spread his arms wide and addressed the whole group. "My name is Constantine, last Emperor of Constantinople and one-time Keeper of Treetops. Long have I been a repentant servant. I have come to warn you. A most deceitful fiend hides in your midst."

Constantine lifted his robed arm and pointed at the ruddy wolf. It was scratching its head vigorously as if trying to put out an invisible flame.

"Imposter, show yourself!" he demanded.

"I thought you'd never ask," snarled the creature in a mocking voice.

The animal's features sparkled and then wavered. As Jackie looked on, the wolf shimmered as it metamorphosized into a boyish-looking man. Fur turned into rosy wavy hair that swept back from his forehead and a canine snout became a human nose that was just a bit too pointed in an otherwise handsome face. He wore a fiery colored tunic and dark boots that wrapped about his feet and legs like winding snakes. The last to coalesce were his dark blue eyes which seemed to twinkle with unpredictability.

"I'm not late, am I?" the stranger asked, a crooked smile plastered across his face. "No, of course not," he said answering his own question. "It wouldn't do to miss Ragnarok."

"Who are you?" Jackie demanded. "And what's a Ragnarok?"

"The end of the world," explained the man stepping forward. "It's what I've been waiting for. As to who I am, well I can be just about anything."

To prove his point the stranger sparkled and turned into a

dragon, then a beautiful mare, a towering giantess, and finally Nimbus.

"Oh! This one's definitely not a keeper," he remarked. Then he shifted back to his familiar form. "Some call me Loki," he said with a bow, "the Trickster."

The detective wrinkled his brow as if searching for a memory. "A wise old woman tried to warn me about you a long time ago, but I wouldn't listen. How did you escape from your chains?"

The god glanced over and sneered. "You are a stranger to me," Loki said, his eyes searching the detective over as if for a secret. "A fool you must be. No prison can hold me. I have come to dance at the end of days."

Hunter clenched his fists at the insult, but he did not move.

"You tried to kill Constantine!" Jackie said, leveling her gaze at the trickster god.

Loki took a step back in mock outrage. "That old has-been? Please. It's the most excitement he's seen in centuries. Serves him right for not freeing me when he had the chance. After centuries of wasting away on that cursed rock all I wanted was a little R&R. When this beastly army loosened my magical chains with all their stampeding, I buzzed around a bit, lying low in case the winged Aesir quested for me while I regained my strength. That's when I found the Last Byzantine."

The trickster god motioned dramatically at Constantine.

"Trouble was, I was so weak that my body was becoming incorporeal. The only thing I could do was grab on to this geezer and possess him before the winds of Hades tore me to shreds. When I regained some strength, I transformed into the big bad wolf to make some mischief."

Dustin didn't try to hide his disgust. "That doesn't sound very nice. Your mother should have taught you better manners."

Loki turned his full attention to Dustin. For a moment Loki's good-natured grin faded.

"Clever little boy, you got into my wolf head. Had a dream of fire and smoke. No harm done. I'm finally feeling like myself again. Worlds to help end and doom to bring about. That sort of thing."

"So this was all your doing then?" Regnal quipped.

"Sadly no," answered Loki. "Still a party's a party. I was only informed of these end-of-days' events recently by Ratatosk. He's a bit unusual for a squirrel. Bright red and a bit of a tongue-wagger. Sort of like me. He climbs up and down the World Tree, listening and sharing what he's learned. Perhaps you've seen him. And unlike this imposter he really *is* a furry rodent. I'm sure he'll tell Odin and all the rest of the gang about me, but by then it will be too late."

The Norse trickster god looked around and grinned. "Time to get this show on the road, don't you think?"

In a blink of an eye he became the towering figure of Flood, only more handsome and dressed in a circus ringmaster's coat and hat.

In unison the bewitched and confused animals turned to him and waited for a final word.

"It won't work, you know," Constantine said with an air of desperation. "You can take the form of Flood, but it's just an empty shell. There's no substance. The denizens of Treetops are smarter than that."

"I'm sure they are," Loki smiled with Flood's broad face. "But thinking isn't what they came here for, is it? To me they seem right on the edge of doing something quite terrible. All they need is a little—push."

Jackie looked over at the renegade Keeper and didn't try to keep the mounting fear that she felt from her voice.

"You used to run this place. Tell them to stop and go back to how they were. Tell them to go home."

Constantine bowed his head.

"They will not hear," he explained with a sigh. "They have a mind only to kill. They must obey the Horn of Calling. But if I was still a Keeper, I would try to make them remember. Yet I am closed to them for my past deeds of coercion and mutiny. They no longer trust me. They barely tolerate my presence."

Jackie looked at the Emperor. Any remaining doubts about whether they could trust him evaporated when she saw the pained look on his face. She made her decision.

"Even so, you deserve to be free for what little time we have left. You've suffered enough."

Jackie reached out and removed the coin that dangled around his neck. Constantine blinked in surprise. In return, the last Emperor of Byzantium bowed deeply and without mockery.

"A symbolic gesture, but one for which I am extremely grateful. With the demise of the last Keeper, however, I am no longer bound. It is ironic that for the second time I am powerless as a kingdom I love falls," he said with melancholy.

Nearby, Loki lifted his great arms like a malevolent conductor to the gathering army, his mischievous smile darkening to malice. In response, they thundered in a cacophony of chaos.

"Tell them to stop Dustin. Please. Try again," Jackie pleaded. "I know you're tired, but they might listen to you."

She stepped away and watched as Dustin closed his eyes, with Gaylon still beside him. Jackie could see the strain build immediately. His small hands clenched into fists and his mouth twisted with the strain. A moment later he opened his eyes and let out a gasp like a diver who's been underwater too long.

"So many," he said in a small voice. "So much hunger. They cannot hear me."

Then Dustin's knees buckled. He fell to the ground. Gaylon reacted swiftly, catching the boy just before his head hit the ground. Flood's former servant cradled the boy in his arms. Jackie stroked her brother's cheek until he rose clumsily to his feet.

Everyone looked at each other helplessly. They had run out of choices. There was nothing more they could do. One by one they turned toward Loki. He right arm pointed directly at them as he spoke to his doomsday troops.

"Kill them!" he shouted. "Kill them all! Then feast on the world below."

With those fierce commands, given by a god in the guise of their appointed Master, the assembled creatures threw off the remaining vestiges of indecision and launched themselves in unbridled fury.

CHAPTER 54

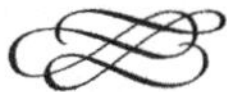

Hunter Greenwold saw it all happen as if he were far away. Each death-dealing fang and talon moved in slow motion. He could see each animal in exquisite detail. There was clarity of sight in his last moments that allowed him to see what had always eluded him in life. Beauty. Everything was precious. How could he have not seen that before? It was as if he were in the eye of the hurricane and instead of destruction, there was only peace. The primitive part of his brain knew something heavy was going down and sent out the appropriate signals, fight or flight. A surge of adrenaline kicked in. Hunter didn't want to die. He didn't want Ashmore's kids to die. Hell, he didn't want anyone to die. But he accepted it. This was his time. And there was nothing he could do about it.

His heart beat one of its final beats, pumping out blood like it had on a thousand other days. Then something strange happened. As Flood's Army rushed in all around him snarling and snapping, something rose unexpectedly from deep inside him. It was something ancient, something forgotten, triggered by his imminent death.

Hunter's world exploded in living green. A shockwave of

power emanated from him, knocking back the charging creatures and sweeping out over the speckled cloudscape. Loki fell back stunned. Never before had Hunter felt so alive. Words alit and then died on his tongue for nothing could convey the transformation. Instead of a voice, vines grew up out of his throat to form a circle that framed his face. Dark emerald leaves, with touches of flaxen and sienna sprang from his head like a living crown. From the tips of his bark covered fingers there protruded like twisted shards of glass long menacing thorns, not yet red.

Of his old clothing nothing remained, no evidence that he had ever been human. Only a small, gold band with familiar markings remained nearby to give evidence of the transformation. Jackie spied it at the creature's feet. There was no doubt as to who the rightful owner was. Kneeling down she scooped it up and put it hastily in her pocket and then backed away.

"Are you a Keeper?" she asked astonished and more than a little afraid.

If the man who used to be Hunter Greenwold heard, he gave no sign.

"He is the Green Man," Gaylon answered in a tone of reverent wonder putting Dustin down gently.

"And should I be envious of that particular hue?" Regnal asked, but his awe was unmistakable. "What has he become?"

Gaylon swallowed and paused. "It's difficult to explain. Nimbus told me about it once. The Keeper said he comes from the wild, untamed part of us when the world was new. Wild and long of tooth, the Green Man remembers."

"I think the lecture will have to wait," Jackie interrupted.

A leopard tensed nearby and made ready to leap at them. Gaylon took a nervous step forward. Raising a hand, Gaylon closed his eyes in concentration. Sparks sputtered from his fingertips and then died as whatever magic he tried to summon fizzled. Sensing opportunity, the leopard sprung for his throat just as the thing Hunter had become knocked the spotted cat out of the air with one swipe from his bark covered hand. For a moment the former detective looked stricken. Then the Green Man pointed his wooden digits at the open ground between Flood's Army and Jackie's companions. Immediately the cloudscape erupted with trees, fully formed, their girths bigger than sequoias. The mighty mass rumbled into the sky creating a thick wall of vegetation that separated Flood's Army from the group. The transformed Hunter stood amidst the towering trees like a force of nature.

"Nice entrance," Loki smirked. "It's a pity you have to be leaving so soon."

Still in the shape of Flood, the Norse god took a giant menacing step forward only to find that he had become entangled in thorny briars. They tore at his flesh and curled around his ankles like living manacles. Cursing he fell over with a crash.

"It will not hold!" Gaylon shouted. "He will simply change his form and escape. You must flee while you still can. Before Flood's Army finds a way through."

Jackie looked at the former apprentice and then at what the man Hunter Greenwold had become. There was so much she wanted to say and so little time.

Thank you, she mouthed to the detective whose alien form bent over the struggling Loki. Then she turned back toward Gaylon. His face was rigid with tension and concern. And something more, she realized, feeling like a fool. He stood there helpless and bereft as if he were losing the best part of him.

"Don't worry about us," Gaylon said as if from far away. "We'll take shelter in the Keeper's old dwelling and try to ride out the onslaught. Speedo is still there if we really need him. Maybe there will even be something of Treetops left when it's all over. Something we can rebuild."

"You're staying?" she asked unable to hide her surprise.

Gaylon hesitated. "Yes," he said as if he had just decided. "Treetops and the world Below need help and I need a new start. Not a

Keeper, though. Something else. Nimbus and Flood are just extremes. There must be a better answer. I'll figure it out."

For a moment they looked at each other as if they were alone atop the clouds.

To Jackie, the spindly figure of Gaylon seemed suddenly taller, more capable. His dark raiment gone, he wore the Nexra's simple white rags like a transformation. "I'm proud of you," she said and meant it. "Take care. I can't thank you enough. You carried me all the way to the Nexra to get healed. I wouldn't be here without you."

With her heart beating quickly, she leaned forward and before she could falter, kissed him gently on the lips for everything he had done, for what he was becoming, and because she wanted to. After the surprise passed, Gaylon kissed her back.

"No more!" screamed Loki who emerged suddenly from a tangle of twisting vines, his chest raked deep with bloody furrows. Nearby, the Green Man pursued the fleeing trickster, running cat-like over the ground and gaining fast. With one desperate leap Loki changed in midair to a red-tailed hawk and took flight, his pained cries echoing over the shaking trees as he disappeared from sight, desperate to nurse his wounds far away.

Gaylon gripped her shoulders hard.

"Go!" he rasped. "While there is still time. Mere trees and a wild man will not hold back Flood's Army long."

Then he motioned to Constantine. Together they turned and fled. There was no time for an avian transformation. No time for goodbyes. Gaylon sped across the cloud-top, his form nearly as graceful as when he flew through the air. Constantine followed behind, his austere robes fluttering as he ran towards the dubious safety of HeartWood, and the waiting Portal inside. Regnal, always a survivor, had already gained the bramble gate, Jackie noticed with passing amusement. She prayed that they would be as fortunate.

Jackie took her brother's hand and ran toward the Portal Tree in the failing light of Helios. It seemed like a lifetime since she had climbed up to Treetops. They had entered the strange realm separately, but they were leaving it together.

Behind them came the horrible sound of shattered wood as the first of Flood's Army burst through the barrier. Jackie turned and looked as she ran, only to wish she hadn't. They poured from the gash with renewed fury as if the delay had only made them hungrier. The only thing blocking their path was the Green Man, and he suddenly seemed very small like a stone in a raging river. He stood with his arms outstretched as if they were branches lifted toward the sun. For a heartbeat the raging army hesitated, sensing a kindred spirit, a powerful connection to the natural world. Perhaps he could have swayed them, at least delayed them by drawing on his innate lore, but he did not try. It could well be that he had lost the ability to reason. Instead he stepped forward into the stampede as if greeting long, lost friends. Then he was gone, swallowed by the thundering abyss. In the wake of his passing, a great wind ushered in as if blown from the four corners of the world. Each creature paused at the spot where Hunter had stood as if paying homage before pursuing their vengeance.

There was little time to waste. The detective had given them a gift. She didn't know if it would be enough. Jackie heard the thundering sound of pursuit and a hundred thousand ravenous cries. They split the air with their fury and stole the breath from her lungs. Somehow her heart kept beating as she struggled across the beautiful vista, pulling her brother after her whenever he faltered. Finally, she saw it, a green jewel sticking out of a white sea. The Earth Tree! Their portal home was almost within reach. It did not look far, perhaps only a hundred yards or more, but it might as well have been a hundred miles. Being only a very small boy, Dustin could not keep up the pace. He staggered out of breath and Jackie ran to him so she could lift him up and carry him in her arms.

As she started forward again, Jackie risked a nervous glance behind her. Immediately, she wished she hadn't. Flood's Army was nearly upon them. A mass of death hurtled toward her without remorse. Creatures great and small joined together by a common malice, forged by the Horn of Calling as well as Flood's power and Loki's mischief. They could not be turned or dissuaded now. That time was past. Nothing would give them pause until every living human being was exterminated, starting with her and Dustin. They were not going to make it. Jackie hugged her brother tighter as if she could shield him from harm.

Beyond the trailing edge of possessed animals, a swirling shape of emerald green came into view.

More animals, Jackie thought with growing panic, imagining an endless landscape of dust kicked skyward by the latecomers to the battle.

She shuffled forward like a doomed pilgrim lurching toward the mirage of a promised land. A pang of remorse seized her as she looked down at Dustin. After everything they had been through, this was how it ended. Then she caught herself. Something wasn't right. There were only clouds in Treetops. No soil existed to be disturbed here. Jackie looked back over her shoulder. The green shape solidified into a vortex. The massive tornado fed off the clouds, gaining strength, and it was heading directly for them.

In panic Jackie realized that she could no more outrun the funnel cloud than she could the marauding creatures. The twister was too fast. Already she could hear the terrible roar and feel its power. Her long hair whipped wildly in the wind. The long strands blinded her as she tried to soldier on, pushing against the gale with Dustin cradled in her arms. There was no hope of escape. Any second they would get sucked away or overtaken by the bloodthirsty army. She just hoped the end would be quick. At least they would go together. Suddenly she didn't want to run anymore. She stopped and looked down at Dustin, his head buried in her shoulder. His eyes were shut tight.

Dustin curled closer, shifting in her protective arms. He felt so light. So incredibly fragile. Flood's Army and the emerald vortex were converging on their spot, each racing to obliterate them first. She felt Dustin lift from her grip as the tempest tried to take him away. With every ounce of her strength she held on.

Then the tornado hit with a fury. She looked over in time to see the trailing edge of Flood's Army simply disappear from sight as the twister plowed through them. In an instant they became merely swirling specks in the great white and green mass, inconsequential shapes ripped from the ground or snatched from the air. Before her unbelieving eyes the emerald tornado cut a horrible swath right down the heart of the advancing horde. Scores of animals that weren't sucked up were scattered and flung. The remnants of Flood's vast army were in temporary disarray. From the center of the storm Jackie caught sight of swirling leaves.

"It's the Green Man or what's left of him!" she shouted to Dustin, her words torn from the air. The wild wind blew her hair into her face, but she didn't care. "The detective's still helping us."

With new found energy and hope, she set her sights on the branches of the nearby Earth Tree and ran. When they arrived at the portal, she risked putting Dustin down and then looked back across the clouds. The Green Man's wind was dissipating, his vortex losing definition as it spun through the mass of creatures. Slowly, the animals were regrouping, beginning the hunt again. If the attack had cost them substantial numbers she couldn't tell. There were still far too many.

"We're going to have to climb down fast," she said kneeling down in front of her brother and putting a hand on his shoulder. "Can you do that?"

Dustin nodded.

Steeling her resolve, she looked into the leafy green world as if she were a scuba diver about to descend into treacherous depths.

"Fall"

CHAPTER 55

Squeezing her brother's hand, Jackie took a tentative step onto the great curving vine. It felt strange to stand on something inherently solid. When it held, she took a deep breath to steel herself against her fear of heights. Then she entered the luxurious canopy of leaves and unexpected filtered sunlight. Blinking, Jackie made her way down the great spiraling staircase back to the world below. When her vision had adjusted to the natural light, she began walking faster and then jogging, casting nervous glances back over her shoulder toward the dwindling high canopy. The rough bark kept her tennis shoes from slipping and the curved wooden lip of the Amarantha plant provided just enough security as she negotiated turn after turn. Soon Jackie felt confident enough to run with her brother in tow. No ground was visible below and no sky could be seen above, only the enveloping green and the growing feeling that she was spiraling down a drain. Little by little the sunlight dimmed until it was replaced by an ominous darkness.

"They're coming," Dustin said.

A moment later she heard the unmistakable sound as Flood's Army reached the tree and began their furious descent. The vibration of countless footfalls reverberated down the living branches and shook the ancient tree to its core. With each passing moment the descending doom became louder and more insistent. Flood's Army was getting closer.

She had already been pulling on Dustin's arm as she negotiated the twisting shadowy path. Now Jackie turned corners with such speed that Dustin flew into the air, tenuously tethered to her outstretched hand. Razor-sharp branches and giant verdant colored leaves whipped past her face as she raced around the trunk on an ever-narrowing path. Dustin's tiny feet barely touched the wood at all as she gripped his hand like a vise and swung him after her. Suddenly, they broke through a dense wall of leaves into brilliant unbroken sunshine. They had made it to the massive trunk of the Portal Tree. A quick glance revealed fissures and growing cracks running through the knotted wood as the weight of thousands of animals bore down toward the Earth below. A silent meadow surrounded the tree. Bending down to a sitting position, Jackie put Dustin on her lap, gripped him tightly by the arms and jumped.

They hit the ground hard and then tumbled over roots and tall grass until they rolled into something sitting at the side of the tree.

"Hey!" exclaimed a man.

The heavy-set stranger was dressed in sagging blue jeans and a faded navy t-shirt with the words "Earl—Rockwood City Employee" stitched above the breast pocket in yellow thread. He had a doughy, but pleasant face. The only thing remarkable about him was a birthmark in the shape of a flame that adorned the back of his left hand. After a moment's uncertainty he stood up, brushing the crumbs from his lunch off. A cigarette butt smoldered nearby.

"Where did you two come from?" he chuckled. "You nearly gave me a heart attack."

Jackie helped Dustin to his feet and steadied him when his knees threatened to buckle.

Earth Fall, she thought. It felt strange to be on the ground again, but otherwise she felt fine. Just another indication that she wasn't special at all.

"Sorry, we didn't mean to scare you," she told the worker. "We were just—playing."

"Good thing I took a break or you might have taken a real fall. I've never seen such a tough customer. Been breaking chainsaw teeth left and right. But I'm close now. This tree is coming down. If it doesn't, I'm as good as fired."

He motioned with his hand towards the tree. Jackie saw it now. A giant red **X** was painted across the trunk like a warning. Looking closer she noticed the deep gash through the center of the wood where he had been cutting. A faded orange chainsaw lay nearby. Sawdust lay everywhere.

"Why are you cutting it down?" she asked in shock, even as the sound of Flood's Army reached her ears from above.

"Don't know and don't care," Earl responded. "Someone marks them and I cut them down. Then somebody else hauls them away."

As she listened, Jackie tried to make sense of how her special place had been discovered. With both the Keeper and Flood gone, perhaps the veil that kept the Portal Tree hidden had failed. Then again, she remembered the families the Nexra and Nimbus had spoken of. Perhaps she and Dustin weren't the only ones nearby who could find such a place.

Beside her, Dustin wobbled on his feet like a weary top and Jackie gripped him tighter.

"Is he all right?" Earl asked.

"Oh, he'll be fine," Jackie said. "Just a little tired from climbing."

Above them in the canopy of leaves, the approaching noise grew louder, turning into an avalanche of fury bearing down.

"Could you finish cutting it down *now*?" Jackie asked with

rising alarm. "Please. Something bad is coming. Can't you hear that sound?"

Earl looked up at the tree as if sensing it for the first time. He frowned and furrowed his brow.

"Squirrels. I've seen it before. Tree is probably infested with the rodents."

"You don't understand," Jackie said in desperation. "We're all in terrible danger."

"Guess you're right. They could be rabid. Might have to call in animal protection. My break will be over in," he paused to look at his watch, "ten minutes. Until then I'm off the clock. Be right back. Nature calls."

Earl walked off into the woods to do his business.

The cracks running through the bark widened as the cacophony of sound above them spiraled downward towards them. The great tree shuddered once and a gash as wide as the city employee ripped through the trunk from top to bottom. Leaves and twigs rained down. It swayed ominously once and then stopped as the tree found a precarious equilibrium.

Jackie looked around helplessly and noticed for the first time the flock of birds all lined up on the branches in the surrounding trees. They formed an ominous circle around the meadow and flapped their wings with impatience, silently watching and waiting in eerie anticipation. Nearby, just past the brush and brambles where the forest met the clearing, a doe looked out at them, foam spewing from its open mouth and nostrils. It took a step closer and then another. Earth's creatures were no longer afraid.

"They don't like us," Dustin said.

Forcing down her anxiety, she turned back to the Earth Tree as if it could somehow protect them instead of bringing doom to everyone. Maybe it could!

Leaping up she grabbed the chainsaw lying against the tree, and pulled the cord. Nothing happened. Jackie tried again. It sputtered once and then roared to life. Holding the chainsaw in her shaking hands, she stumbled toward the massive tree. After a moment's hesitation she placed the teeth of the metal chain in the groove of the ancient bark.

"I'm sorry," Jackie thought silently as the teeth ate into the wood. It felt like she was cutting the great tree's throat. This had been her mother's last gift to her; a gateway to another world. It was inconceivable that she had to destroy it.

Wood chips flew in all directions as blade and bark screamed in unison. Once again the tree shifted as Jackie sliced towards the heart of the wood. Then the chainsaw passed through a rupture in the trunk and a low mournful sound erupted as if the soul of the leafy denizen was escaping. A great final crack sounded, a letting go. Then the Portal Tree, eternal to the Grove, started its slow, ominous fall.

Jackie threw down the chainsaw, grabbed Dustin, and ran towards the dense trees of the surrounding woods, hoping it would provide some small protection. From this slightly obscured vantage point, she watched it come down as if it were a piece of the sky.

The earth below her feet trembled as the mighty tree's last connection to the planet came undone and it came crashing down, a forest unto itself. By luck it tipped toward the open meadow instead of the wooded undergrowth where she and Dustin cowered. They never could have outrun it. The trunk toppled forward like a pillar of the world on which a crown of multicolored leaves sat. Arcing through the noonday sun, the canopy flared once like a torch and then darkened as the mammoth specimen plummeted to the ground. At the instant of contact, Jackie spied the multitude of Flood's Army within the winding branches still racing down, perilously close. Their eyes burned hotly as they made ready for landfall.

Jackie braced for the terrible crash that never came. Instead the tree just disappeared as the last vestiges of bark ripped free.

One instant Flood's Army was leaping in the air towards the battleground, the next they simply winked out of existence along with the Earth Tree. The only mark of its passing was the great depression stretching across the ground where the portal had once stood and the great flock of birds that took flight scattering into the sky above. Into the sudden silence, the chainsaw hummed and vibrated on the ground where Jackie had dropped it.

She breathed a sigh of relief and put her arms around Dustin, holding him close.

From behind a clump of trees Earl emerged adjusting his fly.

"Did I miss something?" he asked.

"Nothing much," replied Jackie. "Just the end of the world."

The city worker went over to the chainsaw and flicked a switch, silencing it. Then he looked up where the tree had been and shook his head.

"Well I'll be," he managed.

From across the clearing the doe reappeared. It seemed shaken, but no longer seemed possessed by unnatural emotions. Timidity ruled the creature again. The connection to Treetops was severed. Cautiously the deer ventured out into the center of the clearing and then stopped.

"Look," Jackie whispered, pointing.

Dustin turned and stepped forward, his hand outstretched as if greeting a friend. The doe tipped its head as if sensing something unfamiliar in the air. Then it walked over toward them until it stood only a foot away. Dustin and the doe stood looking at each other eye-to-eye as his hand gently caressed the creature's warm, furry neck.

"Go play," Dustin said smiling and the deer bounded off as if it already was.

Nearby Earl scratched his head, still trying to make sense of what had happened.

Jackie tousled her brother's hair and then they walked off

together, hand-in-hand, through the woods, disappearing into the trees, following an invisible path back home.

Time hung in the air just out of reach until the maze of branches finally began to thin. Jackie spied an ordinary walkway that angled across the freshly cut grass of Highveil Park. She stood on the edge of the mowed grass, Dustin at her side, looking out across the idyllic setting like a sailor returned safely home after a long and perilous voyage. The smell of rain hung in the air, but the drying ground told her the downpour had moved on. The leaves surrounding them were still lush and green, fluttering in the wind on sheltering maples and stately oaks. Everything looked so commonplace and humdrum. Jackie suddenly felt so happy, she had to fight down an urge to cry.

"I wonder how long we've been away," she asked.

Dustin looked up at her, his wavy blonde hair blowing in the breeze.

"I dunno," he said. "I don't see any flying cars or talking robots so not too long, I guess."

Jackie smiled, but inside she wondered what they'd missed.

Without another word they set off across the park, down the path, and under the wrought iron gate that led to the intersection. Still hand-in-hand they walked across the street and down the sidewalk past neighborhood houses in the afternoon light of high summer, when the days go on forever. A melting popsicle bled red onto the pavement at the foot of the curb; a castaway from the day's bounty. Finally, they rounded the corner and saw their little white house in the middle of the block. Without speaking, both of them walked faster, until they were running, their arms swinging wildly at their sides.

"Beat you!" Dustin shouted as he slapped the old hitching post in front of their home at full gallop.

"No fair," Jackie laughed taking dramatic mouthfuls of air. "Being a pip-squeak, you have less wind resistance. I demand a rematch!"

Glancing around, Jackie took in the details of their Rockwood home, reminded of everyday things and taking comfort in being back. Some things were different. The lawn had grown long with neglect and the flower beds and vegetable garden were overtaken with weeds. Her father, although not an avid gardener, would never let them come to such a state. Tending them honored her mother's memory. Seeing the gardens overrun sent shivers down her spine. With an air of foreboding, she remembered what Hunter had let slip in Treetops. *"Your dad was very brave. You need to know that."*

Taking his brother's hand firmly, she walked slowly up the walk and then stepped into the open porch. The old wooden boards creaked, only reinforcing her growing feeling of dread. *Milky Way should be barking,* she thought.

In a flash Dustin scrambled past.

"Wait!" she said in an urgent whisper.

Dustin's hand hung mere inches from the door knob.

"I feel funny. Let's knock," she said. "Okay?"

Standing on the threshold, she gripped Dustin's shoulder protectively with one hand, while the other grasped the golden ring. Taking a deep breath, she rapped the knocker into the wood.

CHAPTER 56

Jackie shrank back from the door waiting in anticipation. No one came. Swallowing nervously, she knocked again, this time louder. The sound cracked the silence and seemed to echo all around her.

Before she could lift the knocker a third time a shrill symphony of barking erupted from inside.

"At least Milky Way's home," she said with undisguised relief.

The next instant the door swung open. A man she barely recognized stood framed in the entrance, pale and gaunt. His face mirrored the yard outdoors. An unkempt beard sprawled across his face while bloodshot eyes stared vacantly ahead. Both hair and clothes were disheveled. He wore a wrinkled dress shirt, sweatpants and no socks. From the gap where he had mismatched a shirt button, she spied a heavy gauze bandage taped to his side. The figure stood there, frozen in the doorway as tear-filled eyes slowly registered who stood before him.

"Dad?" she asked.

"Is that you?" her father asked.

She nodded and drew back her long hair to reveal the tree-shaped birthmark. "We're home."

Now her father's knees buckled and he gripped the door frame for support. For a moment he said nothing, simply stared at them unbelieving.

"Oh my god. I thought I'd lost you both."

David shook his head as if in a dream and motioned them inside, never taking his eyes off of them. Tears rolled down his cheeks and he sank gratefully to the floor.

"Don't be sad, Daddy," Dustin told him crouching down by his face. "I missed you."

David wiped his eyes and looked at his son.

"I missed you too, kiddo, more than you'll ever know," he said as he gingerly stroked his son's cheek. "Both of you. I looked and looked, but I didn't know what else to do. I just kept hoping you were safe…"

David's voice trailed off into sobs.

"I have something," she said, remembering the object that Hunter had dropped in Treetops just after he had awakened into the Green Man. "It's from the detective you hired."

Digging a hand in her pocket she removed ring and held it out to her father.

"Hunter saved us dad. We wouldn't have made it without him." *And Nimbus and the Chosen and the Nexra and Gaylon.*

After a brief hesitation he took back his wedding ring. He cupped his hand gently around the band, as if it needed protecting, but he did not put it on. Then he closed his eyes as if in silent prayer.

"Thank you," he said. He reached out his arms. "I love you both so much."

Jackie bent down and felt her father's arms encircle her. Returning his embrace, she felt as if she were home for the first time. All the things she had lost were momentarily forgotten. Then Dustin joined in and together they hugged as a family, holding each other as Milky Way sniffed and nuzzled between them, his tail wagging in happy rhythm.

"I'm sorry," Jackie said at last.

"Me too," said Dustin, sniffling.

"Me three," David chimed in and they all smiled a bit at that.

Her father's bandage looked even bigger and scarier up close.

"What happened to you?" she asked. "Hunter said you saved his life. Are you all right?"

"Now that's a story," he began gravely. "I think you have some explaining to do first, though."

"You could say that," Jackie said, sidestepping the issue. "A lot has happened."

"I can hardly believe any of this," David said shaking his head. "How can I? Perhaps I've gone mad. My little girl is all grown up, and I missed it," he said with misty eyes. "How did you become a beautiful young woman while your old man has been wasting away?"

"Is it that noticeable?" she asked turning red.

"Uh-huh. Let's just say the meeting with your principal where we attempt to explain your transformation will be eventful, to say the least."

Jackie took a deep breath. "How long have we been gone?"

"About three weeks. 20 days to be exact."

Jackie looked at him in amazement.

"Is that all?" she asked. "Are you sure?"

The look on her father's face told Jackie everything she needed to know. "You and I must have a different perception of the passage of time," David said with growing emotion. "For me, it's been a lifetime."

Jackie let out a long sigh of relief. "It's not that. I've just been worried that everything would be different here. That more time would have passed."

"My world stopped since you both disappeared," her father said. "It's all I could do to count the hours and not think the worst."

"We're here now," Jackie said.

"Yes, you are," he said.

They hugged again and time really did seem to stand still.

David gazed at his children and then shook his head, chuckling softly.

"Why do I get the sneaking suspicion that somehow your mother had something to do with all of this? That must have been some present."

Jackie looked at her father and tried to smile, but she still had a lot of healing to do. Her voice shook, but she didn't care. "I really miss mom," she said. "There's a hole where she used to be. I don't know what to do."

David looked at his daughter and took her hand. "I know. I miss her too. Every single day. But you know what helps?"

Jackie shook her head.

"I look at your face and see her. She would be so proud of you."

Jackie looked down and swallowed. "I don't know about that."

"I do," her father said without hesitation. "She told me enough times. You too," he added, wrapping an arm around Dustin.

"Thanks Dad," Jackie said, and this time she managed to smile.

At her feet Milky Way began to whine.

"C'mon boy," she said to her puppy, patting his head gently. "Let's take you out and then get you some dinner."

Outside, the sun continued its trek to the horizon until the sky finally blossomed into color with the magic of twilight.

EPILOGUE:

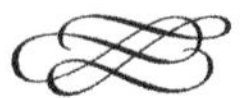

"A NEW BEGINNING"

Seasons change. Time goes on. Memories linger. A late summer breeze, with just a hint of coolness, blew through the austere oak tree nearby. Leaves danced to a silent song, a fragment, perhaps, of the Green Man living on. A small garden grew nearby. It looked well tended.

Jackie watched her daughter Riva put the finishing touches on the birthday decorations around the picnic table and thought again of her younger self, of Earth Trees and Arkanums, KeyStones and Keepers, and kisses atop clouds. In the bright light of an ordinary sunny afternoon, those long-ago events seemed to slip with increasing frequency into the realm of dreams. Yet her adventures had been real, she reminded herself, and every bit as substantial as the hard-won ground she stood on today. Those experiences had made her who she had become: a mother, a wife, and college professor. She remembered and would never forget. Many had sacrificed themselves so she could live to tell the tale. How ironic it was that she couldn't breathe a word of any of it.

The evening she and Dustin returned had been a homecoming. Much, but not all, had been healed. With prodding her father had shared his efforts to find them, of going to the detective out of desperation and the violence that ensued. He had nearly died on the floor of Hunter's office. The doctor told him after the surgery that he was lucky to be alive. If the bullet had shifted even a tiny fraction in its trajectory or if the ambulance had arrived even a few moments later, he would have been in a casket and not a hospital bed. Even so, it had taken over a week before he was sent home and he was still so weak he could barely manage getting up in the morning, let alone going out and searching again. Despite his slow recovery he managed to keep the flame alive by troweling online and sending out inquiries. He called everyone he could think of who might know something or offer advice.

Even so, hope was something he nearly ran out of, her father had confided many years later when he was in failing health. He had tried to believe that Jillian was somehow watching out for their kids when they were missing, but despair had always been close at hand during those terrible days. As always, it was the small things that mattered most. Once, soon after he had returned home from the hospital, a group of young girls came to the door and shared how sorry they were and that they hoped Jackie was okay. It was an unexpected comfort, he said, to know that other people were thinking of his kids too.

When it came time to share their story, Jackie knew that she couldn't really tell the truth. At least not all of it. Her dad would never believe her even though he knew something out of the ordinary had happened. Most of all, she felt secretly ashamed that she has no gift like her mother. So she made up a lie of staying with friends back in Pennsylvania, of running away because there wasn't anything else to do. It was easy since she had daydreamed of it often enough. Dustin simply followed her and then refused to leave unless she came back to Minnesota. To explain her change in appearance, she simply said her mother's mysterious gift had caused a transformation. And in an indirect way it had. Through everything her father gave no indication that he harbored doubts. He simply nodded his head, barely saying a word.

"You could have called," he said awkwardly, like an actor learning unfamiliar lines. "Let me know you were safe. Whatever it was, I would have understood."

"I'm here now," she said, and had meant it.

With effort, Jackie pulled herself back to the present. Her daughter Riva was talking to her, trying to get her attention.

"Mom!" her daughter said again popping her chewing gum bubble. "You've been so spacey lately. Does this look all right?" Riva asked. Bangs of dark chestnut colored hair hung down, framing her green eyes.

"I think you did a great job," Jackie said with encouragement as she scanned the colorful balloons and streamers ringing the picnic table. Her daughter tended to worry a lot, which made Jackie try too hard. "You really have an artist's sensitivity."

"You're doing it again," her daughter complained.

"Sorry," Jackie said. "I'll try not to be so obvious in my flattery next time."

Riva released her fingers from the end of the balloon she held. They both watched as it deflated, an inappropriate sound filling the silence.

Her daughter broke first. A smirk and then a giggle snuck past her defenses before she could stop it.

"That's okay. You're just being a mom. I get it, I guess."

"Thanks for your understanding," Jackie told her dryly. "Let's finish up." She handed Riva some confetti. The guests would be arriving soon. A handful of friends and relatives.

From the table her cell phone rang tunefully. She didn't need to look at it to know who was calling. It was her husband, of course.

"Hi hon. Are you running late?"

"I'll be there soon," said an apologetic voice. "I'm almost off the freeway. Traffic's been a nightmare. Everyone must be heading to Riva's birthday party."

"No worries," she said, loving the sound of his voice. "No one's here yet. We're just finishing up with the decorations."

"I'll be there to cut the cake. I can't wait to see you both."

Jackie took a deep breath. "Okay. See you soon. Love you."

Pocketing the phone, Jackie turned to her daughter.

"Your father is on his way," she said.

Jackie gazed at Riva who was sprinkling colorful confetti across the white tablecloth. A sudden fierceness to protect the only child she had seized her. If only it were that simple. As always, Jackie was drawn to the birthmark which graced her daughter's neck; a tall tree adorned with a crown of leaves. Oh, she had grown too quickly, too soon. Yet it was time. Her baby was thirteen years old today. This moment would not come again. Jackie had been waiting and agonizing so long. Most of her wrinkles and gray hair, she was convinced, were a direct result of worrying too much, but what else could she do? She was a parent and couldn't help but wonder what awaited her child. How would Riva fare? Would she find her place in the world, and perhaps beyond? Most of all, would she come to understand her connection with something greater, a tradition shared by few, and then give back as her uncle had? There were no guarantees. It could be a lonely heart-breaking journey, Jackie knew, where you sometimes had to find your own magic and then try to live with the consequences.

Homesick, Jackie had come back to Rockwood on her first break from college and walked again through Highveil Park, hiking deeper into the woods until she came to the spot where the world had once hung in the balance. It was bare. Ironically, not a living thing grew where the Earth Tree had once stood and no clue remained to suggest that a vast animal armada had almost landed there. Not for the first time Jackie wondered again what had happened to Flood's Army, and if, perhaps, a few of the Treetops creatures had escaped into the world before the rest were returned to their nebulous domain when the Earth Tree connection was severed and the portal destroyed. She hoped so. The thought of a Barbary lion or passenger pigeon alive on 21st Century Earth seemed somehow fitting and a small step towards healing. Perhaps that is why she had come back to the place, to find something, an answer perhaps, a sign that it hadn't just been a story. Jackie didn't know what she was looking for, but she found it just the same. After wandering the clearing for more than an hour she dropped to her hands and knees to feel the earth. Soon after she had been rewarded with a singular prize, glistening like a teardrop, partially buried under the windswept leaves. An Amarantha seed. Even then she had recognized what she had to do.

"Mom! Jeez!" Riva said. She wasn't annoyed, just concerned as if Jackie were a puzzle that needed solving. Thankfully, her daughter was spared the anger that had engulfed her own youth and tended to look at things more logically, more scientifically. "You're doing it again. It's like you're a million miles away. I said I wish Uncle Dustin was coming."

Jackie looked at her daughter and smiled. At the mere mention of her brother's name, Jackie was filled with pride. Already he had done so much in both worlds. She was reminded of her conversation all those years ago with Nimbus when he stated that a Keeper's purpose did not include changing what went on down Below. Thankfully, that kind of thinking was becoming extinct. Dustin had studied with Gaylon, and others, in a new more verdant Treetops, learning all he could about his special talent with animals. He had even led several archaeological expeditions across Treetops to try and uncover secrets from earlier times. Apprentices were finding their way to Treetops, called by a longing to do something to save the living world. Some remained atop the clouds, but most, like Dustin, returned home to use their gifts for good. The Earth needed all the help it could get.

"I wish he was too," Jackie said. "This is an important day. I want all your friends and family to be here. But your uncle's been busy. He just started a new job as an animal rights lawyer, remember? That's why he couldn't fly back, even though he really wanted to."

Riva tried not to let her feelings show, but Jackie knew how disappointed she was.

"He sent something for you, though. Remember?"

"Oh yeah," her daughter said brightening. "That big sparkling box that smells funny."

Dustin's gift seemed to grow in size a little bit every day. Hopefully, they wouldn't need a bigger house.

"I have a present for you too," Jackie continued brightly, trying to hide the shaking in her voice. "I'd like to give it to you now, if that's okay. That way if I cry, no one else will see."

Her daughter looked at her warily.

"It's very special," Jackie explained. "But you'll discover that for yourself. I've been saving it for you for a long time."

Nervously, she fumbled in her pocket and pulled out the small brown velvety jewelry box that her own mother had used. Riva's eyes widened in surprise.

"Hold out your hand."

Jackie placed the tiny present in her daughter's palm.

Riva felt the weight of it as it touched her skin. It was surprisingly heavy yet opened with ease as she freed the small latch and lifted the lid, almost as if it had been waiting just for her.

The End

ABOUT THE AUTHOR

Peter Bremer is a librarian at a small college in Minnesota and the author of almost a dozen published professional articles, none of which feature dragons or unicorns or impossibly tall trees. He lives with his wife and a bearded collie in a very small town and believes the world, on average, is a far better place with more nature in it, not less. This is his first novel.

Made in the USA
Monee, IL
04 March 2021

61770393R00243